ALSO BY SHAUN HAMILL

A Cosmology of Monsters

THE DISSONANCE

The Dissonance

Shaun Hamill

PANTHEON BOOKS
New York

Library of Congress Cataloging-in-Publication Data
Name: Hamill, Shaun, author.
Title: The dissonance / Shaun Hamill.
Description: First edition. New York : Pantheon Books, 2024.
Identifiers: LCCN 2023029790 (print). LCCN 2023029791 (ebook).
ISBN 9780593317259 (hardcover). ISBN 9780593317266 (ebook).
Subjects: LCGFT: Fantasy fiction. Novels.
Classification: LCC PS3608.A654 D57 2024 (print) | LCC PS3608.
A654 (ebook) | DDC 813/.6—dc23/eng/20230703
LC record available at https://lccn.loc.gov/2023029790
LC ebook record available at https://lccn.loc.gov/2023029791

www.pantheonbooks.com

Jacket image: (hands) GreenSkyStudio/Shutterstock
Jacket design by Henry Sene Yee

Printed in the United States of America
First Edition
2 4 6 8 9 7 5 3 1

And Then! An imperceptible flaw is discovered in a hitherto immaculate perfection. A Flaw that "is" Everything perfection is not.

—Grant Morrison, *Multiversity*

Contents

2019: Tremors   1

1996: The Sleepover   33

2019: Homecoming   95

1997: The Conference   117

2019: Reunion   175

1998: Athena's Doorway   193

2019: Memorial   263

1999: Field Trip   281

2019: The Last Adventure, Part One   333

1999: The Day Of (and What Came After)   361

2019: The Last Adventure, Part Two   381

Epilogue: The Next Adventure (2019)   457

Acknowledgments   475

2019
Tremors

Hal

Twenty-one years after killing his mother and one year after killing a man in a bar fight, Hal Isaac stands on the steps of St. Matthew's Catholic Church in Vandergriff, Texas, and smokes a cigarette.

His AA meeting has just let out. The sun has set, but the day's heat remains like a physical force pushing down on his body, juicing him for sweat. He could hop into his car and crank the A/C, but he always gets a headache during meetings, and a cigarette grants his mind a few minutes to unfurl. It's the main reason he took up the habit. Cigarettes give you a chance to press pause on life.

He's not the only one who feels this way. Probably two thirds of the meeting linger on and around the steps, clumped in groups of twos and threes, their tendrils of smoke rising into the oppressive air. Hal doesn't stand with the others, but he appreciates their presence. They're a buffer between him and loneliness. Their chatter washes over him while he studies the expensive-looking houses across the street. Do the upper-middle-class occupants look out their windows at this time of night? What do they think of the tableau of fuckups on the church steps?

"Hey."

He hadn't noticed the woman approach. Susie. A new face. Been coming for a few weeks, since Social Services took her kid.

"Hey," Hal says around his cigarette.

"Congrats." She nods to the chip in his left hand, the one they gave him at the end of tonight's meeting. He's been twirling it between his fingers like a close-up magician ever since. He stops and lets the aluminum circle fall into his open palm. It's the gaudy blue you'd expect to see tossed from a Mardi Gras float, except for the triangle etched around a big roman numeral I.

"One year," she says. "There are days when I think I'll be lucky to make it to six weeks."

"One day at a time." AA's full of these little clichés. *It takes as long as it takes. It works if you work it.* In his old life, Hal, a Jew—if not a very good one—would have rolled his eyes at the pure WASP-y Christianity/motivational poster of it all. Now these trite aphorisms hold his sanity together.

Susie pulls a pack of cigarettes from her purse. She slaps it on her palm a few times before pulling off the cellophane.

"I forgot my lighter," she says. "Help me out?"

Hal gives her his full attention for the first time. She's lying about the lighter. She wanted an excuse to talk to him. Hal's always been able to find company like this when he wants. Jealous friends have called it his superpower. Hal, who knows what an actual superpower looks like, thinks of it as an accident of personality. He's good at reading people, is all.

AA says you're not supposed to start new relationships during the first year of sobriety. And hooking up with a fellow alcoholic? That's a double no-no. But Susie is pretty, and she seems nice, and Hal is feeling low tonight. His lawyer called earlier today to set up a meeting for tomorrow. Insisted they talk in person. That can only mean big news. Likely bad news. So Hal lets this conversation with Susie play out a little further.

"Want to see a magic trick?" he asks.

Susie spreads her hands in a *by all means* gesture. He closes his eyes and pushes past all the worry and anxiety to that deep place in his center that he never visits anymore. He makes an exception tonight because he wants to delight this sad, pretty woman. There's nothing in the blue book that forbids making a pretty woman smile.

He strikes his mind against the spark of pain in his middle. Light flashes behind his eyelids and he opens them in time to watch Susie's cigarette light itself without visible assistance.

This little show is the extent of what he can do these days. He doesn't understand why he has this talent. It isn't one he had as a kid, when he could do far more impressive things.

"Ta-daa," he says.

Susie pulls the cigarette from her mouth and looks like she might drop it, or maybe throw it at him. She's not charmed. She's freaked out.

She jerks a thumb toward the parking lot, where no cars have arrived for several minutes. "My ride is here. I better go."

"Sure thing," he says.

"But congrats on your one year. And thanks for the reminder! One day at a time!"

He raises a hand in farewell as she speed-walks away from him. She drops her cigarette, its cherry winking orange on the pavement. He follows her far enough to stamp out the fire and pick up the butt. He frowns at it, and it bursts like a trick cigar in a cartoon. Tobacco and paper waft through the sticky air, down toward the lawn. Hal looks around, but everyone else seems busy with their own thoughts and preoccupations and conversations.

He decides his mind is as clear as it's going to get tonight. He drives home, to his studio apartment, and tries, mostly unsuccessfully, to sleep.

He rises logy and miserable the next morning and considers calling in sick to work, but his meeting with his lawyer isn't until the afternoon, and he needs a distraction until then. Also, he needs every penny for his stack of overdue bills and attorney fees.

He showers and goes to the auto finance company where he works. He answers emails and phone calls from customers hoping to reschedule their car payments. Everyone he talks to seems to have prepared a speech, a justification for why *they* should be allowed to skip this month's payment or at least be given an extra week to get the money together.

Customers think they have to convince Hal, but the truth is that every one of this company's customers is allowed to rearrange their payment date as often as they'd like, and everyone is also allowed a certain number of skipped payments before the repo men are unleashed. This latter number is based on an algorithm—the unholy union of payment history with the company and overall credit score. Hal's job is mostly to put a human face in front of the algorithm, to create the illusion that the company cares about its customers.

There is *one* decision he gets to make every time he answers a phone call or email. He gets to decide *how* friendly he wants to be. For example, around 11 a.m., Hal gets a call from a man who wants his APR adjusted. Normally Hal would sympathize; he's never been great with money himself, and has often bitten off more than he can financially chew. But this guy? This fucking guy.

"You need to lower my APR," the man says. It's the voice of someone used to issuing orders and being obeyed. "It's too high."

Hal's voice remains placid, pleasant. "That's not a service we offer. I can help arrange your payment schedule—"

"Are you deaf? I don't need to change my payment date. I need to change the amount you're gouging me every month."

Most people's hackles would rise at this tone. Hal's seen it happen with his coworkers. Hal, on the other hand, settles back into his chair and smiles. Call it another superpower, or accident of personality.

"Sir, I would remind you that you took out an auto loan with a subprime lending company," he says.

"Excuse me?"

"You came to us because you needed to clean up your credit," Hal says. "That's an extra risk to us, and an extra risk comes with an extra cost."

"Now listen," the man says.

"We didn't create this situation," Hal says, upbeat and friendly. "We're helping you tidy it up. You're paying us for the favor. You agreed to all of this in writing, and it's not our fault if you didn't bother to read your contract. The APR will not change. But if you'd like to talk about changing your due date or would like to make a payment today, I'd be happy to help you."

"Fuck you, you little prick."

"I see here you're already past due," Hal says. "Would you like to make your payment?"

"Eat shit and die," the man says before he hangs up.

Hal sighs, relaxed for the first time all day. He loves a fight, verbal or physical. He's good at them. Can keep his cool while other people lose theirs.

But the high is short-lived. As the morning drags on and the seconds tick toward his meeting with his lawyer, he fumbles call after call, and eventually asks his supervisor if he can move to emails for the rest of the day.

For lunch, he goes to Taco Bell and orders two bean burritos. He sits in a booth meant for four, and while he eats, he stares into the middle distance, hoping the salt and fat will soothe his nerves. They do, for the few minutes it takes to eat them.

Hal clocks out at 2 p.m., and drives into Dallas. Hal's lawyer, Robert K. Tuttle, has his own building right off I-35. The frosted glass on the front doors bears a crest that reads "LIBERTY OR DEATH." It's the sort of thing a tacky person would mistake for classy.

The inside is every bit as ostentatious, with track lights and large paintings of Southwestern landscapes on the walls. It's a ridiculous place, but the firm's results are impressive. Tuttle's website has a long list of DWI and intoxication manslaughter charges dismissed or refiled as lesser charges. It's why Hal sold almost everything he owned to hire Tuttle.

The receptionist is polite and cheerful as she directs Hal to one of the plush leather chairs in the lobby. Hal tries to play a game on his phone as he waits, but he can't concentrate. After a few minutes, the attorney appears in his office doorway, shaking hands with a middle-aged woman who looks like she's having a bad day. Her sunken eyes are haunted, rimmed by heavy bags. Tuttle waits until she's out the front door before he shakes Hal's hand.

"Hal," Tuttle says. "How are you today?"

"You tell me."

Tuttle leads Hal into his office and takes a seat behind a massive desk with the "Liberty or Death" crest carved into the front. Hal takes one of the small chairs opposite, feeling like a little kid called to the principal's office.

Tuttle steeples his fingers. "You know I didn't invite you here to talk about the weather."

"I figured."

"It's not easy or fun to say this. The DA's office made a plea offer and I think it's the best we're going to get."

"Okay," Hal says. His voice sounds far away to his own ears.

"Ten years, with a chance of parole after the first five years served."

"Five to ten years," Hal says.

"We don't have to take it," Tuttle says. "We can go to trial, but it's a gamble. You might be acquitted, but you could also end up with a longer sentence. And a trial would cost you more, whether you won or lost."

"I see," Hal says, because he feels like he has to say something.

"Take a few days," Tuttle says. "Think about it."

He stands to let Hal know the meeting is over. Hal follows him out of the office. Tuttle pats him on the back but doesn't try to shake his hand again, for which Hal is grateful.

Hal's legs carry him to the edge of the sidewalk in front of the building before they give out and he sits down hard on the pavement. Pain shoots up from his tailbone, and the numbness vanishes, replaced with a sharp hatred of everything about Robert K. Tuttle, that smarmy cartoon of a man. Fucker probably thinks ten years is a good deal. Another victory to add to the list on his website.

Hal spreads his knees and lowers his head. He focuses on his breath, counts from one to ten. He's in the middle of the third round of counting when the earth rumbles. He looks up toward the highway, thinking it must be a truck, but he sees nothing big enough to make the ground shake. Also, the tremble isn't moving like an eighteen-wheeler. It seems to be everywhere.

He tries to stand up, to look around, but the ground beneath him softens, then pulls taut and bounces him like a kid on a trampoline. He trips and falls onto the sidewalk on his hands and knees. The burritos he had for lunch backflip in his stomach. Acid burns up his throat and he vomits all over the pavement. Bile splashes the back of his hands.

When his stomach stops heaving, he realizes that the earth has fallen quiet below him. He tries to stand again, bracing himself against the bumper of his car.

The tint of the world has changed. Everything has turned a burned, brownish tinge. The sky is a fiery red. But on the highway next to Tuttle's office, cars hurtle down the road as normal. No one stops to gape or scream like extras in a disaster movie. Is no one else seeing this? Is it just Hal? Did the plea deal snap his sanity?

His phone vibrates in his pocket. He bends over and wipes his hands on the grass before taking it out. The notification is a Facebook event invitation:

THE CLEGG HIGH SCHOOL
20th ANNIVERSARY MEMORIAL SERVICE

Athena

A couple of hours after Hal Isaac throws up outside his lawyer's office, Athena Watts teaches her sex magic seminar. It's her most popular talk, for obvious reasons, and the one she offers most often. She can teach it on autopilot now, and for much of tonight, that's what she's done, filling the whiteboard with diagrams of magic circles and pronunciations of obscure words, while her mind mulls the meeting she has scheduled after closing.

Athena's Books and Beans, her combination occult shop/café, is located in an old house in what most would call a "dangerous area" of Ashland, Oregon. The parking lot is more pothole than pavement, the front walk a series of broken concrete slabs. A seedy motel stands next door, and the housing projects are only three blocks away, but Athena's never had trouble with her neighbors, and the shop draws a respectable crowd of customers most days.

Said customer base comprises a few overlapping groups: first, people who want a decent cup of coffee not from Starbucks; second, practicing Wiccans and dilettante occultists (people who believe magic can be discovered and practiced with rituals found on the internet or in mass-market publications); and third (and smallest), real-deal Dissonance users. The first group keeps the café full of paying customers. The second group drops disposable income on worry stones and spell kits, and also accounts for most of the students who enroll in the classes, which Athena holds on the second floor of the house. But it's the third, secret group—the ones who know about the real power in this world—who keep the shop in the black. There's money in rocks and herbs and penis-shaped candles, but there's *money* in Dissonant artifacts and texts.

Garrett Thorpe, an old acquaintance and one of her most reliable dealers, called yesterday with a promise of something special. He's prone to exaggeration, but he's never offered her something she couldn't move. Also, he's good-looking for a white guy, and she never minds having his undivided attention for a little while.

Now, as her talk nears its end, she forces her thoughts away from those possibilities and back to the task at hand.

"Remember," she says. "You perform the ritual under a full moon. Outside, in direct moonlight, or the spell won't work. But if you get caught by kids with cameras or the police, you didn't hear any of this from me, okay?"

The students laugh, even the ones who've taken this seminar before. The lame jokes make all the middle-class white women feel more comfortable. As a Black woman in a mostly white community, Athena has had a lifetime of practice making white people feel comfortable.

"And if this goes well and you end up rich and famous, maybe let me wet my beak a little, all right?" She rubs her thumb and forefinger together in the universal sign for *Pay up,* which prompts another round of good-natured laughter. Athena forces a smile at her own joke.

Garrett appears in the classroom doorway—tall, black-haired, in jeans, T-shirt, and a sports coat despite the weather. He looks like the white Hollywood leading man version of a college professor. He sees what's happening, holds up a hand in apology, and backs out of sight. Athena turns toward the whiteboard but freezes as she catches her reflection in a darkened window: sleeves of her button-down shirt rolled up, brown hair barely contained by a scrunchie, Coke-bottle glasses in need of a good wipe-down. She's never felt more like a middle-aged schoolmarm. She swallows a sigh as she faces the class.

"I don't know why I started turning around," she says. "I have nothing else to write. All this sex talk has me flustered, I guess. Thank you all for coming. I mean, thank you for attending. Attending."

It's a weak joke, but it earns a laugh and mild applause. Most of the crowd disperses, but a few students hang back to ask questions. Athena does her best to answer while shepherding everyone downstairs and out the front door. Her barista, Danni, does the same with the last of the coffee drinkers. After Athena locks the front door and flips the sign to "CLOSED," she leaves Danni to clean up and returns upstairs to find Garrett in the classroom, studying the whiteboard.

"I don't recognize any of this," he says.

"It's Wiccan, not Dissonant."

Athena has known Garrett since she was fifteen years old, when they met at a conference of Dissonants. He used to be a straight-up asshole, but in early middle age he's mellowed into a likable blowhard. He's from a Dissonant family, one of those rare lines where the talent passes reliably from generation to generation. Like most old Dissonant families, his is very wealthy. He doesn't have to work, but he does anyway, traveling the world seeking and trading Dissonant texts and artifacts. Most of what he obtains, he sells to affluent collectors, but he offers smaller finds to shops like Athena's. She sometimes wonders if he visits her so often out of a sense of pity, or if maybe there's something more behind his frequent appearances. His visits always feel fraught with possibility, although she's never quite sure if the feeling is one-sided or not. Every time he visits, she inches closer to inviting him back to her place.

Garrett points to the board. "Does it work?"

"Am I selling snake oil, you mean?"

"I didn't mean it like that."

"Yes you did. And yes, the ritual works, but not in the way you're thinking." She walks past him and wipes the board with an eraser. "It's not a Dissonant command line. More like meditation. Directing your energies toward a goal."

"Sounds hippie-dippie," he says.

"To a snob, sure," she says. "It's like prayer. Hospital patients who pray recover faster than patients who don't. It's the layperson's method of drawing power from the universe, or maybe the mind manifesting what it wants by directing its own strengths through some imagined external force." She sets the eraser down.

"Sex magic," Garrett says, his tone more considering.

"Try it sometime," Athena says.

"Couldn't hurt."

"Depends how you like your sex." She doesn't wait for his reaction, but heads downstairs. After she bids Danni good night and watches to make sure the girl gets to her car okay, she and Garrett sit at one of the café tables, drinking beer instead of coffee. Garrett regales her with the story of his most recent adventure, something about a family of cannibals on Mount Nebo in Arkansas. She half-listens with a mix of jealousy and boredom. Garrett is a person impressed with his own experiences, and Athena hates herself a little for pretending to be impressed as well. It's good business—if Garrett suspects she has a crush, he'll underestimate or feel sorry for her, and give her a better price—but it's more than that. This obnoxious blowhard also reminds her of another obnoxious blowhard she knew as a kid. One whom she liked much better.

By the time Garrett's finished his second beer and third anecdote, Athena can't keep her curiosity in check any longer. She drops the façade of polite interest and asks, "So what do you have for me?"

Garrett looks a little startled at the abrupt change in her manner, but rolls with it. He lifts his briefcase onto the table and unclasps it. He removes a gold disc the circumference of a small dinner plate, but thick and solid like a barbell weight. Intricate designs are etched on the surface, making it look a bit like a bronzed circuit board.

"The cannibals were using this as a beer coaster," he says.

He cups his hands around the disc. Warm light shines from the designs on the surface—diffuse at first, and then coalescing into a swirling mass of colors, which then solidify into a three-dimensional image of a creature that could be an otherworldly woman. Her silvery skin shines like the moon, her eyes are solid black orbs, and her dark hair floats around her like she's underwater. Gills ripple on her neck. Her black eyes make it difficult to read her expression, but Athena thinks the creature looks sad. Her right arm bears a dark birthmark in the shape of a spade.

"It's a Dissonant painting," Garrett says. "A creature called—"

"An undine," Athena says. "A cosmic elemental." She scolds herself for interrupting, and for letting on she knows as much as she does.

"You know your stuff," he says, sounding impressed.

Athena chooses her next words with more care. "I thought the Dissonant community considered undine mythical. Part of the 'Many Worlds' heresy."

"They are," Garrett says. "Which is why I'm bringing this to you and not to a more upscale dealer. They'd consider it in bad taste. I thought I could count on your—and your clients'—discretion."

He strokes the edge of the disc, and the image zooms in on the undine's face. She looks familiar to Athena, like something from a dream.

"She seems unhappy," Athena says.

"Because she knows she's not real," Garrett says. It's a joke, but Athena can't fake a laugh for him. She's too exhausted after an evening of playing "teacher," and anyway her curiosity has taken over now. Once she's curious about something, it's hard to be anything else. She puts her hands on the disc and swipes a few times, to examine the image from multiple angles.

"Who's the artist?"

"If you were painting heretical images, would you sign your work? If I had to guess based on the design, I'd say it was done in the late '70s or early '80s, though."

"I'll take it," Athena says. "Usual terms." Meaning consignment. Fifty-fifty split on the proceeds. Garrett sets a minimum price, and Athena will negotiate anything on top of that.

"Cheers," he says. They clink the necks of their beer bottles and drain the remains.

After Garrett excuses himself to the restroom, Athena finishes cleanup. She's debating whether or not to finally take the plunge and invite Garrett back to her apartment when she overhears him talking in the bathroom. The walls in the old house are thin, and in the after-hours quiet, she can hear every word. The polite thing to do would be to make a lot of noise to bury his, or just leave. Instead, Athena stops tying up a trash bag to eavesdrop.

"No, the meeting went well," he says. "She's good. I doubt it'll take more than a few weeks to sell." A pause. "No, you're thinking of the guy in Austin. Whatshisname. This is the woman in Ashland. The one I met as a kid? Yeah, the cute, thick one. She really knew her shit back then, but then something happened to her whole coven, and after that she gave it all up for some reason. Doesn't practice anymore. Yeah." Another pause. "I dunno. Maybe? Fingers crossed. I'll text you and let you know how it goes."

Athena resumes garbage duties as the toilet flush roars. When she returns from the dumpster out back, Garrett is back in the café. He smiles at her, but the expression falters when he sees her face.

"Something wrong?" he says.

"No," she says. "Long day. I'm beat."

His face falls a little, and she feels a little stab of triumph. He was hoping she would finally ask him over, too. He's probably used to being invited wherever he wants. She almost feels sorry for him. Almost.

"Sure," he says, recovering quickly. "Same here. I'll get out of your hair."

She's walking him into the front room, past the display case and cash register, when she feels the tremor. Her first thought is that someone is driving past the store, blasting their bass. Only, unlike a bass tremor, which passes and fades, this one grows. The building begins to shake around her. The portrait disc—the painting of the undine—bounces on the table in the café. Garrett grabs her arm. She assumes he's trying to steady her, but he sways and, as he pulls her down to the floor, she realizes he was using her to keep his own footing. The wooden floor *hurts* when she hits it, and she feels every one of her thirty-seven years. She covers her head with her hands, because isn't that what you're supposed to do in an earthquake? Behind her she hears the portrait disc fall off the table and bang to the floor. But that, she notices, is the only unusual sound aside from the rumble of the quake. There's no shattering of glass, or clatter of pretty rocks falling out of their baskets, or glass jars of herbs shattering on the floor. When the rumble stops, and Athena sits up, everything in the entryway sits where it should—products on shelves, pictures straight on the walls. Like nothing happened.

"What the hell was that?" Garrett says. "Some kind of earthquake?"

"Maybe," she says. "But—" She gestures around the room at the lack of destruction. "You ever experienced anything like this before?"

"No," he says. "That was a first. Are you okay?"

"Yeah." Her heart and mind are both racing. What could have caused this? What does it mean that only she and Garrett and the portrait were affected?

In the ensuing silence, Athena's phone dings from its hiding place behind the counter.

Owen

The morning after Hal Isaac and Athena Watts experience their personal earthquakes, Owen Gilliland steps into the bathroom of his father's trailer in Wellspring, Alabama, sees himself in the mirror, and swears.

When he went to bed last night, he'd hoped he wouldn't look so bad in the morning. But the morning has come, and Owen's face has puffed up with a massive, impossible-to-hide black eye.

This leaves him with three options: he can call in sick; he can skip school without calling in; or he can go like this. None of these sounds appealing, but the first two sound worse than the third. If Owen calls in, he'll have to stay home with his father. The man's currently snoring through a hangover on the couch, but he'll wake up, and Owen doesn't want to be there when that happens.

There is a fourth option. Owen could pack a bag and leave. Sure. He's eighteen, and has a few hundred dollars in the bank. He's old enough to quit school and try his luck somewhere else. A big city where gay kids are commonplace and safe(ish). It could be an adventure. He'd have to sleep in his car until he found a place to live, but as long as he was careful with his money, he could make it, right?

This fantasy—of peace, of being able to breathe—carries him through his morning routine and all the way through his drive to Wellspring High, but it dissipates as he climbs from his car and hears Monica call his name. He fights a cringe as she jogs over to him, a look of concern on her blotchy red face.

"Owen," she says. She reaches for his cheek, but withdraws when he pulls away. "What happened?"

Last night, Owen's father, Bill Gilliland, barged into his son's bedroom without knocking, and got an eyeful of his son jerking off to a video of one man blowing another. Bill stood for a moment, processing the sight through a beery haze, and gave Owen almost enough time to shut the laptop and pull up his pants. Owen had his zipper up by the time his father crossed the room and punched him.

It could've been worse. The old man didn't yell, or lecture, or issue more physical discipline. He didn't ask any questions, or make any comments. After the punch, he left and shut Owen's door behind himself. Within an hour he was snoring on the living room couch. There's even a good chance that, when Bill wakes up, he won't remember the moment at all, and Owen will remain safely closeted to his father. The old man probably won't even ask about the black eye.

"Dad got drunk and I got in his way," Owen says to Monica, as they cross the parking lot toward the front doors of the school. He shrugs like it's not a big deal, but he doesn't look at her when he says it.

To her credit, Monica doesn't poke. She leaves the subject be and they walk in companionable silence to Economics. This is why she's his best friend. She knows who he is. She keeps his secrets like they're her own.

As the day goes on, a few other kids ask about the black eye, but none of Owen's teachers say anything. It's a small town. Most of them have known Bill Gilliland all their lives, and none of them wants to fuck with the man. Owen is torn between sympathy and outrage. They're the grown-ups. Aren't they supposed to do something?

By lunchtime, Owen's feeling almost normal. He and Monica have a booth in the cafeteria all to themselves, and sit across from one another, absorbed in their homework, until Lucy Cushing approaches the table. Lucy is one of the kids who wears all black every day and listens to nothing but metal. She's dating Owen's crush, Cole White, the de facto king of the Wellspring High goths. Owen has been in honors classes with Cole since grade school.

"What's with your face?" Lucy says.

"He got in a badass fight," Monica says, without looking up from her precalculus textbook. "What's your excuse?"

Lucy smirks, acknowledging the point scored. "Are you two busy tomorrow night?"

Monica's head snaps up, and she answers before Owen can: "We are not."

"Do you feel like getting into some trouble?"

"Depends on the trouble."

"Midnight ritual at the cemetery," Lucy says. "We need two more people." She faces Owen now. "Cole thought you might be into it."

Across the cafeteria, all the kids at the goth table stare at Owen. Most look skeptical, and who can blame them? Nothing about Owen or Monica screams *midnight ritual*. But Cole, skinny and pale, stringy black hair in a ponytail, blue eyes bright behind his glasses, wears the same face he wears in English class when he argues with Mrs. Clanton. If Owen had to name it, he would call the expression *amused contempt*. It always creates a little tug behind Owen's breastbone, and it warms his face now.

"We're in," Monica says.

"Great," Lucy says. "We'll pick you up tomorrow around eleven-thirty. Wear black, okay?"

They exchange numbers and Lucy returns to the goth table. Owen scowls at Monica. "What the hell?"

"You have objections?" Monica says.

He has plenty. Monica agreed to this adventure without asking what sort of ritual they're attempting. Owen knows fuck-all about the occult, but he assumes nothing aboveboard happens in a graveyard after dark.

Before he can say any of this, he looks at the goth table again. Cole gives him a smile and a thumbs-up, and his cheeks warm. What *is* the worst that can happen? They're all of them just high school kids, led by an honors student, for fuck's sake. It'll be a bit of mischief, maybe a touch of petty vandalism, and they'll all go home high on the adrenaline.

"No," Owen says. "No objections."

"That's right. Now say 'Thank you, Monica.'"

"Thank you, Monica."

Erin

The day after Owen Gilliland accepts an invitation to a midnight ritual, Erin Porter is running late to her job in Iowa City. The parking deck closest to her job is so packed she has to park on the roof, and when she gets out of the car, she's still two blocks away and five minutes late. She can't afford to wait for the elevator. She sprints down the stairs and between pedestrians on the sidewalk, only slowing when the High Ground Café comes into view.

She stops, wrestles her blond hair back into a semblance of a bun, and walks through the front door, trying to look casual as she maneuvers around a long line of grad students and TAs. From behind the register, Erin's boss, Manny, gives her an impressive frown. He's twenty-six, recently promoted to manager, and treats his new position with deathly seriousness. She hurries into the kitchen to throw on her apron and nametag, washes her hands, and steps back into the café proper.

"You want me to take the register or make drinks?" she says.

"Make drinks," Manny says.

Erin might have a punctuality problem, but once she's at work, she's fast and accurate. She and Manny deplete the mid-afternoon line in under twenty minutes, sending the serious-looking intellectuals to their stools and booths with caffeinated drinks and baked goods.

When the third barista, Cindy, gets back from her break, Manny asks Erin to see him in his office—a closet in the stock area, with a tiny desk and a single chair. Manny takes the chair and Erin has to stand. As he studies her, she fights the urge to cross her arms. She won't show him how uncomfortable this makes her.

"Why are you back here, Erin?" he says.

Because you're an asshole. "Because I was late." She looks him in the eye. She's ten years older than he is. This little creep won't cow her.

"Because you were late." He pinches the bridge of his nose. "Is this job important to you?"

"Sure." Rage tightens her jaw. She can't stand being talked to like a child.

"Times are tough. Do you know how many applications get dropped off every day, 'just in case'?"

She unclenches her jaw through sheer force of will. "I'll do better."

"We'll see." He waves her out.

She spends the next few hours making drinks and warming up pre-made sandwiches for the crowd of graduate students. She's not sure whether she envies or pities her customers. On the one hand, they're in school, doing something with their lives. On the other, Erin knows the job situation in this city. She moved here a few years ago, looking for a change after drifting rudderless through her twenties. What she found when she arrived was a town full of PhDs working in call centers and waiting tables. Erin couldn't get a callback from a temp agency, let alone an interview for an office job. She ended up doing the same thing in Iowa she'd been doing in Texas: serving coffee. Her position here, at the High Ground, is her third coffee shop job in as many years. They fired her from the first for tardiness, and she quit the second to start here.

She had other reasons for coming to Iowa, originally, but she tries not to think about that. Avoidance is the only path forward. Only pay attention to what's right in front of you. It's how she gets through today's shift—the next transaction, the next drink, the next table to bus. She builds a chain of hours to pull herself through the afternoon and into the evening, when the staff lock the doors, stack the chairs, mop the floors, wash the dishes, carry out the trash, and go home.

Erin hurries to the parking garage, stops for drive-through, which she eats on the drive back to her apartment building, and nearly screams when she opens the front door of her third-floor unit and finds a figure looming in the darkened entryway, head and shoulders silhouetted in the light from the windows. She catches herself in time. It's only Philip.

"You scared me," she says.

"I'm sorry," Philip says.

She flips on the entryway light, illuminating his prominent, dimpled chin, aquiline nose, and blue eyes.

"Why are you hanging out in the dark?"

"Am I not supposed to?"

"When the sun goes down, most people like lights. It would make me happier if you would turn them on."

He smiles and Erin experiences a strange mix of sorrow, pity, and lust. She pushes past him into the apartment to hide her expression. The complexity might confuse him.

He follows her from room to room as she turns on lights. "How was work?" he asks.

"Boring. I don't want to talk about it."

They enter the bedroom, and here Erin leaves the light off. She drops her purse to the floor, disrobes, and crawls onto the bed to sit up against the headboard.

"Come," she says.

He undresses, leaving his clothes on the floor by her own, and climbs into bed with her.

She reaches between his legs and finds him hard, ready. She guides him into her. He moves slowly at first, teasing her the way she taught him.

"I've been thinking about this all day," she says.

"Me too," he says, and she understands he means he's missed her and looked forward to her return. That he's eager to please her.

As he slides all the way in, she clenches the back of his neck with one hand and touches herself with the other. She's got pent-up frustration to fuck out, and doesn't need much time. When she finishes and cries out into his shoulder, he remains atop her, erect and calm, until she pushes him off.

He lies down and lifts an arm so she can snuggle on his chest. His breath slows and evens out. He's almost dozed off when she lifts her head.

"Did you enjoy it?" she asks.

He opens his eyes. "Yes." When she continues to stare at him, he adds, "It was very good."

"What does that mean to you? 'Very good'?"

He gives the question some consideration. "I'm happy I pleased you. Am I misunderstanding? Did I do poorly?"

"I don't think you're capable of a poor performance," she says. "What I mean is, did it *feel* good for you? Not in your heart, but in your body."

"I think so," he says, but he sounds confused.

Revulsion runs up her arm from the point of contact. She lets him go and rolls away onto her side.

"Did I say something wrong?" he asks.

"No." She gets up to use the bathroom, where she finishes getting ready for bed. She doesn't meet his eye when she returns and climbs under the covers.

"Good night," he says.

"Sweet dreams, Philip."

It takes her mind a while to settle. She's only just started to drift off when something hits the bedroom window.

Philip stirs beside her. She rolls over to look at him, mind hazy and confused, wondering if he made the sound. Then it happens again: a *whump* against the glass, followed by a skittery flapping noise.

She gets out of bed. As she pads across the bare hardwood floor, another long silence stretches out. She approaches the window and yanks the curtains apart. A greasy gray streak mars her view, but she can see the city street below, the cars at a stoplight, college kids traveling in packs.

Erin opens her mouth to report what she sees when something slams into the window and cracks the glass. She lets go of the curtains and steps back. A pigeon has pancaked across the window, wings spread, head twisted at an unnatural angle. Its beak opens and closes. Its wings twitch. Gravity takes over, and the bird adds its own ghostly streak to the glass. Before it can drop, another bird swoops out of the dark and into the first bird's back. The crack in the window spiderwebs out from the point of impact with a sound like breaking ice.

Before she can decide what to do, another bird hits the glass. And another. And another. The sky, formerly purple black, becomes a live, flapping mass of gray and white that crashes into and through the window with a feathery explosion, a flood of wings and beaks and talons, a legion of angry squawks and cries.

Erin throws herself to the floor. She can't see Philip through the flurry, can't hear her own screams above the din. The torrent of birds hits the headboard and the wall above it. Broken bodies pile up on the bed where she slept a moment ago, then flop onto the floor where she cowers now. Most are dead, but many remain alive. They flap and claw at one another with what looks like blind panic, or rage. One with a broken wing rolls upright and turns its yellow glare on Erin. It hops toward her, squawking. Other intact pigeons close in as well—one missing an eye, one with a leg facing the wrong direction. They hop and drag themselves forward, beaks snapping open and shut, shiny eyes wide and inscrutable, individual cries drowned in the cacophony of this localized apocalypse.

Erin scrabbles back over broken glass and discarded clothing until her head bumps the wall. Birds continue to flood through the broken window, to pile up on the bed and spill onto the floor. The ones who can fly take flight. The ones who can't find other ways to move, dragging themselves on broken wings or by beak.

Philip cowers in the opposite corner, arm across his face to protect his eyes as the horde descends, scratching and clawing and biting and pecking at his flesh. The sight startles the needle of Erin's mind back into its accustomed groove. She stands, raising her hands like a sorceress in a storybook, and draws in the air, leaving streaks of green light behind her.

A great clap tears through the racket, followed by a shuffling sound as every bird in the room drops, dead. Philip uncovers his face and looks at the tableau on the floor in front of him, then at the jagged hole where the window used to be. A humid breeze tickles the curtains.

Erin realizes her arms are still above her head. She lowers them to examine herself. Her pajamas hang off her, shredded. Cuts and scratches crosshatch her arms. Philip's arms are also marked, but his face appears to be intact. She's grateful for this—and ashamed for how grateful she is.

"Are you all right?" she asks.

"I think so," he says. "Are you?"

"Yes," she says. "Not hurt bad anyway." At least, she doesn't think she is. She won't know for sure until the adrenaline wears off. She needs to move before that happens. She tiptoes through a carpet of dead birds to find and put on sneakers, then walks down the hall into the living room. Every window is broken, every surface festooned with dead pigeons. The flatscreen TV hangs in a precarious balance between its stand and the coffee table, its screen cracked from the impact. The hardwood floors are invisible beneath layers of gray and white feathers and unseeing yellow eyes.

She leans out one of the broken living room windows. Hundreds of dead birds line the street below. Their bodies form a trail that leads around the corner at the end of the block. A few pedestrians stand amid the carnage. One or two stare up at her, baffled.

"What happened?"

Erin startles to find Philip beside her. She didn't hear him following. "A fleet of birds suicide-bombed our apartment," she says. "Make more noise when you move. It's unsettling when you sneak up on me."

"I'll try," he says. "What happened to the birds? Why did they die?"

"Because I told them to," she says.

She goes back to the bedroom. She hears his footsteps behind her now, slow and heavy.

"But *why* did they try to hurt us?"

She opens the closet and pulls down two armfuls of clothes. "Someone's trying to kill me." *Or you.* Her thoughts remain diffuse, scattered. She sweeps a blanket of pigeon bodies off the bed and drops a pile of clothes in their place. She turns around looking for her suitcase, then spots her phone on the nightstand. She picks it up and sees the notification she ignored earlier. A Facebook invitation:

THE CLEGG HIGH SCHOOL
20th ANNIVERSARY MEMORIAL SERVICE

Owen

Almost twenty-four hours after Erin Porter flees her apartment with Philip in tow, Owen and Monica change clothes in Monica's bedroom. Once Owen has pulled on jeans and his only black T-shirt, he and Monica sneak out her bedroom window, leaving it cracked for their return. Cole's station wagon sits idling at the curb.

"Remember," Monica says, as they cross the lawn. "The secret is to act like you belong."

The car's hatchback door swings open. There's a boy inside, next to a big picnic cooler. Owen recognizes Cole's best friend, Dean.

"We're almost out of room so you'll have to squeeze in," he says.

Owen and Monica negotiate the space as best they can, and once they're secure inside, Cole gets out of the driver's seat and comes around to the rear to shut the door for them.

"Glad you could make it," he says.

"Happy to be here," Owen says. He hates how lame it sounds.

Cole gets back in the driver's seat. Lucy rides up front with him.

It's a twenty-minute drive from Wellspring to the town of Culver, where the ritual will take place. Owen spends most of the ride in silence, listening to Cole and his friends joke and argue hot takes about the current metal scene. Their boisterousness fades as signs of civilization melt away, until the station wagon floats alone down a two-lane road, hemmed in by long stretches of forest. Occasional homes and churches flash past. The buildings look old, like they've been rotting in the dark for centuries.

Cole turns off onto an old farm road and parks the station wagon in front of a Baptist church. The building sits at the base of a steep hill lined with tombstones, and has an electric sign that might be advertising worship services or announcing the time and temperature. There are too many dead bulbs to tell for sure.

Cole and Dean carry the cooler up the hill. Lucy pulls several tiki torches from the back seat. They walk up the hill to a fresh grave. Dean shines his flashlight on the tombstone: Estelle Schaefer, Beloved Wife and Mother, 1947–2019.

Once they're all gathered around the grave, Cole frowns down the hill at the road. He turns to Dean. "The cemetery's more exposed than I expected," he says.

"You wanted a fresh grave in an obscure location," Dean says. "We're on a farm road in the middle of nowhere. If a cop drives by, then, well, the universe clearly has other plans for us."

Cole gives Dean a sour look but doesn't argue. While they set to work unpacking the cooler, Lucy enlists Monica's and Owen's help setting up the torches in a circle around the grave. When lit, they give the area a spooky old-fashioned feel, although the effect is somewhat muted by the smell of insecticide wafting from the flames. The flashing, inarticulate billboard doesn't help, either.

Owen now also has enough light to see what was in the cooler: a broken rake handle with a sharp point at the end, like the home and garden version of a spear; several Ziploc bags of dried plants; a lighter; a paperback book; a glass jar of dark fluid; and what looks like a real human skull.

Dean shoos everyone out of the torch circle and sets to work with his homemade spear. He scratches a broad circle on the ground, and then draws smaller circles and symbols inside it. Owen is so intent on watching that he startles when someone nudges his right arm. It's Cole.

"Didn't mean to scare you," Cole says. "What do you think?"

"This is spookier than I expected." It's not, but Owen wants to be polite. "It's my first ritual."

"I never would've guessed," Cole says, but he smiles to show he's kidding.

"Have you guys done a lot of these?"

"A few."

"Do you usually do them at a cemetery?"

Cole shakes his head. "Usually we try to manifest good grades with sex magic or whatever we can find online. I know I wear a lot of black, but even I'm not goth enough to fuck in a graveyard."

Owen wonders how this group of goths would conduct a sex ritual. Do they pair off, or do they congeal into a mass of limbs and nerve endings, like that scene in *Caligula*? His face burns in the dark as he considers the possibilities.

"Mary Shelley was that level of goth," Owen says. "She lost her virginity on her mother's grave."

"Queen of the goths," Cole says.

"Okay, so we're not here for sex," Owen says, face burning even hotter now. "What are we doing?"

"Necromancy," Cole says.

The word sounds familiar. Didn't Gandalf spend some time trapped by a necromancer in *The Hobbit*?

"Something to do with magic and the dead?" Owen ventures.

"In ancient cultures, the idea was to seek the wisdom of your ancestors. Or to get information only the dead might have—about the afterlife, or the spirit world, or where you could find some lost treasure hoard."

"And what are you looking for?" Owen asks. "Tonight, I mean. With the ritual."

"Me and Dean have different reasons. Dean has some real questions about the afterlife, since his brother died when he was little. Me? I just want to see if we can do it. I mean, the other stuff we've done before, the other rituals? Maybe they worked, or maybe it was the power of positive thinking or whatever. But with this, it either works or it doesn't. Either that skull over there will talk, or not. Proof, either way."

He smiles at Owen and the goth visage vanishes, leaving the nerdy boy Owen remembers—the one who wore braces and ill-fitting clothes until last summer, when he went all-in on the black wardrobe and death metal.

Owen smiles back, genuinely happy for the first time tonight.

"It could also mean you did the ritual wrong, if it doesn't work. Or maybe used the wrong ritual," Owen says.

Cole nods. "If we get through this without getting arrested and it doesn't work, I'm done. Back to praying to the earth mother before sex or whatever. You can only tempt fate so many times." He squeezes Owen's arm. "I'm glad you came."

"Yeah," Owen says. "Me too."

Dean stops scratching the ground and wipes perspiration from his forehead. "Done," he says, and tosses the little spear into the grass beside him. It rolls down the hill and into the ditch at the bottom.

"I'm not going after that," Lucy says, annoyed.

"No one is asking you to," Dean says, matching her tone.

"Let's get started," Cole says.

Owen follows Cole into the circle. Monica falls in step beside Owen and bumps his shoulder. She must've overheard his conversation with Cole. He bumps her back and feels warm inside.

"No matter what happens, do not step outside of this circle," Dean says. "This is the safe space. Nothing can cross in. Got it?"

Everyone mumbles their agreement as they shuffle into the circle. Cole kneels in front of the tombstone and sets the skull atop it. Dean removes the herbs from the bags, places them in a small bowl, and uses the lighter to set them aflame. Tendrils of smoke drift into the air, filling the space with the thick aroma of sage.

Dean unseals the glass jar and hands it to Cole. A coppery smell joins the sage in Owen's nostrils. Blood. There's blood in the jar. Cole dumps it atop the skull, staining it and the tombstone beneath crimson. He plants both hands on the stone and begins to speak. His voice is strong and clear and carries, but the words are nonsense to Owen's ears until Cole switches to English:

"Thee I invoke, Silver Hunter from the Sacred City of UR! Thee I call forth to guard this North Place of the Most Holy Mandal against the vicious warriors of Flame and the Principalities of DRA!" He continues, invoking guardian spirits for the circle, and Owen makes a disheartening discovery: even a necromancy ritual can be boring. His mind drifts, carried sleepily along on the rhythm of Cole's voice. He thinks about how tired he's going to feel in the morning. Maybe he should call in sick. But the problem is the same as always: then he'd be at home with his dad, which might be worse.

Owen's eyelids are growing heavy when the scent of the air changes.

An acrid, sulfurous stench replaces the incense odor. The switch snaps him back to wakefulness.

The world looks no different—everyone still in the protective circle, the preposterous billboard still flashing at the foot of the hill. But the cicadas have stopped singing. The only things Owen can hear are his breath, Cole's incantations, and a high-pitched whine. Light flickers at the corners of Owen's vision, but when he turns for a better look, he can't find the cause.

The ground shakes, and Owen stumbles back.

"Holy shit," Lucy says. Owen can barely hear her over the increasingly shrill wail.

A hand clamps on Owen's elbow. It's Monica, horrified. Owen doesn't understand, but then he looks down. He's stepped outside of the circle of protection. Although the ground within the circle appears to be soft dirt and grass, the world outside it has been replaced by a dark cave of jagged stone, lit only by firelight. Figures in diaphanous white gowns encircle the ritual participants. These creatures have stitches where their eyes and noses should be. Only their mouths remain open. The whining is coming from them. The sound grows, infiltrates his body, vibrates his insides until he feels like he'll melt into a pile of goo. He covers his ears, but it makes no difference. The whine pierces his mind, relentless.

"Barashakushu, worker of miracles," Cole shouts, barely audible above the din, "kindest of the fifty, we call to thee. Barashakushu, we invoke thy protection during this most dangerous of elixir-based rituals. Please hear our prayer and come to us."

If Barashakushu (whoever that is) is around, they're not taking calls. The eyeless figures encircling the group continue to whine, and raise their withered hands to beat upon the barrier of the circle.

"I don't like this," Lucy says. Gone is her goth-mean-girl attitude, replaced by a small, scared kid out past curfew. "I want to go home."

Dean grabs her arm. "Don't move. This is all part of it. Just stay in the circle."

Lucy stands in place, trembling, tears streaking her makeup. Cole remains in front of the tombstone, braced to keep his balance as the earth shakes. The vibrations move, narrowing inward toward the circle of earth directly beneath the ritual participants. The freshly turned dirt on the grave falls away as the vibrations increase and worsen. Something bursts up out of the ground in a plume of dirt and wraps itself around Cole's ankle. It's a hand, white and withered.

Cole screams and tries to stand. He stumbles in the hand's grasp and hits Monica, Lucy, and Owen. Lucy falls outside the circle and the spirits' whining becomes a screech that stabs into Owen's brain. He falls to his knees and covers his head with his hands. He hears Lucy screaming, and Monica, although he can't make out the words. He hears the sounds of commotion. Of bodies moving. Tearing.

Gradually, the noises taper off. Owen risks a look around. The wraiths outside the circle have vanished. The everyday world of Wellspring has returned, the night sky clear and awash with stars, the Baptist church and its billboard. Lucy, Monica, and Dean all lie partially in and partially out of the circle. All are missing limbs. Dean is missing his head as well. It's nowhere in sight. Maybe it rolled to the bottom of the hill. Maybe one of the wraiths took it for a souvenir. Only Cole appears to be intact. He lies on his back, struggling weakly as the corpse of Estelle Schaefer chokes the life from him. Light seems to flow between her face and Cole's, a vivid, unnatural green.

Owen's body acts without his consent. It turns him around and launches him down the hill. His feet thud on the grass in a sort of hybrid-jog/controlled fall. His breath sounds ragged and heavy. His ears ring with the ghosts of the wraiths' whine. Cole's station wagon is close. The tailgate is open. Owen can't remember if they took the keys when they got out. But if he can lock himself in the car, he might be safe until someone passes. Maybe that one-in-a-million cop will come.

He loses his footing, hits the ground on one shoulder, and rolls the rest of the way down the hill, landing with a splash in the wet ditch at the bottom. Water soaks through his jeans and T-shirt. Footsteps tromp down toward him, as awkward and heavy as a toddler learning to run.

Owen pushes up on his hands and knees and stands. What he sees coming down the hill fills him with relief—it's not the corpse of Estelle Schaefer.

"Cole," he says. "Oh, thank Christ."

Cole looks as though he doesn't recognize Owen. Is the other boy in shock? Before Owen can ask, Cole pulls the car keys from his pocket. They dangle in the air, reflecting the light from the torches that burn on the hill behind him.

"Can you drive?" Cole says. It's Cole's voice, but *not* Cole's diction. Cole's eyes flash yellow-green, and Owen's relief ebbs into something else.

"Yes," Owen says, through numb lips.

The Cole-thing hands him the keys. "Drive," it says, "and maybe I'll let you live."

1996
The Sleepover

Athena

Most days, after art class, Athena Watts met Erin Porter and they made the walk to history together. But on May 17, 1996—the last day of their junior high careers—Athena didn't find her friend in the hall. She was confused, and a little worried. She'd seen Erin at lunch, and the other girl had seemed fine. That had only been an hour ago. Where could Erin be?

Athena was so worried that she did a thing she almost never did: she stood in the busy corridor, waiting for her friend to show up. She counted out one hundred and twenty Mississippis before she gave up and walked toward class alone.

She was momentarily distracted from her concern when she spotted Hal Isaac coming toward her from the opposite direction. She'd been trying to talk to him all day, but keeping him still for more than a few seconds had proven difficult. The end-of-the-school-year energy was infectious, and Hal, already a coiled spring of a boy, was more susceptible than most. He pogoed down the hall now like a real-life Tigger, and she had to grab his arm to keep him from bouncing past without seeing her.

"Athena," he said, throwing up his hands like a circus ringleader and almost smacking a couple of passers-by. "What a pleasant surprise! What brings you to the 300 hallway?"

"History," Athena said.

"It will be soon. Get it? Because it's the last day of school, and that class will be in your past forever?"

"Slow down. Take a breath before you burst a blood vessel."

He closed his eyes, took a deep breath. "Only for you. What's up?"

"Have you seen Erin? She usually walks to class with me."

He shook his head. "Not since lunch. Why?"

Athena had a good reason to worry—or at least, she thought she did. After all, that kid had gone missing just a few days ago. Charlie Simmons. He was only a few years younger than Athena and her friends. But she also knew if she told Hal why she was worried, he'd roll his eyes at her. He'd ask about the odds Erin could be abducted, in broad daylight, at school, and Athena would have a hard time arguing the point.

So instead of pressing, she offered him the yearbook she'd been carrying under her arm all day, and asked the question she'd been too nervous to ask at lunch: "Sign it for me?"

They stepped out of the flow of traffic and to the bank of lockers on one side to trade yearbooks. Athena opened Hal's to find the endpapers jammed with signatures—endless repetitions of *Stay sweet!* or *Have a great summer!* In the crease between the front cover and first endpaper, some wit had written, *Signed your crack!*

She looked from the book to Hal, to make a joke about how silly all of this was, and how silly they were for participating, but Hal wore a look of deep concentration. He appeared to be composing a solid brick of text on Athena's mostly empty back endpaper.

She turned back to his book and tried to decide what to write, how honest to be. She wished she could see what he was writing. If it was something sincere and she made a "signed your crack" joke, that would be the end of the world for her. On the other hand, if he was writing something stupid, and *she* wrote something honest and heartfelt, that would also be the end of the world. So unless she guessed perfectly, life was over.

She decided to err on the side of caution, and wrote *You're a dumbass, but we can still be friends*. She almost added *Happy birthday!* But settled for *Let's have the best summer*. And after a sharp intake of breath, she added *XOXO*.

Hal was still writing even after she finished. The crowd in the hall had thinned, and her inner clock warned her that the tardy bell was coming soon. If they didn't hurry, they would be late to class. Athena was never late to class.

"Come on," she said.

"You can't rush genius." He finished scribbling and offered her the book. "See you tonight, yeah?"

"Unless you go blind before then," she said, as they traded.

"You're weird, lady." He walked backward down the hall and shot finger guns at her. Despite her mounting anxiety, she waited for him to turn around before she sprinted the rest of the way to history class.

Erin wasn't in the classroom when Athena arrived, and Athena's anxiety increased again. She tried to distract herself by looking at what Hal had written in her yearbook.

Between the time when the oceans drank Atlantis and the rise of the sons of Aryas, there was an age undreamed of. And unto this, Conan, destined to wear the jeweled crown of Aquilonia upon a troubled brow. It is I, his chronicler, who alone can tell thee of his saga. Let me tell you of the days of high adventure!

No salutation. No signature. Was it a joke? The name Conan sounded familiar. Did Hal mean the guy on late-night TV? No, that couldn't be right. Maybe these were lines from a movie?

She closed the book, feeling the way she often did after an interaction with Hal—a little hurt, a little nonplussed, a little hopeful. He was a goof. He'd been a goof since they met in kindergarten. He was probably being funny. He'd failed, but Athena could cut him some slack. He'd had a rough week. His birthday had been on Monday and his mother had completely forgotten. No presents, no cake. Not even a *Happy birthday* from dear old Mom. Hal hadn't made a fuss about it, though. He hadn't said anything to Athena. The only reason Athena knew was because Peter Marsh had told Erin, and Erin had told Athena.

She put the yearbook in her backpack but continued to puzzle over it until the tardy bell rang, and Erin Porter—tall, thin, blond, and increasingly pretty—swept into the classroom, face flush.

"I'm sorry I'm late, Mr. Canon," she said, nodding toward the teacher behind the desk.

He barely glanced up from his Tom Clancy novel. "I do not care, Miss Porter. Take your seat, please."

Erin ducked her head, chastised by the lack of chastisement. Like Athena, Erin had always been one of the smart kids. She and Athena had always been in the same honors classes, and still were. The difference was that, this year, Erin had started to look like a cheerleader, while Athena remained short, stocky, bespectacled, and—her biggest social handicap—one of only eight Black students at the junior high in the small town of Clegg, Texas. Erin tried to pretend things were the same as always, but the fact was, doors were opening for her now—doors that wouldn't open for Athena.

"Where were you?" Athena asked.

"I was with Peter, making plans for tonight," Erin said.

"Everything good?"

Erin gave her a thumbs-up as Mr. Canon stood. He put his book down on his desk, open, facedown. Athena winced. Her mother did that with paperbacks all the time, even though it was bad for the spine. She hurt on the book's behalf.

"All right," Mr. Canon said. "Welcome to our last hour together, class. It can go one of two ways. Either we can watch a movie until the bell rings"—he was interrupted by a chorus of cheers—"or we can take a quiz covering every single unit we've done this year." This was followed by a chorus of outrage. A tiny bit of a smile tugged at his lips. He was enjoying this. "This is not an empty threat. I have xeroxed copies of the quiz on my desk. What matters is whether you can keep the volume down for the next hour."

The room fell deathly silent in response.

"I take it you'd like the movie," Mr. Canon said. "Okay then." He put on *1776,* and went back to his desk to continue reading.

Athena wanted to ask more questions about tonight, but she also didn't want to risk Mr. Canon's wrath, so she watched the movie until the bell rang and junior high ended forever. Erin made a quick goodbye—she was going back to Peter's to get ready—and then Athena started the walk home.

She told herself she was wrong to feel stung by Erin's abrupt departure. Athena almost always walked home alone, because her house lay in a different direction than the homes of her three closest (and only) friends. Hal Isaac and Erin Porter lived in the town's only apartment complex and trailer park, respectively, so they tended to walk home together. Peter Marsh, the richest person Athena knew, lived with his grandfather, Professor Elijah Marsh, in a house outside the city limits, so he made his way home alone, too.

If Athena and her friends were the three bears from the fairy tale, Athena would've been baby bear, nestled happily between Peter's wealth and Hal's and Erin's poverty. She and her parents lived in the middle-class part of town, in a one-story brick house with a small, flat lawn. Her mother was a nurse and her father did something in an office in Tyler, although Athena was never sure what. Hers was the only Black family that lived in that part of town. Their neighbors were polite—no one was burning crosses on the lawn—but they held the Watts family at arm's length. Athena felt the distance whenever she saw or heard her neighbors having a cookout or a party, to which her family was never invited. She didn't mind. Most of her neighbors seemed like stupid hicks, and she'd always been an outsider. She didn't need anyone, as long as she had her books, her mind.

She was halfway home when someone called her name. It was Jordan McCormick, jogging up behind her. He was one of her white neighbors. They'd lived on the same street all of their lives. Jordan was two years ahead of Athena and occupied the opposite end of the social spectrum. Where Athena was short and bookish, Jordan was tall and handsome. Where Athena was obscure to most of her classmates, Jordan was popular. He'd been the only sophomore on the varsity football team this year, and had proven himself a dependable linebacker, according to the chatter Athena had heard in town. She didn't know what it meant, but it sounded impressive. More impressive, though: he was kind to Athena, though he had no incentive to be.

"Happy last day of school," he said, as he caught up and fell into step with her. "Is it okay if I walk with you?"

"Sure. You can fend off any attacking players from rival teams." She glanced up at him. "Is that what linebackers do?"

"Sure. Exactly that. Big plans for the summer?"

"Big stack of books to read," she said. "You?"

"Training. And practice. And more training. And more practice."

"With a schedule like that, you should set up a cot in the locker room."

He laughed. "You wouldn't say that if you'd been in there. It stinks of armpit and . . ." He stopped there and pressed his mouth shut.

"Oh come on," she said. "Armpit and what?"

"It's rude," he said.

"I won't wilt. The locker room smells like armpit and . . . ?"

". . . And ball sweat," he finished.

"Oh my God, you're sick," she said. "Why would you say that?"

"I'm sorry," he said, flustered. "I thought you wanted to hear it." He looked like he wouldn't mind a quiet, instant death.

"Relax," she said. "I'm messing with you."

His horrified look changed to confusion, then relief. He forced a little laugh.

"Didn't take you for a kidder," he said.

"I contain multitudes."

Jordan seemed to absorb the joke as a rebuke. She wanted to take it back, but didn't know how. The awkwardness stretched the silence between them until they came to her house, and she turned to him, trying to figure out how to say goodbye and sorry at the same time.

"Want to sign each other's yearbooks?" he asked.

"We don't go to the same school," Athena said.

"We will in a few months. Think of this as a 'welcome aboard' signature."

They made the exchange—her slim blue yearbook for his much thicker, heavier black one. Jordan didn't make fun of Athena's empty endpapers, although his own, like Hal's, were covered in signatures and jokes and doodles. She found a bit of free space inside the back cover and wrote, in the smallest script she could manage: *Have a great summer! Knock 'em dead (yes, dead) at practice.* She refrained from adding, *Stay hydrated,* because he probably knew to do that.

"Be seeing you around this summer?" Jordan asked, as they traded back.

"I live here," she said. "Be hard not to."

"You're not even in high school yet and you're already too cool for me," he said.

Athena waited until she was inside her house before she read what Jordan had written: *Stay sweet!*

Well, it wasn't like she'd written something profound in his yearbook, either.

"How was school?" her father shouted from the living room.

"Fine," Athena shouted back. "You're home early."

"I wanted to see you off, since your mom has to work."

She rolled her eyes, tucked the yearbook under one arm, took her shoes off (the Watts household was a no-shoes-indoors kind of place), then headed for her bedroom. She set the yearbook down on her desk, her mind back on Hal's enigmatic signature. This was how her mind worked. It got hold of a question and wouldn't let go until it got a satisfactory answer. She worked this puzzle as she laid out clothes for tonight's sleepover at Peter's house. She started with pajamas, but for the first time in her life, every sleeping garment she owned looked like little kid stuff. She couldn't let her friends see this foolishness. She picked a tank top and sweatpants instead.

She was on her tiptoes, straining to grab the sleeping bag on the top shelf of her closet when her father entered the room.

"Let me help," he said. He was only a little taller than Athena, but had the better reach. She stepped out of the way and let him hand her the sleeping bag.

"I'm not sure about this," he said.

Athena suppressed a sigh. She'd known this was what he'd meant by *I wanted to see you off*. One last chance at a lecture. At least he hadn't wasted time getting to the point.

"When you four were little," he said, "it was one thing. But you're teenagers now."

"Dad," she said, failing to keep the whine out of her tone. "We already talked about this." Tonight's party—the end-of-junior-high sleepover at Marsh House—had been a hard-fought and hard-won victory, and not one she intended to surrender now.

"I know," he said. "And it's not that I don't trust you. I just don't trust teenage hormones."

"That's the same thing as not trusting me," Athena said. "Besides, it's not like we're unsupervised. Professor Marsh will be home the whole time. You think he's going to let anything wild go down in his house?"

Dad still looked uncomfortable. "That house is too close to the woods. And the Simmons boy is missing."

"Charlie Simmons is ten, Dad. He went into the woods by himself.

There are four of us. We won't go outside after dark, and I doubt anyone's going to try and sneak in to abduct a bunch of teenagers." She felt a little hypocritical, arguing these points, when she herself had been worried about Erin only an hour ago.

A car horn honked out front. Athena shoved the last of her clothes into her bag, along with a Ziploc full of toiletries.

"Gotta go," she said. She picked up the bag and her father reluctantly moved out of the way.

"Please be good," he said.

"I'm always good." She slipped past him, stuffed her feet back into her sneakers, and ran out the front door into the May sunshine. Hal's mom's beat-up convertible stood at the curb, the top up. Hal climbed out of the passenger seat to open the trunk for Athena.

"Whoa, whoa," he said, as she dropped her sleeping bag in. "What do you think you're doing?"

"Putting things in the trunk," she said.

"No no no no no. Mom said your things ride in the backseat. *You* ride in the trunk."

"I'm not riding in the trunk."

He blew a raspberry through pursed lips. "Fine. We can try it your way. But if Mom throws a fit, you can't pretend I didn't warn you."

Athena ducked around Hal and climbed into the back of the convertible before he could offer her shotgun. Sitting shotgun with someone else's parent was like a staged performance, a recitation of grades and plans for a completely disinterested audience. Everyone trying to be polite, nobody giving a shit.

Hal's mom, Lorna, sat in the driver's seat, her dark hair a tangled cloud around her head. She wore big movie-star sunglasses that obscured much of her face.

"Athena, how are you?" she said, in her soft singsong cadence.

"I'm good, Ms. Isaac," Athena said. She always hesitated—she wasn't sure if she should call Lorna *Ms.* or *Mrs.* Hal had never talked about his father, and Athena had never asked. "How are you?"

"Oh, you know," Lorna said. It might have been a complete thought or unfinished. It was hard to tell.

Lorna shifted into drive and almost sideswiped a car moving

through her blind spot. The other driver honked, and Lorna slammed on the brakes. Gravity jerked Athena forward against her seatbelt.

"Fuck, Mom," Hal said.

"Don't swear," Lorna said. With exaggerated care, she pulled out onto the road. She had to keep her head on a swivel because she only had one sideview mirror, on the passenger side. She'd lost the other mirrors (including the rearview) years ago, in an accident, and never replaced them.

"I won't swear if you won't get in wrecks," Hal said.

They drove across the flat, sleepy town of Clegg, seat of Cherokee County, in the heart of East Texas, home to 4,800 souls, most of whom voted Republican like God was watching. The town was a blip on the map, a place you wouldn't notice from the window of a plane. Its biggest building was the high school. The next biggest was the combination City Hall/Firehouse on Main Street.

Aside from the water tower, which declared the town, "Proud home of the Clegg Coyotes," Clegg had one other notable feature: a 546-foot-long wooden footbridge, which had been the nation's longest when it was built in 1861. It had been meant to help residents cross from one side of town to another during the flooding season (back when there still had been a flooding season). The town of Clegg remained proud of the bridge; they'd paid to have it maintained, restored, and, when necessary, rebuilt, over the last century and change.

Athena would never have admitted it, but she loved the bridge. There was something romantic and impractical about it. It belonged in a daydream or a fairy tale, not this hick town. It was one of only two structures in the area she loved.

The other stood about two miles outside the Clegg township, down a long dirt road that started at the outer edge of the woods bordering the town's west side. As Lorna's car pulled onto this dirt road now, civilization disappeared, replaced by a long corridor of trees.

Gravel rumbled and pebbles spanged off the underside of the car as they drove. "This road always gets my car so dirty," Lorna said.

"Yeah, the dirt might hurt the resale value," Hal said.

"It's fine," Lorna said, with a heavy sigh.

Marsh House seemed to emerge from the forest all at once. The corridor of trees parted for the wide circular driveway, behind which stood an old-fashioned white house with a wide front porch and a swing. From the driveway, the house appeared to ramble off into the woods on either side, never-ending. Like the bridge in the park, it seemed to belong to a bigger, stranger, more interesting world than the one Athena inhabited most days.

Professor Elijah Marsh sat on the porch swing, a book open in his lap. He was an elderly white man who wore corduroy slacks and a white dress shirt under a sweater vest. He had thick white hair, a short beard, and a grandfatherly smile. He raised a hand in greeting as the car rolled to a stop. Hal and Athena waved back through the window.

"I don't like that man," Lorna said.

"Yeah well, if I'd been Moses, you'd have drowned me in the rushes," Hal said. "Forgive me if I don't trust your judgment of character."

Athena's mom would've slapped her for the remark. Lorna just popped the trunk. Athena and Hal got out. Athena carried her bag to the porch while Hal leaned in the driver's side window to say goodbye to his mother.

"Hello, Athena," Professor Marsh said, from his spot on the swing. "How are you?" He had a bit of a nasal voice, and incredibly precise diction. He sounded like no one else Athena had ever met.

"Fine, thank you," Athena said. "What are you reading?"

"Joseph Campbell," he said. He was a retired professor of folklore and mythology, so he was always reading something.

"Is it good?"

"It is. What about you? What are you reading right now?"

"I just started *The Wheel of Time* by Robert Jordan," Athena said. "But I'm only in the first book."

"Mm," Marsh said.

"You don't like it?" Athena said.

"I haven't read it," Marsh said. "I never start a series until I know it's finished. I hate cliffhangers, and I think Mr. Jordan still has several volumes to go. But I salute you on your bravery."

Athena glanced back at Hal. He stood up and had barely backed away before the convertible peeled out of the driveway and sent a spray of dirt into the air. Hal coughed and waved at his face as he approached.

"Hello, Hal," the professor said, returning to his book. He was like this. Nice enough, but always more interested in his books than in other people. Athena could relate. She had her copy of *The Eye of the World* in her backpack, just in case things got quiet tonight. "I think Erin and Peter are waiting for you inside. Go ahead and let yourselves in."

Erin

Erin and Peter stood shoulder to shoulder in the kitchen of Marsh House, aprons fastened around their school clothes. They'd been trying to use baker's icing to draw Spider-Man atop a chocolate cake, but all they'd managed so far was a red and blue blob, and what seemed like a terminal case of the giggles.

May had been a tough month for Erin so far. Her parents were going through another rough patch, which meant life at home was a carousel of shouting contests and heavy, poisonous silences. Erin had been walking around with a tight ball of anxiety in her stomach all day, every day. Her frequent smiles at school or in town were practiced, and fake (you got good at fake smiles early, when you were a girl—or you heard about it from every adult you met). But here, in the gentle quiet of Marsh House, beside this gentle, quiet boy, she'd unclenched. Her smiles were genuine, her laughter honest.

Marsh House always put her at ease. When she was inside, time seemed to stop. The outside world ceased to exist. She could forget her parents, the trailer, the pressures of school. This house felt like its own little world, a place that, even though she knew the layout by heart, still felt somehow mysterious and obscure, even now.

But the best part of Marsh House wasn't the peace and quiet. It was Peter. Peter always cheered her up. And here, now, decorating this ridiculous cake, was the most fun Erin had had in weeks, despite her miserable failure as a cake decorator.

"We should probably give up, right?" Peter said.

"Never," Erin said. The middle of the cake looked like a pile of Silly String, but maybe she could draw a smaller, more perfect Spider-Man in the upper corner and pass off the squiggles as an explosion or something? "This is going to be the best Spider-Man cake in the history of comic book character cakes."

She'd just started on this new mini–Spider-Man when she heard the car in the driveway. It didn't improve her line work.

Peter crossed to the window. "Hal and Athena are here."

Peter's grandfather, the professor, had gamely agreed to sit sentinel out front, but Erin knew better than to hope for more than a moment's delay. The old man would say hello, and maybe ask Athena what she was reading (he never asked Erin what she was reading, although Erin read all the time, too), but that was it. Time was up.

Erin dropped the tube of icing as Peter dumped a box of candles on the kitchen counter, and counted out fourteen of them, which he arranged around the circumference of the cake. Erin struck the match and lit the candles. Peter stood near the kitchen exit, as though he meant to bolt if the flames got out of hand. He didn't like fire. It made him nervous. There were never candles on his own birthday cakes. That he'd remained in the room with Erin was an act of real bravery.

She'd almost gotten all the way around the cake when the front door opened.

"Hello?" Hal called. "Why's it dark in here?"

Erin laid the final drop of flame atop the last candle, shook the match out, and hefted the cake platter into her arms. She and Peter exited the kitchen and almost bumped into Hal and Athena as they came to the end of the entryway.

Hal shouted and Erin stepped back, afraid for the cake. Peter steadied her with gentle hands, which also startled her. Peter almost never touched anyone. Big fan of his personal space, that kid.

"Surprise!" Erin said.

Incredulous, Hal looked back at Athena, then at Erin and Peter. They started to sing "Happy Birthday" and walked the cake back to the table. Hal followed, his head ducked, not making eye contact with anyone.

"Happy surprise party!" Athena said, as the song finished and the cake returned to the kitchen table. "Make a wish."

Hal swallowed and looked up. It might've been a trick of candlelight in the dim kitchen, but his eyes looked a little glassy, reflecting more of the flame than Erin would've expected. Then he blinked, gave his friends a lopsided smile and leaned forward, taking a deep breath—and stopped. He frowned at the blob of icing atop the cake.

"What am I looking at?" he said.

"Spider-Man," Erin said.

Hal tilted his head and his frown deepened. "Did he die in a meat grinder? Did Galactus step on him?"

"Blow out your stupid candles and make your stupid wish," Erin said.

He closed his eyes, seemed to gather his thoughts, and extinguished the flames.

"I hope your wish was to learn to be nicer to friends who make you exceptional superhero cakes," Erin said.

"It was not."

"It's okay, you can make that your second wish," Peter said, and, as if by magic, the candles relit.

Hal smirked, and gave Athena a look. Athena raised her eyebrows and made an *Isn't that amazing?* face. It wasn't very convincing.

"Very cute, you guys," Hal said. "Just like magic, right?"

"Go ahead," Erin said. "Now you can get the wish right. Say, 'Dear lord Yahweh, help me learn to be a better friend.'"

"Jewish people don't pray to birthday cakes," Hal said. "It's weird you think we do."

"So help me Yahweh, I will let these trick candles burn this delicious cake to ash."

Hal didn't blow out the candles. Instead, he reached out and pinched the flame atop the closest candle.

"Hal," Athena said.

"Shh," he said. "This is harder than it looks." He continued around the cake, pinching out each candle. His face remained stoic, calm. He got a faraway look in his eye. Erin didn't like it. It was like he wasn't in there at all.

When he finished, he seemed to return. He looked around, gave the group his own *Isn't that amazing?* face, a pretty convincing facsimile of Athena's.

"Didn't that hurt?" Athena said. "Let me see your hand."

He let her look it over. "Neat trick, right?"

"Yes," Peter said. "Now let's cut this cake and eat it."

Hal took the cake knife in hand and started to saw off a piece, but Athena snatched it away from him.

"You're doing it wrong," she said. Hal looked like he wanted to argue, but she proceeded to vivisect the round cake into evenly spaced, perfect wedges, with the same efficiency and blankness he'd demonstrated when touching fire. So instead of arguing, he turned to Peter.

"You told them Mom forgot my birthday?" he said. "Dude, I told you that in confidence."

"No," Erin said. "We've known you for nine years. We know when your birthday is, dummy."

"Yes," Peter said. "I told Erin and Athena." Another thing about Peter. He never lied.

"But don't you go and get pissy about it," Athena said. "He had a good reason. Let us be nice to you, okay?"

"We wanted cake anyway," Erin said. "Your birthday made a decent excuse."

Hal's jaw worked for another moment, but he nodded. "Let's eat cake," he said.

The potential heaviness of the moment passed, and the group's usual mode returned: teasing, and jokes, as they ate their cake and toasted Hal's birth with plastic cups of Dr Pepper. It'd been like this since the four of them had met in kindergarten. They'd all been outsiders, but unlike most outsiders, who tended to go their own lonely way, Athena, Erin, Hal, and Peter had all been drawn to one another. It was hard to explain to anyone outside the group, but when they were all together, nothing was serious. Everything was safe and fun. Erin felt more at home with her friends than she ever did at home. Although she'd never asked, she suspected they felt the same way.

Professor Marsh came in a few moments later, book under his arm. "Everything going all right?"

Erin had been visiting Marsh House since she was five years old, so she'd grown up with Professor Marsh in her life. Despite this fact, she didn't know the old man well. She knew he'd been a professor of folklore and mythology at the University of Texas, but had retired early to take care of Peter when Peter's parents died in 1984. He'd raised Peter, made sure his grandson wanted for nothing, but Peter and the professor had never seemed close. Peter was as likely to call the old man "professor" as he was "grandfather."

"Yes sir," Peter said now.

"Good," the professor said. The ghost of a smile played at his lips. "You'll clean up the mess when you're finished?"

"Yes sir," Erin said. "Scout's honor."

"Would you like a piece of cake?" Athena asked. She already had a piece on a plate and was offering it to the professor by the time she spoke. Ever the teacher's pet, even when they weren't at school. She just couldn't help herself.

"Thank you, Athena," the professor said, taking the plate. "I'll be in my study. You know the rules."

"Yes sir," Peter repeated.

This had always been the deal: Professor Marsh liked to read. He liked to study. He didn't like to be bothered. He didn't seem to enjoy the company of other people, let alone kids. So as long as Peter and his friends didn't make too much noise, and cleaned up their messes, and, most of all, stayed out of the woods behind the house, they were free to do whatever they wanted. Erin had never minded this last rule. It seemed a fair trade for all the freedom granted them. They kept their own hours, watched and ate whatever they wanted. When they were here, Marsh House felt like *their* house. And anyway, since Charlie Simmons had disappeared into those woods a few days ago, the professor's rule seemed like good common sense.

The professor disappeared into his study at the back of the house. The group stayed silent until they heard the door click shut behind him.

" 'Happy birthday, Hal,' " Hal said, in a passable impression of the old man. " 'Many happy returns. Thanks for sharing your birthday cake with me.' "

"I'm sure he meant to say it. He just forgot," Athena said.

"He and my mom could start a club," Hal said.

After cake, they made popcorn and settled into the soft leather furniture in the sunken den to watch a movie. Erin, the group's resident film buff, had selected tonight's VHS rentals. First up was *Mallrats*. Erin didn't know much about it, but it was supposed to be a comedy about comic books, and seemed like the sort of thing Hal might like.

Her instincts proved correct. Hal loved the movie, and so did everyone else. They laughed and clutched their popcorn bowls to their laps to stop them tumbling to the carpet. Erin sat thigh to thigh with Peter on the couch. They shared a bowl of popcorn, greasy fingers occasionally brushing amid the oil and salt. Peter startled each time it happened, like a beaten puppy wary of all hands. Each recoil sounded a little pang against her heart.

"Let's watch it again," Hal said, as soon as it was over.

"Not yet," Erin said. "We have another movie." She'd also rented *Hackers,* which she'd seen in the theater last year and was probably the coolest movie ever made. She loved the scene at the end when Jonny Lee Miller's character said to Angelina Jolie, "You are elite." In Erin's fourteen-year-old heart, those words were the perfect summation of love and admiration.

She got up to switch tapes in the VCR, and only then did she realize Athena had set her popcorn bowl on the floor, and had curled up in her seat with a small green book. She looked utterly engrossed.

"Athena," she said.

Athena exhibited no response. It was as if she hadn't heard her own name.

"Athena," Erin said again, and snapped a couple of times. "Earth to Athena."

Athena tore her gaze away from the book. She looked disoriented and annoyed. "What? What?"

Erin physically backed up, surprised.

"What are you reading?"

Athena closed the book and ran her thumb over the cover. "I'm not sure. I found it in the hallway when I went to the bathroom."

"There aren't any bookshelves in the hallway," Peter said.

"That's what's weird," Athena said. "I found it on the floor."

"The professor would never leave a book on the floor," Peter said. He stood to gather empty popcorn bowls and soda cups. "And he'd yell at me if he caught me doing it. It's a no-no, like not flushing the toilet after going number two."

"First: gross," Athena said. "And second—"

"Number two, you mean," Hal said, from his seat on the recliner next to Athena's.

"—I don't know what to tell you. That's where I found it."

"A mysterious floor book," Hal said. "Perhaps the most boring mystery to ever occur. Either the professor dropped it, or it fell out of his bag. It doesn't make the book interesting. Let's watch the next movie."

"Can I see it?" Erin said.

Athena handed it to her with obvious reluctance. It was slim, like a volume of poetry, and bound in worn green cloth. There was no title stamped on the spine, but the front cover bore an embossed golden symbol: a gnarled thing of sharp angles and branches, what you might get if the letter A and a tree had a baby. It looked familiar, something Erin felt she ought to recognize.

"Hello?" Hal said. "Birthday boy, making a request over here."

Erin's concentration broke and she huffed in annoyance. "Shut up a second."

Athena pointed to the symbol. "Looks like something you've seen before, doesn't it?"

Erin opened the little book. The pages felt even older than the binding, stiff and yellow. The text inside was handwritten rather than typeset. She experienced that same sense of recognition, but multiplied exponentially. An intense wave of déjà vu.

Hal got up from his chair with a heavy sigh, and looked at the book over Erin's shoulder. "Looks like a bunch of nonsense to me."

"I don't think it is," Erin said.

"Me neither," Athena said.

"Then what is it, exactly?" Hal said.

"I don't know, because I keep getting interrupted," Athena said.

Peter returned from the kitchen, drying his hands on a dish towel. "Let me interrupt you one more time before you start concentrating again. I want to see it." He stood next to Erin. His body was so warm. Was it her, or did he generate more heat than most people?

He narrowed his blue eyes at the text, and his mouth curled to one side. "Oh," he said. "Hal, clear your head and just look at it for a minute."

"Try relaxing your eyes," Erin said. "Like the hidden picture in the movie, when Willam's trying to see the sailboat."

"It's slower than Magic Eye, though," Athena said. "I missed most of the movie staring at this book, and I can see a few things, but they're fuzzy." She took the book back from Erin, flipped to the first page, and pointed to the first character. "I think this one means 'place.' Or at least 'place' is part of the meaning."

"You guys are fucking with me," Hal said. "I still don't see anything."

"I promise we're not," Peter said. "We wouldn't mess with you that way. Or I wouldn't."

"Let me make it up to you, Hal," Athena said. "Why don't we play a game?"

Hal

Hal knew Athena pretty well, felt like he could read her expressions and moods. But he'd never seen this particular look on her face before. Playful, but also mischievous. It made his stomach feel funny.

"What kind of game?" he asked.

"You know. Your average American teenage slumber party game."

"Truth or dare?" Hal said.

"No to that," Peter said. "I'd prefer we all still be friends by the end of the night."

"It's not what I had in mind anyway," Athena said. "Have you ever played 'light as a feather, stiff as a board'?"

Hal knew the game. He'd seen it in a movie. A group of kids huddled on the floor. One kid lay down and the rest of the group tried to lift—to levitate—that person using only their fingertips. It was silly, but the sort of thing that can feel true after dark, when you're up too late. Like saying "Bloody Mary" in the bathroom mirror three times. He had that same unease now.

"Truth or dare sounds more fun," he said.

"Not if we use this," Athena said, gesturing with the little green book.

"I thought you couldn't read it," Hal said.

"I said I couldn't understand *all* of it. I think I understand enough to try something cool."

"Define *cool*."

"You'll see. C'mon, let's go into the yard."

"No no no no no," Peter said. "The professor only has like three rules, and one of them is that we stay inside and away from the woods at night."

"They're woods," Hal said. "What's the worst thing they could have in them? A bear or something? We'll hear it coming from a mile off. We should be fine in the backyard."

"It'll be okay," Erin said. "We'll turn on the porch lights and stick close to the door." She put a hand on Peter's shoulder, and Peter, who usually hated to be touched, didn't even flinch.

"This is still a bad idea," he said.

The group went out the back door onto the flat patch of lawn behind the house. The mown grass marked the borders of the yard. There was no fence, no barrier between the woods and the house. Peter turned on the porch light, which gave the grass plenty of illumination, but made the woods beyond look darker and more sinister.

Hal wondered if the professor could see the light from his study window. Wasn't the study on this side of the house? He had a hard time remembering the layout from the outside.

"Hal, you lie down," Athena said. "Flat on your back, arms over your chest like a vampire in a coffin."

Hal obeyed. The freshly mown grass pricked at the backs of his arms and neck. He would itch like crazy later.

"Peter, Erin, you have to pretend Hal is dead," Athena said. "This is his funeral. We're here to pay our respects. You two deliver the eulogy while I go find a stick."

"What's the stick for?" Hal said.

"To smack you if you don't shut up. Now shut up and play dead."

Hal faced the sky and closed his eyes. The backs of his ears already itched. He heard and felt Athena walk toward the tree line.

"Dear Hal," Erin said. "We hardly knew ye."

"What can we say about Hal?" Peter said.

"He was loud," Erin said.

"Energetic," Peter said.

"Some might say hyperactive," Erin said.

Nearby, Athena continued to hunt, grass and leaves crunching underfoot.

"Some have suggested Hal might have had ADD. That his was an undiagnosed case."

"If only he'd seen a doctor," Erin said. "Maybe he wouldn't have sprinted so hard into the side of that building."

"He flattened out just like a pancake," Peter said. "I didn't know that could happen in real life."

"I hate you guys," Hal said.

Something whistled through the air and gave his shoulder a painful smack. Athena had found her stick.

"Ow!" Hal said.

"I warned you, dead boy."

Hal's shoulder stung and his temper split two ways. Half of him wanted to grab the stick and whack her back, ask her how she liked it. The other half admired her bossiness, was intrigued by this side of her he'd never seen before. He listened to the dictates of this second half, and lay still.

"But despite his many, many failings," Erin said, resuming her eulogy, "he was an okay friend."

"Loyal," Peter said. "Had your back, even if you were wrong. Because he was so used to being wrong himself."

It sounded like Athena was using her stick to scratch in the dirt above Hal's head.

"He was funny," Erin said. "Not as funny as he thought he was, but still."

Athena scratched something in the earth to Hal's left.

"I'll miss him," Erin said.

"Me too," Peter said.

"Me three," Athena said, as she scratched something near Hal's feet. "But there comes a time in every life when we have to say goodbye. Say goodbye to Hal, kids."

Something in her voice: a sharp, frosty edge. It sounded wrong, and Hal felt an icy stab of fear. She hadn't actually told him what they were planning to do out here. But he was being silly, right? Athena wouldn't hurt him. And anyway, magic was fake. What was the worst she *could* do?

"Goodbye, Hal," Peter said.

"Good journey," Erin said.

Athena scratched something to Hal's right, then tapped him on the forehead and both shoulders with the dirty stick. She leaned over and whispered in his ear: "Have a safe trip, birthday boy." His ear, already itchy, tingled from the proximity of her lips, and because of the physiological response to such a near-intimate gesture, it took him a moment to realize the sensation of the grass beneath him was changing. It went from a sharp poke to a gentle tickle, and then the feeling disappeared altogether, and instead of lying on the lawn, he felt like he was floating on the surface of a calm body of water.

"Oh my god," Erin said.

Hal opened his eyes as she jumped to her feet and stepped back. He experienced a moment of vertigo. His perspective was all wrong. Erin ought to have loomed over him, but instead, although Hal remained on his back, he seemed to be at eye level with her. He wasn't on the ground anymore. He turned his head to look down, and the gesture tilted his body into a slow, lazy roll. The earth was at least four feet below him, and inching farther away.

"Um," he said. "Am I flying? I feel like I'm flying."

"You're floating," Athena said. "So, almost."

"Holy shit," Erin said. "Holy shit. Athena. Holy shit." She paced back and forth, hands on her face.

"Breathe," Peter said. "Just breathe."

"Are you kidding me?" Erin said. She waved her arms at Hal in the air. "Athena just did fucking *magic*!"

"I was talking to myself," Peter said. His mouth hung open in a sort of goofy smile for a moment before he turned to Athena. "But Erin has a point. How did you do that?"

Athena watched Hal slowly rise through the air for a moment before she seemed to realize Peter had asked her a question. She licked her lips and focused with visible effort before using her stick to point at the etchings in the dirt. "It's all from the book. This symbol means something like *presence*, or *mass*? And this one over here is *lack*, or maybe *absence* or *zero*. And on either side, I think this says *barrier*. To prevent him from drifting side to side."

"Holy shit," Peter said, a note of wonder in his voice as he echoed Erin. "And it worked."

"It fucking worked," Athena agreed. A giggle escaped from her throat.

Hal thought the giggle was adorable. Athena never giggled. And he felt like he understood her sense of wonder. He felt it, too, although his mingled with unease as he continued to rise. He was at least six feet off the ground now. He could see the tops of his friends' heads. On the ground below, he could see the characters Athena had scratched into the dirt. They glowed a bright yellowish green.

"And what symbol did you use," he said, "to keep me from floating up into the atmosphere and suffocating or freezing to death?" He tried to make it sound like a joke, but in another few moments he'd be able to see the roof of Marsh House.

"Um," Athena said. She licked her lips, then bit the bottom one.

"You didn't think of that, did you?" Hal said.

"I didn't think it would actually *work*," Athena said. "Or, at least not this well. I can fix this, though. I'm sure of it." She dropped the stick, pulled the book from her jeans pocket.

She was still rifling through the pages when something exploded out of the tree line, wrapped two hairy appendages around her torso, and yanked her into the woods. She didn't even have time to cry out. All that remained behind was one of her sneakers, and the little green book.

Peter and Erin screamed. And Hal continued to rise, and rise.

Athena

The rough, bristled appendages held her tight as her abductor sped through the trees, footsteps loud and sure as a galloping Clydesdale. Brush crashed around her. Twigs and leaves slapped at her face, but she couldn't lift her hands to protect herself. She squeezed her eyes shut and prayed she didn't stab out an eye on an errant branch. They were going fast enough to make it seem like a valid possibility.

Her abductor smelled oddly pleasant: cottony, like laundry cleaned with unscented detergent. In other circumstances, it would've been soothing.

Sometime later—maybe seconds, maybe minutes—the thing stopped and dropped Athena. She landed on soft earth, dizzy and nauseated. She hunched on hands and knees, waiting for the next terrible thing to happen.

Silence stretched out, lasting so long that her stomach settled. Nothing had happened yet. She risked a look.

What she saw was a silhouette out of nightmare, a creature taller and wider than any human being she'd ever seen. It made a chittering noise that might have been a question. She let out an involuntary grunt and fell backward, and the thing jutted forward at her.

She scrambled away, but the silhouette kept pace with ease, and the two of them moved out of the dark and into a treeless patch, bright with moonlight. Here her abductor was drawn plainly: a creature arachnid in shape, but standing upright on two legs. As if a tarantula and da Vinci's Vitruvian man had had a baby. Its huge, multifaceted black eyes reflected back dozens of reproductions of her own terrified face. It continued to chitter its questions at her.

This couldn't be real. This couldn't be happening. She made straight As, and knew the difference between fantasy and reality, and spider-monsters *did not exist.*

But only a few minutes ago, you sent your friend Hal floating into the sky. Using magic. So why not spider-monsters?

She looked away, wanting to see something—anything—else. She'd been dropped in a small bowl in the forest floor, and had backed herself up against a wall. It felt too smooth to be natural. This creature must've dug this space out. The floor was littered with uprooted grass, sticks and leaves, even though there was no tree cover above—Athena could see the night sky, clear and full of stars.

"Hello? Is someone there?" The voice came from her left, high-pitched and terrified. A little kid's voice.

Its owner lay nearby, propped up against the wall, only his head visible above a blanket of forest debris. Athena recognized the face. She'd seen it in the papers all week. Charlie Simmons, the little white boy who'd gone missing. His head faced forward. He stared at the sky as he spoke. It might have been a trick of the moonlight, but he looked deathly pale.

Athena opened her mouth, then stopped and swallowed, afraid she might throw up. She closed her eyes, and silently repeated his name to herself, drawing her focus into a tight beam: *Charlie Simmons. Charlie Simmons. Charlie Simmons.* She wouldn't think about anything but Charlie. If she could keep him calm, she could keep herself calm. She hoped.

She managed to speak on her second try. "Yes, Charlie, I'm here," she said.

He continued to stare at the sky. If he weren't blinking and talking, he'd look dead. "How do you know my name?"

"Everyone's been looking for you," Athena said. She worked to keep her tone upbeat. "Your mom and dad are so worried."

"I got lost," Charlie said. "And now I can't move. Can you help me?"

Athena tried to stand, but the spider-thing crossed the bowl before she was half-up. She opened her mouth—to reassure the creature, or maybe scold it for getting in her personal space, she wasn't sure which—but white pain lanced through her before she could make a sound. One of the creature's lower legs had stabbed her left calf, passed all the way through, and thrust into the earth beneath.

She tipped over onto her back, too startled to scream, and so there was nothing to prevent her hearing the meat of her leg tear on the creature's appendage.

She was pinned like an insect. Pain coursed through her, radiating out from her leg. She fought a gray wave which threatened to pull her down into unconsciousness. The creature stared at her, chittered something, then finally withdrew from her body and stepped away.

"That's what they did to me," Charlie said.

They?

The pain was already fading. Was she going into shock? She felt like she was still thinking clearly. Did people in shock think clearly? Or maybe she only thought she was thinking clearly.

"Charlie," she said. Her voice sounded normal enough to her.

"Yeah?"

"You said 'they,' How many of these things are there?"

"Two," he said. "I call the one you met Daddy. Mommy's somewhere close by, sleeping."

"How can you tell them apart?"

"Mommy's much, much bigger than Daddy. She lays the eggs."

For the first time, Athena noticed fine threads strung between the trees. They held aloft clouds of fluff about the size and shape of basketballs. Eggs. She lifted her head to look for Mommy. It felt like lifting someone else's head, and looking through someone else's eyes. She abandoned the effort, and dropped her skull back to the hard earth. Even in this drugged state, it was clear enough what was going to happen. The eggs would hatch. The babies inside would be hungry. She and Charlie would be their first meal.

"Are you going to help me?" Charlie asked.

Athena looked past the webbing and into the night sky. Hal was up there somewhere. She might have killed him with her weightlessness spell. Was that why this monster had grabbed her? Had the magic drawn its gaze? Or was it a coincidence, a cosmic joke? She wondered whether she or Hal had it worse. Him, freezing to death and suffocating? Or her, paralyzed and eaten alive.

An egg twitched on its line above her.

Hal

Hal was so far up now he couldn't make out the yard below. His breath came in little white clouds, and when he blinked, ice crystals jostled between his eyelashes. His hands and feet throbbed the way they did on an extra-cold winter morning. Soon they'd go numb.

Hal had heard somewhere that when you froze to death, your body tricked you into thinking you were warm. Then you sort of went away. Like falling asleep. That didn't sound too bad. It sure as shit sounded better than falling to his death behind Marsh House. Up here, alone with the stars, he could let everything go. His mother. The crappy apartment where they lived. His shitty grades. The constant hum of discomfort in his stomach, the sense of everything being seconds from collapsing all the time.

But it also meant he had to let go of Peter, Erin, and Athena, and that part didn't sound so good. Sure, they'd sent him up here, but not because they wanted to hurt him. They did it because they wanted him to be happy. It wasn't their fault it had gone wrong. He wished he could help them with whatever was going on down on the ground. Pay them back for the kindness they'd shown him. Tell them they were the best things in his stupid life.

One nice thing about dying like this: for the first time he could see the night sky without distraction, without tree or cloud or streetlight or building to interfere. As he went numb, he felt true wonder at the spill of the infinite above.

Then a strange thing happened. The stars disappeared. The world above and below went black. Hal's body lurched as his ascent stopped and gravity reasserted itself. Then he fell. He plummeted, not toward earth, but through a black, spinning, featureless void.

The right side of his body slammed into something and knocked the wind from him. He tipped again and fell once more, but a much shorter distance this time. He hit another surface with his left elbow and shouted at the pain. At least the falling seemed to have stopped. He was back on a solid surface, and gravity had returned. He curled into a fetal position and tried not to throw up all the popcorn and birthday cake he'd eaten earlier.

He focused on his breath. His hands and feet tingled with the return of sensation. He flexed his fingers and toes and endured the pins and needles that followed.

When he felt able, he rolled up onto his hands and knees. The ground beneath him was smooth and cold and uneven, like stone, and the darkness around him was broken by a faint light. The stone absorbed and reflected the glow and revealed the shape of his whereabouts.

He was in a vast chamber, lined with massive pillars stretching up to a vaulted ceiling so high it barely caught the light below. Everything seemed to be made of the same glossy black stone as the floor. The design reminded him of European cathedrals he'd seen in movies—but without pews or pulpit or choir box or stained glass windows. There were statues though—grotesque, monstrous shapes that seemed to emerge and wrap themselves about the pillars in frozen agony. The faces, where Hal could see them, might've been human once. If this was the afterlife, it sure didn't look like heaven.

At the head of the chamber, a short set of stairs led up toward the small, faint light. It glowed weakly but steadily. It grew no larger as Hal crested the stairs, but remained a chip of illumination which hung in midair, like a firefly stuck in "glow" mode. He reached for it with his left hand. Was it warm? Was it a bulb of some kind?

The light dilated as his hand grew close, from the size of a quarter to the size of a small plate. The strength of the illumination grew in tandem, flashing into a bright glare. Hal had to shield his eyes with his right hand.

His left-hand fingers met no resistance as they touched the light. They passed into the circle, and for a moment were bathed in a glorious warmth. It was the purest pleasure he'd ever felt.

Then the circle clamped down on his wrist like the jaws of a predator.

Hal grunted as the light's warmth became a burning sensation. It started in his fingertips and spread up his arm like flame. He tried to withdraw his hand, but the light held him fast and tightened its grip painfully. His knees weakened. He wanted to fall over, but if he did so now he would dislocate his shoulder or break his arm.

He steadied himself, clamped down on further vocalizations of pain and the threat of tears. He'd had years of practice. Heck, it was in his blood, wasn't it: Jews certainly knew a thing or two about suffering. So this thing—this bizarre hole in this nonsensical dark world—might kill him, sure. But he wouldn't give it the satisfaction of his weakness, his pain. That was for Hal and Hal alone.

Scream. The command entered his mind like a radio signal, adrift in static.

"I won't," he said.

Beg for mercy, the voice said.

"I won't," he repeated.

The static grew fuller, crowded into Hal's head. Images formed. Hal saw himself as if watching from across the room. He watched the light chomp down and sever his hand at the wrist. He watched himself stagger back and fall, arterial blood spraying from his stump. He watched his face go pale as he entered shock and bled out on the temple floor. The stone seemed to absorb his blood, like earth soaking up rain.

I will kill you, the voice said.

"Then do it already," Hal said.

I will do it slowly. Another mind-movie came through the static. In this one, Hal saw himself through a series of time-lapse images, a flip-book in which he starved to death on his feet. He thinned and paled; his hair and teeth fell out. His pants dropped around his ankles, revealing knobby knees and graying pubic hair. He wept tears of blood and begged for death, his words incoherent in a toothless mouth.

The real Hal, the one watching, laughed. "I've never seen someone starve to death, but I'm pretty sure that's not how it works, you dumb fuck."

In this place, I determine the rules. I decide how you die, the order in which your body fails.

"It's your party, pal," Hal said. He made himself sound bored and annoyed. He couldn't make the thing release him, but maybe he could piss it off, and that was the next best thing. "Is this all you do? Float around in some sky temple and catch random people in mid-flight, for torture? Or am I the first human being you've ever met?"

The voice didn't answer, but the pain in his arm intensified. Black tendrils appeared beneath the skin of his forearm and crawled toward his shoulder. Agony flowed into him. He closed his eyes. He focused on his friends. Erin. Peter. And Athena. He wondered what had happened back on earth. He hoped they were all okay.

"Athena," he said. Saying her name didn't stop the pain, but did make it more bearable. He pictured her rolling her eyes at him, because it was the face she made most often.

The tightness on his left wrist loosened a little. He could now wriggle his fingers a bit. They bumped into an object. There was something in this hole with his hand. He poked it a couple more times, but it didn't move. Probably not a living thing, then. He opened his trapped fist and closed his fingers around the object. It was soft, like old leather, and cylindrical. The handle of something.

"What is this?" Hal said. "What's going on? Is this an elaborate 'pull my finger' bit?"

"You can withstand great pain." It was the voice from the static, but no longer in his head. Now it echoed in the chamber. *"You are worthy. You shall be our champion."*

Before Hal could ask for some sorely needed clarifications, the hole widened, and pulled him into the light.

Athena

Before tonight, Athena had never wondered what it sounded like when a spider egg hatched. Since egg sacs were round and puffy like cotton balls, it seemed like it should be a soft, gentle sound. And perhaps that was the case for regular spiders. But when the large egg sacs suspended above her began to jostle and twitch, they made a heavier noise, like a sheaf of paper towels being shredded, as the newborns inside ripped and tore their way free.

She couldn't feel much of her body. Everything below her nose was a vague, heavy tingle. With effort, she could still turn her head and see across the bowl of the forest floor, where Charlie lay trapped and paralyzed beside her. He mewled with terror as the egg sacs closest to him shook.

Daddy emerged from the dark as a sac above Charlie broke. A multi-jointed limb flailed in the air, searching for purchase. Finding none, it retreated into its cotton sac, which sheared down the middle and spilled its cargo onto Charlie's torso with a splat.

The hatchling looked like a cross between a slimy newborn calf and a cockroach. It tried to stand, but slipped in the fluid of its afterbirth and hit the dirt next to Charlie. There on the ground it made its first sound: a high-pitched chitter which could have been surprise or indignation.

Daddy responded with a chitter of his own. He scuttled forward and bent low, face level with the hatchling. The hatchling looked at its parent with a tilted head. They chittered at one another, the baby high and excited, Daddy low and almost melodic. A voice of calm. Reassurance. Love.

Perhaps in response to this exchange, the other sacs above Charlie rattled and tore. Four more hatchlings spilled onto Charlie. The trapped boy gasped as the little creatures found their feet and one another. They tumbled, intertwined, and played. Athena wished Daddy's venom had worked on her nose. The afterbirth smelled awful.

Daddy leaned down between the hatchlings and interrupted their play. They gathered around his face, and he held their attention as he leaned in over Charlie.

"Please let me go," Charlie said. "I'll do anything. I'll bring back other people for you to eat, whatever you want. Please."

Daddy tilted his head as if considering the proposal. He chittered.

"Do you—do you understand me?" Charlie said. "What I'm saying?"

Daddy turned back to the hatchlings. They scattered off Charlie's body, leaving his midsection exposed. Daddy's face thrust forward, and his mandibles ripped open the boy's abdomen. Charlie screamed, and Athena wondered if the scream was born of pain, or from the terror of understanding what was happening to him, even if he was completely numb.

Daddy lifted a bloodied face to look at the newborns. They scuttled forward and, mimicking their father, bit into Charlie's arms and legs. The runt of the group, too slow to get at the meat of Charlie's torso, went for his face. Charlie's screams became more urgent and panicked as the runt pushed its pincers into his open mouth and clamped down on his tongue. Charlie's head jerked back and forth as the runt tugged its prize free.

Even through her venom-induced delirium, it was the worst thing Athena had ever seen. She would have given anything, would have given her own life, to make it stop. She turned her head away, looked past the eggs and up into the sky.

The screams eventually tapered off, overtaken by wet sounds of eating. Finally these slowed and stopped as well. The creatures had finished with Charlie. The scuttling, rustling sounds drew closer. If Athena's body could shudder right now, it would've.

A hatchling's face loomed into view above her. How much was this going to hurt? She tried not to think about it. She looked past the monster above her, to the starry night sky. It was a pleasant thing to see, the last nice thing she would ever have. She could focus on the sky and hope things turned out okay for Hal.

But maybe the poison had screwed with her vision, too. Caused a hallucination or something. Because the starry sky wrinkled like a bedsheet yanked out of place. Stars warped, distending, or, in some cases, disappearing altogether. In the middle of this wrinkle, a dazzling light flashed, and something up there screamed—but this scream was different from Charlie's scream. This was a happy sound. Like what you'd hear on a roller coaster. A cry mingled with laughter and exhilaration.

The sound distracted the hatchlings. They, too, looked at the falling, screaming thing. Athena had no trouble placing the voice. It was Hal, who she'd accidentally sent into the sky. Now he plummeted back toward earth with something gripped in his left hand—something long and bright. A blade, bathed in a yellow-green glow.

He hit the ground feet-first, hard enough he ought to have broken every bone in his legs. The earth shook and cracked beneath his feet, but somehow he remained upright. He raised the sword and smiled at Athena. The green-yellow light lent his face a sinister aspect.

"Look what I found," he said.

Daddy skittered away from Athena and put himself between Hal and the newborns. He swiped at Hal with one razor-sharp foreleg. Hal sidestepped and swung. He caught Daddy mid-swipe, and the sword severed the creature's limb at the joint. Daddy fell forward, balance compromised, and hit the ground face-first. Hal didn't prolong the thing's suffering. He stepped forward, raised the blade over the creature's head, and stabbed down.

All of Daddy's limbs twitched and flailed in a final, futile attempt to ward off harm. The hatchlings charged toward Hal en masse, chittering with terror and rage. Hal cut through them like scissors through butcher paper, turning the entire brood into ichor and blood.

Hal stood, breathing hard for a moment, covered in the creatures' remains, smiling in a dazed sort of way, as if he couldn't quite believe what he'd just done. Then he looked at Athena, seemed to remember what was going on, and dropped the sword. The eldritch light of the blade winked out as he knelt beside her, his smile replaced with a look of grave concern.

"Are you okay?" he said. "Say something if you can."

She tried, but couldn't make a sound. Daddy must've given her a bigger dose of venom than he'd given Charlie, or maybe Charlie's had started to wear off. Robbed of all but the most basic of motor functions, Athena did what she could. She blinked.

"Good enough," Hal said. He looked her over, running his hands over her arms and legs. It was the most he'd ever touched her, and she couldn't feel any of it. Just one more complaint to add to the pile tonight—maybe less dire than the injury to her leg, but that didn't mean this numbness didn't suck.

Hal sucked air through his teeth when he found the wound in her left leg. "Oh man. Okay. This is bad. I'm going to have to carry you." He slid his arms beneath her and lifted her with a grunt. "Don't suppose you know the way back to Marsh House?"

She almost allowed herself to experience relief. She'd been rescued. Her knight in shining armor had appeared. But another part of her—the practical part, who knew nothing is ever as easy as it looks or seems—continued to dread. Something gnawed at her. Something was wrong.

Behind Hal, part of the darkness shifted, and separated from the rest. It moved forward silently, so Athena could see it, but Hal remained oblivious as Mommy appeared behind him. She was as massive as Charlie had claimed—easily double Daddy's size—and held her extra weight and girth on four legs instead of two. Like Daddy, she had two forelimbs that hung like arms at her sides, but hers were larger, the serrated edges longer and sharper. The fur covering her segmented body rippled in the still air as she tensed to leap down onto Hal.

Athena was helpless to do anything but watch.

Mommy raised a forelimb over Hal's head, casting a shadow in the moonlight. Hal finally noticed something amiss. He turned toward his attacker, but too late. The deadly limb was already arcing toward him, and he was defenseless. Hal braced himself, shielding Athena with his body, and closed his eyes.

Only the forelimb didn't hit Hal. Instead, yellow-green light flashed and there was a hollow *bonk* noise as the blow bounced away, harmless. The light left tracers in the air, leading out of the clearing and into the trees. Athena turned her head. It was slow, difficult work, and the tracers had almost faded by the time she spotted their point of origin: Erin, standing at the edge of the clearing, arms raised like a sorceress out of legend, the yellow-green light flowing from her fingertips. She wore a strained look, like whatever she'd just done pained her. As though she'd received the blow meant for Hal. Behind her, almost invisible in the dark, stood Peter, looking quite astonished.

"It won't last," Erin shouted. "Let's go."

Hal opened his eyes, saw Erin, and didn't waste time with questions. He tightened his grip on Athena and ran toward their friends. Athena's head lolled to one side, and she had a clear view as Mommy pursued them, somehow silent despite her incredible speed.

Hal passed out of the clearing and between the trees. Erin fell into step beside him and they rushed forward.

Peter remained behind, however. He stood directly in Mommy's path, and Athena worried she would run him down, but the creature stopped just short of the boy, apparently confused. Maybe she was used to prey running away—or maybe she was fascinated by the drawing Peter made in the air now, his fingertips trailing yellow-green light.

Erin stopped running as she noticed, too.

"Peter!" she called.

"You go on," Peter said.

Erin did the opposite of what he asked, and ran toward him. Hal stopped and turned to watch. Athena's head lolled in the right direction for her to see.

Something shot up out of the earth between Peter and Mommy: a single stick that quickly unfolded into a sapling, and, in an additional span of instants, thickened and lengthened into a tree from a dark fairy tale, with long, skeletal branches and huge, far-reaching roots. The branches folded outward at all angles, completely blocking Mommy's way. She slammed into the tree but it held fast. She backed up, found a different break in the trees to her left, and ran for those. Another tree shot up out of the earth, blocking her way again. She loosed a high-pitched, chittering scream of frustration.

Peter continued to draw, and as he did, the trees continued to grow and fold around the clearing until they had completely boxed Mommy into the bowl in the earth. She had enough room to move around a bit, but she couldn't go anywhere. When she finally ceased searching for an escape, Peter stepped back and put a hand to his head. He staggered to the side, caught himself on a nearby tree trunk, and vomited into the grass. He wiped his mouth with the back of one arm, like a little kid.

"Are you okay?" Erin said.

"I think so," he said.

"Yeah, you look terrific," Hal said.

Erin laughed. It was a bright, happy sound amid all the darkness, and proved contagious. Before long, Hal and Peter joined in as well. The giggles became full-bellied laughs, and rose toward the verge of hysteria before they were interrupted, not by an otherworldly creature, but a very human voice.

"What the *hell* is going on here?"

Professor Elijah Marsh stepped out of the dark, flashlight in hand, wearing work boots with his pajamas, his white hair a frightful cloud around his head. He looked *pissed*.

Erin

Erin had never seen Professor Marsh angry before, and found it surprisingly frightening. Despite the old man's absurd appearance, there was a harsh glow in his eyes that made his gaze difficult to meet. Erin looked at the ground instead.

"Professor," she said. "We were—" She flailed for a good excuse, then glanced back at the giant spider-monster trapped in the trees behind her, and realized there was no easy path out of this situation.

"I'm sure you were," Professor Marsh said. "Let's get back to the house before something else decides to make a meal of us."

They followed him back through the woods. Erin fell into step alongside Hal and shone her flashlight on the ground in front of him to help him keep his footing. Hal, who usually turned everything into a joke, held Athena to his chest like something both precious and fragile. Erin wanted to ask him if Athena was okay. How Hal had found her. How, for that matter, he'd gotten out of the sky. Why he seemed to be covered in blood and guts. But she could feel Marsh's stormy mood from several feet back, so she kept quiet.

The porch light was still on when the group emerged from the woods and into the backyard of Marsh House. Marsh had Hal lay Athena in the grass, and knelt to examine her with a penlight. He took special care with the bloody hole in her leg.

"I assume this was the work of that thing Peter trapped?" Marsh said.

"I'm pretty sure, yeah," Hal said. "Well, maybe not that thing. There were other things in the clearing. Like smaller ones. I killed them. There was a sword. I had a sword for a minute. But I dropped it back there, so it might be in the cage with the monster still."

Marsh continued his inspection of Athena.

"I know how it sounds," Hal said. "But it's true."

"It's a shame you and your sword didn't get to Athena sooner," Marsh said. "You might have prevented her injuries."

"I was in the *sky*," Hal said. "I didn't have an ETA on my return to solid ground."

Marsh began drawing symbols in the air over Athena, more complex and intricate than those Erin had seen earlier in the little green book. These also glowed brighter than her own or Peter's. Well, that answered the question of whom the magic book had belonged to.

Athena exhibited no visible change as a result of Marsh's ministrations, but it would be hard to tell out here in the dark, since she was drenched in blood and monster guts.

"The venom is serving as an anesthetic now," Marsh said, "as well as keeping her paralyzed. We won't know the extent of the damage until it's out of her system." He beckoned to Hal. "Let's get her inside."

Hal lifted her again. She hung limp in his arms like a damsel on an old-timey movie poster. They followed the professor inside, and Marsh directed them into his study. Erin had never been in the study before. None of them had, aside from Peter. She'd only ever glimpsed it through a partially open door.

The entirety delivered on the promise of those glimpses. A huge desk dominated the large octagonal room. Floor-to-ceiling bookshelves lined six of the eight walls, and the seventh wall, opposite the door, contained a bay window with a plush cushion across it. A large brown leather sofa and reading chair stood in front of the desk, alongside a freestanding dry erase board on wheels. The board was jammed with bizarre symbols, like an endless, undecipherable math equation. An old bar cart was pushed up against one side of the desk, but instead of liquor, it was stocked with bottles of powders and dried leaves.

Hal set Athena on the cushion in the window. He stood over her for another moment, flexing his hands, arms held out at an awkward angle as though unsure what to do next. Then he clenched his hands into fists, ducked his head, and joined Peter and Erin on the sofa.

Marsh leaned against the front of his desk, arms and legs crossed. Even in his pajamas he radiated stern authority.

"Athena won't be able to speak for a while," he said. "Which means there will be gaps in your story. But go ahead and tell me what you can."

Peter started. He told his grandfather how Athena found the little green book; the ensuing game of *light as a feather, stiff as a board* in the yard; the symbols scratched in the dirt; Hal untethered from gravity. When he came to the part about the monster emerging from the trees and grabbing Athena, Hal took over and told how he'd floated up and up, getting colder and colder; the sudden fall into a bizarre temple of black stone; the trial of pain he'd endured, which granted him access to a crazy glowing sword like something out of a fantasy novel; how, once he had the sword, the temple expelled him and he'd fallen out of the sky and into the clearing with Athena; how he'd slaughtered all the monsters in the clearing with her.

"They were about to eat Athena," he said. "And it looked like they'd just finished eating someone else, too."

Erin picked up the story from there: how, after Athena was taken, she'd tried to dash into the woods after her; how Peter had stopped her; how she'd tried to smudge out Athena's symbols in the dirt under Hal; how Peter had stopped her again, worried that breaking the spell would cause Hal to fall and die; how she and Peter studied the little green book and the spells they'd found for a shield; and how, when they finally found their friends, Peter had grown an entire orchard's worth of trees on command.

"I can't tell you how I did it," Peter said. "I drew a symbol I thought meant *growth* or *garden*. I didn't know that would happen."

"And then you showed up, Professor," Erin said. "You know the rest."

Marsh's arms remained crossed. He frowned at the ground. "Athena needs more care. Erin, I'd appreciate it if you stayed and helped. Boys, I'll need your help with the creature you trapped. We'll all talk more in the morning."

Erin wanted to object. She was the one who'd saved Hal and Athena from being stabbed to death by the monster. She could be of real use if they were going back. Why was she being singled out to stay behind and help? Because she was a girl, and it was a girl's job to be a nurse?

Peter stood. "Yes sir," he said, looking at the floor. Erin realized he never made eye contact with the professor. He'd grown up in this house, but he and Marsh didn't *seem* like family. She hadn't given it much thought until now, because Peter had never talked about it. He was the only member of their little clique who never complained about his parents (or parental stand-ins). But then, Peter had never talked much anyway. He'd always been the quietest.

Hal remained on the couch. "I'd like to stay with Athena."

"No," Marsh said. "You'll come with me."

"I don't want to leave her. I can help here. Take Erin."

"I'll go," Erin said.

"Young man," Marsh said. "If you're interested in being welcome in this home past sunrise, you'll want to leave this room now and wait for me near the back door." Marsh's volume didn't go up, but his tone grew hard-edged.

Hal's mouth worked. He was about to say something ugly. Peter shook him by the shoulder.

"Come on," he said.

Hal gave Erin a questioning look. She gave him a tiny nod and jerked her head toward the door. She would take care of Athena.

Hal stood and let Peter lead him out of the room. When they'd gone, Marsh let out a long sigh, some of the tension leaving his body. He'd been ready to say more to Hal—maybe *do* something. Who was this man? Erin had known him all her life, but now understood she hadn't known him at all. The doddering professor had been a mask, and now she saw the real Marsh. She didn't know how she felt about this new, keener, meaner version of him.

Marsh pulled a book off his shelves, flipped through it until he found the page he wanted, and carried it over to the bar cart. He set the book down on his desk, then removed two jars, a pair of latex gloves, and an earthenware bowl from the cart. He put on the gloves, then poured bottled water and a pungent brown powder into the bowl. He mixed them using a mortar and pestle, and produced a rust-colored paste that Erin could smell from the sofa. It stank like the fake eggs they served for breakfast in the school cafeteria.

He handed the stinking bowl to Erin.

"What do you want me to do?"

"I knit her flesh back together," Marsh said. "But the venom in her blood could cause nerve damage. This paste will ameliorate the after-effects. Rub it into her skin."

Well, that explained why Marsh had asked her to stay behind. It would have been completely inappropriate for him or Hal to undress Athena, especially when she was incapacitated like this. Erin was the only person in the house who could do it. It was a relief it wasn't some patriarchal sexist thing, but it was also disappointing—part of her had been hoping she'd been kept back because she was special.

Marsh brought in more bath towels and they spread them on the floor beneath the bay window. Together they lowered Athena onto the makeshift pallet. Erin could scarcely believe this limp body had life left in it. Athena's skin was cold to the touch.

"Work as fast as you can," Marsh said. He shut the study door behind him as he left.

Hal

Peter and Hal stood near the back door. Even in his sulky rage, Hal did his best not to touch anything or spread the mess of blood and bug guts to anything in the house. He might not like Marsh, but he liked Peter and he liked this house, and he didn't want to give the old man an excuse to throw him out. Hal had the feeling they were about to embark on something extraordinary, and he didn't want to miss it.

The boys didn't have to wait long. Marsh emerged from his bedroom and met them near the back door a few moments later. He'd changed from his pajamas into shorts, hiking boots, and a polo shirt.

"Come with me," he said.

The trio of late-night explorers stepped into the backyard, where Marsh drew some more indecipherable symbols in the air and created a yellow-green ball of light, which traveled with them through the yard and into the woods. They walked in silence, Peter and Hal following the professor, who seemed to know exactly where he was going despite the dark, dense forest around them. It never even occurred to Hal that Marsh might get them lost. He seemed too confident.

Finally, they came back to the clearing. The way in was blocked now by Peter's insta-forest, and the spider-monster stalked its cage. It stopped when Marsh and the boys approached. Hal couldn't read its expression, which somehow made its absolute stillness more horrible.

"You did well," Marsh said, "killing most of the creatures and saving Athena, but there's still the matter of this last, biggest one." He pointed to the thing, which came closer to the barrier of trees.

"Peter has it trapped. It's not going anywhere," Hal said. "Why did we have to leave Athena?"

"Look closer at the trees Peter created," Marsh said. He beckoned his ball of light forward, and the spider-creature retreated, as though afraid.

Hal stepped forward and peered at the trees. They looked ashy and dark, although it could've been a trick of the light.

"Oh," Peter said. He sounded sad.

"What?" Hal said.

"They're dying," Peter said. He turned to Marsh. "You knew they would die?"

"Don't blame yourself," Marsh said. "Creating and sustaining life using the Dissonance is an incredibly complex and difficult proposition. It would have been nothing short of a miracle if you'd created living trees that could survive out here."

"What are we going to do?" Hal asked.

"We're going to kill the monster," Marsh said.

"What?" Peter said, offended. "It's defenseless and trapped. We can't just murder it."

"I just told you your makeshift prison won't hold it," Marsh said. "And I don't have a better way to deal with the problem. Now. Shall I deal with the issue, or will you?"

Peter stepped back, and in the eldritch light from Marsh's ball, Hal saw him swallow hard. "You want me to do it?"

"Call it a test," Marsh said.

"Call it what you want," Peter said. He crossed his arms and glared at the ground. "I'm not going to kill that thing for you."

Marsh scowled, but Hal interjected before he could reply: "I'll do it."

Marsh's scowl changed to a look of curiosity. "You're up for it?"

"I killed the rest of them," Hal said. "I might as well finish the job."

"As you said, you had a sword when that happened," Marsh said. "But you dropped it in the clearing. Can you even see it in there?"

Hal squinted through a gap in the trees. There was definitely nothing aglow, no telltale yellow-green light.

"I can't," Hal said. "But maybe it just loses its light when it gets dropped? Like it needs a wielder to glow?" He thought it was too bad the sword wasn't like the one Bilbo had in *The Hobbit*, which would glow blue when bad guys were nearby. It would be lit up like a beacon right now.

"Are you willing to risk your life to go in there and find out if your theory is correct?" Marsh said.

Hal shrugged. "If I don't kill it, you will, right?"

"I'll certainly try," Marsh said. "But I can't guarantee your safety once you're in the cage with the creature."

Hal continued to watch the monster. It had lost interest in its visitors for the moment and was searching the far end of its prison for a likely exit. It moved so quickly and so quietly, Hal couldn't help but shudder.

He knew it was a dumb idea to go back in after the sword. It was a needless risk, since it sounded like Marsh had the power to terminate the creature right now. But the truth was, Hal already missed the sword. He'd loved holding it. Loved using it. He wanted it back.

"At least let me try," he said.

"It's your choice," Marsh said. "I'll part the trees for you, but then I'll close them behind you. Call if you want my help."

Hal jumped up and down a few times to get his blood pumping, then nodded at Marsh to show he was ready. Marsh twiddled his fingers in the air and two of Peter's trees leaned away from one another, creating a space just large enough for Hal to squeeze through.

The creature still had its back to Hal as he entered the clearing, but it stopped moving at the sound of the trees parting. It turned slowly, looked at Hal, and made a deep chittering sound. Hal swallowed and bit his lower lip. This was truly the stupidest idea he'd ever had.

The spider-thing lunged at him, and Hal backed up into a wall of trees. He realized the mistake almost too late as the creature swung a giant, razor-sharp foreleg at him, but he ducked just in time. The foreleg wedged into one of the trees as Hal dove out of the way and landed on his face in the bowl in the middle of the clearing. It was dark out here. The moon was no longer directly overhead. He scrambled about in the dark, feeling for the sword but finding only leaves, sticks, and dirt.

The spider-thing tugged its forelimb free and scuttled around to face Hal. Hal stood up and backed away from it.

"Professor," he said. "Now would be a good time to intervene."

He looked past the creature to a break in the trees where he could see Marsh and Peter. Marsh watched Hal with avid eyes, and Hal had little doubt the old man had heard him. Had heard him and elected not to answer.

Hal's left arm—his sword arm—ached with a strange pins-and-needles feeling. The way it felt when he slept on it funny and it woke up both numb and not-numb. He flexed the hand and bumped into the wall of trees on the far side of the clearing. Marsh continued to watch. Was the son of a bitch smiling?

The spider-thing moved slowly now, enjoying itself, sure of its imminent victory.

"Fuck you," Hal said, both to the monster and to Marsh. He flexed his hand again, and was surprised to find he couldn't make a fist. His fingers closed around something soft and leathery, and he smelled a strange ozone odor in the air. He looked down to see the glowing sword in his left hand, scorching the earth, setting some of the forest debris aflame.

The spider-thing seemed to realize what was happening at the same moment as Hal. It tried to back away, but Hal stepped forward, and in one simple, angry stroke, severed the creature's head from its body, sending a spray of blood and gore right into Hal's face. Hal backed up, sputtering, as the head hit the ground with a thump and then rolled against his shins like a furry bowling ball. Somehow he managed to keep his grip on the sword as he fought not to puke all over himself and the forest floor.

The spider-thing's body danced about for another couple of moments, a solo waltz beneath the starlight, before it finally collapsed in the middle of the clearing. Hal waited until it had stopped moving entirely before he crossed back to Peter and Marsh and cut his way free. Peter and Marsh backed up to make room, but Hal continued forward toward Marsh, sword up, tip pointed at the old man's chest.

"You left me in there to die."

"Nonsense," Marsh said. You had to give it to the old man—he really kept his cool with a deadly weapon pointed at him. "I had a command at the ready, but I needed to see if the sword would come when you needed it."

"You almost let me die—"

"I let you *think* you were about to die," Marsh corrected.

"—as part of an experiment?"

"And it worked," Marsh said. "The sword comes when you call it. So sure, you can kill me, but really you should be thanking me, and asking me to make all of this make sense for you. I can't do that if I'm dead, now can I?"

Erin

Erin unfastened Athena's jeans and worked them down off her hips and legs. She didn't look at Athena as she did it. Erin knew that if her friend was aware of what was happening, she was mortified. This was just too damn weird—rubbing paste onto a living person who looked and felt like a dead person. Out of respect for her friend (and for her own comfort), Erin tried to think of it as manual labor as she pulled on latex gloves and began to work. Wax on, wax off. Not a body or a life at stake. A task. She filled the silence with chatter, to help dispel the weirdness.

"When I got up this morning," she said, "no way did I expect we'd be casting spells and playing *Mists of Avalon* in the woods. Anyway, how are you? Not so great, I expect. Me? I'm okay. I probably had the easiest time of any of us tonight. No injuries, no tests of pain, no throwing up. I guess that makes me the natural choice to rub this fart paste all over your leg. That and being the only other girl in the group. I need to do my part and suffer, right? I hope this gunk works. If I covered you in stinky goop for no good reason, I'm gonna blow my stack."

She shifted Athena onto her right side and applied the paste to the back of her injured leg.

"Maybe this is more than my fair share, though," she said. "I'm pretty sure I'm the only one of us who lives in a house of constant yelling. I imagine it's pretty quiet at the Watts and Marsh houses most of the time. I don't know about Hal and his mom, but she's working nights at Kinney's convenience store, so they probably don't see much of each other. You don't realize what a luxury silence is until you don't have any." She laughed as she realized the irony of what she'd just said. "You'd probably appreciate a bit of silence now, yourself. Don't worry, almost done."

She finished rubbing the paste into Athena's leg, laid her flat on the towels, then peeled off her latex gloves. She covered Athena's legs with spare towels, then went to the bathroom to wash the powdery feeling off her hands. On her way back to the study, she noticed Athena's backpack, dropped in the hall when they'd first arrived. The bag was unzipped and open. A Clegg Junior High yearbook poked out the top. Erin grabbed it and returned to the office.

She showed the yearbook to Athena as she settled next to her on the floor. "I hope you don't mind. I didn't get a chance to sign it at school today."

In truth, Athena hadn't asked Erin to sign it. Erin hadn't known Athena *had* a yearbook until now. She'd assumed Athena skipped the tradition, the way she skipped most fun school-related stuff. And yet, here was said yearbook, in Erin's hands.

Erin opened it now, pen in hand. The endpapers were almost bare, save for two signatures. In the front, one from someone named Jordan. In the back, a brick of text. Erin recognized the handwriting as Hal's. She laughed as she read, and Athena kicked her in the shin.

"What the hell?" Erin said. She dropped the book as Athena kicked her again. The other girl's body shook, and her hands beat out an unsteady rhythm on the floor. Was this a seizure?

"I'll get help," Erin said, but Athena grabbed her wrist before she could stand.

"Don't go," Athena said. She winced as a wave of tremors wracked her body. "Please."

Erin settled back onto the floor. She took Athena's hand off her wrist and held it in her own. Together they rode out each wave of shakes, each a little less intense than the last, until they stopped altogether.

Athena groaned as she let go of Erin and rubbed her eyes with clenched fists. She seemed to have regained control of her body.

"Why were you laughing at my yearbook?" she said. "Is it because nobody signed it?"

"I was laughing at what Hal wrote," Erin said. "And did you *ask* anyone to sign it? I would have. Shit, I still will."

Athena flattened her hands on her face and massaged her cheeks. "What Hal wrote. What does it mean?"

"It's from that Arnold Schwarzenegger movie—*Conan the Barbarian*. It's the voice-over from the beginning."

Athena frowned. "Why would Hal put a quote from *Conan the Barbarian* in my yearbook?"

"You'd need to ask him," Erin said, but she didn't want to get sidetracked. "Why didn't you ask me to sign your yearbook?"

Athena closed her eyes. "I don't know. I didn't think you'd be interested."

"Why wouldn't I be interested? We're friends."

"Can we talk about this later? I got stabbed in the leg tonight."

"You can talk to me alone right now, or you can talk to everybody at once. I can bring the whole group in now."

It was a bluff—Marsh and the boys were still gone—but it worked. Athena groaned. "Can I have some water at least? Some aspirin?"

Erin headed for the kitchen. On her way, she met Peter, Hal, and Professor Marsh reentering the house. Peter looked harrowed and Hal perturbed. Hal also seemed to have fresh gore on his clothes. Only Marsh seemed to have his usual equilibrium.

"You're back," she said, stating the obvious.

"Snoochie boochies," Hal said. His eyes were bloodshot. "How's Athena?"

"Cranky. Asking for water and aspirin."

"So back to normal then. I can bring her that stuff," Hal said.

"No," Marsh said. "I'll take it to her. You and Peter need to shower and change clothes. Then we'll all meet in the study and talk."

Hal made a face but did as he was told. He bent to open his bag, pulled out his change of clothes, and headed for the bathroom. Marsh headed down the hall with water and pain relievers, leaving Peter and Erin alone. Peter looked awful.

"Are you okay?" Erin said.

He shook his head.

"Is it okay if I hug you?" she asked.

He nodded, and she stepped forward, pulling him into an embrace.

"Do you want to talk about it?" Erin said.

"Later?" Peter said, plaintive.

She didn't push, but rather tightened her hold on him.

"You smell good," he said.

"Liar," she said.

"Yeah okay, you smell like rotten eggs." He let her go and rubbed his eyes. "How about we get cleaned up and join the others in the study?"

"Sounds like an excellent idea," Erin said.

Hal

A little while later, all five of them gathered back in the study. Hal, Erin, and Peter squeezed onto the sofa, and Athena sat alone in the leather chair, a towel wrapped around her waist, bare legs crossed in front of her. She usually wore long pants and sneakers, so Hal couldn't remember the last time he'd seen her legs. They had grown shapely in the meantime. Was Athena hot now? Hal thought maybe she was. He had to force his gaze toward the professor, who leaned against his desk, arms crossed. Through the window behind Marsh, Hal could see the sky turning gray with predawn light.

"How do you feel, Athena?" Marsh asked.

"Tired. And my leg hurts."

"Hopefully that will stop soon, but you might carry it for the rest of your life. We'll know more in a few days."

The information clearly hit Athena like a blow. Hal, still annoyed at having been sent away earlier, swallowed what he actually wanted to say to the old man. How hard would it have been to break the news gently?

"Can't you use magic to fix it?" he said instead.

Now Marsh flinched as if struck. "We don't use that word in this house."

"What, 'magic'?"

"Give us the right word, then," Erin said.

"I don't think that's a good idea," Marsh said. "You've already seen too much."

"You can't make us unsee it," Athena said.

"I can, actually," he said.

A cold stone settled in Hal's gut. Tonight had been crazy, but in a good way—mostly. A doorway had opened, revealing a new world, and now Marsh was threatening to close it.

"I'd prefer to do just that," Marsh continued. "But I won't. Because I think there's more at work here."

"What do you mean?" Athena said.

Marsh crossed to his dry erase board and flipped it so the blank side faced the room. He wrote the word MAGIC on it, then crossed it out. "First day of class. 'Magic' is a word charlatans use to explain stage illusions and peddle children's stories. It disguises measurable phenomena as incomprehensible mysticism."

Beneath MAGIC, he wrote DISSONANCE THEORY.

"Dissonance theory is based on the hypothesis that something is broken in the foundation of creation: a gap between how things should be, and how they are. A disharmony. Most people feel this disharmony. It's why they aren't happy, why we're all preoccupied with visions of *could* or *should*. It's why so many world religions have a 'fall' or 'original sin' narrative. They want to make the brokenness make sense. What these religions don't know—or allow themselves to admit—is this broken foundation creates a friction, a sort of energy users call the Dissonance."

"And the symbols in the book," Athena said. "They're code for harnessing that energy?"

"Very good, Athena," Marsh said. "The major branch of Dissonant study is centered around the accumulation of strands of this code. Practitioners hoard manuscripts and books and sell them at a high price. What I've paid for the contents of this room"—he gestured at his bookcases—"could put all four of you and your children through college, even accounting for inflation. And what I own represents maybe a toenail in the body of knowledge that exists, which is likely a fingernail on the body of knowledge yet to be discovered. I've spent my life in pursuit of this knowledge. It's why I built a house here—at the edge of an area rich in Dissonant energy."

"Is that why those monsters were out there?" Hal said. "Were they drawn to this place, too? Or is this place rich in Dissonant energy because of their presence?"

"It's sort of a 'chicken or egg' question," Marsh said. "In truth, I don't know. I just know the woods here are wondrous, strange, and dangerous."

He flipped the board back to the side jammed with writing and pointed at a string of symbols.

"To most people this looks like nonsense. But certain people—intelligent, sensitive people—carry more pain than others. They have a stronger sense of the gap between what is and what should be. They mourn it. Some of these people can make sense of this language. They can read and write Dissonant. It's what you discovered about yourselves tonight."

"And because we can read it, you feel morally obliged to tutor us?" Erin said.

Marsh actually laughed. It was a nasal sound, and not a kind one. "No. Not even a bit. Talent doesn't entitle you to education. But the Dissonance *does* sometimes seem to exert a will of its own, and I believe that's what we're seeing here. The book you found last night? I believe it sought you out. I can't think of another explanation for how it got from the shelf in my study to the hallway floor. The Dissonance has put a path before you, but also before me. In my experience, it's best to go along with its wishes, whether I want to or not."

"Gee, thanks," Athena said.

"You're getting what you want," Marsh said. "Don't be a sore winner."

Hal had probably been up too long without sleep. His head hurt. He set his empty mug on a side table to rub his temples. "I'm sorry, guys, but those characters—the Dissonance symbols—still look like gibberish to me."

"That is an interesting wrinkle," Marsh said. He flipped the board again. "You can't read Dissonant. But based on your story, it sounds like you were summoned to the Temple of Pain, withstood the Trial of Agony, and were chosen to wield the Blade of Woe." He wrote those three terms down: TEMPLE OF PAIN. TRIAL OF AGONY. BLADE OF WOE.

So the sword had a name. *The Blade of Woe*. Which sounded totally metal and badass. Hal approved.

"It could be your comprehension of Dissonant is delayed," Marsh went on. "But either way, you are part of this. You'll take lessons with the others. But before I become your teacher, there are conditions all four of you will have to agree to."

"Anything," Erin said.

"Never agree to something until you know what you're agreeing to," Marsh said, but he smiled a little. "First: until I indicate otherwise, you are only to employ Dissonant under my supervision. Second: you come straight to me if further Dissonant phenomena present themselves to you—be they books like the one you found tonight, or another family of strange creatures. If you are attacked, you may defend yourselves, but otherwise do not engage with each other or anyone else unless I give you permission to do so. Third: from now on, you stay out of the woods unless I accompany you. Fourth, and most important: no one outside this room can know about this. That means no showing off. No using your gifts to impress a girl or win a schoolyard fight."

Hal and his friends exchanged glances, casting silent votes. Peter spoke for them: "We swear."

"Good," Marsh said. "Take today to rest. Summer school starts tomorrow."

Hal and Erin started to get up, but Athena remained seated.

"Charlie Simmons," she said.

"What about him?" Marsh said.

Athena looked wan, and spoke softly—much more quietly than usual. "His body is still out there. We have to bring it back."

Marsh started shaking his head before she even finished her sentence. "No."

"Why not?" Hal said. It sounded like good sense to him.

"If we go back into town with his body, we'll have to answer a lot of uncomfortable questions," Marsh said. "We become people of interest in the investigation of his disappearance. I'm surprised the police haven't asked to search this house already." He shook his head again. "No, best to leave Charlie where he is. Let his parents have the hope he's still alive somewhere."

This sounded right to Hal. Practical. But it felt wrong. Immoral.

Erin and Peter didn't look happy about it, either, and Marsh took note of their expressions.

"There are people you can help," he said, "and there are people who will drag you down with them. Half of surviving and thriving as a Dissonant is learning to tell the difference."

Athena

Athena remained weak and stiff, so it fell to Erin to help her into and out of the shower. It was mortifying, but Erin was nice about it, and as she helped Athena dress in the guest bedroom, Athena found the courage to speak: "Thank you for your help. I don't know if I could've done the same for you, if our positions were reversed."

"Sure you could," Erin said. "You'd have complained out loud the entire time. I just did it silently."

They both smiled, but Erin's looked flimsy, and Athena assumed the same was true of her own. She scraped the bottom of her heart to produce her next words—the important ones, the ones harder to say.

"I'm sorry about the yearbook. I felt shy."

"Why?" Erin said. "We've known each other since we were babies."

"I don't know. It's different now. When we were little, that was one thing, but now we're almost in high school, and you keep getting taller and prettier, and I'm still a short, chunky Black girl. A bunch of cool stuff is about to happen for you that isn't going to happen for me. And now you're hanging out with Peter all the time?"

"So?" Erin said. "You've always spent a lot of time with Hal."

Athena waved it away. "That's different and you know it."

"I don't know any such thing," Erin said. "But I don't want to talk about boys." She put her hands on Athena's shoulders. "Look me in the eye while I say this, okay? I can't help my height, or the way other people look at me. But even if I grow to be the most beautiful woman in the world, and men start wars over my looks, I will still want to sign your yearbook. I will always want to be your friend. You and Peter and Hal are my real family."

Athena managed eye contact through Erin's speech, but dropped her gaze to the carpet as soon as it felt permissible. "I'm sorry for assuming."

"Don't mope about it," Erin said. "Hug me, already."

Athena was not and never would be much of a hugger. But she raised her arms and allowed herself to be pulled into an embrace now. Despite her discomfort, she had to admit it felt better than expected— and unlocked something in her she hadn't even realized was locked. Her throat constricted and her chest ached and her eyes stung. She squeezed Erin back and tried not to make a sound, but her shoulders shook as she breathed, and Erin's T-shirt blotted with her tears.

"Hey," Erin said. "What is it?"

"Charlie" was all Athena could manage. Charlie Simmons. Who'd died screaming. Who she hadn't been able to save. Whose parents would always wonder, and hope, in vain. Who hadn't been lucky, as Athena had.

Erin held her tight, and stroked the space between her shoulders, and told her everything would be okay. That there was nothing she could've done.

It was the first death that would weigh on Athena for the rest of her life. It would not be the last.

"Thank you," she said again.

When Athena had cried herself out, she and Erin joined the boys in the kitchen for cereal and orange juice. It was like the morning after any sleepover: they joked, teased one another, cleaned up after themselves—but there was a new energy among them. They all buzzed with it, and it went a long way toward lifting Athena's spirits.

Lorna came to pick up Hal and Athena around ten. Hal carried Athena's bags and insisted she ride shotgun. Athena's leg hurt too much to argue this time. She sat up front with Lorna while Hal squeezed into the tiny backseat. Lorna mumbled a hello to Athena, but it was barely audible. She looked exhausted.

As the car pulled out of the driveway, Athena turned in her seat to look back at the front porch of Marsh House. Erin and Peter stood on the steps, watching them leave.

"You think they're going out?" Hal asked.

"If they aren't, they ought to be," Athena said.

When the dirt road ended and they'd returned to Clegg township, Lorna swerved through light Saturday morning traffic, skidded around corners, and somehow—through either a miracle or genuine driving skill—made it to Athena's house without causing any accidents. Hal helped Athena out of the car, and carried her stuff up the walk for her. It would've been sweet if she hadn't needed the help, but her left leg burned with every step. She hoped Professor Marsh had been wrong when he'd suggested the pain might never fade. She couldn't imagine enduring this forever.

"Do you need any help getting inside?" Hal said, once they had everything on the porch.

"I've got it, thanks."

"What will you tell your folks about your leg?"

"Are you kidding? I'm going to say it was all your fault."

"And what do I tell your dad when he comes to my house and yells at me?"

"That you're sorry and it won't happen again."

"Won't it, though?" he asked, stuffing his hands in his pockets.

"What, me being injured? I hope not."

He picked a loose thread on his jeans. "We're on a path now. Who knows what sorts of horseplay might lie ahead?"

Athena's face warmed. She felt like they were right on the edge of something.

"Why did you write a quote from *Conan the Barbarian* in my yearbook?"

He smiled. "You got the reference!"

"Erin had to explain it to me," she said. "But she couldn't tell me why you wrote it."

He looked away, like he was checking on his mom. "I mean. *Conan* is my favorite movie, and you're my favorite person, so it felt right somehow. I don't know. It probably sounds stupid."

"It does," Athena said. "So very dumb."

"Right," he said.

"But you're my favorite, too, you know."

He backed away, off the porch and onto the lawn, hands clasped to his heart. " 'All the gods, they cannot sever us. If I were dead and you were still fighting for life, I'd come back from the darkness. Back from the pit of hell to fight by your side.' "

"Is that from *Conan,* too?"

"Movie night at my house soon!" he said. "And tell your dad to go easy when he comes over to yell at me!"

He ran backward across the lawn back to his mother's car, not breaking eye contact until he bumped the passenger side door and turned to get inside.

2019
Homecoming

Owen

Owen drives Cole's station wagon through the night and into the next morning. As the blood and mud dry on his skin and clothes, he pushes forward without direction, without stopping. The thing in Cole's body rides shotgun, bloodstained seatbelt across its chest. It stares straight ahead, not breathing, a sickly-sweet smell wafting from it. Whatever is keeping the body upright isn't keeping it alive.

Owen wonders about his phone. He lost it somewhere in the carnage at the cemetery. Maybe the police will find it soon. Maybe Cole's parents have called them. Maybe there's an APB out on the station wagon. Also, he and his passenger look *terrible*. That ought to be enough to get them pulled over, right? But they pass cruiser after cruiser on the side of the road, and nothing happens. Why? Why won't someone do something?

When the fuel gauge drops to "E," Owen is distracted from his ruminations. "We need gas if you want to keep going," he says.

"Stop at a filling station," the Cole-thing says.

Owen takes the next exit and pulls into the empty parking lot of a Citgo. He parks by the pump closest to the convenience store.

"I don't have any money," he says.

The Cole-thing stares ahead for so long Owen wonders if it's heard him.

"Stay here," it finally says. It unbuckles its seatbelt, climbs from the car, and takes awkward, ungainly steps across the lot. Owen has an unobstructed view as his abductor enters the store, so he sees the clerk behind the counter back up into the wall of cigarettes behind him, and raise his hands as though the Cole-thing has pointed a gun at him.

The Cole-thing limps around the counter to stand beside the clerk. The clerk lowers one hand long enough to point at something Owen can't see. The Cole-thing presses keys on the cash register, then waves to Owen and twirls a finger in the air. *Proceed.*

Owen fumbles with his seatbelt, and the car door, and the gas tank, and the pump and nozzle. By the time he manages this simple string of actions, the Cole-thing is already almost back to the car, carrying two plastic bags. Owen looks past the thing, into the store. He can't see the clerk anymore. A dark stain runs down the wall of cigarettes.

"I brought you food," the Cole-thing says.

"Thank you," Owen says. His voice sounds farther away than usual. Like someone beside him is speaking. "I'm not hungry."

"You will be."

"I have to use the bathroom."

The Cole-thing waves him toward the store. "Don't try anything. I'll know. You'll regret it."

Bells jingle over the door as Owen enters the store. A radio behind the counter plays a commercial for a local car dealership. Owen tells himself not to look back there, then does it anyway. From outside, the red smear on the wall of cigarettes could've been paint. Up close, it takes on more dimension. The cartons are crushed where something slammed into them. Small bits of meat and bone slide through the sticky fluid, creeping toward the floor.

Owen runs to the bathroom, vomits in the sink, then pees for what seems like an hour. He washes his hands, scrubs his face as best he can, and steals a stick of deodorant on his way out the door. The store only has women's brands, so he takes Dove. His father would make fun of him for this choice. Owen wonders where his father is right now. Is he even awake yet? Is he answering questions for the police?

In the car, the Cole-thing has already cleaned the blood off its face, and donned a pair of sunglasses to hide its unblinking eyes. It looks almost human.

Owen starts the car. "Where are we going?"

The thing tilts its head like it's listening for something Owen can't hear. "Where are we now?" It's beginning to sound more human. Like it's learning to play Cole's vocal cords.

"Northern Louisiana."

"Keep going south. Follow signs for Texas."

Please, Owen prays, to whatever might be listening. *Someone please help me.*

Hal

Hal puts in for PTO at work and calls the Saunders Inn, Clegg's one hotel, to reserve a room for the memorial. He has to call because the inn has no website and doesn't take online reservations. He wonders how they stay in business.

He speaks to a woman named Barb, who keeps up a steady stream of happy chatter until Hal gives his name. Her ensuing silence stretches long enough Hal pulls his phone away from his ear to confirm they haven't been disconnected.

"Hello?" he says.

"Hal Isaac," Barb says, her voice warmer but far less peppy.

"Yep," Hal says. His heart sinks. He should've known this would happen.

"How are you? How have you been?"

"I'm fine," Hal lies, employing the same upbeat tone he uses when he wants to sound friendly to customers at work. "Can't complain."

"You're coming for the memorial."

"I am."

"Oh, you sweet boy." Her voice tightens. "That's so thoughtful."

"Thank you," he says, because it seems rude to say anything else.

He hears typing on Barb's end. She quotes him a price, takes his credit card information, and confirms his reservation in a voice like a wet rag. She blesses him a couple more times, and he thanks her and lies about needing to get back to work, so he can end the call.

He tries not to let the experience bother him, but it does. He hadn't even considered the town's collective memory. He'd hoped to slip into Clegg anonymously, attend the memorial service, see his friends, and then leave. Was that phone call a trailer for the full experience? A preview of every interaction to come?

He hasn't had a good night's sleep since the night he killed a man, so he wakes up before dawn on the day before the memorial. He guzzles a pot of black coffee in his studio apartment kitchenette, eats some antacids to fight the inevitable heartburn, and, out of useful distractions, starts the drive at 6 a.m.

It's stupid to go this early. The drive from Vandergriff to Clegg takes about three hours, and check-in at the Saunders Inn isn't until noon. Even with piss and gas breaks, he'll arrive between nine and ten. What the hell will he do for two hours? Make the rounds and soak up sympathy from people who don't know any better? That sounds awful.

But he can worry about it once he's in Clegg. For now, he only needs to move forward, look at what's right in front of him. As long as he's moving, he doesn't have to think or feel too much. Stillness is the problem.

Maybe he'll get lucky and Erin or Athena will arrive early, too. Both responded to his DM to say they were coming, but he hasn't talked to either of them since. He suspects none of them know what to say. Moreover, the earth is quaking and the sky is intermittently turning red. Both things have happened twice more since Hal tossed his cookies outside Tuttle's office. Red skies and earthquakes. With that shit going on, how is he supposed to make Dad jokes and send them "hey, remember when?" messages?

Despite the foreboding sky, it never rains, and he gets to town around ten. Clegg has changed little in the last twenty years. They've repaved the streets, the cars are newer, and the storefronts on the main drag advertise different goods, but the squat buildings housing them are the same. City Hall still shares a building with the fire station. Trees still wave from the city park, and the "world's onetime longest wooden footbridge" still crosses the creek (dry this late in the summer). The only truly, jarringly different thing is the high school and its immediate environs.

He knew it would be different. He googled pictures of the building to prepare himself. It's still a shock. The brown brick box where he struggled to stay awake in science class has been replaced with a bigger brown box that looks like a fortress. The windows are narrow and high, the athletic fields surrounded by tall fences wrapped in mesh fabric, to keep outsiders from seeing in. As Hal drives past, a coach escorts a gaggle of teenagers out of the building and onto the field. He uses a keycard to unlock the fence gate.

After what happened in 1999, Hal gets it. The town wants to protect their children. They want to make the school impregnable. But none of these measures would do a damn thing if there were a repeat of that day. It wasn't a loner with a pipe bomb or a disgruntled student who destroyed the school. It wasn't a thing you could stop with keycards and metal detectors.

The area around the school has changed, too. The streets have been repaved, and a few of the closest buildings have been rebuilt as well. There are still vacant lots where some of the owners elected not to rebuild. Hal finds these empty spots difficult to look at, too, empty spaces where his mind tells him there *ought* to be something.

His mind drifts as he navigates the sparse Friday-morning traffic. He thinks about the months ahead. He owes Tuttle an answer about the plea bargain. He tries to imagine what five years of prison, at a minimum, would look like.

In this dour version of autopilot, he drives to the Saunders Creek apartment complex, where he lived as a kid. As he pulls into the parking lot, he decides "complex" is too generous a word for this loose grouping of two-story buildings and its cracked lot of battered cars.

He parks and gets out to look around. The spirit of the place remains unchanged. The cars are banged up and filthy. Broken blinds dangle in the windows. The building that burned down in 1999 remains an empty concrete lot. A pall of desperation and resignation hangs over all of it.

As Hal takes it in, a Mazda with a missing headlight sputters in off the road and parks too close to another car. The driver—a woman so young she might still be a girl in high school—gets out and retrieves a toddler from the car seat in back. She and the boy have the same red hair and fair skin.

The boy wriggles and fusses in the woman's arms. She sets him on the pavement, steadies him by the shoulder, and smacks him across the face.

Hal puts a hand to his cheek as though he received the blow. The boy's features scrunch together as he takes a shaky breath, prelude to a miserable wail.

"See what happens when you don't mind me?" the woman says. Her voice is that of an older woman, rough with the ghosts of cigarettes.

The toddler wails louder, and the woman raises her hand in warning.

"Shut up, or I'll give you something to cry about."

Hal takes a step away from his own car and toward her, unsure what he means to do. He catches the girl's attention, and she scowls at him.

"What do you want?"

"Hi," Hal says. "You shouldn't hit your kid."

"You should mind your own fucking business," the girl says.

"You might regret it, is all I meant."

He doesn't mean the words as intimidation. More like friendly advice. This girl and kid are young enough to reverse course. Have a decent relationship. That's all Hal means to say. But as soon as the words escape his mouth, he knows he's fucked up.

The woman picks the kid up and holds him on her hip. She runs a hand through the boy's hair. It's the first time she's shown concern for his wellbeing, and his sobs taper into snuffles against her neck.

"I'm going inside now," she says. "If I look out my window in sixty seconds and you're still here, I'm calling the cops."

"I'm leaving," Hal says.

The woman hurries into one of the first-floor apartments. Hal returns to his car. At least he stopped her from hitting the kid for a few minutes anyway. Maybe the peace will last a whole day.

He starts the engine and glances skyward. No red in the heavens, but there are some heavy-duty storm clouds up there.

Erin

Erin flees her apartment after the bird attack on Wednesday night. Her plan is to make the drive to Clegg in one straight shot, but by noon on Thursday she can barely keep her eyes open. She and Philip check into a motel in Kansas and Erin casts a concealment command on the room before they go to sleep. The rain that's followed them out of Iowa spends the night and early morning rumbling and booming over the motel, and follows when they resume the journey Friday morning.

She's thankful it's only rain so far, but suspects it's the intermezzo between acts. Whoever is after her has more cards to play. Erin's one hope—the closest thing she has to cards of her own—are her old friends from Clegg. Maybe they can help her. Maybe.

Philip has remained quiet since they left the apartment. He doesn't speak unless spoken to, and answers in a hollow, absent way. He's in shock from the bird attack, but Erin doesn't have the bandwidth to help him through it right now.

They reach Clegg late on Friday morning. It looks much the same as it did when Erin and her father left back in 2001. It's still a *Friday Night Lights* sort of town, mostly white, architecturally flat, rural, and forested at the edges. The Dairy Queen has graduated from a stand to a full sit-down restaurant, and the dollar theater where she snuck into *Jackie Brown* is still in business, but now the featured attractions are all superheroes and cartoons and space wizards made by the same studio.

"This is where you grew up?" Philip says.

"It is."

"Where we'll meet your friends?"

"I hope so."

"Do they know I'm coming, too?"

"Yes," she says. It's a half-truth. She mentioned a plus-one in her DMs with Hal and Athena, but nothing else. It would've been too hard to explain via text or phone. Also she didn't want to risk someone using Philip as an excuse not to come. Better to just show up and force the group to deal with it.

They drive past the Saunders Inn and the new school. Erin avoids looking at either. Instead, she keeps her eyes on the road until she reaches the gravel driveway of the town cemetery. It's not the only cemetery in town—there are a few churches with yards for interring their own dwindling congregations—but it's where most of Clegg's dead end up.

"Can I come, too?" Philip asks, as Erin gets out of the car.

"Okay," she says. "But be quiet. No questions for a while."

They enter through the black iron gate, rain pattering on the bright fabric of their gas station umbrellas, which look garish among the tombstones and muddy earth.

For most of Erin's life, this lot was half-full. After the high school was destroyed, the town had to buy more of the surrounding land to accommodate the influx of headstones and empty boxes—there weren't many bodies left intact. The cemetery's iron fence had to be taken down and rebuilt to encompass the expansion. The recent additions had been an eyesore at the time—the headstones shiny with finish, the graves freshly dug. Now Erin has trouble telling where the old lot ends and the newer one begins. It doesn't matter, though. The Marsh family plot is fenced in near the back.

There are four graves inside. The first is Peter's mother, Sophie, 1959–1984, *Loving daughter, wife, and mother.* The second, Peter's father, Lawrence, 1957–1984, *Loving son, husband, father.*

The third belongs to Peter Marsh. 1982–1999, *Taken too soon.* Erin looks at it with a twinge. This was the last place she stopped when she left back in 2001, and it feels right to start her return to Clegg here as well. At the marker commemorating Peter's too-short life.

The fourth and final headstone takes her by surprise, however, distracting her from her mourning: Elijah Marsh, 1938–2010. No epitaph. Only a name and dates.

Erin hadn't known the professor had died. She wonders if Hal or

Athena know. The old man outlived his grandson by a decade. What must that have been like? To spend the winter of his life alone. Probably lonely. Acutely sad at first, gradually fading to a dull, constant throb in your chest. Erin doesn't need to imagine the pain. It's been her life for twenty years now.

Philip lingers outside the fenced-in area with his back to her, umbrella tipped up so he can look at the sky. He was supposed to ease her suffering. And he does, kind of. When they make love, she can forget the loss for a few minutes. The rest of the time, however, he's mostly a disappointment. More of a ward than a companion.

He seems to feel her watching, because he turns and offers her a puzzled smile. She gives him her barista customer service smile in return—the one she produces on command to get better tips at work. The one unconnected to actual feelings.

She faces the grave. Marsh didn't *have* to die alone. He could have reached out. Erin would've kept him company. Athena and Hal might've come, too. Yes, they'd all parted on bad terms, but surely they missed one another the way she's missed all of them?

But even as she tells herself this, she knows it for a lie. Marsh was firm in their last conversation. Their coven was finished. Their careers as Dissonants were at an end.

That had been the day of the funeral. The second-worst day of her life. Is this why she came here? To make herself feel worse?

No. She came to center herself. To touch the nexus of her pain and her joy. To remember good things. Like the night they learned about the Dissonance, or the flyting tournament in Dallas, or the morning Peter found her on the bridge—or even that one night in the tent, that final summer.

She squats in front of the tombstone and runs her fingers over the engraved letters of Peter's name.

"Dude," she says. "I miss you. Like all the time. Every day. How stupid is that?"

Pain explodes at the crown of her head. The world flashes red, then dulls to gray. When Erin comes back to herself, she's on her side, on the ground, soaked to the skin. She lifts her head out of the mud and sees Philip a few feet away, also prone. The cheap blue fabric of his umbrella has ripped. A red trickle runs down the side of his face. A softball-sized rock lies on the earth beside him, also stained red.

No. It's not a rock. It's a ball of ice.

She starts to get up, but something hits her between the shoulders and knocks her back down. A chunk of hail plops into the mud beside her. Her umbrella lies a few feet away, the fabric slashed and useless. They're caught out in an impossibly intense hailstorm, at least twenty yards from her car, with no tree cover. The sky above has turned blood red. The clouds look like a slow-rolling wall of flame.

"Philip," she croaks.

His eyelids flutter and his mouth moves, but his words are buried in the roar of thunder and clatter of ice. Erin forces herself onto her hands and knees. Ice chunks pelt her shoulders, back, and legs, but somehow she stays upright and gets to Philip.

She touches his temples. His eyes flutter again, but don't open. Erin, weak and woozy, manages a quick, sloppy version of Haley's Dome. The ice bounces off the invisible shield with hollow *bonks*. Erin grabs Philip under the shoulders and drags him toward the car. He outweighs her by at least fifty pounds, and it's all deadweight. Her arms and back protest with each step.

She makes it almost all the way to the gate before the bubble makes a tearing sound like a pep rally banner. The first ice chunk to break through bounces harmlessly off her shoulder. The next is not as kind, hitting her left arm like a baseball bat. She stumbles forward as another smashes the small of her back. Stupid, worthless dome. Stupid, worthless Erin.

She endures the beating and gets Philip through the gate. With great effort, she stuffs him into the backseat of her car before collapsing into the driver's seat. She leans on the headrest and closes her eyes. She's probably in a great deal of pain, but she can't feel it now. What she feels right now is *awake*. More present than she's been in a long time.

She catches her bruised, bloody reflection in the mirror and finds herself smiling. Not the barista smile, but the real one. She feels high. Stoned on adrenaline and possibility. The way it felt in the old days, with Peter. In the midst of this rush, she can almost believe if she turned her head, she'd see Peter in the passenger seat, also bruised, also smiling.

But when she opens her eyes, of course he's not there. There's only Philip in the back, semiconscious, moaning, eyes twitching behind closed lids. She starts the car and heads toward the Saunders Inn, praying this shell of glass, plastic, and metal will hold together for the rest of the trip.

Athena

The first place Athena stops in Clegg isn't technically part of the township at all. She goes to Marsh House, where it all started. Who lives there now? What became of Marsh's library of Dissonant texts? She looked Marsh up online before her trip here, and learned the old man had died in 2010, but when she looked through old Dissonant catalogs from the time, she found no record of a large book sale. His collection—worth several fortunes—either passed to new owners in private or was sold in small lots, which would make it harder to track.

Or, the whole collection could be in the house, untouched. If Athena can take possession of that collection, she can retire. Buy an island and a jet. Never talk to another person again if she doesn't want to.

About a mile down the dirt road that connects Clegg to Marsh House, she comes to a closed metal gate bearing a sign: PRIVATE PROPERTY—NO TRESPASSING. There's no surrounding fence, but trees grow too close on either side of the gate to drive around it.

Athena parks, gets out, and walks around the gate to make the rest of the trip on foot. Her left leg already aches from sitting in a car, and the sky is heavy with rain clouds, and as usual, she's forgotten her umbrella. All of this makes the prospect of a long, wet march unappealing, but the truest part of her—the part that grabs on to puzzles and won't let go without answers—won't let her turn back.

She walks up the middle of the gravel road, bordered on both sides by the Clegg woods. How many times did she and her friends make this walk as kids? If she closes her eyes, she can almost feel them beside her, probably on a summer afternoon. She and Hal bickering, Erin and Peter walking behind, wrapped in their own private world.

The rain still hasn't started when she emerges from the woods into Marsh House's circular driveway. She's a bit surprised the building still stands. She half-expected to find it burned down or collapsed. The paint is peeling, and the windows are crusted with years of filth, but the house looks much as she remembers it. Large, somehow foreboding and comfortable at the same time, seeming to grow up out of the surrounding woods like something from a fairy tale.

She walks around back, her sneakers squelching in the soft earth. The old toolshed still squats in the backyard, near the trees, the doors held with a rusted padlock. Peter's greenhouse stands beside it, overgrown, branches winding through its broken windows. The porch furniture—metal chairs and tables where they sat and cooled off between exercises—has rusted as well, but remains arranged as if expecting occupants to return at any moment.

She approaches the house, stops at the bay window of Marsh's study. She cups her hands around her eyes and peers through the murky glass. The room is dark, and the view less than perfect, but she doesn't see any furniture, or books, or a bar cart full of mystery powders. Just a big empty room.

Why doesn't anyone live here now? It's a nice house. Surely somebody would want it. But who in this town could afford it? And who outside of Clegg would want to move here? Both questions have the same answer: nobody.

She sighs, the expected disappointment arriving at last. The house is still here, but it's just a house. She walked all this way for nothing, and now she gets to do it in reverse. She makes the return journey as fast as her uneven stride will carry her.

As she nears the gate again, she finds a Sheriff's Department cruiser parked behind her car, blocking her in. A tall white man in a khaki uniform bends over to peer through her driver's side window. Her insides tighten the way they always do when she knows she'll have to interact with a cop. But he stands up as he hears her feet on the gravel, and Athena recognizes him. She wonders if he'll recognize her, too. She's not sure which outcome she'd prefer. Whichever one gets her in the least amount of trouble, she supposes.

"Good morning, deputy," she says.

"Ma'am," he says. "Is this your vehicle?"

"Yes."

"Did you see the sign on this gate?" He points in case she missed it.

"I did," she says. She steps around the gate and its sign and wonders how much trouble she's in. Isn't this place outside his jurisdiction? She doesn't say so, but slips the idea in her back pocket in case she needs it later.

The deputy gives her a stern frown, but it quickly melts into puzzlement. "Athena?" he says. "Athena Watts?"

Athena's unease melts into relief as she recognizes him. "Jordan McCormick," she says. Her old neighbor. A couple of years ahead of her in school. Kind when he didn't need to be. Still good-looking, in a small-town sort of way, dark hair graying, a hint of middle-age paunch over his belt. She's suddenly aware how she must look and smell after hours and hours on the road. She resists the desire to mess with her hair.

"How are you?" he asks.

"A little achy," she says. "Tired."

"Leg still giving you trouble?"

He remembers that? "Gets worse every year."

"I know that game," he says. "Some days I can't even with my lower back." Then he seems to remember he's at work, and rearranges his expression into sternness. "What are you doing out here?"

"I'm in town for the memorial. I wanted to see Marsh House while I was here."

"Guess that makes sense," he says. "You and your friends practically lived out here when we were kids." He puts his hands on his belt like a TV cowboy. "Far as I'm concerned, you're off the hook, okay?"

"Thanks," she says. She tries to sound grateful, like she wouldn't have made his life difficult if he'd tried anything. The ups and downs of dealing with police while Black.

"I want to get that out of the way, so you know before I ask my next question." He remains serious, but now also looks a little embarrassed.

"All right?" she says.

"Can I buy you a cup of coffee while you're in town?" he asks. "Or dinner or whatever?" He looks like a nervous seventeen-year-old despite the graying hair, crow's-feet around his eyes, and laugh lines around his mouth. "Totally okay to say no."

It's been a while since someone looked this anxious asking her for a date. It's been a while since anyone asked her for a date, period, she realizes. Closest she's come is Garrett, angling for a hookup.

"Coffee would be nice," she says.

"Okay." He grins. "Okay, great."

They exchange numbers, agree to firm up plans tomorrow, then get into their separate cars. As Athena waits for Jordan to turn his cruiser around, her phone dings with a text from Hal:

DINNER 2NITE?

Owen

After telling Owen to head to Texas, the Cole-thing falls silent. It stares forward, and with the sunglasses on, Owen can't tell if its unnatural yellow-green eyes are open or closed. He focuses on the road, the highway stretching toward Texas beneath a stormy dark sky. Rain patters on the roof of the old station wagon, and an invisible blanket of calm wraps itself around Owen's mind and heart. He must be in shock, or maybe dissociating. One of those terms he sees online, and in his psychology textbook. Doesn't matter which one. What matters is the invisible blanket shielding Owen from emotions or concerns about what has happened or will happen next. The blanket allows him to drive, soothed by the gentle, steady patter of rain.

All of this is ruined, however, when somewhere on the road between Vicksburg and Monroe, Owen's passenger takes a deep, hoarse gasp—maybe the first breath Owen's heard this thing take—and goes taut in its seat.

"Are you okay?" Owen says.

The Cole-thing jerks to the right and its head slams into the window hard enough to crack the glass. Its left hand flies up and slaps Owen's right arm, causing him to turn the steering wheel and swerve in the heavy rain. A car in the next lane over honks as it passes on the left.

"Hey," Owen says. He sounds more like himself. Angry. Present. "What the fuck?"

"Stop. The. Car," the Cole-thing manages.

The rain falls so heavily now that Owen can't see past the hood. He swerves onto the shoulder and parks. The Cole-thing throws open its door, letting in the full fury of the thunderstorm. It tries to stand but instead falls onto the wet pavement with a splat.

Owen gets out and runs around the front of the car. He bends to take the Cole-thing by the arm and helps it to its feet. He doesn't know why he's helping. Part of him is screaming he needs to stop right now, goddammit, let this thing, whatever it is, figure out its own shit or die. But through the fog in Owen's mind, the idea feels wrong. It's the same part of him that feels bad whenever people are sentenced to death, even if they committed the crime. The part of him that hates to see anyone suffering, whether they deserve it or not.

The Cole-thing holds on to his arm like an old man. Together they stagger off the road, leaving the car door open behind them. The earth is saturated with rain, and wetness soaks through Owen's sneakers and squelches between his toes, and for some reason this bothers him more than the thought of the living-dead creature beside him.

They stop a few feet shy of the barbed wire separating them from a patch of gently rolling grass. Here the Cole-thing uses Owen's arm for balance as it leans away from him and retches. A thick, chunky red splatter rockets out of the thing's mouth, hits the wet ground, and splashes back onto the thing's filthy jeans. The Cole-thing lets go of Owen, leans forward with its hands on its knees and makes a sound like a cat with a hairball. Its sunglasses slide off its nose and into the unmown grass. One of its hands goes to its throat, and a look of panic flashes in the thing's yellow-green eyes.

Is it choking? Is that possible? The thing doesn't breathe. Owen feels panic, but it's distant through the brain fog—a vague sense he ought to do *something*, but what? The Heimlich? He doesn't know how, and anyway, would it work on a creature that doesn't use airways?

He's still debating when the Cole-thing's mouth opens wider than any human mouth should. Another gout of blood and some fat, slimy objects spill forth onto the ground. Owen tries to understand what he's seeing—an endless sausage casing, a lump that expands and contracts on its own—and then he does understand and wishes he didn't. His abductor has just thrown up all its organs into the grass.

The thing dry heaves, thick rivulets of blood, saliva, and snot running out of its mouth and nostrils. The skin on its face looks wrong somehow, too—stretched too far, now hanging too loose like the neck of an old T-shirt.

"Are you okay?"

Owen turns to see a woman with an umbrella at the edge of the road. The Cole-thing lets go of him and he holds up a hand like a traffic cop. *Stop.*

"We're okay," Owen says.

"Are you sure?" the woman says. "Your friend doesn't look so good."

The Cole-thing keeps its back to the woman, hands on its knees. It has fallen still. Unnaturally so. Like an animal waiting to pounce.

"Just a stomach bug," Owen says. He works to keep his voice steady, reassuring. Not to let his sudden terror for the woman show. He smiles and does a *what are you going to do* shrug. His heart pounds and he tries not to think about the beating heart slowing on the ground beside him. Cole's heart.

"We're fine," Owen says. "It's nice of you to stop and ask, ma'am."

The Cole-thing, still leaning forward, not looking at her with its bloodstained face, raises its right arm in a thumbs-up. It's almost funny. Owen almost laughs.

"See?" he says. "We'll be back on the road in a minute, and honestly I'd hate for you to catch what he's got if it's contagious."

The woman at the edge of the road wrestles with herself. Owen sees it. She doesn't want to leave it alone. Then her eyes widen and her nostrils flare. She's noticed something—something she hadn't noticed before.

"Okay then," she says. She gives Owen a sharp little wave and hurries back to her SUV. As she gets in, Owen can make out other figures behind the tinted windows. Small figures. Kids. The woman drives off and disappears into the rain.

"You saved that woman's life," the Cole-thing says.

"I know," Owen says.

"But you also helped me."

"I know."

"Why did you help me?"

Owen opens his mouth, closes it. Considers. "I don't know," he finally says. "It feels wrong not to help."

"Normally I'd tell you that's an idiotic instinct—one you ought to ignore. But in this case it saved your life." It turns Cole's face up into the downpour, and lets the rain rinse off some of the blood and gore. With its eyes closed, and its face clean, the monstrosity starts to look a little like Cole. When it looks at Owen again, the illusion is shattered.

"I chose to spare you," it says. "But I'd have killed you if you hadn't helped. And I won't hesitate to kill you if you ever hesitate to help me with anything moving forward. Do you understand?"

Owen can't speak. So he nods.

"Good," the thing says. "Now let's go. We need to find a place to rest and prepare."

Prepare for what, exactly? Owen wonders.

1997
The Conference

Erin

Erin couldn't sleep the night before the conference. She spent the dark hours between Thursday night and Friday morning in her bed, rolling from one side to the other, alternating between flashes of excitement and sheer terror. She had never been and would never be a strong sleeper, but when her alarm went off at six and she shuffled into the bathroom, she could see dark bags beneath her eyes.

At fifteen, she was still young enough to hide a lack of sleep with judicious makeup application, and to shake off her weariness with a can of Surge. These tasks accomplished, she double-checked the contents of her backpack, then tiptoed through the living room of her parents' trailer so as not to wake her father.

He was sleeping on the couch again, after another shouting match with her mother last night. Erin paused before him now. He lay on his side, wrapped in an afghan blanket, brow furrowed. Even unconscious, he seemed troubled. Erin could relate.

She forced herself to turn away and let herself out the front door as quietly as she could. Once outside, in the early-morning sun, her mood brightened immediately. The trailer, and all those problems, were now behind her for two whole days.

She made the short walk to Hal's apartment complex, where she found him on his way out the door of his unit. He clomped down the stairs wearing a sour expression. Erin wondered why, then realized his mother's beat-up black convertible wasn't parked out front. Lorna was supposed to be their ride to Marsh House today.

"Where's your mom?" Erin said.

"Your guess is as good as mine," Hal said. "I called Peter. They're going to pick us up."

They sat on the bottom step while they waited.

"Excited?" Hal asked.

"Nervous. You?"

"Also nervous."

Professor Marsh's SUV pulled into the parking lot then, saving them from having to elaborate. They hoisted their bags onto their shoulders and ran to the SUV, where they joined Athena in the backseat. Marsh sat behind the wheel and Peter rode shotgun. Of the three, only Athena looked excited—almost uncharacteristically so.

"Oh my god," she said, as Hal slid into the middle seat beside her. "Could you sleep last night? I couldn't sleep last night."

Hal rolled his eyes. "I slept fine, you nerd."

Athena gave his head a playful shove to one side, and looked at Erin through the gap she'd created. "Did you sleep?"

"I didn't," Erin said.

"See?" Athena said to Hal. "Do you see?"

"Hi Peter," Erin said.

Peter had a small potted cactus in his lap. He moved the fingers of his right hand through the air over the plant, like a puppeteer, and the cactus reached and swayed in response. He glanced back at her, then away again, as if embarrassed.

"Hey Erin," he mumbled.

It was about what she'd expected, if less than she'd hoped for.

They made the drive in relative quiet. For more than a year now, Erin and her friends had been studying the Dissonance under Professor Marsh. It had been a year of afternoons and weekends in Marsh's study, or out in the backyard of Marsh House, practicing what Marsh called "the Dissonant alphabet": twelve symbols that formed the basis of most Dissonant commands. Erin and her friends had memorized these symbols.

Marsh had them reflect on each symbol's "surface" meaning (air, entirety, time, etc.) but also what he called "the deep meanings"—the subterranean associations and truths attached to the symbols.

"Some Dissonants spend their entire lives in contemplation of a single character," Marsh had told them. "They write treatises on the idea of water, or motion, or breath. Sometimes these deep studies yield surprising new insights, new ways of seeing and using the Dissonance. But more often these ascetics are content to spend their lives in reflection upon mystery. Not looking for definitive answers."

Luckily Marsh had not insisted upon such a course of study for his students, although he *did* insist upon daily meditation exercises, focusing on breathing, on *noticing*—not just the physical world, but the interior emotional landscape as well. "Notice your discomfort. Your pain. Use it. It's the source of your power."

It was by noticing—and then harnessing—this pain that Erin and her friends had begun to reliably draw on the Dissonance, and reshape the world around them in small ways. At least, that was how it'd gone for Erin, Peter, and Athena. Despite showing up to every lesson and studying alongside the others, Hal still couldn't read or write Dissonant. Even though he'd grown to recognize certain shapes, his understanding remained shallow, and no amount of breathing exercises, meditation, or reflection seemed to help. He could now summon the Blade of Woe at will, but he couldn't cast even the simplest Dissonant command.

Erin was progressing much faster, even though Dissonant study was far from the only thing going on in her life. She'd kept up with her regular schoolwork, and, in March, had gone out for the Clegg High cheerleading team. She'd done so without telling the rest of the coven. Partly because she was worried about what they might say, and partly because it meant she wouldn't have to admit to them if she hadn't made the team. But she *had* made the team, and so she had had to tell the others.

"I suppose this means I'll have to start working around the Clegg High cheer team calendar," Marsh had grumbled.

Athena's only remark had been, "Why would you waste your time on that?"

Erin hadn't had a good answer at the time—at least, not an answer she thought might satisfy Athena. In truth, she'd done it because she wanted something completely *normal* in her otherwise chaotic (at home) and bizarre (at Marsh House) life. It was the same reason that, not long after joining the cheer squad, she started dating a football player named Randy Taylor. Randy was nice, and fun, and unlike Peter, very up-front about wanting to be Erin's boyfriend.

The car ride was three solid hours, and there wasn't much to see out the window, aside from small towns, stretches of farmland, and billboards advertising churches, personal injury lawyers, and fast food. Eventually, mercifully, they entered Dallas. Erin had been here before, on day trips with her mother, but it never ceased to amaze her, the press of other people, the roads clogged with cars, the sky blotted as they passed between canyons of concrete and metal and glass. It was so much bigger than Clegg, and its sheer scale pulled her out of her own head and into the present as they arrived at the Hyatt Regency hotel. It was the fanciest hotel she had ever been to.

The lobby was packed with other travelers, and there were long lines both at the hotel check-in desk and the conference registration desk, which sat beneath a banner: WELCOME DISSIDENTS. Erin's mouth twisted in a smile. A simple typo to disguise the purpose of the gathering to outsiders, and hotel management. She glanced at her friends. Hal and Athena remained deep in the throes of argument, but she did manage to catch Peter's eye. He even gave her a little smile of his own, and for a second, it was the way it used to be—the way it always had been. Then he seemed to remember he wasn't part of the Erin Porter fan club these days, and he frowned down at his cactus. The cactus shivered beneath his gaze, as though suddenly cold.

They waited in line, registered, got their badges, then checked in at reception. The boys had a room on two, the girls had another on three, and Marsh was alone up on the tenth floor.

"I tried to get three rooms together," Marsh said, as he handed out room keys. "But it was impossible." He gave his pupils a hard stare. "This means I am trusting you to behave this weekend. Please honor my trust."

Erin and her friends all murmured their assent as they accepted the keys. They agreed to meet Professor Marsh back in the lobby in an hour so they could attend the conference's opening remarks, then split up. The boys took the stairs up to two, while Marsh and the girls took the elevator to their own floors. Erin would've liked to take the stairs, but didn't want to aggravate Athena's leg. A year later and the injury she sustained in the Clegg woods still hadn't fully healed. She moved around easily enough, but always winced when standing up or sitting down, and often took stairs slowly, like a grandma or someone with arthritis.

"Can I carry your bag for you?" Erin asked, as they stepped off the elevator onto their floor.

Athena shook her head. And then, perhaps trying an olive branch of her own, she added, "I've been training. Trying to stay sharp for the tournament."

She was referring to the Dissonant flyting tournament that would take place this weekend. It had been one of the central selling points of the conference, to attract younger Dissonants: a chance to test their skills against their peers. Marsh had insisted Peter, Erin, and Athena all participate. "It will be a worthy challenge," Marsh said. "And will provide me with useful benchmarks for your development."

Erin had been excited at the prospect, as had Athena, but Peter had objected strenuously.

"Why do we have to use violence to measure ourselves?" he'd said. "It seems barbaric."

"Hey," Hal had said. "Ouch."

"Sorry," Peter said.

"Make no mistake," Marsh said. "This power, this energy, this Dissonance? It's born from discomfort. From unhappiness. From pain. The world we occupy, and which we hope to control, is a broken, violent place. I can think of no better test for you."

So that's exactly what the coven had been practicing since the spring.

Flyting was an old Scottish word dating back to the 1400s. It referred to a verbal contest, an exchange of insults as a measure of one's wit. Dissonants had adopted the term for their own style of formalized dueling. In a Dissonant flyt, two opponents entered an arena and used their mastery of Dissonant to try and knock the other down. Since Dissonant was a language, the term still applied, although perhaps more literally than originally intended. A flyt was scored best of three rounds. The first opponent to fall twice lost the duel. It was more than a physical brawl. It was a contest of wits and wisdom. So far Erin hadn't had much luck with it. In practice bouts, she could usually best Peter, but always lost to Athena.

In their hotel room, Erin flopped onto the bed. It felt impossibly big and comfy compared to the squeaky twin in her room back home. She wanted nothing more than to close her eyes and take a long nap.

"Are you excited about the tournament?" she asked Athena, forcing herself back to wakefulness.

"Very," Athena said. "I've been training every day, even at home. Not just my Dissonant forms, but my physical strength."

Erin cast an appraising look at her friend now. Athena did look thinner and more toned than usual. Erin had assumed it was puberty reshaping her body, but apparently it was sheer willpower and discipline.

"You look great," Erin said now.

"I don't know about all that," Athena said, brushing the compliment off. "What about you. Are you excited?"

"Sure I'm excited," Erin said. "Just nervous, too. I mean, every time you and I duel, you destroy me."

Athena waved this remark away, too. "Only because you're distracted."

Erin rolled up on one side. "What's that supposed to mean?"

Athena kept both hands up, as if at gunpoint. "Don't make a whole thing out of this."

"Who's making a thing? You said something and I want to know what you meant."

"You've got a lot going on this summer." She averted her eyes, dug for something in her backpack. "If this was all you had to do this year, our duels would be more evenly matched."

Erin could've pushed. Could've rolled Athena's little faux pas into a great big fight. But what would be the point? Athena was like this. And Erin had to share a room with her for the next two days. If Erin had learned anything from her parents, it was how to keep the peace. Some things you didn't talk about, because talking about them made them real. Better to say nothing, so everything stayed more comfortable and everyone got along.

So Erin let out a silent sigh and smiled. Athena would be Athena, regardless. She sat up.

"C'mon," she said. "We need to get downstairs if we're going to make the keynote."

Hal

Hal, Peter, and Professor Marsh met in the basement of the hotel, where all the conference rooms were located. The opening keynote was taking place in the largest room, which was packed with rows of chairs. They managed to find five chairs together near the front of the room.

Hal looked around at the crowd and sighed. When he'd heard the coven would be attending a gathering of the Dissonant community, he'd anticipated something akin to his first (and, to date, only) trip to the Temple of Pain. He'd pictured mysterious figures draped in dark, hooded robes, conversing in vast, dark chambers. Instead, he sat in an uncomfortable chair in a hotel ballroom, the modular walls folded back to make room for a crowd of disappointingly normal-looking people.

"We could be at an accounting convention," he grumbled.

"What did you expect?" Peter said. "I mean, look at us. It's not like we stand out in public."

"I was hoping we'd be the exception," Hal said.

The girls entered the ballroom, and Hal waved them over to the seats they'd saved. Peter sat between Hal and Marsh, and the girls sat to Hal's right. Peter didn't even look at them as they sat. Erin looked pained, but only for a moment. It passed so quickly it might never have happened at all.

Not wanting to make things worse, Hal decided to look through the catalog he'd been handed at registration—a schedule of everything taking place at the convention over the weekend. Aside from the flyting tournament, it mostly appeared to be panels or presentations. "Silverman's *Music of the Infinite* in the 1990s." "The Many Worlds

Heresy." "Mysteries of the Temple of Pain." The first two sounded dull as dirt, but Hal was excited about the third one, because it was Professor Marsh's presentation. Marsh would tell Hal's story. And perhaps someone at the presentation would have some idea *why* Hal had been chosen by the Temple.

The roar of conversations died down abruptly, and Athena nudged Hal with one elbow. He looked up from the catalog to see a man now stood on the stage behind the lectern. He looked like he was in his thirties or early forties, handsome in a sharp-featured sort of way, with a head of receding brown hair.

"Good afternoon," the man said. "My name is Richard Thorpe, and it gives me great pleasure to welcome you all to the Convocation of Dissonants, 1997." He paused as the room filled with applause, and gave it a moment to die down before he spoke again.

"I wish I could say this was the annual Convocation of Dissonants, but that's not the case. This is actually the first large gathering of the community since World War II, and the best we can do for a meeting place is a Hyatt in Texas. It makes a sad sort of sense. The nature of the Dissonance attracts users who tend toward solitude and privacy—small, intimate groups of friends rather than large communities. We like to hide, and we tend to hoard our knowledge, because, for us, knowledge is quite literally power. And yet—I'm hoping this weekend we can start to change our collective attitudes toward one another. To realize we're stronger together than we are apart. To share our knowledge and grow together as a community. After all, we're an Abrahamic sect, are we not?"

"Speak for yourself," Marsh murmured.

"And what did Christ say?" Thorpe went on. " 'For where two or three gather in my name, there I am with them.' We're meant to be together. So please, don't hide in your hotel rooms this weekend. Come to the panels and presentations. Ask questions. Share knowledge. Each and every one of you is a valuable member of this community, and when we work together, I believe we can accomplish anything. Let's make this weekend count, and try to turn these gatherings into something more frequent than once every half-century. Thank you."

The room broke into another round of applause. Hal and Peter and the girls joined in, but Marsh remained unmoved, hands in his lap. Hal and the others stopped clapping and looked to the professor, questioning, as the people around them stood and shuffled out of the room.

"That man is the single most powerful and well-connected Dissonant on the continent—perhaps even in the world," Marsh said, leaning over and speaking low. "It's well and good for him to ask others to share knowledge, because he already has most of the knowledge available. It's the equivalent of a millionaire running a canned food drive."

"So why are we here?" Hal said.

"Because there may still be things to be gained from it," Marsh said. "Make no mistake, this *is* an opportunity. But remember to view opportunities with skepticism, and apply critical thinking. Don't let emotions cloud your judgment."

The words sank over Hal like a sheet of snow. He'd been studying with Marsh for a year now, and the old man was free with his advice—but the advice often took more than it gave in return. Every maxim or truth Marsh uttered seemed to make the world a smaller, meaner, sadder place.

Hal knew he ought to expect this. It was the basis of the Dissonance—the broken world—and for fuck's sake he'd been chosen by the *Temple of Pain* as a champion. Of course disappointment and sadness would be the prevailing emotions. It still hurt, though.

"Apparently there's a youth mixer tonight," Erin said, pointing to a page in the catalog. "Sort of a get-to-know-you thing, before the tournament starts tomorrow?"

Marsh frowned. "You need rest before the tournament. And by making friends with your opponents ahead of time, you forfeit any psychological advantage you have over them."

"But they forfeit their psychological advantages as well," Athena said. "So it sounds like we'd break even."

"You *hope*," Marsh said. "I won't stop you. Your time tonight is your own. Just don't give me cause to regret bringing you."

An hour later, Hal and Peter met Erin and Athena in the lobby, so they could go to the party together. Athena was wearing her usual uniform of jeans and a T-shirt, but Erin had changed into heels and a dress. Hal had always known Erin was pretty. He'd known it in an abstract and disinterested way, the same way he knew T. rexes were carnivores and tomatoes were plants. But all dressed up, she looked more than pretty. She was statuesque, and looked almost like a grown woman. He felt a pang of sympathy for Peter, but said nothing.

Like the keynote, the youth mixer was downstairs in the hotel basement, although it was being held in one of the smaller conference rooms. The chairs had been stacked against the wall, and snacks laid out on long tables near the doors. The lights were dimmed and music played on the PA. Most of the kids stood along the walls, but a few couples danced in the middle of the room.

"So these are our peers," Hal said.

He glanced at Athena, her mouth twisted in disappointment. "We might as well be at the Homecoming dance back home," she said.

"It's not so bad," Erin said.

"Yes it is," Peter said.

"C'mon," Hal said. "Let's go mingle."

They headed for the refreshments table, but were about halfway there when they were intercepted by a handsome boy with dark hair and a half-smile on his face.

"Hi," he said, over the music. "I'm Garrett Thorpe." He offered his hand to shake, which they all did, introducing themselves. When Peter gave his name, Garrett's eyes widened in recognition.

"Are you Elijah Marsh's grandson?" he said.

"Yeah," Peter said.

"I heard about what happened to your parents. Awful thing."

"Thanks," Peter said. "I don't really remember it, so it's not like a whole big thing for me."

"Sure," Garrett said. "Well, I'm glad you guys could make it! My dad organized the whole convention, but this part was my idea. The mixer, I mean."

"Your idea was to put on a shitty high school dance at a convention of the most powerful people in the world?" Athena said.

Hal stifled a laugh, and Peter smiled. Only Erin looked aghast.

"I think it's nice," she said.

Garrett gave her a toothy grin. "Thank you so much," he said.

Hal didn't like that smile one bit.

"So I know this is a totally lame, cliché thing to ask, but—do you want to dance, maybe?" Garrett asked Erin.

"She has a boyfriend," Peter blurted.

Athena raised her eyebrows, but said nothing. Erin looked slightly mortified.

Garrett opened his mouth, then shut it, smiling. "I'm not asking you to go steady," he said. "Just if you want to dance." He turned his winning smile on Peter. "No funny business. You have my word."

Erin shrugged. "Sure. Let's dance." She let Garrett take her arm, and they walked out to the dance floor.

As soon as they were out of earshot, Athena turned to Hal and Peter. "This is lame. I'm leaving."

"Me too," Peter said.

Hal didn't have the heart to argue.

"You coming?" Athena asked.

"I think I'm going to stick around," Hal said. "Soak up the atmosphere."

The others left. Hal drank his punch, and stood at the edge of the crowd. Every now and then he caught a glimpse of Erin and Garrett Thorpe, dancing. Even in the dark he could tell she was enjoying herself—smiling and bouncing on the balls of her feet, head thrown back in laughter. He watched her and the other couples dance, and felt a mix of boredom and envy.

He'd just about decided to head back to the room when a girl walked up to him out of the dark. She was small and fair, with dark hair and brown eyes and a slightly upturned nose. She wore a simple blue dress and sneakers.

"Do you want to dance?" she asked.

Hal felt a moment of sheer terror. Wasn't this supposed to go the other way around? Shouldn't he be the one working up the nerve to talk to her?

But Hal Isaac was nothing if not brave.

"Sure," he said. "I'd love to."

She took his hand and he let himself be led out onto the dance floor. He was keenly aware of the feel of her fingers in his own.

The song was a slow number, and Hal knew the basics from junior high—one hand on her hip, the other intertwined with her own.

"I'm Kelly," she said, leaning close to be heard over the music. Her lips brushed his ear and his flesh goose-pimpled around the spot.

He leaned over, suddenly very conscious of his own breath, wishing he'd brushed his teeth before he'd come down, and also that he'd avoided the fruit punch at the refreshments table. "I'm Hal," he said. "Where are you from?"

"Des Moines," she said. "You?"

"Here. Well, more or less," he said. "From the area."

"Cool."

After that, they turned their awkward, shuffling circles during the slow numbers, and bounced around during the fast ones. Holding Kelly's hand, touching her waist, trying not to step on her feet, Hal couldn't help but remember carrying Athena out of the Clegg woods the summer before. He tried to banish the thought from his head, to focus on the girl in front of him. He wondered if Kelly was thinking about someone else, too.

As the songs progressed, Kelly drew closer and closer to him, leaving less and less space between their bodies as they moved. Hal thrilled and worried, as his heart raced and his breathing sped up. Did she know how excited he was getting? Could she tell?

Finally she leaned her head on his shoulder but pressed herself against his groin and sighed happily. She backed off after that, but when the event ended at ten, and the overhead lights came on, and everyone was told to go get some rest, Kelly stood on tiptoe to kiss Hal on the cheek.

"Maybe I'll see you tomorrow?" she said.

"I hope so," he said.

She ran off to join a group of girls across the room, and Hal turned to head to the elevators, breathless, confused, and more turned on than he'd ever been in his life. He startled to find Erin standing in front of him, barefoot, holding her shoes in one hand. Her hair was slightly disheveled. Her face was red, and she was smiling, and sweaty.

"And they were worried about *my* behavior," she said, raising an eyebrow.

They walked down the hall together in companionable silence, Hal with his hands in his pockets, Erin dangling her shoes over one bare shoulder.

As they got into the elevator, she sighed and leaned against the back wall. "You know this is the most fun I've had in months?"

"Really?" Hal said. "You always look like you're having a good time."

"'Look like,'" Erin echoed. "Do you ever feel like you're being tugged in like four directions at once?"

"No," Hal said.

"I do," she said.

The elevator opened and she got off. Hal rode the rest of the way up by himself. Peter had taken the bed farthest from the door, and lay with his back to Hal as Hal entered. He'd left on one of the little lamps for Hal and his cactus sat on the table between the beds. It might've been a trick of the light, but Hal could've sworn the plant swayed at him in a greeting.

Hal undressed as quietly as he could and lay down. As he leaned over to switch off the light, Peter said:

"Did she dance with him a lot?" He didn't turn around, or move at all.

"Not really," Hal lied. "She got bored with him pretty quick. You should've stuck around—would've been fun."

Peter made no response. He let Hal kill the lights, and they lay in silence until Hal passed out.

Athena

On Saturday morning, Athena rolled over and checked the clock on the table between her bed and Erin's: 5:55. Five minutes before the alarm she'd set for herself. She reached over and turned it off. She'd set it more as a precaution than anything else. This had always been her own personal superpower. Her internal clock always woke her without fail.

This morning, however, the hunger pangs would've done the job all by themselves. They'd woken her every ninety minutes all night, and her stomach growled as she got out of the bed now.

She'd been dieting all summer long, trying to slim down, to look like the other girls in her classes at school. She'd never been a skinny kid, but in the past couple of years, as her friends lost their baby fat, she'd widened at the hips and bust. She wasn't fat, exactly, but she wasn't far off from it, either. So she'd been eating frozen Weight Watchers TV dinners, guzzling Diet Coke, and chewing sugar-free gum, all in an effort to curb her body's inclination toward girth and fullness. She'd lost ten pounds since the end of the school year, but each pound had been a battle. She'd had to grit her teeth and say "no thanks" to every snack her parents offered, every cheeseburger her friends wanted to go eat at the diner in town. In short? She was miserable. But she wasn't a quitter. She *could* do this.

As she showered, she stretched her left leg and winced. It was always stiffest in the morning, and even at the best of times it never felt quite right. She'd managed to hide the extent of the injury from her parents—thanks to the professor's paste, there was no scar, and she could conceal her limp if she was determined—so they had no idea how much discomfort she endured daily.

She dressed as quietly as she could. She could probably have made more noise—Erin was out cold on her stomach and sawing logs into her pillow. She snored through Athena's preparations and exit.

Athena took the elevator to the lobby, then the escalators to the basement, where she found Professor Marsh engaged in conversation with a middle-aged woman who only came up to about his shoulder. They spoke in low, but friendly-sounding voices, yet when Marsh caught sight of Athena, he put a hand on the woman's arm, and the conversation stopped as the woman turned to look.

"We'll talk later," the woman said.

"Indeed," Marsh said.

Marsh didn't introduce Athena, and the woman didn't seem to expect him to. She gave Athena a curt nod and walked away, back toward the elevators.

"She's not going into the presentation?" Athena said.

"I don't think she could stand it," Marsh said.

"Why not?"

"Because she's a woman of considerable intelligence, and she has a weak stomach for nonsense."

They entered the ballroom, passing a sign on the placard: THE VOICE OF GOD, THE DISSONANCE, AND JUDEO-CHRISTIAN APOLOGETICS.

"If it's nonsense—" Athena started to ask, but Marsh shushed her.

"Keep your voice down," he said.

"If it's nonsense," Athena murmured, "why are we up so early to be here?"

"Think of it as reconnaissance," Marsh said. "Intelligence gathering. It's important to know how your opponent thinks."

"Why are these people our opponents?" Athena asked.

"Not here," Marsh said. "After."

Athena fell silent, but not happily. If Marsh wanted Athena's help gathering information, he could have at least briefed her on why they were here ahead of time. That would've been helpful.

The panel was sparsely attended, mostly by men around Professor Marsh's age. This apparently wasn't a subject of much interest to most Dissonants younger than Moses, which would explain why it was taking place at 7:30 on a Saturday morning. The panel was made up of three older men, one younger man, and one middle-aged woman.

They dressed like Marsh, in conservative tweeds and sweater vests, despite the summer weather outside.

The moderator took the lectern at the end of the long table. He was the first other Black person Athena had seen since they arrived. Why were there so few Black people here? Lord knew Black people had enough pain to contend with existing in this world. They ought to out-number the white attendees by two to one at *least*. And yet, Athena and this man appeared to be the only spots of color in an otherwise pasty population.

"Good morning," he said. "My name is Lucius Hannon, and I want to thank you all for being up so early to attend what I think is a very important conversation." He made eye contact with Athena as he said it, and smiled a little. Athena forced a little return smile, because it seemed the polite thing to do.

Hannon introduced the panelists: Joseph Means, retired professor of theology from Texas Christian College; Daniel Allen, Old Testament scholar from somewhere in Oklahoma; Jeb Hart, a graduate student at a small Bible college in the Midwest; and Cordelia Wehmeyer, a retired schoolteacher from Wisconsin.

Each panelist said hello to both Mr. Hannon and to the audience before Hannon presented them with the first question:

"For most of its history in North America, Dissonant use has been tied to the practice of Christianity. Do you still feel this is a worth-while, relevant bond?"

Next to Athena, Marsh crossed his arms and sighed, loud enough that some other people in the audience turned to look at him. Athena fought the urge to shrink in her seat. The professor had specifically asked her to attend this panel with him. This was her invitation to the grown-up table. She was proud to be here, and she would act like it. She resquared her shoulders and held her head high. She stared straight ahead like she was interested in the panelists' answers—and caught Jeb Hart's glance. He smiled a tiny bit before he spoke.

"That's something of a softball question," he said. "The five of us wouldn't be gathered here on this stage right now if we didn't think this was important." His voice was surprisingly deep, and he spoke in a flat, unaffected way. "You might as well ask a duck if it thinks water is relevant."

Soft laughter rippled through the sparse crowd.

"I disagree," said Daniel Allen, an overweight man with a few wisps of white hair in frozen exodus from his skull. "Not that we all think this is important—but I take umbrage with Mr. Hart's flippant tone. Look at the time of day the convention scheduled this panel. First thing in the morning on a Saturday, when most attendees are still sleeping off last night's parties. Look at the crowd we've drawn." He swept a hand out at the three-fourths-empty ballroom. "We agree this is important, but I believe the larger Dissonant community has dismissed us in deed, if not yet in word."

"If only," Marsh whispered.

The panel rolled on from there, and Athena did her best to keep up. She'd known before now that many Dissonant users believed Christianity was somehow tied to the Dissonance, but Marsh had never presented it to their coven as (ha ha) gospel truth. Marsh had spoken about Christian Dissonants as a sect, rather than the majority. Apparently the professor had downplayed this sect's power in the community. She began to wonder in what other ways Marsh might have given her a skewed, imperfect picture of this world. And yet he'd brought her here, hadn't he? He wanted her to see. Why?

She couldn't follow some pieces—the arguments regarding obscure points of theology, books of the Bible she'd heard of but never read. One thing she did catch, however: repeated references to the first verse of the Gospel of John:

In the beginning was the Word, and the Word was with God, and the Word was God.

The scholars on the stage seemed to believe the energy force Athena called the Dissonance was the selfsame Word mentioned in the book of John. Now it'd been years since Athena had been to Sunday school, but she'd been taught that "the Word" meant Christ, not a magical power wielded by humans.

Finally, after about forty-five minutes of conversation, the panel opened up for audience questions. Professor Marsh was the first to the microphone. From the looks on their faces, Athena guessed some of the people onstage recognized her teacher.

"Hello, Professor Marsh," Lucius Hannon said. "Kind of you to join us."

"The pleasure is mine," Marsh said. Athena couldn't see his face from where she sat, but she heard the smile in his voice. "My question is for the entire panel."

"This ought to be good," Daniel Allen said.

"So far, you've made repeated references to the idea of Christian Dissonants as a minority. Do you honestly believe you're a minority in this community?"

"Indeed," Cordelia Wehmeyer said. "When I was a girl, the *only* way to be introduced to the mysteries of the Dissonance was to join the right church, make the proper show of piety. Put in the work, let yourself be vetted. And only then, *if* the practitioners in your congregation thought you were the right sort, would they take you on as a pupil. Now we're incidental. A fringe group. A minority."

"And yet a very powerful minority," Marsh said. "A minority that exerts a stranglehold on Dissonant education and worldview."

"I'm not hearing a question in there," Lucius said, a slight warning in his tone.

"And anyway, there are other people standing behind you, waiting for a turn," Jeb Hart said. He gestured and Marsh turned to see there were two people in line behind him.

"Then I'll make this quick," he said. "Why does the Council of the Word refuse to entertain the Many Worlds theory, despite mounting evidence?"

Murmurs of conversation passed through the auditorium, then hushed as Joseph Means straightened in his seat and peered at Marsh through thick glasses.

"'Mounting evidence' is an overly generous way to phrase it," he said. "'Proliferation of misinformation' is more accurate. The Council of the Word reviews all claims of Dissonant discovery with an unbiased eye, and incorporates new knowledge into its canon upon verification."

"A verification process with zero transparency," Marsh said, almost talking over the other man.

"I understand you're upset," Means said, "that your repeated attempts to undermine or hijack the process have been frustrated. But the fact remains, your claims have no basis in fact. There is no substantial evidence that there are other realities than the one we inhabit, or that the Dissonance isn't related to the Word of Yahweh. I am sorry your life's work has been a failure."

The room fell silent, waiting for Marsh's response.

"Enjoy your obsolescence," he said. He turned and walked back up the aisle, beckoning to Athena as he passed. She got up and followed him out of the room. She had to hurry to keep up with his long-legged strides.

They took the escalators to the ground floor, and there he finally paused and looked back at Athena. His shoulders rose and fell with his heavy breathing, and his lined face was scrunched with anger. He stood up straighter, took a long, calming breath, and then gave her a half-smile.

"Do you want to get a coffee?" he said.

They crossed the lobby to the café, and ordered two large black coffees. They sat at one of the small tables near the back of the shop while they drank. Athena felt terribly grown-up with the paper cup in her hand. The rush of caffeine sent a flood of questions through her mind, but she only dared voice one of them:

"Why are there only two Black people at this convention?"

Marsh nodded, as though he'd been expecting this. "There are in fact many different Dissonant communities—a Black community, a queer community, and so on—that refused to take part in this conference."

"Why?"

"You saw that panel in there. They have a very conservative worldview, one not necessarily welcoming to those other communities. I don't blame those other communities for staying away. Perhaps when you're older, and a little more seasoned as a Dissonant, I'll introduce you to some of my other contacts. There's much you can learn."

"If there are so many different communities, why are you participating in this one?" Athena asked. "It seems hostile to you, and vice versa."

Marsh sighed. "As a straight white man, I might be less welcome in some of those other communities, which is only fair. But, even setting that aside, the primarily white, Christian Dissonant community is still the most powerful in the world. It attracts the most people, and gives me the most opportunities to find like-minded individuals who can help me on my search for the truth. You're beginning to see that there's much more to the Dissonant world than I've perhaps led you to believe."

"I feel like I'm in that dream," Athena said. "The one where you show up for a test and then realize you forgot to come to class all semester?"

He gave her a small, rare smile. "A good teacher does more than offer knowledge. A good teacher gives shape to the knowledge, leads the student through it in the most effective way. I wanted your coven to see the Dissonance the way I see it, before you got bogged down in the dogma those people downstairs would want you to believe."

"You see it as a power," Athena said. "Agnostic. A tool. They see it as a part of their religion."

"Very good," Marsh said. "And it's the biggest problem facing the Western Dissonant community today. It's the thing that estranged me from my mentor. When I was only a few years older than you are now, I was studying linguistics in college. I had a teacher who took an interest in me. A man I loved like a father. He kindled my interest in ancient languages and convinced me to pursue my doctorate. He chaired my dissertation. This man was convinced there was a written language which preceded even most ancient spoken languages. A primordial code. His ideas weren't popular at the university or in the field, but I believed him. And because I believed him, he showed me the little green book you discovered in my hallway last May."

"My first Dissonant text," Athena said.

Marsh fiddled with the paper sleeve of his coffee cup, turning it in a slow circle so the Starbucks logo slowly rotated in and out of view. "My teacher had kept it all his life, a secret even from his family. He'd hoped to decipher it and publish his findings, but had never been able to crack the code. He was more than a touch unnerved when he realized I *could* read it. That the symbols in the book made more and more sense to me, the longer I studied them. When I began to copy out the symbols—to scratch them in the earth, or draw them in the air—I realized I had discovered more than a language. I had discovered the power to reshape the world. I tried to show my mentor, but he was a religious man. He rejected me, said what I was doing was wrong. So I stole the book and set out to learn more on my own."

He picked up his coffee, blew on the opening in the lid, then took a sip. "Hoping to learn more, I started work on a second doctorate, in folklore and mythology. But despite all my study and reading, that book was my only peephole into a larger world. It was years before I met another practitioner, and learned the proper name for what I was doing. Unfortunately, we turned out to be in the minority. Most North American Dissonants believe this power should be used in accordance with the teachings of the Christian Bible. That the Council of the Word is the foremost authority, and their prescribed use of this power is the correct and *only* proper use. They also believe that, because the Christian Bible doesn't make explicit mention of other worlds, ours is the one and only."

"Is this Council of the Word powerful?" Athena said.

"Yes," Marsh said. "They've managed to keep a monopoly on use of the Dissonance for the last two hundred years."

"So why haven't they come knocking on our door yet?" Athena asked, but the answer came to her before Marsh could speak: "Because you built your house next to a powerful Dissonant area. Next to the Clegg woods, they would have a lot of trouble detecting what you were doing."

Marsh nodded. "Very good again. But that's not the whole of it. I also spend a lot of money on bribes every year, to keep Council enforcers away."

"Why? What are you doing that's illegal?"

"There's . . . more to my work than you have seen so far, or are likely to see anytime soon."

"What could happen if you were raided by the Council?" Athena said.

"My library could be confiscated," Marsh said. "I could be arrested, thrown into detention, to await Council trial. And if I were convicted, they could break my connection to the Dissonance."

Athena sat back. "They can do that?"

Marsh nodded. "They can. And worse, it's an irreversible process. Once the connection is severed, it can't be reforged."

Athena took a sip of her coffee but barely tasted it. "That sounds worse than dying."

"I agree," Marsh said. "And that's why it's so important we be discreet and careful in our dealings. Most of the people at this convention are not our friends. They would neuter or destroy us if they could."

"Why did you bring us here, then?"

"Because there are still opportunities to learn," Marsh said. "And there are a few people here who have information I need. Information that could bring down the Council and its foolish notions."

She made an intuitive leap, then, remembering something Marsh had said during the panel. "The Many Worlds theory?"

Marsh said nothing, but winked at her as he took another drink of his coffee.

"Is there someone here who can confirm its existence?" she asked.

"There are conversations to be had."

"And if you can prove it?"

"Everything changes," Marsh said.

Erin

Erin woke in an empty room and guessed that Athena and the professor must be off seeing a panel or something. She was grateful for the quiet and the space, because it allowed her to ease into the day in her own time. She stretched, drank some water, then showered and dressed in jeans, sports bra, and T-shirt. She had been disappointed when she'd learned that there was no formal costume for the flyting tournament. She'd imagined something like the Gis from *The Karate Kid*. Costumes would've made it feel more dramatic and theatrical.

She knelt on the floor of the room, bowed her head, and silently moved through her forms. Athena and the professor thought her a traitor for choosing to be a cheerleader this year, but she knew her Dissonant characters better than she remembered the moves of any cheer routine. She'd worked her ass off.

It doesn't matter. They've already made up their minds about you.

This was the voice she heard constantly now. The voice of her own doubts and fears. It was a persistent little thing. She took a deep breath, pulled the voice into the center of her chest, and then released it through parted lips.

She finished getting dressed, then made her way to the basement. The ballroom for the flyting tournament had been lined with plastic mats, and all the kids from last night's mixer were already spread around the room, drinking from water bottles, bouncing on the balls of their feet, talking to their chaperones. Erin looked around for her own coven, and found them near one corner of the room—Hal, Peter, Marsh, and Athena, all huddled and talking. Hal waved to her and she approached. Peter looked absolutely miserable. He hadn't been keen on this tournament from the beginning.

"Why didn't anyone tell me we were meeting up beforehand?" she said. "Thanks for letting me know."

"We didn't plan it," Hal said. "We all just got here at about the same time." *So please calm down,* his look seemed to add.

"Yeah," Peter said. "Get over yourself."

He couldn't have hurt her more if he'd slapped her.

"Enough," Marsh said. "Save it for your duels. Hal and I just came to wish you luck before we go to our own panel."

"Can I just come with you?" Peter said. "I don't want to do this."

"You're going to do this, Peter," Marsh said. "It's important."

"To who?" Peter murmured.

If Marsh heard, he gave no indication.

The coven split up then, going to their designated spots. Erin was grateful to be far away from Athena and Peter. They'd only be a distraction, a drag on her ability to concentrate.

Erin's opponent in the first match was a girl named Jane Hughes. She was as tall as Erin, but broader and more muscular. She had a strong jaw and heavy-lidded eyes, and when she shook Erin's hand, she squeezed hard enough to cause pain.

Erin took care not to let her discomfort show. She'd always been good at keeping a tight lid on her feelings.

The adult referee stepped between them, pushed them apart, explained the rules: No physical contact. No audible speech. The goal was to knock your opponent off their feet, not harm them. Any obvious attempts at causing your opponent bodily harm and you would be disqualified and ejected from the tournament immediately. The referee asked Erin and Jane if they both understood. When they said they did, she sent them to opposite sides of their mat, gave them a three-count, and then set them loose.

Jane's fingers moved so fast she might've been stuck on fast-forward like a VHS tape. Yellow-green light flashed between her hands, and Erin was lifted off her feet and tossed backward. She hit the barrier at the edge of the mat. All the air seemed to explode from her mouth in a stupid-sounding "Oof!" and she barely experienced her fall.

The world came back with her first whooping inhale of breath. The referee was kneeling next to her on the mat, her hands on Erin's shoulders. The ringing in Erin's ears faded and she heard the woman ask: was Erin all right?

Erin nodded and tried to wave her off.

"I need a verbal 'yes,'" the referee said.

Erin took in another deep lungful of air, and continued to nod. "Yes," she said. Her voice sounded surprisingly strong. "Yes, I'm still here. I'm okay."

The ref stared hard at Erin, then made an *If you say so* face. She stood and turned toward Jane.

"I'm going to let the match continue, but I'm warning you," she said. "That was borderline, at best."

Jane gave the ref half a smile. "Sorry, ma'am," she said, although she didn't sound it, not one bit. "Guess I don't know my own strength."

Erin got to her feet. She walked back to the center of her side of the mat. She stretched and looked across the room, and saw Peter Marsh in his own match. He'd been paired against Garrett Thorpe. They stood across the mat from one another. Garrett seemed to have an entourage of friends hanging out near him. Peter had no one. He was alone over there.

The referee stepped back. Peter began moving his hands, but Garrett was faster by an order of several magnitudes. Peter's arms had barely risen above his head before he was smashed forward onto the mat. It looked like something from a Road Runner cartoon. Wile E. Coyote flattened into the ground by an anvil. It had the cadence of a sight gag, and a single laugh escaped Erin's mouth before she could catch it.

Peter stayed facedown on the mat for a long time—long enough that his referee came over to check on him. The ref rolled Peter over, and any humor in the moment vanished. He looked like he'd been punched square in the face. His nose was clearly broken, and he had the start of two black eyes. Even over the roar of the crowd, Erin heard Garrett's entourage make an "ohhhh," sound as they saw the damage their friend had inflicted. Garrett bobbed on the balls of his feet and grinned.

We're outmatched here. The thought came unbidden into her head, accompanied by a sinking feeling in her stomach. Marsh hadn't prepared them properly. He'd given them no real idea what they'd be up against. He'd probably had no idea himself.

Do you really believe that? Another unwelcome thought, accompanied by a suspicion. Had Marsh deliberately undertrained them for this? Had he wanted them to come here and be humiliated? Was it some bigger lesson he was trying to teach? And had he undertrained all of them, or just Erin and Peter—Peter, because he hadn't wanted to be here, and Erin, because she'd had the nerve to go out for cheerleader, to do one fucking normal thing with her life?

I'll bet Athena got plenty of training.

And as soon as the idea took hold in her mind, the sinking feeling in her stomach turned to a hard knot of anger in her chest. She looked away from Peter, and Garrett Thorpe, and back at Jane and the ref. The ref gave her a questioning look, and Erin gave her a curt nod. She was ready to go again.

The ref threw her hand down in the air between them, signaling the beginning of the new round. Jane moved just as fast as before, the light flashing between her blurred hands. This time, Erin let her anger do the work. She let it take control. Her hands moved faster than she'd realized they could, and light flashed around her as she conjured a giant hammer blast of air. She sidestepped Jane's missile as her own hit her opponent like a hard shove to the shoulders. Jane teetered on her heels for a second and then fell down hard on her ass, with a look of mingled outrage and disbelief. Disbelief at having been knocked down. Outrage at the method of her defeat.

"That's it?" she said to Erin. "That's your big move?"

Erin didn't respond, tamping down on her own delight. Whatever was happening right now, she didn't want to screw it up. Instead, she stretched, and fought to hang on to her own anger. She pictured Garrett Thorpe's face, the little smirk as he bloodied Peter. She hoped Peter had won that match by default. That Garrett had been disqualified for unnecessary roughness. She wanted to look at him, to see how it had turned out. But this would be over in a moment, and she could check then.

The ref helped Jane to her feet. Although Jane clearly didn't want to be helped, she was too discombobulated to prevent it. She stood up, shook her head as if to clear it, and told the ref she was fine, ready to go on to the third round.

The ref started the final round, and this time Erin didn't even need to move quickly. Jane was off balance, off her game. Erin had the momentum. So instead of using a basic hard wind command, she reached for something else: the command for a hook. She extended it slowly. Jane had plenty of time to throw up a dome, but Erin's conviction, her grasp of the language, was deeper and stronger, her construct more powerful. It pushed through Jane's dome like a hand through fog. Jane tried to dance out of the hook's way, but it darted forward, wrapped around her ankle, and yanked. Jane did an unwilling backflip through the air and landed hard, facedown on the mat.

"That's match!" the ref said. She turned to Erin. "Congratulations."

Erin nodded her thanks, and went to help Jane to her feet. The other girl allowed herself to be helped up. She was still a bit dizzy and disoriented, and needed Erin's help to stay upright.

"Respect," Jane said. "Where'd you learn to flyt like that?"

Erin looked around. It would've been nice to see a friendly face, to have someone to celebrate with. No one was in sight. Peter was gone. Garrett was already across the mat from someone else.

"I'd say I had a good teacher," Erin said. "But I'd be lying."

Hal

Hal would've liked to stick around and watch the first matches of the flyting tournament, but had to leave to help Professor Marsh prepare for their presentation. He and the professor went to their appointed room forty-five minutes early, so they could do a speed run through the presentation ahead of time.

They'd been working on it for weeks—or rather, Marsh had been working on it for weeks, while Hal mostly waited around or did gofer work (taking down notes when Marsh stopped mid-rehearsal, refilling the old man's coffee mug). Most of the presentation consisted of Marsh telling the story of Hal's trial at the Temple of Pain. Hal's only part was near the end, when Marsh asked him to summon the Blade. When Hal had pointed this out, hinting to Marsh he might like to have a larger role, Marsh had dismissed him.

"You're the grand finale," the professor had said. "You're what they'll remember after the fact."

Hal recognized the appeal to his vanity, but had to admit it was effective. He had to admit something else to himself as well: he was pleased that the professor wanted to work with him. Most of the old man's teaching time was devoted to Peter, Erin, and Athena. After all, there wasn't much call for a magic sword during lessons, and the coven hadn't had any real adventures since the first one. Hal's superpower had begun to feel more like a parlor trick than a useful part of the group.

So today he helped Marsh move through the stages of the presentation. He switched out transparencies on the overhead projector, containing copied pages from Dissonant texts as well as Marsh's and

Hal's own renditions of the Temple and the Blade. If Marsh gave Hal a note—to speed something up, or slow it down—Hal didn't argue. He listened. He obeyed. And as the clock ran down to the start of the presentation, Hal found himself experiencing another unusual sensation: nervousness. He'd always thought of himself as fearless—willing to jump off the swing set at the highest point, or be the first off the high dive; the one unafraid to make an ass of himself in front of other kids at school, if it got a laugh. But now, as a crowd of Marsh's contemporaries shuffled into the room with their matching expressions of skepticism, Hal's stomach did a flip-flop.

The doors shut, and the lights went down. Hal took his place onstage, in a chair next to the podium.

"Thank you all for coming," Marsh said. "To what is sure to be a revelatory presentation."

He then launched into a narration of the events of last May. Athena's discovery of the Dissonant primer. The game of *light as a feather, stiff as a board* in the backyard. Hal's rise into the night sky. He brushed over the events on the ground, instead following Hal's narrative, as he landed in a darkened temple. Hal rose from his chair every few minutes to switch transparencies on the overhead projector. He'd practiced it so often, he could do it on autopilot. But when Marsh got to the part of the story about the Trial of Agony, and Hal put up the transparency containing his sketch of the temple, the pain began. It started in Hal's fingertips, and crawled up through his wrist and forearm. The memory of the burning sensation. The pictures the temple had given him: images of himself suffering, dying comically terrible deaths.

"And," Professor Marsh said, "when Hal refused to concede to the voice's wishes for the third time, the temple itself conceded. It told Hal he had the ability to withstand great pain, and would therefore be a worthy champion." Marsh turned and nodded to Hal.

Hal walked downstage so that he was slightly in front of the professor. He extended his left arm, and called the Blade. His arm, which had started tingling during Marsh's telling of the story, now burned with invisible fire. There was a gasp as the weapon materialized in his hand, a burst of light and heat in the darkened ballroom. In that brief illumination, Hal recognized a face in the audience: Kelly, the girl from the dance the night before. She smiled up at him, wide-eyed, and his stomach did a triple backflip of nervousness and physical desire. He fought not to grin back. This was a serious academic proceeding, after all.

"The Blade of Woe," Marsh said. "A supposedly heretical legend, but here before you in reality. You probably can't see it from where you're sitting, but the blade and pommel bear the intricate markings first described in the work of Rebecca Ness. It is an exact match. Moreover, without any prompting, Hal's description of the temple is a perfect match for Ness's own descriptions and sketches." Here Marsh switched out the transparency himself, putting up a reproduction of a crude sketch from an old journal. "Rebecca Ness has been considered heretical. Her work non-canon. And yet here we have irrefutable proof she told the truth about the Temple of Pain—a location which, as near as we can tell, exists outside the reality in which we live every day. When are we going to stop using the word *heretical* to describe objective truth?"

"This is absolute nonsense." The voice came out of the dark, and caused a ripple of murmured conversation. Marsh shielded his eyes with one hand and peered into the crowd.

"Hello, Dr. Allen," he said. "I'm flattered you could make it."

An old man—older-looking than Marsh, with blotchy skin and barely any hair left—hobbled toward the stage, leaning on his cane.

"How *dare* you come here and present such absolute hogwash," the old man said. "Delivering your pet theories and hearsay as fact."

Marsh's smile didn't budge. "I guess we can move on to the Q&A portion of the presentation," he said. "Did you have a question, Dr. Allen?"

"Indeed," Allen said. "What is your proof that this blade is in fact what you claim it is? Will you submit it to inspection?"

"The Blade only remains material while Hal holds it," Marsh said. "If he lets it go, it returns to its place in limbo."

"How convenient," Allen said.

"You're welcome to examine it while he holds it," Marsh said. "Hal, why don't you get down offstage so Dr. Allen doesn't have to hobble up and embarrass himself in front of all these people?"

Hal hopped down lightly and landed before Dr. Allen. Here was another benefit of holding the Blade—gravity seemed not to have such a tight hold on him. He could jump higher and farther, and falls hurt less.

Hal held the Blade out, the flat side up so Allen could examine it. The old man bent forward and squinted through his glasses, murmuring to himself, occasionally glancing up to compare with the slide on the projector depicting Rebecca Ness's sketch. He spent a long time comparing the two.

"Thank you, young man," Allen said. Hal nodded and took the stairs back up onto the stage.

"It's very convincing," Allen said. "I'll give you that. But how do we know your student hasn't conjured a blade by abusing the Word?"

"Because Hal Isaac is not a Dissonant," Marsh said.

Another murmur of surprise ran through the audience. Hal experienced a strange sensation, as if a hundred invisible index fingers were poking him at the same time. They must be trying to ascertain the truthfulness of Marsh's claim. It was deeply unpleasant, and Hal fought to stand still through this low-key assault. It ended after a moment, replaced by increased murmuring.

"Did you have any further questions, Dr. Allen?" Professor Marsh said.

"Plenty," Allen said. "But I've wasted enough time talking to you for one day. And I've wasted enough of my life trying to teach you. There comes a time when a man has to say 'enough.'" He left the microphone and walked, not back to his seat, but all the way out of the room. Everyone—Marsh included—watched him go.

"That was certainly dramatic," Marsh said. He nodded to a woman at the audience's microphone. "Yes ma'am."

"Hi," the woman said. "So we've established, at least informally, that the boy isn't Dissonant. But he was with Dissonants before he went to the Temple of Pain, and he was under the sway of a Dissonant command when he arrived at the Temple. My question is: Could the Temple have made a mistake? Could it have assumed he was a powerful Dissonant and chosen him under false pretenses?"

Marsh listened and sipped water from a glass before he answered. "That's been my working hypothesis for some time now. After all"— and here he spread an arm in Hal's direction—"why else would the Temple have chosen such a profoundly unremarkable boy?"

Athena

Athena breezed through her first three flyting matches. She knocked her opponents down, gently but firmly, in the first two rounds each time. Her opponents were good sports. They shook her hand after each match and said gracious things, like how they wouldn't like to meet Athena in a real duel. Athena was gracious, too. She refrained from saying *I wouldn't want to fight me, either.*

She was directed to another mat for her fourth match. Now that half of the entrants had been eliminated, there were a lot more kids standing around and watching. She looked for her friends, trying to tell how they'd fared. She didn't see Erin, but she did spot Peter, sitting on the floor against the wall, an icepack pressed to his face. The icepack made it impossible to see his expression, but she didn't have to wonder how it had gone for him. He'd been trounced.

She ought to feel sympathetic. He was her friend, and one of the nicest people she knew. He hadn't wanted to compete in the tournament, had only done so because his grandfather had insisted. But in truth, the sight of him slumped against a wall sent a silver thrill of exhilaration through her chest. Professor Marsh's own grandson hadn't been able to cut it, but Athena had. She'd done the work. She had the talent.

I can win this tournament. The thought made her giddy, and it took an effort not to bounce, Hal-style, all the way to her next match. She wished he and Marsh had been here to see her victory. It would've made the whole thing so much better.

This ebullience lasted until she actually got to the mat and saw her opponent: Erin, wearing a shocked expression of her own.

"Okay, then," Erin said. "This ought to be interesting."

That was certainly one word for it. Athena was surprised Erin had made it to the fourth match. As distracted as she had been for the last few weeks, Athena had expected her to be quickly dispatched. Maybe she had gotten lucky, gone up against someone even less experienced? Three times in a row? Anything was possible, Athena supposed.

She decided right then. She would go easy on Erin. She would beat her, but not humiliate her. Their friendship was too important to risk, and also, Athena felt sorry for her.

"It'll be fun," Athena said, keeping her voice light.

The referee made them shake hands, then sent them to opposite sides of the mat. When he gave the signal, Athena moved slowly on purpose. She luxuriated, weaving a pillow out of glowing lace, which she intended to use to knock Erin on her ass. She was still in the midst of her ethereal crochet when something grabbed her around the ankles and yanked hard. Her legs flew into the air and she landed on her back, her Dissonant projectile dissipating back into the ether as the air was knocked from her body.

She rolled onto her side, pulling air back into her lungs in great whooping gasps.

"Holy shit!" The words came from Erin, but sounded like they were coming from a radio in another room, faint and crackly. Athena barely registered it. She was too shocked that Erin had not only knocked her down, she'd knocked her *on her ass*.

Athena felt the ref's footsteps on the mat as he approached, but she waved him off.

"I'm okay," she said, but it came out as a croak that belied the words.

She got back to her feet. Erin gave her a crooked, apologetic, and embarrassed smile.

"Sorry about that," she said. "I didn't mean to."

Athena waved this off, like she'd waved off the ref. As the level of air in her lungs returned to normal, she began to feel more herself again—and herself, it turned out, was *angry*. How *dare* Erin make a fool of her this way?

The ref signaled the start of round two. Athena didn't try to play nice this time. She was fucking *pissed*, and ready to show Erin which of them was the stronger Dissonant. She moved as fast as she could, sketching the command for a veritable sledgehammer, her fingers leaving jagged streaks of light in their wake.

Maybe she was still dazed from the first round. Her brain still scrambled, her reflexes dulled. Whatever the reason, she just wasn't as fast as she wanted to be. Not nearly fast enough. Her gust of hard wind formed and shot toward Erin, but Erin ducked it and sent a gust of hard wind of her own.

Erin's hard wind knocked Athena down for the second time in as many minutes.

She was still trying to get up, still trying to prepare for the next round when the ref took Erin's hand and raised it into the air. The crowd broke into cheers, but Athena's head was still so rattled, it took her until she'd gotten to her feet to fully understand: there would be no third round. Erin had won. Athena had been eliminated from the tournament.

Erin

When Athena got up from the mat, Erin shook her hand, and congratulated her on a good match. Athena wouldn't meet her eyes. Then the referee came between them again, shuffling Erin off. She was taken to a table near the doors of the auditorium, where her scores were updated, and she was informed that she was one of two finalists. The final match of the tournament—the championship match—would take place tomorrow morning.

When they finally let Erin go, she looked for Athena, but couldn't find her anywhere. There were plenty of other people hanging around, however, waiting to wish Erin well, to tell her what a good job she'd done. She shook hands and accepted the compliments, feeling bashful all the while. The person with the most effusive praise was her dance partner from the evening before, Garrett Thorpe.

"Looks like it'll be you and me tomorrow morning," he said, shaking her hand. "Final match."

"Oh god," Erin said.

"Tell me about it," he said, with a bashful smile. "I saw your matches. You wiped the floor with those other kids."

"So did you," Erin said, remembering Peter's bloody face with a twinge of guilt.

The handshake felt like it ought to be over, but Garrett kept his hold on Erin's hand, and moved closer to her.

"Listen," he said. "We're having a party up in my suite tonight. A real party. Not like the mixer, if you know what I mean."

Erin, who'd been to her share of pasture parties since she'd started dating Randy, thought she understood.

"You should come," Garrett said. "I'd really like it."

I have a boyfriend. The words popped into her head but stayed locked behind her lips. Riding high on the adrenaline of her win, slightly punch-drunk on this handsome boy's looks and attention, suddenly her boyfriend didn't matter. The only thing that did matter was the twinge of guilt she felt for the others—her two friends who'd been eliminated, but also Hal, who couldn't have competed at all.

"Can I bring my friends?" Erin asked.

Garrett's smile twitched a little. "Well, it was supposed to be for people who made it to the second match. Kind of an exclusive thing. But yeah, sure, bring them along. If that's what it takes to get you there."

He finally let go of her hand, and she took the elevator up to her room, planning to shower and change. When she let herself in, she found Athena on the bed, still wearing her tournament sweats and tank top and staring up at the ceiling.

"Hey," Erin said. "Good match down there."

"For you, maybe," Athena said.

"I just got lucky, is all."

Athena didn't respond, but continued to stare at the ceiling. After an awkward moment of silence, during which it became apparent Athena didn't mean to say any more, Erin went and showered. By the time she got out, feeling clean and refreshed, Athena was gone, so she dressed and put on her makeup alone, before heading down to dinner in the hotel restaurant. There, she met with Peter and Hal and Marsh. Peter's face was a mess of bruises, radiating outward from his nose. Hal looked glum, too.

"Where's Athena?" Marsh asked.

"I guess she's not feeling well," Erin said. "How was your presentation?"

Thankfully, Marsh accepted the subject change with ease. "It was . . . illuminating. Wouldn't you agree, Hal?"

Hal nodded. "It sure was."

Marsh didn't offer any more on the subject, but Hal's expression suggested there was a story there. Probably a painful one. She made a mental note to ask him later.

"But I want to hear about the tournament," Marsh said. "How did you fare?"

Peter scowled at the table. "I told you I didn't want to compete," he said.

"It hurts to fail," Marsh said. "And it hurts me to see you fail. But it's also an important part of your education. I brought you here to test your skills against other Dissonants your own age. And now you know where you stand."

"Why, though?" Peter said. The words were low, almost a growl in his throat.

Marsh cocked his head at his grandson and Erin tensed up as well. She didn't think she'd ever heard Peter question his grandfather.

"Excuse me?" Marsh said.

"Why is it so damned important that we fight? Are we soldiers? Are we going to war? Or are we clinging to some outmoded form of violence because you can't think of a better way to test us?"

"You want to watch your tone, young man," Marsh said, a warning in his voice. "I didn't want to have this conversation here, but you started it. In truth, I am bitterly disappointed in you right now. Ashamed you share my last name. But that doesn't mean you can speak to me without respect. Do you understand?"

Erin had never been afraid of Peter in her life, but she felt frightened now. His anger seemed powerful. The Dissonance rolled off him in hot waves. He could break the dinner table with his glare.

"Answer me, Peter," Marsh said.

Hal reached over and touched Peter's arm. Peter shrugged him off.

"I understand," he said, through gritted teeth.

"You want to do something about this failure?" Marsh said. "I suggest next time I tell you to start training, you take it seriously. You prepare, instead of playing in the garden. I have my reasons for wanting you combat ready, and they are not trivial. I am not ready to reveal them, but I will also not have a Marsh, the last of my own bloodline, beaten down like a punk."

Erin wanted to protest, but could think of nothing to say.

"Erin," Marsh said. "Good job today. From all reports, you were extraordinary."

"Thank you, sir," she said. Luckily their food arrived and the conversation broke off. They ate in uncomfortable silence, and then Marsh dismissed them for the night. Hal and Peter started to head back to their rooms, but Erin caught up to them at the elevator. She reached for Peter's shoulder, but something about his posture, the way he was hunched, made her grab Hal instead.

"Hey," she said. Both boys turned to look at her. "Marsh was completely out of line."

"What else is new?" Hal said.

"There's a party tonight, up in Garrett Thorpe's suite," she said. "You guys should come."

Peter looked aghast. "Why the hell would I want to go there?"

"Show him he hasn't scared you off," Erin said. "Show him it's all in good fun. Come for whatever reason you want, but please come."

"Think I'll pass," Peter said. He turned his back on Erin. "You have fun, though."

"Sure," she said. She couldn't stand this coldness from him. "Sure, I will. You too. Have fun, I mean."

The boys got into the elevator, but Erin hung back. Hal had the good sense not to hold the door for her. Instead he gave her a sympathetic little nod. She forced a smile and nodded back, trying to show everything was just fine and dandy, thanks.

Hal

Hal went up to the room with Peter. As soon as they were through the door, Peter flopped onto his bed and faced away from Hal.

Hal was torn. He could tell Peter was in pain, and needed a friend. On the other hand, there was a party happening tonight. Hal hadn't been to many parties. Maybe he'd see that Kelly girl again. Just the thought made a pleasurable heat rise up his neck into his cheeks. But Peter just looked so pitiful over there, curled up on the bed like a forlorn little kid.

Hal sat on the edge of his bed, hands down beside him.

"I know you had a bad day," Hal said. "I get it. My day was bad, too. You know what happened at the panel?"

"Hal, I know you're trying to help, but can you please just shut the fuck up?" Peter said.

Peter never swore, and the force of it hit Hal like a blow.

"Sure," he said. "I can shut the fuck up."

He freshened up, and when the clock finally hit eight and he was readying to leave, Peter rolled over onto his back and said, "Wait. I'll come with you."

Hal's heart felt a little lighter at this. "Good."

When Hal knocked on the girls' door, Erin answered it, and Hal was surprised to see Athena standing with her. Okay. Maybe this night wasn't going to be so bad after all.

Together, the coven went up to the twentieth floor, where Garrett's suite was located. Even if they hadn't had the room number, they would've been able to tell—the door was open and people were crowded into the hall. As they grew close, Hal noticed all three of his friends wincing.

"Jesus," Athena said.

"I'm sure the neighbors love that," Peter said.

"Love what?" Hal said. He looked around, confused.

"The music," Erin said, raising her voice. "It's deafening!"

Hal shook his head. "I don't hear anything!"

Athena and Peter shared a look.

"All right, I have to admit, that's pretty cool," Athena said.

"They must have set it up so the music only plays for Dissonants," Peter explained. "It's blasting our eardrums out, but you can't hear it."

"Oh," Hal said. "Terrific."

They entered the suite, crowded with other teenagers. Not an adult in sight. Garrett Thorpe stood in the living room, leaned back against the couch, red plastic cup in hand, talking to a pretty girl. Hal recognized Kelly with a simultaneous burst of excitement and jealousy.

Garrett noticed them and stood up to wave.

As he approached, Peter said, "This was a bad idea." Hal didn't need Dissonant powers to tell that Peter wanted to turn around and run.

"Hello!" Garrett said, smiling. If Peter was radiating discomfort, Garrett was radiating charm. In that second, Hal forgave him for bloodying Peter's nose. Accidents happened, after all. The guy must've not known how weak Peter's defensive skills really were, and come on too strong. It was the most obvious explanation. So when Garrett offered a hand to shake, Hal took it.

"Hal, right?" Garrett said. "I didn't see you at the tournament today."

"I was taking part in a presentation," Hal said, raising his voice to match Garrett's. It felt strange in the seemingly silent room.

"That's too bad," Garrett said. "I would've loved to see the so-called champion of the Temple of Pain in action, you know?"

"The night is young," Hal said, and Garrett laughed.

Next Garrett turned to Peter. "Peter. I'm really glad you're here. It's big of you to come after what happened this afternoon."

Peter shook his hand with a curt nod.

"If I'd been in your position, I don't know if I'd have done the same," Garrett said.

Peter's stoic expression curdled as Garrett turned to Athena. "Athena. I saw your first bout today. Impressive. My father says a lot of stuff about you. Says you're going to be the most distinguished Dissonant of our age, if Marsh doesn't ruin you first."

"Why would he ruin me?" Athena said.

Garrett answered with a simple shrug. Then he turned to Erin, with his most winning smile. "And Erin—good to see you again."

Erin's smile back at Garrett was dazzling. Peter looked away, his mouth a tight little line.

They went deeper into the party, where they were given beers from a keg. Athena gave Hal a wary look when he tried to hand a cup to her.

"We could get in big trouble if Marsh finds out," she said.

"What's he gonna do?" Hal said. "You heard Garrett—you're going to be the most distinguished Dissonant of our time."

"That kid blows so much smoke you might think your ass is on fire," Athena said. But she took the beer.

Hal had never had beer before. It didn't taste very good, but he made himself finish it, and get a second one. And the second one tasted a lot better. So he went on and had a third, and after that, he felt lighter. Almost like he could step into the air and fly away, like he'd done last summer. He started to understand alcohol's appeal.

He'd spent all three of the beers hanging out in a corner with Athena and Peter, and waiting for Kelly to approach him again, like she had last night. But so far, she'd mostly been dancing, and although she'd looked at Hal a couple of times, she'd always looked away again quickly.

After his third beer, Hal decided she must be waiting for him to come to her. He made his way to the dance floor, surprised at the extra effort it took to walk in a straight line.

Kelly didn't look at him until he touched her on the shoulder. Even then, it was a quick glance up, and then away.

"Hey," he said.

"Hey," she said, her voice raised over the music he couldn't hear.

"I've been waiting for you to say hi," he said. "Are you avoiding me?"

She stopped dancing. "No," she said. "It's just—I don't really mix with non-Dissonants."

"I'm sorry?"

"I saw your panel today with Professor Marsh," she said. "I know you're only here by accident."

"We don't know that for sure," Hal said. He hated how pathetic it sounded when it came out of his mouth.

A hand landed on his shoulder. Garrett Thorpe, winning smile gone. White knight concern in its place. "Everything all right here?"

"We're fine," Hal said. But Kelly didn't speak up.

"The lady looks uncomfortable," Garrett said. "Maybe you go back and sit with your friends, and if she wants to talk to you, she'll come do that?"

"What—"

"It's time to go," Garrett said. He put himself between Hal and Kelly, clamped a hand on Hal's shoulder and marched him out of the suite. "Get some sleep," he said again. "You'll feel better tomorrow. Maybe apologize to Kelly, if she'll talk to you."

"What did I do wrong?" Hal said.

"It's my fault," Garrett said. "This is a party for Dissonants, not freak accidents. I wanted to be big and inclusive, but I see now it was a mistake. Why don't you run along now? Sounds like you've been embarrassed enough for one day."

Hal stood in the hallway as Garrett returned to the party. He was too shocked to feel anything for a moment. Then he went back to the elevator and took it down to Marsh's floor, meaning to give the old man a piece of his mind.

As the elevator doors parted and Hal stepped out, the hallway vanished before him, and he found himself in a vast, dark space. It was cold and, as near as Hal could tell, completely empty. In the distance, he could make out a tiny pinprick of light.

Even through the beery haze, Hal thought he understood what had happened. A year later, he'd finally returned to the Temple of Pain.

His rage abated somewhat, replaced with wonder and curiosity. His footsteps echoed on the stone floor as he walked toward the pinprick of light. He stopped just short of it, in no hurry to put his hand inside again.

"Hello?" he said.

The Temple made no reply, so Hal tried another question:

"Why am I here?"

You have questions. The voice reverberated inside him, creating a buzz in his chest like the bass at a rock concert.

"That's true," Hal said. "Are you going to answer them?"

We'll tell you what we want to tell you, when we think you need to know it, the voice said.

Now Hal took a turn with the silent treatment. If the Temple was only going to tease him, he would just refuse to play its game. He waited long moments in the following silence. He focused on his breathing, the way Professor Marsh had taught him.

You must be patient, Champion, the voice finally said. *The old man seeks to provoke you, and by extension, us. You were not chosen by accident. You were destined to come to us and endure the Trial of Agony, and you are destined to further our great work in the future.*

"And what would that great work be?" Hal said.

You will know, when the time comes.

The words were still buzzing in Hal's chest when he suddenly found himself back in the Hyatt Regency, in the hallway on Professor Marsh's floor.

Athena

Athena also tried beer for the first time that night. Like Hal, she didn't much care for the taste, but she *did* find that her mood changed, the more she drank.

It wasn't that she felt better, exactly. She still felt lousy. But as she grew increasingly drunk, she was able to *marinate* in her feelings. To soak up her humiliation and anger, to convince herself she *had* been cheated during the day's duel.

As Athena drank, she watched Erin mingle and dance, watched her smile and laugh. Everyone loved Erin. Everyone always had, for as long as Athena could remember. She was white, she was blond, she was pretty. She'd more or less won the lottery of life. She *had* her thing. The Dissonance was supposed to be Athena's thing. What she was best at. And Erin had wiped the floor with her today, in front of all these people. These people, who were now laughing and dancing and making out and ignoring her. It wasn't right. It wasn't fair that Garrett Thorpe was escorting Erin around the party, introducing her to other Dissonants, while Athena sat in the corner and stewed.

She was so angry, and so drunk that by the time Erin finished making the rounds and, practically hanging off Garrett Thorpe's arm, came to check on her, Athena's temper was at a low boil.

"Hi," Erin said, voice bright. "How are you? I wanted to make sure you and Garrett got a chance to really talk." She turned to Garrett. "Athena is the most brilliant person I know. She's going to be a big deal."

"Is that right?" Garrett said, sounding faintly amused. Athena felt warm with embarrassment—both for herself and for Erin. Garrett had already given her that compliment tonight.

Athena opened her mouth, and was surprised by what came next:

"The fuck is the matter with you?"

Garrett took an abrupt step back, hands raised. "You two clearly have business. We'll talk later."

"Why did you yell at me?" Erin said.

"Why are you eye-fucking that boy?"

"I'm not cheating on Randy."

"I don't care about Randy," Athena said. "Garrett kicked the shit out of Peter this morning. He and his friends laughed at Peter when he did it. He was rougher than he needed to be, and he probably should've been disqualified, but because Garrett's daddy is important, he doesn't have to face any consequences. And here you are, practically humping him on the dance floor."

Erin's hand stayed on her cheek throughout Athena's speech, as though she'd been struck. When Athena ran out of steam, she finally let the hand fall back to her side.

"Peter had his chance with me," Erin said. "He had lots of chances. I got tired of waiting for him."

"He's still your friend," Athena said.

"Does he know that?" Erin said. She licked her lips, eyes glassy. "Oh, forget this. You're just mad I beat you today." She shoved Athena, hard, and disappeared into the crowd. Athena stumbled backward into a dresser and dropped her (thankfully empty) plastic cup. Her insides sloshed around, and she felt sick.

Air. She needed air. She left the suite, got in the elevator, and took it down to the lobby. She walked/ran past the reception desk and through the sliding glass doors, making it all the way to the sidewalk before she threw up. She managed not to do it right in front of the hotel entrance, but she still wasn't as far away as she might've liked.

Not much came out. She'd skipped dinner, so it was mostly beer and bile. It burned like hell coming up, and just kept coming until it was nothing but dry heaves.

She started when a hand landed on her shoulder. It was Peter, holding out a bottle of water.

"Thought you might need this," he said. He smiled a little, and somehow the bruises on his face made it even more endearing.

They sat on a bench outside the hotel, Athena taking careful sips of water. To his everlasting credit, Peter didn't try to talk. He didn't try to jolly her out of one mood and into another. He was the opposite of Hal, who could never shut up. Peter seemed completely at home in silence. And as Athena sipped her water, she *did* start to feel a little better—so good, in fact, she laughed a little bit. Then the giggles turned into great whooping sobs of laughter. She buried her face in her hands.

"I'm so embarrassed," she said. "Acting like a clichéd teenage girl, drunk at a party and picking a fight with her best friend." She lifted her face to look at him as something occurred to her. "How'd you know to find me out here?"

"Lucky guess," he said. "I needed some air, too, and had a feeling you might be here."

"A feeling?"

He licked his lips, then pressed them together. "A strong feeling."

She considered. Was it a lucky guess? Or somehow related to the Dissonance? She'd never felt another presence in the energy field, but each member of the coven did seem to have their specific, unique gifts.

"I overheard what you said," Peter said. "At the party. Thank you for sticking up for me."

"Sure thing."

"Although, I have to say—" His head perked up, almost like a dog. "Hal's coming."

And sure enough, Hal walked out the sliding glass doors a moment later. He also had two bottles of water in his hands.

Athena murmured, "You have to show me how to do that trick."

"What are you two doing out here?" Hal said.

"We came to mope," Peter said. "What about you?"

"Same," Hal said. He offered Peter one of the bottles of water, which Peter accepted, then sat down on Athena's other side and opened his own. He took a long drink.

"Aren't we a sorry sight," Hal said. "To think I was *excited* about coming here."

"What happened to you?" Athena said.

"I'll tell you later," Hal said. "Still trying to get my head around it."

"Seems like all we've done since we got here is get our asses kicked," Athena said.

"Not Erin, though," Hal said.

"No," Athena admitted, grudgingly. "Not Erin."

Hal set his water down and leaned forward, elbows on his knees, hands together. "Look. I know how you both feel right now, because it's how I feel, too. I'm jealous. I'm angry. I'm confused. But I know if the tables were turned—Athena, if you'd beaten Erin in the tournament today, or Peter, if you'd started dating someone else before Erin did—Erin would still be here for you."

"She's not here now," Athena said. "She's up there, partying with that spoiled rich boy."

"I know," Hal said. "I don't like it either. And I know, if positions were reversed, she wouldn't like to be left out, like we've been. But whether you partied with Garrett Thorpe all night or not, she'd still show up to the final match of the tournament tomorrow morning. She'd still cheer for you both. So here's what I'm proposing: we all go to bed, sleep, and try to get over ourselves, and then, tomorrow morning, we act like a goddamn coven again. Good night."

He didn't wait for them to argue, but got up and went back inside. Athena sat in the balmy night air and thought about what he'd said.

Erin

Erin stayed out late, partying with Garrett, enjoying being the center of attention. It felt good. Everyone wanted to meet her and be her friend. She had a handsome boy to dance with. For the first time in a long time, she really felt like she completely *belonged*.

She got back to the hotel room around two in the morning. Not wanting to wake Athena, she undressed in the dark and collapsed into the bed, too much a rookie drinker to think to have some water first—a mistake she would make later, to greater consequence, but from which she recovered easily at fifteen.

She slept fitfully, and woke before the predawn alarm. The first thing she saw when she opened her eyes was Athena, sleeping in the room's other bed. She lay on her stomach, and snored softly into her pillow. Erin felt a stab of rage—at Athena's cruelty and callousness, her inability to let Erin have this one thing. She was tempted to turn on the lights, and the radio, and force Athena to wake up with her—but then Athena would have more chances to be mean, and she was better at it than Erin was. So Erin showered and dressed as quietly as she could, then went downstairs, where she bought coffee and a croissant, and ate them alone at a little table in the nearly deserted lobby.

When she'd finished eating, she took her coffee downstairs to the basement. The doors to the tournament room were unlocked, so she went inside.

Such a drab room. So very ordinary. So different from the lively backgrounds in fighting video games. In *Mortal Kombat* the characters dueled on stone bridges over a pit of spikes. In *Street Fighter II*, they fought inside Japanese dojos and on American air force bases.

This ballroom, on the other hand, was the sort of place where insurance executives would gather to listen to long, boring presentations on advancements in actuary tables.

The only thing interesting about this room was the smell. After a day of teenagers sweating inside, there was a definite *funk* to the place. No wonder they'd left the doors open. They needed to air the room out.

Still. This was where the final bout would take place. So it was here, in this drab, funky-smelling room that she sat, straight-backed, cross-legged, open palms on her knees, and meditated on her Dissonant characters, the way Professor Marsh had taught her.

In traditional meditation, he'd told them, *you're supposed to focus on your breath. You notice your thoughts, but you let them go. It's a way of clearing your head, claiming calm. In Dissonant meditation, you don't try to remove the clutter from your mind. Instead, you embrace the clutter: the confusion, the hurt feelings, the annoyance, irritation. Everything abrading your peace of mind. You fixate on it. It's fuel. Your pain is what makes you strong.*

This morning, she thought about Peter and Athena. Both of whom had been so cold, so cruel this summer. She thought about Marsh, so dismissive of her desire to be a cheerleader. Telling her she was wasting her time. She thought about her parents, the icy discomfort beneath every single conversation between them. The coldness of the home where she lived. The new coldness of her home away from home, Marsh House. It seemed like there was nowhere she could turn anymore.

She felt the wetness on her cheeks. Tasted the tears as they gathered at the edges of her mouth. She breathed the pain in, and decided: this Dissonant stuff sucked. It was all about discomfort, and suffering. The worse you felt, the better you were at it. Why would she hurt herself this way? She would finish the tournament today, because she'd made it this far, and she was committed. After that, she'd tell the others she was finished. They were welcome to their clusterfuck of misery. She would start doing things that were good for her. She would find her way to happiness. The other girls on the cheer squad seemed welcoming. She could probably make lasting friendships there if she wanted. She could have a nice, normal life.

"Hey there."

She opened her eyes. She hadn't heard Garrett Thorpe enter. He was halfway across the room to her now. She stood up and wiped at her cheeks, self-conscious.

"You okay?" he said.

"Fine," she said, and smiled to show him just how good she felt. "What are you doing here?"

"I wanted to do the scene from *Rocky*," he said. "You know, where he goes to the arena and looks around, before the big fight?"

She nodded. She knew the scene, and guessed on some level that's exactly what she'd come here to do as well.

"It's a good scene," she said.

He stopped a few feet away. "Look, maybe it's none of my business, but I've seen the way your coven has been acting for the last couple of days."

"Yeah?" she said, voice guarded.

"They've been absolute shits," he said, "when they should be down on their knees thanking God they have you. And you're all studying under this crackpot old man who's always trying to sell the Council on his Many Worlds theories. You're too good for them, Erin."

She thought of something Marsh had said to her last summer. That there were people you could help, and people who would just drag you down. Is that what her coven had been doing? Holding her down?

"I know you're stuck here," he said. "In Texas. But when you're older, maybe think about coming to Boston. I think you'd fit in with us."

And as quickly as that, her thoughts of leaving the Dissonant life were abandoned. Maybe there was a chance for a different life? Something better than normal. "What if I could make my way out there sooner?" she said.

He raised his eyebrows, opened his mouth, and shut it again as he considered. "I bet we could find a place for you, if that happened," he said.

She pulled him into a fierce hug. He laughed as he put his arms around her. "You have no idea how much that means to me," she said.

He reached up and brushed a stray bit of hair behind her ear. "There's too much talent here to waste."

She was still trying to find a way to gracefully accept the compliment when he leaned in to kiss her.

She jerked away. "What are you doing?"

He looked genuinely surprised. "I thought we were having a moment."

"I have a boyfriend."

"Still with this shit?" he said, incredulous. "I told you, none of these people deserves you—and that includes whatever hick you're dating back home."

She held him away from her firmly, until he got the point.

"Right," he said. He let her go. "My bad. Can't blame a guy for getting carried away."

"Guess not," she said, because it was easier to lie.

"Anyway. I'll see you again on the mat," he said.

Since there was only one mat for the final match, organizers had used the rest of the space for chairs, and soon enough, those chairs began to fill with spectators. There were a lot of vaguely familiar faces from the parties on Friday and Saturday night. A few waved to her or gave her a thumbs-up, and she smiled and waved back.

Then something happened she did not expect: her coven arrived. All of them—Peter, Athena, Hal, and even Professor Marsh—came walking in together. Peter carried something that looked like a folded-up bedsheet under one arm. Rather than take some of the empty seats near the back, they came up to the front row, which was already full. Marsh leaned forward to say something to the kids sitting there, and whatever it was must have sounded convincing, because the kids moved, opening four chairs just to Erin's left.

Peter raised a hand in sheepish greeting. Erin nodded, but didn't go over to say hi. The last thing she needed was those four getting in her head.

Finally the ref arrived, and signaled the start of proceedings. He called Erin and Garrett to the middle of the mat. As Garrett approached, he looked off to his right, then looked at Erin with barely suppressed laughter.

"What's so funny?" Erin said.

"I'm sorry," he said. "Just—the string bean in the front row. The one from your coven. He went down like a bitch yesterday morning. It makes me laugh every time I think about it."

Erin turned to look at Peter. He was unfolding the bedsheet across his, Hal's, and Athena's laps, but stopped to meet her gaze. He smiled sadly and mouthed *I'm sorry*. Something in her, something which had begun to harden, softened.

Garrett took Erin's hand and pumped it twice. "I'll go easy on you," he said.

"Don't," Erin said.

He raised his eyebrows as they backed into their individual corners of the mat. The ref remained in the middle, arm raised to signal readiness, then brought it down in a sharp motion.

Garrett's fingers were almost a blur as he cast. Erin didn't give herself time to think. She cast Hypatia's Vengeance. A wall of green flame flowed from her fingertips and rolled, roaring, across the mat. It blocked her view of Garrett, so she didn't see what happened next, but she heard the crowd's sharp intake of breath, followed by a collective "ohhhhh."

The flames shot skyward and dissipated somewhere close to the ceiling, and Erin saw Garrett down on one knee. He'd deflected the blast, but it had cost him his balance. The rules were clear. If even one knee hit the mat, it counted as a loss.

All the good humor was gone from his expression. Erin had broken one of the cardinal rules of being a girl: she'd humiliated a boy. And she'd done it in public, no less. He didn't just look angry. He looked furious as he went back to his corner of the mat.

Erin felt a wriggle of discomfort in her stomach. She'd achieved a narrow, technical victory in the first round, against someone who'd been trying to get on her good side. Now she'd embarrassed him, and he would want payback. She could see it in his eyes. No warmth.

She took a deep breath, tried to use the discomfort to strengthen herself. She put her hands at her sides and nodded to the ref that she was ready. The ref nodded back his understanding, then dropped his hand, signaling the start of round two.

Erin tried something else this time—the hook snare she'd used to defeat Athena the day before. She was fast enough to fire it off, but

Garrett was just as fast. He spread his hands, and a pack of huge, bright green lions appeared. They tore through Erin's snare like toilet paper and hit her all at once, a missile of muscle and sinew and teeth. She didn't have a chance to lose her footing. She was knocked backward through the air and crashed into the front row of spectators behind her before rolling off their collective laps and onto the carpeted floor.

Erin got up onto her hands and knees. She was vaguely aware of the sound of the ref's shrill whistle, and when she looked up, the ref was in Garrett's face, yelling at him. It all sounded far away. There was a ringing in her ears, and when she tried to stand, she felt a sharp pain in her right ankle. Was it sprained? Broken? Just twisted? She wasn't sure.

The ref came over to help Erin up. She did her best to hide her discomfort as she regained her feet.

"Are you all right?" he said. "Do we need to call the match? Garrett will forfeit right now."

Erin tried to put the words together, to make them make sense. She looked around the auditorium, at all the faces staring back at her. Then her gaze landed on her coven, and she noticed for the first time they'd unfolded the bedsheet, holding it up just under their chins so that it hung down to the floor. They'd found paint somewhere, and written two things on it in red. The first was *ERIN IS #1 FOREVER*. And the second was one of the Dissonant characters Marsh always made the group meditate on. One of the few characters that didn't completely branch off like a tree, but rather looped around at both ends to touch. It was the character for *whole* or *entire*.

Her friends wore expressions of concern. Peter looked around, as if waiting for someone to put an end to this. Only Athena looked calm. She met Erin's gaze, and nodded slightly. The message was clear: *You can do this.*

Erin looked back at the ref. "No. Don't stop the match. Win or lose, I want to finish."

"You're sure?" the ref said. "It's your call."

"I'm sure," Erin said.

The ref helped her hobble back to her side of the mat, and the audience clapped. Making sure Erin could stand on her own, the ref walked back to the middle of the mat and raised his hand in the "ready" signal.

Erin looked at Garrett. He murmured something, too low to actually hear, but she read his lips fine: *White trash bitch*.

Erin glanced at her friends again. At the character they'd painted on the bedsheet. She closed her eyes, picturing the character in her mind's eye. She took a deep breath in, and experienced something she had never experienced before: three bright sparks in the darkness, just off to her left, exactly where Peter, Athena, and Hal all sat. They burned like fires in the dark, and as she watched, their flames joined together, and ran toward her. Gooseflesh covered her arms as she felt her friends, not just beside her, but somehow *with* and *inside* her, too. When she breathed in, she felt huge. Almost invincible. She opened her eyes and looked at her friends one more time. They seemed as confused as she felt, but also excited; hopeful. Something new was happening here. Even Marsh seemed to sense it. He looked confused for the first time since Erin had known him.

She faced forward. The ref dropped his hand. And instead of trying to guess what her opponent would do; instead of trying to meet his aggressiveness and anger with her own, Erin stepped back, and threw up a shield—the same one she'd used last summer, to protect her friends from the spider-creatures in the Clegg woods. Haley's Dome. A defensive command.

She felt it rise and solidify around her even as Garrett unleashed his final attack—a massive blast of hard wind. Erin's shield rose to meet it. The blast bounced off the dome with such force that it ricocheted right back at Garrett. It hit and the audience's heads all turned to watch his body fly back and up like a rag doll, soaring over the crowd and landing somewhere near the ballroom doors.

The ref didn't even wait to see if he was okay. He came over to Erin and raised her hand, declaring her the victor. The Dissonant flyting champion, 1997. Then her coven were out of their seats and rushing toward her, shouting and screaming. Peter wrapped his arms around her waist, picked her up, and spun her around. Everyone was smiling and laughing and cheering—even Athena looked happy—and Erin knew that despite their fights and imperfections and misaligned points of view, these three were her real people. The ones she deserved, and who deserved her. Her forever people. The ones who sparked with her in the dark.

She let herself be subsumed in the flame of their love, and as they huddled around her and hugged her, for a moment, one perfect moment, she disappeared into that amazing warmth.

2019
Reunion

Hal

As a kid, Hal always wondered what the Saunders Inn was like on the inside. The outside looked like a rich grandma's house, with ostentatious pillars on the front porch and tastefully clipped hedges bordering the property. Large windows into the inn's restaurant presented a tableau of candlelight dining beneath a chandelier.

Now returned to Clegg as an adult, Hal finds that his initial guesses about "rich grandma interior" were basically correct. It's a pleasant enough place. Hal's room is on the second floor, opposite a wall of packed bookshelves. The books, when Hal examines them, are "mom" and "dad" material. History. Right-wing political commentary. Spy novels. Christian inspiration. But if he stands back a bit and squints? The illusion of a nice library is almost convincing.

The room is larger than he expected, with a king-size bed, two reading chairs, and a gas fireplace. The curtains are drawn against the rainy afternoon, making it dim and cozy.

He leaves his suitcase by the door and collapses onto the bed. After the drive and his encounter with the woman at his old apartment complex, he needs a nap. He kicks off his shoes, plugs in his phone, and texts Athena:

DINNER 2NITE?

He watches the three dots in the messaging app do their "she's writing a response" dance.

Sure. 6 PM at the diner?

He sends back a thumbs-up emoji and dozes off. He sleeps hard and wakes in the late afternoon, fuzzy-headed and dry-mouthed. Funny how you can give up drinking and still get hangovers. Funny, but not really funny.

He showers, shaves, and brews some awful sludge in the room's coffeemaker. As he drinks it, the storm clouds hanging overhead burst. It starts as a gentle rain, but then the roof and windows rattle with the telltale signs of hail.

He thinks of his poor car in the open-air lot in front of the inn, but reminds himself it doesn't matter. He'll have to sell it soon anyway. Not like he'll need his Kia in prison.

He unpacks and tries to find appropriate clothes for dinner. Aside from the suit he packed for the memorial, all he has are jeans and T-shirts. Not a single button-down. Nothing with a collar. Only slob clothes.

He's trying to pick out the least slobby items when the earth heaves. He's pitched forward onto the bed, then tossed backward. He grabs at the blankets, but the floor bucks and hurls him into the dresser. A drawer knob punches him in the kidney, and he hits the floor with a cry. He rolls into a ball and covers his head with his hands. Every breath hurts, but pain can be useful. He focuses on the discomfort, and in turn blocks out the rest of the world.

When the room's phone rings a moment later, he realizes the shaking has stopped, and his insides don't hurt quite so much. He picks up the receiver. It's the receptionist downstairs, asking if everything is all right. The genuine concern in her voice is almost nauseating. Hal says the storm startled him, and he tripped and took an embarrassing fall, but he's fine now.

His cell chimes with a notification. It's Athena:

Have you looked out the window?

Hal goes to the drawn curtain and pulls it aside. The gray clouds from this morning have turned blood-red. They look ready to spit flame rather than ice.

This is some biblical shit, he writes back.

The hail lets up a little later, although the rain continues, and the sky remains a worrying shade of red. Hal goes outside to check on his car. It looks as if it's been attacked by a thousand tiny gremlins swinging a thousand tiny baseball bats. At least all the glass remains intact.

Although he assumes both he and Athena are staying at the inn, he drives to the diner by himself. Before he leaves, he texts Erin to let her know where they'll be. He hasn't heard from her since she first RSVP'd to the memorial early Thursday morning, so who knows if or when she's even coming.

He's glad they decided on the diner. It's more neutral than the inn's restaurant. Fewer romantic implications, and therefore less pressure. As he enters, he finds little has changed. The white tile floor is more scuffed and faded, and the booth seats seem deflated. Photos of more recent sports team rosters hang on the walls. Most of the patrons are older people, although a few teenagers sit at a booth in the far corner by the bathrooms. No one seems to have noticed the red skies.

Hal takes a booth by the window and wonders if this place was so depressing when he was a kid. He remembers it being a fun spot to grab a burger. Is he a victim of nostalgia, or has the entire town somehow deflated in the last twenty years?

He's lost in contemplation of the dark crimson sky when the bell over the front door jingles and Athena walks in. His immediate impression is that she hasn't changed since they were seventeen: short and broad, her brown hair drenched, her glasses rain-spattered, purse the size of a diaper bag slung over one shoulder. She wears a man's button-down shirt with the sleeves rolled up, tucked into a pair of jeans. The one real change—the thing that carries him from 1999 to the present day—are her shoes. She's traded in her black Converse All-Stars for more comfortable Nikes.

He stands. She approaches, then stops a couple of feet away, looking conflicted. Is she trying to decide whether to hug him? He takes the risk and wraps his arms around her. She's soaked, her skin cold in the diner's frigid A/C, and it sends a wave of gooseflesh across his back.

"Hey," he says.

"Hey yourself," she says into his chest, returning the hug after a classic Athena hesitation.

Despite the cold and the awkwardness, his eyes sting and he squeezes her tight. When he lets go, it's not because he wants the moment to end, but because he doesn't want to creep her out. He sits, and she eases into the booth across from him with a wince.

"Leg?" he says.

"Worse every year," she says. "And worse than that when it rains."

"Maybe——" he says.

"I was——" she says at the same time.

"Go ahead," she says.

"No, you, please." He feels like he's on a first date. An awkward first date, at that, which is unusual. Hal kills it on first dates. His long game is the problem.

"I forgot what I was going to say," she says, more to the table than to him.

"I was going to ask if you wanted some Tylenol," he says. "I keep some in my glove box."

"I've got Tiger Balm and CBD back in my room," she says.

"Big partier," he says.

Athena doesn't get a chance to answer, because the bell over the door heralds Erin's arrival. She's thinner and taller than Hal remembers, her ears ringed with piercings, her arms sleeved with tattoos. Like Athena, she's soaked, but also covered in bruises.

"Hey guys," she says.

Hal stands to hug her. Athena looks like she can't decide what to do, and seems miserable with indecision by the time Erin slides into the booth next to Hal. Erin takes Athena's hand and squeezes.

"It's good to see you, Athena."

"What happened to you?" Hal says. His first, unhappy guess is the plus-one she mentioned in her text—but he himself is a veteran of many barroom fistfights. He knows what a punch looks like. These bruises aren't it.

Erin touches a black bruise on her neck, self-consciously. "I was at the cemetery when the storm started. Had to run to my car." Her chin dips. She picks up a menu off the table and makes a show of reading it. "Philip took a bad hit on the top of his head, so he decided to call it an early night. He's excited to meet you all tomorrow, though."

"Yeah," Hal says. "We're excited, too." He doesn't have to ask why Erin was at the cemetery. He's surprised and ashamed he didn't think to stop there, too. He could have visited Peter instead of the apartment complex. He glances at Athena, and from her dour expression, guesses she feels the same way.

"How—" Athena says. "How did it look? The plot and all."

"About twenty years older," Erin says. "Otherwise the same. Professor Marsh is buried there now."

Just as the moment starts to feel too acute, their server, a girl who must be about seventeen, stops by the table to drop off glasses of water and take drink orders. It's a nice distraction, a natural-feeling transition, and once the girl is gone, the three members of the broken coven segue into the traditional Adult-Catch-up Checklist. Hal tells his old friends about life in Vandergriff: the call center where he works, the apartment where he lives alone. He doesn't mention the bar fight, or the plea deal on the table. He's not ready for these people—the best friends he ever had—to know that about him yet. To see the looks in their eyes as they realize what he's become since they knew him.

Erin sketches a life that sounds similar to Hal's, if less lonely, thanks to Philip.

"I hear there's a big underground Dissonant community in Iowa City," Athena says.

"I blew my savings to move there for exactly that reason," Erin says.

"And?" Athena says.

Erin breaks the seal around her napkin and silverware. She unwraps the paper napkin, removes the silverware, and sets it on the table— knife on one side, fork on the other. She flattens the napkin between them, and begins to shred it. "And . . . I wish I'd saved my money. There's a community there, but it's insular. They're not looking for new recruits, especially people like . . ." She stops shredding the napkin long enough to gesture at herself, and then at Athena. "So now I'm stuck in Iowa City, where it gets cold as balls in October and stays cold as balls until April. It sucks. I serve coffee to grad students and hipsters all day."

"Well, if you feel like coming to Oregon, you could at least serve coffee in a slightly warmer climate," Athena says.

"Are you offering me a job?" Erin says.

At which point, Athena takes over, and tells them about her life in

Ashland. Of the three, she seems to be the only one successfully living an adult life. She owns her own business and by her account, it's doing well.

"So you want me to move all the way to Oregon to sling coffee for you?" Erin says, eyebrows raised.

"I'll pay you better than whatever you're making there," Athena says. "Also, not just coffee. There's a whole shop attached to the café, and a side business I think you'd be interested in. It's my favorite part of the job, anyway."

"Hey," Hal says. "How come Erin gets a job and not me?"

"What? You already have a job," Athena says.

"For real," Erin says. "You get to sit down all day, and don't have to make *anyone* coffee."

"Yeah, but I get yelled at by people who can't afford their car payments," Hal says. "I want to come serve coffee and sell penis-shaped candles or whatever. I'll move to Oregon. Shit, it can't be any worse than the Dallas–Fort Worth area."

"You're right on that count," Athena says.

"You're your own boss at a job that keeps you in touch with that other world," Hal says. This seems a good opportunity to spring the question he's been wanting to ask since they sat down. "Do either of you still feel anything at all?"

Erin looks like she wants to speak, but Athena interjects. "No. We were severed, same as you. Why? Have you reconnected?"

Hal thinks about his cigarette trick. It probably doesn't mean anything. A little leftover piece of a long-dead connection.

"No," he says. "But my thing was always a little different from yours anyway, right? I thought there was a chance something had happened for you. And lately I have been . . . experiencing things."

Athena leans forward, conspiratorial. "Like earthquakes that don't seem to shake anyone or anything but you?"

"Or red skies that no one else seems to see," Hal says.

"My apartment was attacked by thousands of pigeons," Erin says. The words emerge in a rush, like an embarrassing confession.

Athena's expression of surprise mirrors Hal's feelings perfectly.

"Thousands of pigeons," he says.

She gives a curt nod, as the server comes back to take their orders.

When the girl departs again, Erin leans forward like Athena had a moment ago. "I was asleep. They just came crashing through the windows. They nearly killed me and Philip, but I—" And here she hesitates. Hal glances around, but no one else in the diner seems to be eavesdropping. "—but we got away before anything too awful happened. Just some scratches and bruises."

"What did Philip think of that?" Hal says. "Does he know about us? What we are? Or were?"

Again Erin seems to weigh her words, and again Hal wonders why. "He was pretty freaked out," Erin says. "Before that happened, he didn't know anything. Now, he knows a little, but not everything. I didn't want to tell him too much at once and overwhelm him."

"But he still decided to come here with you," Athena says, sounding impressed.

Erin stops shredding her napkin to consider. "He's loyal. Also I think he's curious for answers."

"Me too," Hal says.

Erin smiles. "Can I just say how good it is to see you guys again? I haven't felt this happy in a long time."

"Yeah," Hal says. "Same here."

Athena says nothing, but also doesn't deny it, which Hal knows is her version of agreement.

Athena

After dinner the rain continues to pour, so Athena gets soaked running from the diner to her car, and then from the car to the Saunders Inn. She and the others go to their own rooms to change clothes, and meet back up on the covered back porch. They sit in wicker chairs around a round white table and stay up late talking.

Both Erin and Hal seem preoccupied. Athena also feels a vague dread, a tightness in her chest. Something is wrong, and now that they're not in a public place, they can actually talk about it.

"Okay," Hal says. "The earthquakes. The red skies. The fact we're the only ones who seem to experience them."

"It's not *only* us," Athena corrects him. She tells them about Garrett's reaction to the first quake.

"You still talk to that douchebag?" Hal says.

"He's useful," Athena says. "And middle age has mellowed him a bit."

"So it's not just our coven," Erin says. "It's people who have a connection to the Dissonance. The fact that we feel it has to mean something, right?"

"Phantom limb syndrome," Athena says. "People say they feel pain in a missing hand or foot. Doesn't mean the limb is still there."

"But other Dissonants are experiencing it, too," Hal says. "I've never heard of a person experiencing someone else's phantom pain."

"So it's an imperfect example," Athena says. "But it points to the same basic idea—just because we're experiencing these events doesn't mean our connection to the Dissonance has been restored. It could be a leftover nub from the severing—the way some mostly blind people can still make out motion and color."

"You don't think it's weird?" Erin says. "We start feeling these earthquakes, and then suddenly we get an invite to come here?"

"It's weird. Coincidences are weird," Athena says. "It doesn't make them significant."

"Is that what you really think?" Erin says. "Or are you playing devil's advocate?"

"I don't want to get my hopes up. Hope is a poison. It clouds judgment, and impedes rational decision-making. If we find concrete proof all of this is connected, then I'll change my tune."

"Those birds tried to kill me the other night," Erin says. "I came here because I was hoping you could help me."

"And maybe I can," Athena says. "But I don't know how much good I can do here. Maybe I should go back to Oregon. I know people in the Dissonant community."

"Like Garrett Thorpe?" Hal says, a sour note in his tone.

"Yes, like Garrett Thorpe. He might be able to help," Athena says. "Do you have any better ideas?"

"I want to stay, at least for now," Erin says. "Even if there's nothing we can do here. Tomorrow is the twentieth anniversary of Peter's death. I want to be here. And I'd like it if both of you were here with me."

It feels wrong to Athena. She doesn't dare hope the feeling comes from the Dissonance. She hasn't felt the Dissonance since 1999. It's a garden-variety human instinct, telling her to flee. But she looks at Erin, beaten and bruised, and Hal, slump-shouldered. She can't walk out on them. Not yet. They need closure.

Maybe I do, too, she thinks. She can ignore this anxiety for an extra day. For their sakes.

"Okay," she says. "But we leave right after the service."

Hal glances at Erin. "Okay," Erin says. "Yeah, okay."

Athena picks up her phone and is surprised to find it's already almost eleven. They've been out here for hours.

"I know that look," Hal says.

"What look?" Athena says, glancing up.

"It's your 'it's time to go to bed' look. Oh, wait, no, now it's changing."

"Yeah," Erin says. "Now it's her 'you don't know so much, you asshole' look."

Hal laughs and Athena tilts her head with a humorless smirk. "You're not funny."

"I'm pretty sure we are," Hal says.

"It's been confirmed by a panel of experts," Erin says. "I'll show you the test results in the morning."

"In the morning, yes," Athena says. "Because I have had enough of your bullshit—that goes for both of you—for one night."

"I need to check on Philip anyway," Erin says.

They let themselves inside. Erin bids them a quick good night, then ducks into her first-floor room. As soon as the door clicks shut behind her, Athena becomes acutely aware of herself occupying a body in space, next to Hal's body in space.

He appears to come to this same conclusion at almost the same time. He clears his throat, meets her gaze, then looks away.

"You upstairs?" he says.

"Yeah," she says. "You?"

"Yeah. So it's not weird if I walk up with you, right?"

"Why would it be weird?"

"Exactly? Why would it be weird? Who would think it's weird? Only a psychopath."

"Or someone bad at social cues," Athena says.

"Awkward people and psychopaths," Hal says. "Overlapping circles in the Venn diagram of humans who think it's weird to walk upstairs with you right now."

"You're an idiot," she says, and starts up the stairs, quickly so he can't see her smile. Her limp slows her down, and he catches up with ease. They make the climb in silence, the conversation's momentum stalled. She has time to notice the way he moves. It's the same as when they were kids, but a fraction of a second slower. His breath is more labored. There are lines around his mouth. His hair is thinning, starting to gray, but when he smiles, he looks like the boy she remembers.

He stops at the top of the stairs and stuffs his hands in his pockets. He jerks his head toward the door behind them. "That's me."

She points to the door down the hall. "I'm down there. If you need anything." The second sentence is out of her mouth before she realizes what she's said.

Hal's eyebrows rise. "Yeah. Same. They gave me a fancy room with a fireplace, so if you need a place to dry off or whatever."

She can't tell if it's a joke or an invitation, and she's pretty sure she'll die right here on the landing if she has to ask. She dips her head and turns down the hall toward her door, mad at herself with every step, but committed now.

"Athena," Hal says, and she stops outside her door to look at him. "It's been too long."

"Has it?" she says.

"For me, anyway."

She leaves her hand on the doorknob, opens her mouth, then closes it again. She smiles, almost against her will, and finally finds the right words: "Good night, Hal."

Erin

When Erin lets herself into her room, she finds Philip asleep in the king-size bed. Apparently mindful of their conversation about turning on lights after sunset, he's left every bulb in the room blazing.

She goes into the bathroom, undresses, and scrubs off her makeup. Without it, her bruises come into sharper relief. She looks like Robert De Niro in *Raging Bull,* or Stallone in the third act of any *Rocky* movie. She certainly aches like someone who lost a fight.

She takes care getting into the bed, because every movement hurts, and she's unable to suppress a pained grunt. Philip stirs and makes an interrogative sound as she spoons up to his back.

"Just me," she whispers, and runs a hand through his sandy hair. "Go back to sleep."

"I was dreaming about you," he says, voice sleepy. "But you were younger. And I wasn't me. It was scary." Erin doesn't know how to respond, and before she can, he says, "Did you see your friends?"

"I did." She runs her hand down the back of his neck and traces a finger along the contour of one shoulder.

"Was it fun?"

"It was," she says, and realizes it's true. She smiles in the dark.

"Do you think they'll like me?"

Her finger stops near the bottom of his biceps. She squeezes his arm. "Of course they will. Go back to sleep."

She lies with him until he begins to snore—softly, never too loud, just enough to be cute. When she's sure he's drifted off, she climbs out of the bed and goes to the window. It looks out on the street in front of the inn, slick with a deluge of rain. She sets to work putting up a protection command over the building. She hopes it's stronger than the dome she used at the cemetery this afternoon. She hopes it can hide her (and her lover, and her friends) from whatever might be after them, at least for one more night.

Owen

Owen's supply of terror-fueled adrenaline is running out. He's exhausted. His eyes are bone-dry, and he's battling a nasty case of highway hypnosis. He's afraid to admit this to the Cole-thing, but it notices anyway.

"You need rest," it says.

Owen is grateful for the observation, although he knows he shouldn't be. It's this thing's fault he's exhausted. Nevertheless, Owen could cry with gratitude. He's desperate for sleep.

"Maybe we can find a parking garage," he says.

"You need a bed," the thing says.

It directs Owen to an old motel in Fort Worth called the Sleep Inn. The building has the desolate, faded look of a place that's been out of business for at least a decade. Some of the windows are jagged holes of broken glass, and the parking lot is a garden of weeds and fast food garbage. It's the sort of place where bad things happen.

Owen parks behind the motel, to hide the car from the street. He and his abductor walk around to the front, where the Cole-thing jimmies the lock on a room with the windows intact. It's too dark to see much inside, but at least it doesn't smell like anyone or anything has used this place as a toilet. It's musty, but Owen can live with it. Not like his bed back in the trailer in Alabama is a grand accommodation, anyway.

He shakes the blanket on the bed to dispel any dust, or to startle anything sleeping beneath the covers. Nothing scurries between the sheets. Satisfied, Owen lays down on the mattress. He does so slowly, because he's afraid to make sudden moves around the Cole-thing.

Again and again for the last two days, he's been unable to stop pictur-ing the dead clerk from the convenience store. The bits of blood and brain that marked the body's slide to the floor. He tries to banish the image now, and fails.

"Are you comfortable?" the Cole-thing asks.

The blanket is thin, the sheets brittle and starchy against Owen's sweat-sticky skin. But Owen could sleep in a tub of rusty nails right now, if not for the heat in the room.

"It's a little stuffy," he says.

The Cole-thing kneels in front of the room's A/C unit. Yellow-green light sparks from his fingertips, and Owen has to cover his eyes to protect them from the brightness as the A/C roars to life and a wave of heavenly cold air washes over him.

The Cole-thing settles into a chair by the window and regards him. "The people I killed in the cemetery. They were friends of yours?"

"Yes," Owen says.

"I wasn't in complete control when that happened," the thing says. "If I had been, I still might have killed them, if it suited my purposes. The way I killed the man at the gas station. The way I will kill you if you cross me. But I don't do it to be cruel. I do it because it's necessary."

Owen pictures the scene at the cemetery. Cole chanting over the grave. The body that sprang up out of the dirt and choked him to death. That hadn't looked necessary. There had probably been a quicker way to kill Cole.

No, he thinks. *You enjoyed that.*

"Who are you?" he asks.

"No one you'd know," the thing says. "What's important is why I'm here."

"Okay, then. Why are you here?"

"To save the world."

1998
Athena's Doorway

Hal

On the first Saturday of summer break in 1998, two years and two days after Hal Isaac entered the heavens and returned with the Blade of Woe, he spent the afternoon getting the shit kicked out of him.

It sucked.

He and his coven were arranged on the back lawn of Marsh House, beneath a hazy blue-white sky. The professor sat on the back porch, beneath an umbrella, sipping from a tall glass of iced tea and looking very much at his ease. The coven, in contrast, were all panting, sweaty, and cranky after two straight hours of combat drills.

Last summer had been flyting practice, in which Hal could not participate. This year, they were engaging in physical duels, with practice blades *and* Dissonant. For two hours now, Marsh had been pairing them off. One partner wielded a blade against an opponent, while the other cast defensive commands to protect and assist. It was a new technique Marsh had implemented after Erin's victory at last summer's flyting tournament, when he'd realized the coven could pool its collective power and present a united front. It had happened instinctively that day in the hotel basement, but Marsh wanted them to be able to call upon it at will.

While the other members of the coven switched up roles, Hal always had to run offense. Since he couldn't read or cast Dissonant, it was the only role he *could* play. And yet, somehow, today, despite the fact Hal was actually, literally bonded to an immortal, otherworldly sword, and also despite the fact Erin was the group's best protective caster, *and* the fact Peter was the least aggressive and violent member of the group, Athena and Peter had trounced Erin and Hal all afternoon.

It wasn't a fair fight. The rest of the coven got to use the Dissonance, but Hal wasn't permitted to summon the Blade of Woe during drills. Marsh said he wanted Hal to learn how to wield a sword without having to lean on its Dissonant properties. So during these duels, Hal used a practice sword like everyone else.

Across the lawn, Athena spun her blade in a fancy little move. She was showing off a little. Under normal circumstances, Hal would've loved that. He loved her confidence. But today, after endless hours of defeat, it bummed him out. Shouldn't *he* be better at this? This was his one supposed superpower. He'd been named *champion* by an otherworldly power. Shouldn't he be the best at sword fighting, after two years of training?

Hal leaned to look past Athena, at Marsh in his comfy, shaded seat. "Can we call it, Professor? I'm beat."

Marsh took a long sip of tea before he answered. "If you have the energy to complain, you have the energy to fight. Square up."

Hal and Athena met in the middle of the lawn, leaned forward in slight bows, then stepped back and raised their blades.

A breeze swept across Hal's exposed arms and neck, wrapping him in an unseasonable cool. Erin had cast her protection command. She'd already mastered Haley's Dome, and now she was experimenting with ethereal armor commands.

The ethereal armor was neat, but posed the same basic problem as physical armor: protection equaled weight. The more freedom you wanted, the weaker the armor needed to be. You could choose to be a tank, or take your chances with speed and hope you were fast enough to outmaneuver your opponent.

Hal wriggled his shoulders, and felt weight press back against him. Heavy armor, then.

Behind Athena, Peter finished casting his own command. Hal had no idea what it was, so he decided to let Athena make the first move, hoping she'd give something away. She was fast, despite her bad leg, and closed the distance with a thrust to his chest. He knocked it to the left. Compared to her, he felt like he was moving in slow motion. Athena's speed meant her armor must be light. He'd have to hope he could outlast her.

One thing he *could* and *had* studied was his swordplay. He took an *oerhaw* swing now, wide and powerful. Athena ducked out of the way, darted back in under his sword, and slapped his stomach with the flat of her blade. The blow registered as a shock through his body—not painful, exactly, but not pleasant either.

She tried to step back, so Hal stabbed at the open space between her legs, striking her left calf. Light flashed at the point of impact. He'd damaged her armor.

She staggered from the blow, and Hal pressed his advantage. He swung sideways in a *mezzano* slice, but Athena managed to regain her balance and dance out of reach. She waited until his swing had passed its midpoint, then took a huge overhand swing of her own. It hit Hal's left shoulder. The shock of the blow shook his whole body, and his fingers went numb for a second.

He staggered back, right arm in front of his face for protection, and almost lost hold of his sword.

"Follow through!" Marsh shouted from across the yard. "Don't let up."

Hal would happily have killed Marsh in that moment. He'd asked if they could stop. He was tired. This fight—and, to be honest, all the ones before it—hadn't been fair.

Athena hit Hal's raised forearm and sent another tremor through his body.

"Fuck!" he shouted. He'd had enough. Fuck Marsh's rules. He threw his practice sword into the grass, swung his empty left hand through the air, and grabbed Athena's blade. His armor vibrated, registering another hit, but he kept his grip and squeezed tighter.

"What are you doing?" Athena said. "Let go."

But Hal didn't let go. The practice blade wasn't sharp. It was the sword equivalent of safety scissors. It felt and sounded like metal, but couldn't cut butter, let alone bread. He clenched his fist around it as tightly as he could. Yellow-green light fizzled out from between his fingers—probably his stupid useless armor taking *more* damage. He yanked on the sword. Athena lost her grip and fell forward. Hal turned the sword around so the hilt was in his hand, and he jabbed right into Athena's stumble. Light burst from her chest and the impact sent her reeling. She lost her balance and hit the ground with another flash and a shout.

She glared up at him from the lawn as he pointed the blade down at her. "Yield?"

"Like hell." She gestured at him and a gust of hard wind hit him like a wall. He flew backward through the air and slammed into Erin. They both went down.

"Goddammit, Athena," Erin groaned, as Hal rolled off her.

"Cheating!" Hal said. "We're only supposed to be using swords. That's cheating!" He looked to Marsh for confirmation.

Marsh leaned forward and clasped his hands between his legs. His mouth quirked in a half-smile. "You cheated first, Hal. Don't misunderstand—I've been waiting for one of you to be smart enough to try cheating. But you can't be mad at Athena for using your own tricks against you."

"She has access to all her tools," Hal said. "I have one tool. One. And I'm forbidden from using it."

"Young man, there are people who complain, and there are people who get things done," Marsh said. "You'll need to be smarter if you're going to fight opponents more powerful than yourself."

Hal laid his head back on the grass and closed his eyes against the sun until a shadow blocked the light. He squinted up at Athena, who offered him a hand up, along with a half-apologetic smile. Some of his frustration dissipated. It was tough to stay annoyed with her. He accepted the hand up.

"That's enough sparring," Marsh said. "There's something else we need to discuss before we finish for the day."

He stood and opened the back door to Marsh House, and they all crossed the lawn to follow him. As they approached the door, Athena bumped Hal with a hip. Was it Hal's imagination, or did she feel bonier these days? It had been two years since he'd last carried her, so maybe this was just her body growing up?

"I thought grabbing the sword was a badass move," she said.

"Not as badass as using superpowers to knock me over like a bowling pin," Hal said, but he appreciated the olive branch.

They went inside, stopped in the kitchen for water (no sodas until they'd rehydrated, per Marsh's orders), toweled off the sweat and grime, and then gathered in the professor's study.

Marsh leaned back on his desk, arms crossed, and studied his students. Out of his usual khaki slacks and button-down shirts, he should've looked ridiculous, but somehow, even in sandals and shorts, he remained an intimidating presence. He stared at his students until Hal lost patience.

"Professor?" he said. "What are we doing here?"

"You four are waiting," Marsh said. "I am considering."

"And it's important for us to sit here and do nothing while you consider?" Hal said. He used his needling *I'm fucking with you but not really, but kind of, actually, let's see how far I can push this* tone.

"Yes," Marsh said. "And the more often you interrupt me, the longer it will take me to decide, so please learn the value of patience and shut up."

As if to reassert his authority, Marsh let the silence stretch on for several minutes more—so long that the last of Hal's adrenaline ran out, and he began to feel more sleepy than irritable. His eyelids were growing heavy by the time Marsh spoke.

"I've been tutoring you for two years now," he said. "And I think you're ready, as a group, to advance to the next level of your education. So far, we've dealt primarily with basics. Practical uses for the Dissonance. Flyting. Dueling. But now, this summer, I think it's time to look to your individual strengths. I've come up with assignments for each of you." He walked around the back of his desk, where he'd piled a stack of books. He picked up the biggest one off the stack.

"Athena, you have two assignments. The first is to read Anne Silverman's *Music of the Infinite*. It's long and difficult and should take even you some time to finish. Second, and more important, this summer I want you to write your own Dissonant command. You can use everything you've learned, but the end result should be your own creation."

Athena accepted the book with a skeptical look, as though unimpressed by its considerable length.

"Am I allowed to borrow more books from your library?" she said. "To help me make the command?"

"No. Only what you already have." He returned to the stack of books and picked up three smaller volumes. "Peter, you've demonstrated skill with the natural world. Read these books on botany and biology. I want you to cultivate a new plant—one that can live and thrive in your greenhouse."

"I don't have a greenhouse," Peter said.

"Yet," Marsh said. "The builders are coming later this week."

Peter's mouth dropped open in delighted surprise. He regained composure quickly. "Yes sir," he said, taking the books.

Next Marsh turned to Erin. "Erin, you and Hal will share an assignment. I want the two of you to practice the combat and defense sequences you've learned. This is your specialty, and yet today you were beaten soundly by two less-gifted opponents. Today you're embarrassed, and you should be. But there may come a time when it's not about saving face in front of your teacher, but about saving all our lives. You need to be perfect."

Hal's fingers dug into the fabric of the couch armrest. Pins and needles ran from his fingertips to his elbows. The Blade was waking in the void, opening the passage between Hal and itself.

Hal took deep breaths. He would not lose control in front of Marsh. He wouldn't.

"But that's not the only thing," Marsh said. He picked up a tiny red-leather-bound volume and looked it over. "Last summer, at the convention, I spent a considerable amount of money on this little book. This summer, Erin, I'm entrusting it to you."

"What is it?" Erin asked.

"Call it a legendarium," Marsh said. "Or a book of fairy tales, or a collection of anecdotes. A book of stories about the Temple of Pain, and one of the only works of literature I've ever seen written entirely in Dissonant. I want you to translate it for Hal, and I want you both to study and reflect on the narratives inside. We need clues surrounding Hal's connection to the Temple. What is this destiny he's been promised? Is there a larger narrative in play here?"

Not once during this speech did the old man look at Hal.

Finished handing out books, he leaned back on the desk. "We'll continue drills this summer, and I want all of you to take the independent studies seriously. How seriously you take them will be a gauge of how seriously I consider continuing your tutelage. Do you understand?"

All four—even Hal—said they did.

"Good," Marsh said. "Now get out. I have work of my own to do."

Athena

The coven retreated to the back porch, flopped onto the deck furniture, and stacked their assigned reading on the table between them. It was late afternoon, and almost unbearably hot, but out here they'd have at least a little bit of privacy.

"Independent study," Athena said. She picked up *Music of the Infinite*, enjoying the heft of the book in her hand.

"Did you know about this?" Erin asked Peter.

Peter shook his head. "You know he never tells me anything. When you three aren't around, he keeps the study door shut and only comes out for meals." He glanced at the closed door behind him, then leaned forward. "Lately I've been hearing him in there. Talking on the phone, I think."

"He sure is a mysterious old fuck," Hal said.

They stashed their books in backpacks and Hal drove them into town. His mom had just started a new job as the night shift DJ at the local radio station, which meant he had access to her car most days. Athena rode up front with Hal, and Peter and Erin squeezed into the backseat.

On the drive, Hal continued to bemoan their summer projects.

"Aren't you a little disappointed? I thought after two whole years we'd get into some epic shit this summer. A quest. Battles. Save-the-world stuff where I might be useful. Instead it's more practice for me, and book reports for the rest of you. My job is to let Erin read me children's stories. Oh, and I guess protect the rest of you from paper cuts."

"Paper cuts are no joke," Peter said.

"What kind of quest did you envision this summer?" Erin said.

"Maybe like *Conan the Barbarian* meets *National Lampoon's Vacation?* We could go across the country in an RV, stop at shitty motels, barter for Dissonant texts, and battle inexplicable horrors?"

Hal laughed. "Then there'd be some mix-up where Peter gets a room to himself and the professor and I have to share."

"The two of you arguing over what to watch on TV," Athena said. "Who gets the first shower. Who farted."

They arrived at the diner just ahead of the dinner rush, and managed to snag their favorite window booth, in the corner farthest from the front door. They all ordered cheeseburgers, Cokes, and milkshakes, except for Athena, who ordered a salad and ice water. It was all charged to Professor Marsh, who had accounts at pretty much every business in Clegg. Athena watched her friends feast, her stomach growling, as she mechanically worked her way through her salad. She'd been unable to drop any substantial weight since last summer, and was hanging on to her diet plan by sheer willpower this year.

After dinner, they piled back into Lorna's convertible. When they arrived at Marsh House, Athena got out and pulled the seat forward to let Peter climb out. Instead of running up the steps, he stood beside the car, shoulders hunched, as though caught between two conflicting impulses. Athena heard the click as Erin unbuckled her seatbelt and scooted toward the open door. Athena understood then: Peter was trying to decide whether to invite Erin in, and Erin was trying to make it easy for him.

Instead, he stepped back as Erin came toward him. "Good night everyone," he said. "Talk to you tomorrow." And then he ran up the steps.

Erin buckled herself back in. Athena avoided eye contact as she climbed back into the car. Better not to let Erin know she understood what had just happened.

"What time is it?" Hal said.

Athena checked her watch. "Almost six-thirty."

"Oh shit," Hal said. "I have to get home and wake up Mom for work." He glanced at Athena. "Would you be okay hanging out at my house for a little bit and having your parents come get you?"

It was the first time Hal had ever invited Athena over by herself.

She tried to take it in stride, like it was by no means exciting and/or a big deal.

"Sure," she said. "No problem."

The drive to Erin's was more subdued than the drive to the diner had been. Erin radiated a silent melancholy from the backseat of the car. She and Peter had been doing a strange sort of courtship dance for almost a year now—ever since they'd returned from the conference last summer, and Erin had promptly quit the cheer squad and broken up with Randy. They seemed to be stuck in a pattern where they would get a little closer, and then a little farther apart again. And worse, Athena knew things weren't getting any better at the Porter house. She'd heard the rumors about Erin's mom, stepping out with Fire Chief Alan Sturgess.

When they got to Erin's trailer and Athena let Erin out of the car, Erin walked up the front steps with her head down, her stride slower than usual. Athena wanted to say something kind and reassuring. What would Erin say, if their positions were reversed?

The best she could manage was, "Good work today."

Erin looked back, incredulous. "You beat my ass."

"Yeah well, you had it coming after you beat me at flyting last summer," Athena said, but lightly, so Erin would know it was in good fun.

"I guess I did at that," Erin said, and finally smiled, before she let herself into the trailer.

"C'mon, let's boogie," Hal said, beckoning Athena back to the car.

As soon as she stepped into the Isaacs' apartment, she had an almost immediate, visceral desire to go back outside. It felt hotter in here than it had outside, and the air reeked of cigarettes.

Hal gave her a sympathetic glance. "There are Diet Cokes in the fridge if you want one. You might be more comfortable out on the balcony."

Athena went into the kitchen while Hal went to the master bedroom. She found a few Diet Cokes on the bottom shelf of the fridge, almost hidden behind a case of Coors. It was one of the big cases, with twenty-four cans of beer. Athena had seen them at the store but never at someone's home. Her own parents weren't against a drink every now and then, but they preferred to mix cocktails, or sip wine from fancy bulb-shaped glasses. She peered into the case of Coors now, and saw it was more than half-empty. Part of her—the part that would straighten stacks of books in a bookstore display—wanted to unload the cans and free up space in the fridge. She might even have done it, too, if she hadn't been interrupted.

"You can try one, if you want."

She started and stepped away from the fridge, letting the door swing shut. A man stood in the kitchen entryway. He was white and rail-thin, with blond hair, blue eyes, and a couple of teeth missing from his grin, which was somehow unkind.

"Sorry, I don't think we've met," Athena said.

"Reggie," the man said. "Lorna's true love." He spared a glance toward the apartment's master bedroom before returning to his study of Athena with a gaze both familiar and strange. The familiar part was just part of being Black in Clegg. No matter where she went, white people stared at her like an oddity, a not-entirely-welcome curiosity. Usually, the nicer ones tended to catch themselves after their initial surprise, and then go back to minding their own business. Others though, kept staring, unashamed, like she was an animal in a zoo.

The *un*familiar part of the stare was something that had only begun in the last year, as Athena had started to starve and exercise herself down to an acceptable weight. Now, in addition to curiosity, discomfort, and occasional hostility, she felt a certain *hunger* in the gazes of boys and men. Desire. The nicer ones had the decency to only stare when they thought she wasn't looking. Other people, like this Reggie, openly leered, as if waiting for an invitation. No, that wasn't quite right. They didn't want anything as nice as an invitation. They were waiting for an *opening*. Athena met Reggie's gaze, keenly aware of the cold can of Diet Coke in her hands, the mass of his body blocking the kitchen exit.

"You a friend of Hal's?" Reggie said.

"That's right," Athena said. "It'd be pretty strange for me to be in here otherwise."

"I'd have to call the cops," Reggie said. "Tell 'em there's a stranger in my home, breaking in and stealing sodas." He laughed, and Athena managed a polite smile in return. It was what you did when a white person—especially a white man—made a joke.

Hal appeared in the kitchen entryway behind Reggie. "There you are," he said to Athena. "What's taking you?"

"I was just offering your little friend a beer," Reggie said.

Hal's eyebrows went up and he pursed his mouth as he considered the offer.

"No thanks," Athena said firmly. "Diet Coke will be fine for both of us." She reached back into the fridge to get one for Hal as well.

"Aren't you going to introduce me?" Reggie said to Hal.

"Sounded like you were introducing yourself fine," Hal said.

"Excuse me?" Reggie said, and Hal flinched back. It was tiny, and Hal recovered from it quickly, but Athena saw it, and she would have bet Reggie did, too.

"I said it sounded like you two were already old friends," Hal said. "But in case it hadn't come up yet, Reggie, this is my best friend, Athena. Athena, this is Mom's boyfriend, Reggie."

Athena would've been touched by the *best friend* thing, if Reggie hadn't taken the opportunity to leer at Athena again.

"Best friend, huh?" he said.

"That's right," Hal said. He ducked under Reggie's blocking arm, and put himself between Reggie and Athena. He started making a pot of coffee for his mother, and acted casual, as though this were the only reason he'd come into the room, but Athena felt safer already.

"Give me one of them beers, Hal," Reggie said.

Athena pulled a silver can from the case and handed it to Hal, who handed it to Reggie. Reggie didn't say thanks. He cracked it open, and continued to stare at Hal and Athena. Hal returned to the process of making coffee.

Reggie finally *(finally)* took the hint and left the doorway. A moment later Athena heard the sounds of pro wrestling from the living room TV. It was, of course, turned up way too loud.

As Hal fixed the pot of coffee, Athena called her parents and asked for a ride home. Hal finished the coffee and left it on the table by the front door, where Lorna couldn't miss it. Then they crept through the living room, past Reggie, who was smoking on the couch, beer cradled in his lap, and out onto the balcony.

It wasn't much of a balcony—just a slab of concrete bordered by wood, with a view of the crappy parking lot below. There weren't even any chairs up here. Athena and Hal leaned on the barrier and surveyed the shitty surroundings.

"Fucking Reggie," Hal said.

"Fucking Reggie," Athena said, and they clinked their soda cans together.

Hal took a long pull from his can before he spoke again. "I'm sorry about him. Usually when Mom gets a boyfriend, it only lasts a few weeks, but this guy just keeps lingering."

"I'm sorry you have to put up with him," Athena said.

"Stinking up the house with his cigarettes. Always watching the TV."

"Yeah, but he's watching wrestling. I thought you liked wrestling."

"I do," Hal said. "But somehow, having to watch it with him ruins it."

He looked out at the parking lot. If he was aware his right elbow was pressed up against Athena's left, he gave no indication. Athena tried not to stare, but couldn't stop picturing it in her mind, even as she looked away.

"It makes sense," she said. "It matters who you do things with."

"Exactly," he said.

"It's sweet of you to get your mom up," Athena said.

"More like self-preservation," Hal said. "If I don't literally drag her out of bed, she'll oversleep and miss work."

They stood in silence for a little while. Athena finished her Coke, and glanced at Hal surreptitiously. Out in the heat, away from the cigarette smoke and the others, she felt well and truly happy for the first time all day. Together, they watched Hal's mom exit the apartment, run down the stairs to the parking lot, get into her car, and drive away.

"I keep the radio on until I fall asleep now," Hal said. "To make sure she's still working. Like I can't fall asleep unless I hear her voice."

"That's kind of sweet," Athena said.

"It's not like that. It's like I need to know she's making money and we'll have enough for rent and groceries. And I know that when I hear her voice on the radio." He waved the subject away. "Anyway, enough about Lorna. What are you going to do for your project?"

"I'll have to think about it," Athena said. "I want to do something grand. Something no one has ever done before. But all we've learned in the last two years are basic characters and simple commands. Kid stuff. You can't build the Great Wall out of Lego bricks, you know?"

"You could," Hal said. "But I don't know why you'd want to. It would be a terrible wall. Maybe you could superglue the bricks together to reinforce it?"

"Maybe, but that's not my point."

"I know. Marsh is probably expecting the Dissonant equivalent of a science fair volcano. Think of it like homework. You don't have to paint the Sistine Chapel on your first go."

Athena didn't concede the point. Hal scoffed.

"You want his approval so very badly."

She scoffed back. "And you don't?"

"No," Hal said. "I want to keep him off my back."

"He pushes us to help us grow."

"He pushes because he's a fucking prick. He does his best to humiliate me in front of other people."

She peered at him in the dark. He stared forward, shoulders hunched, head down.

Hal and Athena were rarely in the same classes at school. Athena was on the college track, and Hal was with what he liked to call "the rest of the dummies." He wasn't stupid. He was maybe the sharpest person Athena knew. It was more like he was uninterested in school. And because he wasn't in honors courses, he didn't understand how hard you had to work at a thing to be good at it. How, if you wanted to be extraordinary, you had to allow your teachers to drive you past frustration, past exhaustion.

"He's harsh," she conceded. "And maybe not the best teacher for you."

"Not like I have a lot of options. No transfer forms available. And after his presentation at the con last summer, I don't think anyone else is going to step up and offer to teach me."

She swallowed hard. "Maybe I could help you."

Hal looked up, his gloomy countenance a little faded. "What, like do drills on our own? Without Marsh?"

"Maybe some regular Dissonant study, too. Maybe we need to come at it from another angle. My parents are taking a day trip to Vander-griff on Saturday, but I'll probably stay home to work. You could come over. Protect me from paper cuts."

There it was. She'd just invited a boy to come over while her parents were out of town, and, shockingly, it had sounded like the most natural thing in the world. Panic flooded her chest.

"If you're bored or whatever," she added. "We could order pizza, invite the others over, watch a movie." She winced inwardly. She hadn't meant to make it a group activity.

Hal looked back out at the parking lot. "Yeah. Yeah, maybe that could be fun."

"Cool," Athena said, and tried to sound it.

"Cool," he agreed.

Erin

A couple of weeks passed. Erin and Hal showed up at Marsh House and ran their drills. Erin's shields and ethereal armor grew stronger. She got better at varying density and weight on the fly. Marsh seemed pleased with her progress. Less so with Hal's.

Hal remained fierce. Every swing of his practice sword seemed designed to split Erin in two, and Marsh complained that Hal needed to learn finesse and patience; that swordplay wasn't about power, but intelligence and instinct. The more Marsh nagged, the harder Hal fought. Erin had always known her friend had a temper, but there was an anger swelling in him now that worried her.

One Wednesday in early June, as they sat on the back porch of Marsh House after drills and rehydrated in the shade, Hal said:

"All this combat training. Why do you think it's so important? What's Marsh training us for?"

Erin started to answer—standard Dissonant training, etc.—but it struck her as false before it even left her mouth.

"It's nice for me, since I'm included," Hal said. "But Marsh is pushing combat way harder than usual."

"I'm not sure," she said. "I mean last summer, there was the tournament, but this? It doesn't make sense."

The door to Peter's greenhouse opened, and Peter stepped out, drenched in sweat, face beet red. He waved to Erin and Hal, and Hal beckoned him to the table.

"Come drink some water," Hal said. "You look like you're about to have a stroke."

Peter flopped into one of the empty chairs and accepted a bottle of water. He cracked it open and drank half of it in one pull, then set it down on the table. Hal was right: he didn't look good, and he was breathing hard.

"Peter, how long have you been in there?" she said.

"Dunno," he said between breaths. He sounded like he'd been running. "Lost track of time."

"Come here." Erin scooted her chair closer to his, so her right knee was between his legs and vice versa. She picked up her own cold bottle of water, slippery with condensation, and pressed it to his forehead, and his cheeks. He leaned forward and dropped his head, let her roll the bottle across the back of his neck. She couldn't help but be aware of his proximity, the heat of his body, the top of his head only inches away from her chest. He was so damn close.

He sat up, looking a little better. "Thank you," he said. "That helped."

"Now do me," she said. The words were out of her mouth before she made a conscious decision to say them.

Peter looked as startled as she felt, but after a brief hesitation, he took the bottle from her. She leaned forward, dropping her head. Her hair was up in a bun, so her neck was already exposed.

"I think I'm going to head home," Hal said.

Erin lifted her head to glare at Hal. Hal looked uncomfortable, which, okay, fair, but couldn't he see that she and Peter were having a moment? Hal lifted one hand, but only slightly, the gesture equivalent of a whisper meant for one person.

"Peter, can you give Erin a ride home?" he said. "Reggie said I can bring Mom's car by the garage where he works and he'll change the oil for free. I was gonna do that."

Peter had turned sixteen last week, the youngest of the coven, a summer baby. He'd only had his driver's license for a few days, but he was the first of his friends to have his own car. It wasn't a fancy thing—a Honda CRX that only had two seats and a hatchback—but Peter didn't need anyone else's permission to use it.

"Sure," Peter said, then looked from Hal to Erin. "I mean, if that's okay with Erin." While Peter's head was turned toward Erin, Hal gave her a quick wink.

"Yeah, that's okay with Erin," Erin said.

"Okay, then," Hal said. "I'll see you guys later." And he got up and left the yard, and Erin was alone with Peter for the first time in—well, she wasn't sure how long it had been.

She dropped her head again, leaning forward with her elbows on her legs.

"Enough stalling," she said. "Cool me off, dammit."

"Yes ma'am," Peter said.

The water bottle was a shock of cold against the back of her neck. She gasped and squeezed Peter's thighs as goose pimples ran in a wave across her entire body, and her nipples hardened to stone.

The bottle left her neck. "Are you okay?" Peter said. "Do you want me to stop?"

"No," she said, with a shaky little laugh. "I'm fine. Keep going."

The cold returned, a pleasurable icy spike distracting her from the extreme heat in her body. She felt hotter now than she had while she and Hal were still working out. It should work the other way. She should be cooling off now, right?

She relaxed into the feeling, but didn't move her hands off of Peter's legs. Those she left exactly where they were. He kept his legs absolutely still. Like unnaturally still. Was he uncomfortable? She let him run the bottle over her neck, shoulders, and arms for a few minutes before she finally let go of him and sat up.

"Thank you," she said.

He smiled at the table. "You're welcome."

They sat in the suffocating heat, silent for a moment, before Peter fanned his face and said, "I don't know about you but I'm still burning up. Want to go inside?"

She followed him through the back door and into the kitchen, where they grabbed more water, then went into the sunken living room. Peter and his grandfather had cable, so Erin put the TV on one of the movie channels. It was some sort of courtroom comedy, starring Jeff Daniels and the guy who played Kramer on *Seinfeld*. It wasn't very good, but the comedic cadence of the dialogue and the score was comforting to Erin all the same.

"This okay?" Erin asked.

"Sure, if that's what you want to watch," Peter said.

Erin loved the sound of movies and TV shows—especially movies and TV shows that weren't heavy on action or violence, but rather dialogue and human relationships. She loved the patter the same way some people loved the sound of a rainstorm or a waterfall. She wished she could have a TV in her bedroom at home, because she would fall asleep with it on every night. So far her parents had denied her this, so she had to settle for naps in other people's homes. The Jeff Daniels movie made a soothing aural wallpaper now as she and Peter collapsed next to one another on the couch and basked in the waves of central air.

There, in that space of perfect contentment, Erin fell into happy, exhausted, dreamless sleep.

She woke up cold, the sweat on her skin having long since dried beneath the A/C's steady, gentle ministrations. There was no clock in the living room at Marsh House, but Erin had an idea several hours had passed. The light through the windows had changed, and a different movie was playing on the TV: *Major League II*, with Charlie Sheen and Tom Berenger. She was leaning her head on Peter's shoulder. Peter was asleep, sitting up, head leaned back, snoring softly. She wiped her face with the back of one hand, suddenly sure—like deep-down, bone-sure—she'd drooled all over him in their sleep. But her hand came away from her face dry.

She got up, went to the bathroom, then to the kitchen for more water. She brought two bottles with her to the living room. Peter had woken up in her absence. He rubbed his eyes with the heels of his hands.

"Where'd you go?" he asked, his voice still sleepy.

"Here," she said, and handed him one of the waters.

He took a long drink and then said, "What time is it?"

"About six," Erin said.

"I should get you home," he said.

She tried not to let her disappointment show. She'd thought they were making progress today. She'd thought he'd want to spend more time with her. Maybe ask her to do something with him, like go to a movie, or at least rent something from Blockbuster. Or come up with literally any excuse to keep this intimacy, this closeness going. But here he was, pushing her away again.

"Yeah," she said. "My dad will be wondering where I am."

What she didn't say was, *I gave up my chance at a normal life for this. Why won't you let me get close to you?*

Hal

Marsh had broken up the coven's training into a regimented schedule that summer. Tuesdays and Thursdays were combat drills for Erin and Hal at Marsh House. Mondays, Peter spent in the garden with the professor for botany lessons. Wednesday was group training day, which left Friday for Athena's one-on-ones with Professor Marsh. So Hal started going to Athena's house every Monday. Together they sat and read, and Hal practiced his Dissonant alphabet, and listened to Athena read passages she'd copied out of Marsh's books.

Hal continued to struggle. He could look right at the Dissonant alphabet written out before him, then close his eyes and be unable to picture the characters. He could make shapes when Athena guided his hands, but nothing actually happened. No sparks. No minor miracles. Just an idiot making funky hand gestures like an interpretive dance major.

Athena turned out to be a patient teacher. Although he'd always known her to be a grumpy, irritable person, she never lost her temper with him. She held his hands, went through the motions again and again and again. When *she* did it with him, he could feel *something*. A thrum in the air, a crackle of power.

Or, at least, he *thought* he could feel something. Maybe it was just how he felt when she touched him? Could that be possible? He wasn't sure. Despite the way it ended, his initial interactions with Kelly last summer had left him confident enough to go after a number of girls. He'd put his hands all over these girls and vice versa, but he'd never felt anything like this. It had to be the Dissonance, right?

After the first week of training, Hal had pretty much given up hope of advancing as a Dissonant, but he continued to show up at Athena's. It beat being at home. Reggie had basically moved in, and now everything Hal owned reeked of cigarette smoke. There was no escaping the stink in the apartment, and whenever Hal brought it up to Lorna, she always made a vague promise to talk to Reggie. Nothing, of course, ever happened.

He found other ways to be out of the house, too. One afternoon after a Thursday session with Erin, he lingered at Marsh House to hang out with Peter. He was hesitant to interfere with Erin and Peter's alone time, but Erin had to go shopping with her mother, which gave Hal a good excuse to stay. They watched a lot of MTV, and played a metric fuck-ton of *Super Smash Bros.* and *GoldenEye*.

After a couple of hours, when Hal felt he couldn't take another thrashing in either game, he asked Peter about his work in the greenhouse. They were sitting in Peter's bedroom, Peter on the bed, Hal on the floor.

Peter set down his controller and sighed. "Still stuck," he said.

"On what?"

"Come on. I'll show you."

Hal followed Peter out into the backyard. Peter pulled a key chain from his pocket to unlock the padlock on the greenhouse door, then held it open for Hal. Hal passed inside, into a space so stiflingly hot it seemed to suck the air from his lungs. Sweat broke out over his entire body.

Peter entered behind Hal, and put the padlock on the inside of the door, locking it again.

"You lock yourself in here?" Hal said.

Peter nodded. "After what happened to Athena with the spider-thing, it seemed safest. I'm out here alone a lot. What if something senses me working and tries to get in?"

"You think a padlock is going to keep out a monster?"

"No, but it'll slow it down and give me time to react," Peter said.

Hal conceded this was a fair point, and looked around. The greenhouse wasn't large—there was room for Hal and Peter to move around, but barely. The rest of the space was taken up with plants of various types. Hal couldn't have named most of them. A narrow workbench stood in one corner, and on it were a bunch of more exotic-looking plants. Fantastical, colorful things, like something off the cover of a trippy 1970s rock album—or they would be, if they weren't all shriveled, faded, and obviously dead.

"All of this stuff," Peter said, gesturing to the living plants, "is basic. These you can buy at any nursery. They're pretty easy to grow and take care of. Call it the 'control' group. The stuff over here?" He walked over to the workbench. "Call this the 'experimental' group. These are my attempts to grow something new."

Hal stood beside Peter at the bench. There was just room for the two of them to stand shoulder to shoulder.

Peter picked up a shriveled purple watermelon. "I do everything right, according to the books. I cross-pollinate. I use the Dissonance to make sure the soil is fertile and full of energy. And at first, everything seems okay. But at a certain point . . ." He set the little watermelon back on the table and spread his hands to encompass all the dead things.

Hal picked up what seemed to be an ordinary potato. "What's wrong with this one?"

A ghost of a smile haunted Peter's mouth before it disappeared. "That was supposed to be a glow-in-the-dark potato. Like a potato you could use as a reading light."

"That's awesome," Hal said.

"It would've been," Peter said. "If it worked."

Hal looked the potato over. He tried to picture it sitting on his nightstand at home, a comforting warm glow illuminating the pages of a comic book, or helping him find his way to the bathroom in the middle of the night.

As he did this, something strange happened—so faintly he didn't realize it at first, at least not on any conscious level, but only became aware gradually. A slight *thrum* in the air around him, that seemed to pass into and through the flesh of his arm, up to the fingertips holding the potato.

Assuming it was something Peter was doing, Hal looked at the other boy, but Peter's hands were flat on the table, and he gave Hal a questioning look.

"What are you doing?" Peter said.

"I'm not doing anything," Hal said. "I thought this was you."

Peter shook his head slowly. Hal looked back at the potato. It had grown larger and firmer, and was warm to the touch. Even its skin was more vibrant. No, not just vibrant. It was *aglow*. Emitting light.

"What the hell?" Hal said.

Roots pushed through the skin of the potato and reached into the air, searching for a place to take root.

"Quick," Peter said. "We need to plant it." He pushed past Hal deeper into the greenhouse, and returned a second later with an empty planter full of soil. He dug out some space, and Hal gently lowered the potato into dirt. He would've sworn the thing actually *jumped* out of his hand and into the planter, its roots continuing to grow. Once it touched the soil, its glow turned into a glare, so bright Hal had to shield his eyes, then look away. He and Peter stepped back from the workbench and squinted at the miracle, throwing up an ungodly amount of light.

"What the hell?" Hal said again. He could think of nothing else to say.

"I'm not sure," Peter said. "But I think the potato just came back to life. Like Lazarus, risen from the grave."

"A zombie potato," Hal said. He laughed. "This is insane. So totally random." He glanced at Peter, and his smile died. Peter was giving him a very serious look.

"Yeah, maybe," Peter said. But he didn't look convinced. Not one bit.

Athena

Although she and Professor Marsh were scheduled to begin private lessons at 10 a.m. on Fridays, Athena liked to arrive early, to sit and read quietly in Marsh's office while he finished up his own morning work. She could have hung out with Peter, but studying with Professor Marsh felt very grown-up and professional. It was how she imagined college would feel, someday.

One Friday morning in early July, Marsh sat at his desk, poring over an old volume and making notes in a notebook, while Athena sat in her favorite chair, legs curled beneath her, Anne Silverman's *Music of the Infinite* open on her lap. Despite having had the book since the end of May, she continued to struggle with it.

It is a fact long-acknowledged by most Speakers of the Word (at least, any Speakers we care to trust) that language is the root of the Word's power. In the Abrahamic religions, God spoke the sky, the oceans, the fish, the birds, the land animals, and finally, human beings into existence. The good Speaker—the trustworthy Speaker—accepts the literal and mythological truth of this story. We are after all a Christian sect, praise God, and when we lose sight of that, we lose sight of the source of the power the Lord has granted us, and thereby fall into the sin of Dissonance.

She stopped, rubbed her eyes, and tried to recenter her attention.

"Are you feeling all right?"

She blinked and found Marsh watching her.

"I'm fine. Just having trouble with the reading."

"Oh?"

"You hadn't noticed?"

"I'd noticed you'd had the book for longer than usual, but it's also summer break, and you are a teenager. I can't expect you to study full-time."

"I am, though," she said. "This is all I'm doing. Reading this damn book. I don't understand why it's giving me so much trouble. The prose isn't difficult. It's almost—" She broke off, embarrassed by the next thought.

"Go on," Marsh said.

"It's almost as if the book would prefer not to be read. Like it's throwing up barriers, making itself as boring as possible. Like the textual equivalent of a maze with a series of gatekeepers guarding the path to the treasure in the center."

Marsh took off his glasses and polished them with a rag. "That is an *interesting* idea."

"Is that—something that happens?" she said. "With Dissonant texts, I mean."

"Not that I know of," Marsh said. "But I don't know everything." He replaced his glasses and gave her a faint smile.

"Then why am I having so much trouble?"

"Do you want my opinion?" Marsh said. "I'm not sure you do."

"I do," Athena said. She sat up straighter in the chair.

"I don't think there's a problem with the text. I think the problem is you. You're distracted."

"Distracted? By what?"

He stood and walked around the front of the desk to lean back in his usual spot, arms crossed. "You tell me."

"I don't know what you're talking about," Athena said.

"If you don't want to tell me, don't. But if you won't tell me, I can't help. So let's move on with what I can teach you. How is your original command line coming?"

A thread of unease ran like a ribbon, up from her stomach into the back of her throat. "I have some ideas," she said.

"Ideas," he said. "Do you have anything to show me? Concepts for us to review?"

She closed *Music of the Infinite* and pulled a blue-and-white composition book from her bag. The title *Athena's Cookbook* was written on the cover in black marker. This was her grimoire, her book of shadows, the place where she took her notes and copied out pertinent passages from Dissonant texts the professor loaned her. She flipped through the book now, looking for anything she could pass off as an idea for a command, but all she could find were other people's work. No bailouts on offer.

She slumped back in her chair, and Marsh smirked. "So, nothing to review, then."

She glared at him. It was like he had X-ray vision or something, could see right through her. "I'm worried about Hal."

He watched her, but said nothing. She took this as a sign to continue. "We've been spending a lot of time together this summer," she said.

"How is that different from any other summer?" Marsh said. "You, Hal, Peter, and Erin have always been inseparable."

"This is different," Athena said. "We've been spending time just the two of us. I've been tutoring him, trying to help him catch up on his Dissonant comprehension." And there it was. She'd just admitted to tutoring Hal behind Marsh's back. Would she ever be able to keep a secret from this man? "And he's not making progress. But worse, there's something . . . dark growing in him. An anger."

"Hal is struggling," Marsh said. It wasn't a question, but a plain statement. "That's how it goes, for Hal. It's the type of life he has, the sort of person he is. Do you remember what I told you when you first started studying with me? After the coven discovered their power, and you saw that boy eaten by those spider-monsters. You wanted to go back for the boy's body."

"Charlie Simmons," Athena said. She would never say so to her teacher's face, but it bothered her how he never said Charlie's name. It was always *the boy*. "And yes, I remember. 'There are people you can help, and there are people who will drag you down with them.'"

"Much of surviving and thriving is learning to tell the difference between those types of people," Marsh said.

"You think Hal is going to drag me down."

"I think it's possible, if you let him." He raised a hand to ward off potential objections. "When he wields the Blade, he's powerful. But consider the evidence empirically. Despite his supposed vision last summer, I am still baffled why an otherworldly entity would pick Hal to visit the Temple, let alone give him such a powerful weapon. Without it, he can't beat you—a permanently handicapped girl—in a fair fight."

"Those aren't fair fights," Athena said, caught somewhere between flattered for herself and angry on Hal's behalf. "And the Temple did test him and give him control of that Blade."

"It did. And I know you care about him. But I also urge you to think about your potential versus his. You, Erin, and Peter are special in a way he never will be, and you, Athena—I believe you're the most special of all. You have incredible potential. Do not let anyone—not my grandson, or Erin, or least of all, Hal Isaac—ruin that potential. Do you understand me?"

She wanted to argue. To defend Hal. But in that moment, no counterargument would take shape. She felt outmaneuvered by unassailable logic.

Marsh crossed his arms again. "If you learn anything from me, it should be this: put yourself first. It is immoral to do anything else. If, along the way, you can help someone without diminishing yourself? Terrific. But if you want to be a great Dissonant—one of the legends— serve yourself first. You have a noble heart, but also a wide pragmatic streak. Let the streak lead, not your heart. Do you understand?"

She didn't want to. She wanted to argue. It sounded right, but felt wrong. But no cogent counterarguments would take shape.

"Yes sir," she murmured.

"Good," he said. "Unfortunately, because you're falling behind on your project, there isn't much for us to do today. So go home, and get to work, and don't you dare come back without finishing the Silverman book and having at least five ideas for your original command line."

Erin

A couple more weeks passed, and on a mid-July morning, Erin found herself sitting outside the trailer at 5 a.m., awake quite against her will. The air was balmy, and the sky was still mostly dark. She sat on a lawn chair, trying to translate her book using only the trailer's front porch light.

Most of the trailer park was still asleep. Only Erin and her next-door neighbor's dog were up. The dog sat and stared at her through his chain link fence. Erin waved at him every now and then, and the dog thumped his tail on the ground with pleasure.

Aside from the dog and the book, her only other company was the radio on the porch steps beside her, volume low, tuned to KART. Erin didn't like country music, but listened because Hal's mom DJ'd the night shift.

Unfortunately, Lorna wasn't a great DJ, especially for a country station. She didn't have a Texas accent, and always sounded spaced out, like her mind was on other things. Sometimes a block of songs would end, and instead of a commercial or some chatter, there would be dead air. Sometimes the silence stretched long enough the "emergency tape" began to play a loop of songs at least a year out of fashion. Then, suddenly, the songs would stop and Lorna would be back, introducing a more current country hit.

What did Lorna think about during those long silences? What could absorb her so completely?

Hal's mom had always been absentminded and weird. When Erin and her friends were little, Lorna only ever showed up to about half of the school concerts and plays, and Erin had lost count of how many times Lorna had forgotten to pick Hal up after school. Hal had always been embarrassed and frustrated with his mother, but this morning, Erin would happily have traded with him.

Her own mother had gone out last night around seven, to "meet friends for drinks." That had been ten hours ago. She hadn't come back and hadn't called to say where she was. Around three in the morning, an hour after the bars closed, Erin's dad had started calling all the hospitals in the area to see if her mom had been admitted. She had not. At least Lorna eventually remembered to start another song or commercial. Danielle Porter was currently maintaining radio silence.

Erin had heard the rumors around town. Her mother cheating, going behind her father's back with Fire Chief Alan Sturgess. The girls at school had told Erin that her mother and Chief Sturgess weren't even discreet when they were out together. Shameless. These girls framed their gossip as concern or helpfulness, but Erin had seen the cruel delight on their faces. One reason she was glad to have left behind the so-called normal life for the Dissonant path.

For the last two hours, Erin had been sitting outside on the lawn chair with her radio, trying to understand the book Professor Marsh had assigned her. It was a slow process, because Dissonant was imprecise and rich with implication, and she wasn't at all confident in what she'd transcribed so far:

Mysteries of the Hidden Truth

1. *No one knows why life began. So-called "holy men" made guesses and named them Truths.*
2. *And humanity, eager for comfort, flocked to these guesses. They built temples and waged wars against others who believed in different guesses. They slaughtered and died believing they would be rewarded in another life.*
3. *These fallen, these heroes and martyrs and saints and tyrants, served a Truth, although they knew it not. This truth is Pain.*
4. *Pain is the originator, the first cause. Only those who accept this one Truth shall ever find solace.*
5. *Herein are gathered accounts given by saints, adherents, and heretics. Each presents a different aspect of the Truth.*

Although some may seem to contradict one another, all are true.

6. *May you meditate upon these Mysteries and find the wisdom within.*

She shouldn't have been surprised at the tone. The Dissonance was generated by the friction between what should be and what was. Only people in psychic discomfort seemed to have access. But this book seemed extra dark and Erin didn't like the idea of reading it to Hal, who wasn't a cheery person anyway. Could this be good for him?

She shifted in the lawn chair and it made a squeaking sound. Her eyes itched and her mouth tasted like fuzzy carpet. She needed to brush her teeth, but couldn't bring herself to abandon her vigil. She didn't know how her father slept on nights like this. Maybe he didn't. Maybe he was awake in bed right now, waiting for the sound of his wife's Mitsubishi in the driveway. This summer, for the first time, Erin spent a lot of time thinking about how little she *really* knew about her parents.

As if responding to her thoughts, the air was suddenly full of the high-pitched squeal of a car in dire need of service. Erin's mother's car swung into view at the end of the street and weaved up the path, narrowly avoiding accidents with the neighbors' vehicles. It pulled into the Porter driveway too fast, tearing up the grass on the lawn, hitting the carport pillars, and scratching Jacob Porter's pickup.

From where Erin sat, she could see her mother through the passenger side window. Mom looked happy in a way Erin hadn't seen in a long time—but when she looked over and saw Erin watching, her beatific expression soured, and she looked more like her usual dour, preoccupied self.

Mom climbed from the car with exaggerated care, and made a smooth, dignified line for the front steps.

"You're up early," she said.

"Haven't been to bed yet," Erin said. "What about you? Spent any time in a bed tonight?"

The diffuse quality of her mother's gaze sharpened. "Excuse me?"

Erin stood and got in her mother's face, blocking her way to the front door. Mom smelled clean. Her hair was a little wet, and smelled of Head & Shoulders instead of the usual Pantene. Head & Shoulders was Peter's shampoo, and she hated that this awful woman now smelled like her favorite person.

"Dad called every hospital in three counties, looking for you," Erin said.

Her mother sighed. "He's just being dramatic. You both are. You don't know what it's like being married to that man."

"No, but I know what it's like being your daughter, and it's fucking embarrassing."

Mom hit Erin. Not hard, but Erin wasn't expecting it. Usually, her mother slapped her for backtalk, but this was more like a punch, and it knocked her back. She tripped over the lawn chair, and landed in the grass. She touched her cheek, and her fingers came away bloody. Her mother's engagement ring had broken the skin.

Mom dropped her purse and covered her mouth with her hands, horrified.

"Oh baby. Oh sweetheart, I'm sorry. I didn't mean it."

She shambled forward to help Erin up, but Erin got up on her own, and shoved her mother away. She left her book and notebook in the grass as she ran across the street and through the neighbors' unfenced yards.

Danielle called after her, but Erin didn't stop. She ran as hard and fast as she could. When she stopped, breathing hard, covered in sweat, with a painful stitch in one side, she found herself in the town park. The sky was now gray with predawn light. In a couple of hours, little kids and their parents and babysitters would overrun the place, but for the moment, Erin had it to herself—the playground, the walking path, the basketball/tennis courts, and the world's onetime longest wooden footbridge. She was tempted toward the swings, but skipped them and headed for the bridge instead.

Erin, like Athena, loved this bridge. She walked to the farthest end, the wood groaning beneath her feet before seeming to sigh with relief as she stopped at the center, over the low creek, and braced her hands on the railing. She took deep breaths and tried to stop crying. Nothing her mother did was worth crying over. Erin would not break now.

Except she already had. The tears had come. Erin couldn't discard the memory of her father's resigned, heartbroken expression. She couldn't stop hearing her mother, calling after her as she'd run away.

So she cried, and swallowed the scream she wanted to let loose—and nearly choked on her own breath when a hand squeezed her shoulder.

She turned, fists clenched, but it wasn't her mother. It was Peter Marsh, soft blue eyes lit with concern. He was wearing his PJs—basketball shorts and a white T-shirt—and flip-flops on his feet. She must have been crying harder than she'd realized, because she hadn't heard his approach.

"You scared the shit out of me," she said. "What are you doing here?"

"I woke up early. I had a feeling I should come here." He smiled a little, embarrassed. "I know how it sounds."

Erin wrapped her arms around him and squeezed him close. He didn't ask her why she was crying. He didn't tell her everything would be all right. Instead he hugged her back and caressed the space between her shoulders.

In the grip of such acceptance, the fist around her heart loosened, and when she let Peter go, she felt a little less overwhelmed. She leaned on the railing. He joined her, and together they surveyed the park, their little kingdom for at least the next little while.

"You're so calm," Erin said. "I know my pain. I know Hal's got mommy issues up the wazoo, and, if his relationship with Marsh is any indication, daddy issues, too. Athena is the only one of us who seems to get along with her family—but even she keeps so much stuff from them. You, though. You're just . . . distant. Hard to know."

Peter stared forward, face betraying no tension. "Do you know how my parents died?"

"Sure," she said. "They were in a car accident."

"Did you know I was in the car when it happened?"

"No." Peter had never talked about it, and Erin had never asked.

"I was two years old," he said. "Most people don't remember stuff that young, but I remember this, at least. I was in my car seat in the back. It had been snowing. The roads were icy. Dad lost control. The car flipped, and somehow caught fire. I watched my parents burn. I heard their screams. I smelled their cooked flesh."

"Why weren't you killed, too?"

"I should've been. But when they found me in the back of the car, I was the one thing that hadn't burned." He gave her a brief smile.

"They called it a miracle. My grandfather became my legal guardian. It was like growing up in a boarding school, but without other kids. I learned early that crying or screaming wouldn't get me anywhere with the professor. He wasn't a hugger or a soother. He only listened to logic. Reason. So I learned how to be quiet. To keep a lid on things. I think that's why I'm . . . a little distant. I'm not good at being around other people."

"I can't even imagine what that must have been like," Erin said. "To see your parents die. And here I am crying about my mom stepping out on my dad."

"We all have pain," he said. "Just because mine is real doesn't mean yours isn't."

She leaned closer to him until their elbows touched again.

"I hate it here," she said. "We should leave. Get jobs in Austin. Take the GED and start college early."

"We'd have to give up the Dissonance," he said. "I doubt the professor would start a correspondence course for us."

Erin laughed. "Garrett Thorpe offered me a spot in his coven last summer—but that was before I beat his ass into the earth."

"Would you want that?" Peter asked. He moved away, just far enough their elbows stopped touching.

She leaned closer so they brushed again. "No. I wouldn't want that. I'd rather go without the Dissonance than have to spend another day hanging out with that asshole. I asked *you* to come with me, dummy." She sighed. "But you're right. We need Marsh for now. So maybe we stay long enough to learn everything he has to teach us, and *then* we bail?"

"Deal," he said.

She bumped his shoulder with her own. "I'm serious."

"So am I," he said.

"But you always seem so far away," she said. "I gave up Randy for you, you know. I gave up cheerleading for you. You and the Dissonance, anyway. But every time it feels like we're about to get close, you pull away."

He seemed to have no answer for that. As they stood in the quiet, the sky turned from gray to pink, and the view from the bridge looked like a Norman Rockwell/Thomas Kinkade mashup.

"It's almost pretty right now," she said. "The park, I mean."

"What would make it all the way pretty?"

She glanced down at the creek. It was July, so there was still a bit of water, but come August it would become a ditch, a dry divot in the earth. Even now, it was difficult to believe this tiny body of water could ever rise above its banks, let alone flood the park and necessitate the bridge.

"Water," she said. "I wish I could see this place flood like it did in the 1800s."

Peter's gaze remained fixed on some distant, far-off spot, but his eyes narrowed and his jaw tightened with concentration. Yellow-green light sparked in the air and Erin startled, realizing only belatedly that his fingers were moving—and because she was focused on that, she wasn't paying proper attention to the quiet roar when it began behind her, disrupting the morning stillness. She barely turned in time to see the wave of water accelerating up the length of the creek toward the bridge. It stood at least eight feet tall, and seemed to hasten as it approached.

Erin didn't have time to brace herself, and shrieked as the wall of icy water broke against the bridge and soaked her from head to toe. For the second time that morning she was knocked backward—but this time, Peter was there. She stumbled back against his chest, and he grabbed her by the arms to steady her as the water passed and calmed, spreading out to flood the entire park and turn it into a giant puddle.

He let go of her and she turned around to look at him. His blond hair was plastered to his head, and his clothes were stuck to his body. She realized the same must be true of her, and felt her entire body prickle into a mass of gooseflesh. She tried not to look down, and admirably, for once, Peter maintained perfect eye contact.

This was his gift—the earth, the water, the things that grow and flow. He'd put it to work for her, given her a little tsunami to cheer her up and drown her tears. He opened his mouth and closed it again.

"Is there something you want to say to me, Peter?" she said.

He nodded, took a deep breath and sighed heavily. "I think about you every day when I wake up, and I dream about you when I go to sleep at night. All I want to do is touch you. Like all the time. But I'm scared. I don't know how to start unless you do it first."

"It's easy. Like this." She grabbed his face and pulled it close to give him a practical demonstration.

Soon the humidity would start to pick at her. She would want dry clothes, a shower, a nap, and the comforts of central air. But that was in the future. Right now, she had everything she wanted. It was the most perfect her life had ever been or would be: soaking wet and kissing Peter Marsh for the first time on that wonderful, stupid bridge.

Hal

A week after Peter and Erin's first kiss, Hal dreamed of the Temple of Pain. At least, it seemed like a dream at first. One moment, he was sighing into his pillow, and the next, he found himself in a great empty space, lit only by a tiny speck of light. And yet, this didn't *feel* like a dream. It didn't have that distant, hazy quality. This all seemed too real.

"Am I really here?" he asked.

His question was met by silence.

"You know, I've gotta say. My favorite part of being your champion is this easy back-and-forth we have," he said. "Open communication is the key between human pawns and supernatural powers, that's what I always say. Just look at God and Abraham. Thick as thieves, those two."

Your destiny approaches, the Temple said, in that vibrating internal voice that sent shivers down Hal's spine. *Inch by inch.*

"Terrific," Hal said. "Any chance you can tell me more?"

A wave of agony rippled across Hal's shoulders and sent him to his knees. He caught himself with his hands and gritted his teeth.

Your insolence makes you strong, the voice said. *But do not mistake your place. You are our servant, and will address us with respect.*

"This shit again?" Hal managed, through the pain. "You know, you and my mentor should start a club. You could call it 'People and Things Who Condescend to Hal.' I already told you. Kill me if you want to. I'm not going to beg."

The pain stopped immediately. Hal remained on his hands and knees, breathing hard for a moment.

The woods, the voice said. *Look to the woods.*

Hal wanted to ask more questions, but as he lifted his head to do so, he found himself back in his bed, facing his alarm clock. It was 5 a.m., and there was a sound of someone fumbling with the front door. At first, Hal thought it must be a burglar, and he stretched his left arm into the air to summon the Blade. Then he woke up a little more and realized he'd heard the deadbolt turn. A burglar wouldn't have keys. Also, what the hell did Hal and his mother have that a burglar would want? Hal's Nintendo 64? The VCR that ate one quarter of all the tapes you inserted?

He dropped his arm and got out of bed. He arrived at the front door as his mom shuffled through it, a cardboard box balanced in her arms. A framed photo of Hal stuck out of the box like a cherry atop this shitty sundae, and he understood what had happened before she opened her mouth.

"They fired me. Didn't even let me finish my shift."

"Mom," he said. This was the third job she'd lost in the last four years.

She picked the picture of Hal up out of the box. It had been taken when Hal was six. He wore a Hawaiian print button-down shirt and khakis and grinned a gap-toothed smile from beneath a chili bowl mop of dark hair as he pointed a water pistol at the camera.

"You were such a sweet little boy," she said. "So loving. So happy."

"Mom," he repeated. He didn't want to look at the picture, at the awful shirt and asinine haircut. The kid whose mother dressed him like a villain on *Miami Vice*. "What happened?"

She dropped the picture in the box. "My boss came to the station. He said I was sleeping on the job."

"Were you?"

"No," she said, indignant. "I was resting my eyes."

"Mom," Hal said.

"You don't know what it's like!" she said. "Working that job. You're all alone in this dark little booth with nothing but bad music to keep you company."

Except for the bad music part, it sounded to Hal like a dream job. No one to bother you, and all you had to do was send songs and commercials into the ether, maybe run your mouth for a few minutes an hour. Seemed like an impossible job to fuck up—and yet his mother had found a way.

"What are we going to do?" he asked.

"I'll find another job."

"And when you get fired again?" Hal said. "This isn't a big town. You're running out of possible employers."

"If it's so easy, maybe you should go get a job. I'll stay home and criticize you every day. How does that sound?"

Hal was sixteen. Sixteen was the *earliest* most places hired. They preferred seventeen. Hal knew because he'd checked, tried to prepare for this exact situation. He'd put in an application at Kinney's convenience store, hoping they wouldn't blacklist him since Lorna had worked there for a little while, as well as the Winn-Dixie in town, but had never heard back. It would probably be at least a year before Hal could "help out" with the rent, and although he knew the day was coming, he dreaded it. His mother would start to rely on him. He would become the family earner, and if he let it, this would become his life: living with his weird, unemployable mother, paying rent on this shitty apartment. No college. No escape from Clegg. He'd seen it happen to kids ahead of him at school—tied to a job at Winn-Dixie at seventeen so their parents didn't end up on the street, or worse, on welfare. He'd seen the lights go out of his classmates' eyes once they gave in and let inertia and poverty do their things.

As he searched for a way to explain this to his mother, Reggie wandered out of Lorna's bedroom, shirtless, scratching his stomach and blinking.

"What's going on out here?" he said.

Hal leaned around his mother to look at Reggie. "Your girlfriend got fired from another job."

"Oh shit. For real?" Reggie said.

Lorna nodded. She looked so pathetic with her box full of possessions. Hal felt an irreconcilable mix of pity and disgust.

Then she put the box down on the dining room table and ran into Reggie's arms.

"Oh baby," Reggie said. "That job was shit anyway."

Something about Reggie's words—and the image of the two of them holding one another—flushed all the pity out of Hal, leaving only the disgust. He went back to his room, shut the door, dressed with numb hands, and put his favorite Bad Religion album in his Discman. When he came back out, his headphones were on and the volume was turned all the way up. He slammed the front door behind himself.

He didn't have a destination in mind. Where could he go anyway? The sun wasn't up yet.

He could visit Athena. He was supposed to go over to her house later today. But she liked to sleep in, so she might yell at him if he showed up now. And Hal wouldn't be any fun anyway. Athena shouldn't have to put up with him in this state. He needed to be alone. He needed to keep moving.

For a while, the wailing guitars and insane punk rock percussion did their job. Hal moved at a good clip, bobbing his head, the sidewalks of town all to himself. But there was only enough town for about an album and a half of listening. When he hit the middle of *Stranger Than Fiction* for the second time, he found himself at the edge of the Clegg woods.

Hal suddenly remembered his dream/vision from the Temple. *Look to the woods*. The woods Professor Marsh had made the coven promise to stay out of.

They didn't look dangerous today, but if they were? So much the better. Hal wanted trouble. He wanted an excuse to summon the Blade. To chop something in half. To see some more of this destiny which had been promised to him.

He barreled ahead into the trees, walking forward and looking for a fight.

He was still looking for that fight when his Discman's batteries died. Frustrated, he kicked a bunch of leaves and sticks, and plopped down on a fallen log to catch his breath. He was covered in sweat, and his shirt was already soaked through, so he couldn't even wipe his forehead clean. Christ, it was hot. He wished he'd brought some water. Why did he have to live in such a fucking oven of a town? When Hal graduated high school, he planned to move somewhere cold. Somewhere it snowed six months a year. He'd buy a house with a big back deck and a Jacuzzi where he could sit toasty as a bun, watch the snow fall, and relax.

Relax with who?

The question came from deep inside. It sounded playful, as if the speaker already knew his answer, but wanted him to admit it. *Who do you see when you close your eyes? Cynthia Brofur? Denise Hunt? Samantha Rone?*

"Shut up," he said, out loud.

Have you seen Athena in a bathing suit since you were little kids? She's probably a one-piece sort of gal, but maybe not? If she felt safe, and it was just the two of you, maybe she'd try something a bit more revealing?

"Shut up," he said. It wasn't that he didn't like to picture girls in scanty outfits. It was one of the major vocations of his life. He was sixteen. His body was on fire all day every day. But when Athena entered his mind's eye, when he thought about how it had felt to carry her through the woods two summers ago, how warm and soft and full she felt, he grew nervous and unhappy. He didn't understand why, but he also never examined the feeling too closely.

And now, working so hard at *not* picturing Athena in a bikini, he'd pictured her in a white bikini that shone like sunlight against her dark skin. Goddammit.

He was trying to decide what to do about it (if a man jerked off in the woods, and no one saw it, did it even happen?) when he heard the song. At first he thought his Discman must've found a little extra juice, but then he realized 1) the music sounded nothing like Bad Religion, and 2) it wasn't coming from his headphones, but from somewhere close by. It was a high, clear sound like the ringing of a bell, out of place here among the dirt and fallen leaves. It didn't sound human.

He experienced a second's wariness—this was probably the sort of thing Marsh had warned them about, when he'd told them not to come back in here—but put the wariness aside. He'd come into the woods looking for destiny. This seemed to fit the bill.

The sound led Hal to a wide hole in the forest floor, perfectly round, as though carved by a stencil. Despite the sunlight streaming through the trees above, the hole was pitch-black, inscrutable. Hal stood and listened to the aching melody until it stopped.

"Hello?" he said. When a few seconds passed without reply, he added, "Is someone down there?"

A voice echoed up out of the hole—deeper than the song, but still unmistakably the singer: "Are you going to stand out there all day, or are you going to come in?"

A thrill of simultaneous fear and excitement unfurled in his gut. This was probably a terrible idea. He could get himself killed if he dropped into this hole.

Or you could go back to your unemployed mom and her shitty boyfriend.

He stepped off the edge. The daylight disappeared, and he fell a short way before he landed, feetfirst, on hard stone. He grunted as pain shot up from his feet into his calves and knees, but the pain passed quickly, and he forgot about it as his eyes adjusted to the darkness.

He was in a small, round cave. Half the chamber was stone floor, and the other half was occupied by a sunken circular pool. Blue light shone up from beneath the surface of the water and danced on the crystalline ceiling, creating a psychedelic riff on the starry night sky. The water rippled as a figure glided across the surface toward him, silhouetted against the blue lights. It halted at the edge.

It looked like a woman, but with black orbs for eyes and silvery skin that glinted with thousands of tiny reflections of the light. The creature propped herself up on the edge of the pool. The insides of her elbows were webbed, but the fingers seemed human.

"Hello," she said. Her speaking voice had the same otherworldly quality as her singing, and something in Hal trembled, and he felt pinpricks of tears in his eyes. He tried to blink them back. Why would a voice, no matter how lovely, make him cry? It made no sense.

"Hi," Hal said. His own voice sounded thick, and he cleared his throat. It occurred to him that the woman in the pool might be naked, and he experienced a flash of his aborted hot tub fantasy about Athena. He turned his gaze up toward the sparkling ceiling and willed his hard-on not to return. If it did, this creature with the beautiful voice would have a front-row seat, and how disrespectful would that be?

Very, he decided, with a deep breath.

"You should sit, if you mean to stay awhile," the woman said. "Get comfortable."

Hal sat cross-legged, far enough from the edge of the pool that the woman would have to get out if she wanted to grab him.

"What is your name, traveler?" she asked.

"Hal Isaac. Who are you?"

"My name is Morgan."

"Do you live here?"

"I've been imprisoned here. So yes, I live here, but not by choice."

"Imprisoned?"

"By an evil wizard who wants to make use of my gifts."

"You mean your singing voice?"

Hal had read stories where people threw back their heads and laughed, but he wasn't sure he'd ever seen it in real life. That changed now, as Morgan tilted her face up and laughed. Again the space behind his eyes tingled with threatened tears. What the hell was going on here?

When her laughter died away, she spoke again: "You don't know, do you?"

"Should I?" Hal said.

Her apparent puzzlement grew. "How did you get here?"

"I went for a walk in the woods outside the town where I live," Hal said. "I stopped to catch my breath and heard you singing. I followed your voice, and found a hole in the ground, and, well—" He gestured at the ceiling, where there ought to be a hole, but it had sealed behind him. He could see no way out. It was troubling, but best to deal with one thing at a time. "Well, you saw the rest," he finished.

She let go of the edge of the pool and floated backward, head partially submerged, so only her eyes were visible above the surface. Her black hair floated around her like an inkblot, and she narrowed her eyes at him.

"This isn't a trick," he said. "I think I'm trapped in here now, too. Tell me—did you see the enormous hole in the ceiling when I came through?"

Morgan continued to study him. She swam back to the edge of the pool and raised her head above the lip. "You are clueless, aren't you?"

"That's me. A regular grade-A dummy. Well, grade-C if we're being honest."

If she understood the joke, she didn't find it funny.

"I'm an undine," she said.

"What's an undine?"

"A cosmic elemental. I swim the deeps between worlds."

"What, like in outer space? Like the Silver Surfer?"

"I haven't met any silver surfers," she said.

"He's a made-up character," Hal said. "He rides a surfboard through outer space, hunting for planets for his boss to eat." He shook his head as he finished. "I'm sorry, I know it sounds silly. I'm just trying to understand."

"You're equating 'world' with 'planet,'" she said. "Let me try another, more accurate phrasing: I swim the deeps between 'realities' or 'universes.'"

"There's more than one reality?" Hal said. So Professor Marsh was right. Holy shit.

"There are infinite realities. A wizard from one of these realities captured me because he wanted to steal my gifts. When I refused, he locked me in here. He's trying to wait me out."

"Oh my God," Hal said. This could be the answer to the Dissonance. The reason why the universe—or multiverse—was broken. This could be huge. "Wait, though," he said, as the rest of what she'd said sank in. "Surrender your gifts?"

"An undine can make that choice, yes."

"But you swim between realities. Why not just swim to one where this wizard can't find you?" *And take me with you,* he didn't add.

"This place dampens my power," she said, gesturing at the cave. "But not yours."

"I don't have powers," he said. "Not like you, anyway. All I can do is this." He extended his left arm and concentrated. The prickle started in his fingertips and rolled burning up his arm. The Blade materialized in his hand, its green light bright and strange against the blues of the cave.

Morgan backed up from the edge of the pool, eyes wide. Hal stepped away from her.

"No, it's okay," he said. "I won't hurt you."

"How did you come to possess the Blade of Woe?" Morgan asked.

"I was chosen as champion."

"Who are you?"

"I told you. Hal Isaac." He shrugged. "I'm nobody."

"You can't be nobody," Morgan said. "Not if you're in thrall to that weapon."

She started to say more, but her voice became distorted, then dropped away entirely, as if the world was on mute. After the sound, the color drained away, and everything seemed to slow down, so that Hal seemed to be looking at a photograph rather than occupying a real space. Then, something invisible grabbed hold of his body and yanked him backward, hard. He let go of the sword as the cave disappeared, and he flew through darkness. It felt less like falling and more like he'd been thrown up in the air. He closed his eyes and braced himself for the inevitable landing.

The fall itself actually wasn't too bad—less like plummeting off a skyscraper and more like tripping while walking. Hal landed in dirt and leaves and filtered sunlight, and gasped in a lungful of stifling heat. He'd returned to the forest floor.

He sat up. The hole in the earth—his path to Morgan—had disappeared.

Athena

In the weeks after her "come to Jesus" talk with Professor Marsh, Athena grew increasingly frustrated. First, Hal stopped showing up to their one-on-one tutoring sessions. He still came to the group training, but stopped hanging around after and instead took off right away. She tried to tell herself that this was a good thing. That Hal was relieving her of any responsibility for his future. That he wasn't going to try and drag her down with him.

And maybe that thought would have cheered her up, if she'd made any real progress with her original command line. In the past few weeks, she'd had dozens of ideas, and still possessed no clue how to make any of them work. She spent day after day pacing the length of her bedroom, trying to force inspiration to take hold.

"Brand-new Dissonant command," she murmured to herself, as she paced. "Only characters I already know." It had become a mantra. Characters she already knew. Simple characters, like the elements, darkness, light. Kiddie stuff. Nothing that would put her in the history books.

She was in this state of ecstatic agitation one Sunday morning when her thoughts were interrupted by the doorbell. She wasn't expecting any visitors, especially not this early. She ran across the house and threw open the door, half-hoping and half-dreading that she would find Hal on the front porch—but it was Erin, eyes puffy, shoulders slumped, backpack over one shoulder, purse over the other.

"Hey," Athena said, after an uncomfortable moment of silence. "What's up?"

Erin leaned in so fast that Athena thought the other girl was falling, but then Erin's arms closed around Athena, and she understood she was being hugged. As usual, Athena's first reaction was alarm and discomfort, but she hugged back, trying to match Erin's grip, to show she did understand and care.

"Mom left," Erin said. "Took her bags this morning. She's going to live with Alan Sturgess."

It was about time. Shouldn't Erin be feeling relieved the tension was finally over? The worst thing had happened. Now she could move on.

"I'm sorry," Athena said.

"I'm not," Erin said, into the top of Athena's head. "Good fucking riddance."

Athena wasn't sure how to respond. *You don't mean that?* Or *Yeah, fuck her?* What would Emily Post recommend?

"Do you want to come in?" she said instead.

She led Erin into the house. She offered her a cup of coffee, which Erin accepted, and then they went to Athena's bedroom. Erin set her backpack down on Athena's desk. "I thought maybe we could study together," she said. She pulled a spiral notebook from the bag, along with the legendarium about the Temple.

"How's it coming?" Athena said. They were back on safe ground. Homework. Academic stuff. Dissonant.

"Slow and awkward," Erin said. "Why would someone write a narrative in Dissonant? It's a language of function, not communication. It would be like writing an entire book in math equations. Worse, a lot of Dissonant characters offer multiple interpretations, and I'm worried I'm losing things in translation. At this point I might as well stand next to Hal while he reads and interrupt him after every sentence to explain other possible meanings. But you want to know what the worst part is?"

"What's what?"

"This Temple? I think it's dangerous."

"It *is* called the Temple of Pain."

"Ha-ha. But seriously. There's this weird undercurrent in the stories," Erin said. "It's hard to explain. This sense of something bigger. But I can't find an explicit mention or explanation of what the threat might be. You'll laugh, but it's almost like the book is—"

"Taunting you?" Athena said.

"Yes," Erin said. She set down the books on the desk and crossed her arms, looking for a moment like Professor Marsh. "How did you know I was going to say that?"

Athena explained her own struggles with *Music of the Infinite*. How the book seemed to push her attention away. Promising secret knowledge but refusing to impart any. Clouding her mind every few sentences.

She picked up *Music* off her desk. "I thought this would be easy. I thought I'd have been done a month ago."

"Me too," Erin said. "For you, I mean. Not for me."

"Can I see what you have?" Athena said.

Erin handed over the notebook with her translation in it. "Remember, I'm no poet."

Athena sat on the bed and flipped through the pages until she came to the last narrative Erin had transcribed.

The Tale of Artigue

1. *In those days, in a land with a long-forgotten name, there lived a woman named Artigue. She was unsatisfied with the gifts of earthly life. Her ambitions extended beyond the pleasantries of food, drink, and flesh. She wanted more. More life, more knowledge, more pleasure.*

2. *She visited the temples of her land, listened to the wisdom of the hierophants. Their words sounded like lies told by the powerful, to keep the powerless obedient.*

3. *Artigue suspected the Truth, but no one she spoke to understood. They were content with life as it appeared to be. In despair, Artigue ate and drank to excess. She brought men and women to her bed, often at the same time, and paid them to fulfill her every lustful daydream. She might have spent the remains of her life this way, but for one chance encounter.*

4. *One woman Artigue brought to bed was secretly a priestess of the Temple. This priestess recognized in Artigue a kindred spirit, and invited her into a secret organization of seekers, those who knew that pain and discord rule the universe. They called themselves the Scarred Congregation.*

5. Artigue rose quickly in the Scarred Congregation. She allowed herself to be Marked, her earthly beauty transformed into something truer, so the pleasures of the flesh could not distract her.

6. She studied at the feet of the priests and priestesses. She read all she could, especially about the Temple of Pain. Some Scarred believed the Temple legend, but Artigue sought its location. This, she thought, would be the heart of the truth she sought.

7. It is whispered that the Temple was intrigued with this mortal, as it had not been intrigued in ages. And so, when Artigue's years on earth reached the count of fifty, the Temple presented itself to her and offered her entrance.

8. Artigue entered the Temple and prostrated herself. She made promises to bathe the world in Pain if the Temple would bless her with Wisdom.

9. The Temple offered Artigue the Trial of Agony, and she agreed. She was proud and considered herself an expert in pain. But when the test was upon her, she found herself unprepared for the Holy Anguish.

10. Artigue wept and screamed and begged for release. The Temple balked at this rebuff of its sacred gift. It released Artigue, but not before severing her right arm and tearing the tongue from her head, and leaving a mark on her face, one its followers would read as "Imperfect."

11. Artigue returned to this world with no way to tell her story. When the Scarred found the Mark of Imperfection upon her, they stripped her of rank and cast her out of the Congregation. No tales tell of what befell her after.

12. The Temple waits for its next champion, the one who will pass the Trial and draw the Blade of Woe, and spread the one Truth.

When Athena finished reading, she handed the notebook back. "I don't know about the fidelity, but the writing is good. Although—if this Artigue had no way to tell her story, how did it end up in this book?"

Erin looked relieved. "Your guess is as good as mine. And thanks."

She riffled through the pages. "The book's full of stories about people who see or go to the Temple or do its bidding, but it's all second- or thirdhand information. Like, in the gospels, we're supposedly getting the accounts of people who traveled with Christ and saw everything or could confirm with primary sources. This is more like scripture by way of tabloids. It's someone who heard something from someone else. The stories are creepy and vague, but there are never any rules or laws or explanation of what the Temple is or where it came from or what it wants. Whoever recorded these stories doesn't offer commentary. Only a prefatory note which explains fuck-all."

"What does Hal think about it?"

"I haven't told him yet," Erin said. "Every time I call his house, his mom says he's out."

"Probably a new girlfriend," Athena said. Trying to sound like she didn't care.

"I don't think so," Erin said. "I was with Peter the other day, and he said he'd seen Hal heading into the woods at least three times in the last week. All by himself."

"Did he say what Hal was doing out there?"

"Peter didn't follow him. He said Hal will tell us when he's ready."

"Are we talking about the same Hal?" Athena said. The Hal she knew would die before surrendering a secret. He never came to the group with his feelings or problems.

"If only we could just teleport into the woods and spy on him," Erin said.

And as soon as she said it, Athena's brain fog burned away. In one intuitive burst, she had her summer project.

"What?" Erin said. "What is it?"

Athena shushed her. She sat at her desk and began to write in her *Cookbook,* only stopping to check previous notes. She copied a character here, combined a few others there. Once she was sure of the characters, she rearranged them, then rearranged them again. And again. On the fourth try, they looked right.

She stood. "Think of a place you want to go right now," she said. "Someplace you've been before."

"I never mind going to the movies," Erin said.

Athena stood in the middle of the room, the *Cookbook* open in her left hand while she drew in the air with her right. The air warmed and crackled around her. Her yellow-green characters lingered and pulsed with energy. She set the *Cookbook* on the floor, and used both hands to draw a rectangle that started above her head and extended down to the floor. She stood and pushed at the empty space in the center. A hole opened in the middle of the room. Through it, Athena peered into the cool dark of an auditorium at the movie theater in Tyler. Some film was already in progress.

Athena picked up her *Cookbook* and leaned around the hole to look at Erin sitting on the bed. "Come on."

Erin stood and joined Athena before the door. She gaped, then grinned.

They stepped into the auditorium, and Athena closed the door behind them with a clench of her fist. They took seats near the back of the mostly empty theater. None of the other midday patrons turned to look at them. No one noticed.

The movie was about a bunch of teenagers trying to get laid, and working out their feelings about high school graduation and love. Not Athena's kind of film, but Erin, who enjoyed most movies, already looked—not happy, exactly, but content. The open despair she'd worn on Athena's front porch had vanished, at least for a little while. Athena settled in, relaxed, and let the comedic melodrama unreel before her.

But although she remained calm with her eyes on the screen, her mind moved back to their conversation about Hal. About what it might mean that this Temple had chosen him.

And what the hell was he doing out in the woods?

Erin

On a weekend in late July, Professor Marsh went out of town for a few days. He told the coven to keep at their assignments, and promised to give them their final summer evaluations upon his return.

"Where are you going?" Erin asked.

"Two places. First, I have to meet with the Council of the Word."

"What for?" Athena said.

"An 'intellectual audit,'" Marsh said, throwing up quote signs with his fingers. "Something they subject me to periodically, to try and wear down my resistance to their way of thinking."

"And you have to go?"

"If I don't cooperate, they're more likely to send someone out here for a true audit," Marsh said. "And let's just say I'd rather not have some Dissonant accountant poking around in our business."

"What's the other place you're going?" Hal asked.

Here, Marsh smiled. "For the past three summers, you've been helping me investigate perhaps the largest mystery in existence. The same mystery I've been investigating since I was only a little older than you are now. I'm going to meet some associates. If I'm lucky, I'll be coming back with a clue. One of the big puzzle pieces we still lack. If I get it, it will change everything."

He'd refused to say any more about it at the time, but rather dismissed them.

The day after he left, Erin and Athena called a coven meeting. They gathered in the backyard of Marsh House, where Peter showed them his greenhouse. Even though Erin and Peter were officially together and had been for weeks, this was the first time he'd asked her into the greenhouse, to show her his experiments.

The interior was cramped, and far more colorful than Erin would've guessed—clumps of technicolor flowers next to a purple cactus and a bush covered in crimson berries, amid a profusion of lush green plants—all of which seemed to be thriving and healthy despite the brutal Texas heat. Peter really did have a gift.

He picked a few of the crimson berries off the bush and handed them around.

"You can eat them," he said. "They're good."

Erin popped one in her mouth, as did the others. It was mushy like a blueberry, but sweet like a grape. She made an appreciative sound, and followed Peter to a tree at the greenhouse's edge. It looked like an ordinary Virginia pine, the sort you'd cut down and throw up in your living room at Christmastime.

"Stand a little closer," Peter said.

All three visitors shuffled into the tree's personal space. Its branches wobbled and a blast of cold air washed over them, gifting a chill to the sweat on Erin's brow, arms, and legs. It felt like standing in front of a window-mounted A/C unit.

"You made an air-conditioning tree?" she said.

"I call it a Douglas Brrr," he said. "It breathes in carbon dioxide like any other tree, but chills oxygen before exhaling it out into the air."

"That's amazing," Athena said, sounding truly impressed.

"For real," Hal said. "You've been busy."

"Since you helped out, sure," Peter said.

"What do you mean?" Athena said.

"I mean," Peter said, "Hal performed a small miracle earlier this summer." He launched into a story then, one Erin hadn't heard before. How Hal had come into the greenhouse, picked up a dead glow-in-the-dark potato, and how said potato had suddenly come back to life again. How Peter and Hal had replanted the potato in soil. How, as long as Peter pulled soil from the planter with the revived potato, everything he planted had taken root and grown.

"So everything," Peter said, gesturing at all his wondrous creations, "everything I've been able to do this summer? It runs on potato power."

"How did you do that?" Athena said to Hal.

"I have no idea," Hal said. "I'm not sure it was me, to be honest. I just happened to be holding the potato when it came back to life."

"That's what makes it a miracle," Peter said. "It's a mystery."

"And an interesting one," Erin said. "But it's not why we're here."

"No?" Hal said. "Are there further wonders to behold? A carrot that will give me a handjob?"

"Hal," Athena said.

Hal looked around, and appeared to realize everyone was staring at him. He dropped the smile.

"What?" he said.

Athena and Peter looked at Erin. Since the intervention had been her idea, she was acting as de facto spokesperson for the rest of the coven.

"We know you've been going into the woods by yourself."

"You've been spying on me?" Hal said.

"Not on purpose," Erin said. "Athena and I told Peter how we've been trying to reach you lately, but you're never home. Peter told us he's seen you coming and going while he's working in the greenhouse."

Hal's expression fluctuated. "Traitor," he said to Peter. Peter looked appropriately stung as Hal turned to the girls: "I've been going into the woods. So what?"

"You know we aren't supposed to," Athena said.

"I know Marsh told us not to," Hal said. "That's not a moral imperative."

"You want to argue technicalities?" Athena said.

"No, I want to know why you're all ganging up on me. Marsh gave you projects. I got nothing."

"What are you doing out there?" Erin asked, recentering the conversation.

"Why do you care?"

"Because you're part of this, you asshole," Athena said. "This coven. We leave you messages, you never call back. We want to know why you're ignoring us."

Hal's expression fluctuated into confusion. "You left messages?"

"Two or three times a week," Erin said. "For like three weeks now. Always with your mom."

His shoulders tensed as his face softened. "God*dammit*, Mom."

"You haven't been getting the messages," Athena said, realizing the truth as she said it.

"Not a one," Hal said. "I figured you'd call if you needed me, and as far as I knew, it wasn't happening."

"Why haven't you been home?" Erin asked again.

"I've been working on a project of my own," Hal said. "Independent study I made up for myself. And maybe it's good you ganged up on me, because I'm stuck right now."

"Tell us," Peter said.

So Hal performed his own verbal "What I Did on Summer Vacation" essay. He told them about the trapped undine and how he'd been searching for the cave's entrance again ever since, with no luck.

"Luck?" Athena said. "You're lucky you got out of there alive. That thing could've eaten or drowned you."

"I don't think so," Hal said. "She seemed okay."

"What about this evil wizard who imprisoned her?" Peter asked.

"I don't know," Hal said. "She's an interdimensional being; comic books have taught me those tend to make a lot of enemies."

"*If* she's telling the truth," Athena said. "Did it ever occur to you the whole thing could've been a trap? Or that whoever imprisoned her did it for a good reason? And whatever yanked you out of the cave saved your life?"

"Sure, it occurred to me," Hal said. "And everything you're saying makes logical sense. But I don't know. I have a gut feeling, you know? All that suspicion feels wrong somehow. And I had another vision of the Temple. It told me to 'Look to the woods.' That's where I found Morgan. It all seems to connect, you see?"

Athena scoffed and rolled her eyes.

"The Temple has not exactly established itself as a benevolent force," she said. "You should see what Erin's been translating this summer. I don't think we can trust it."

Hal tensed up and Erin foresaw the onset of a verbal battle. After weeks of listening to her parents yell at each other, first through the papery walls at home, and more recently, on the phone, Erin refused to listen to more shouting. She put herself between Hal and Athena and raised her hands. For a wonder, they both held their tongues.

She allowed several seconds of silence to lapse before she asked, "What do you want to do, Hal?"

"Whether I was breaking the professor's rules or not—whether I was acting like an idiot or not—I found someone in distress," Hal said. "And what is the point of all of this"—he gestured at the group, the house, the woods, and the power that hung invisible but tangible in the air around them—"if we don't help when we can?"

"We can't go into the woods without Marsh," Athena said. "We have no idea what an undine is or can do, or if this Morgan is telling the truth."

"Of course you'd stick up for Marsh's rules and parrot his bullshit," Hal said. "You're his favorite."

Now Athena tensed up, her shock hardening into anger. "You're just mad you got caught breaking the rules. And you also resent me because I always beat you at the only thing you're supposed to be good at."

"The only reason you win those duels," Hal said, "is because your beloved old wizard makes me fight with a massive fucking handicap."

"Or maybe you're a lazy student," Athena said.

"Athena," Erin said, in a tone that sounded amazingly like her own mother's scolding voice.

"He started it," Athena said.

"Enough!" Peter shouted, so loud he startled the rest of the group into silence. Glowering at the coven, he looked a lot like his grandfather: dour and authoritative. "Athena, my grandfather clearly favors you, and rides Hal like a donkey. He may have good reason for it. It might be how he's training each of us, tailoring to our strengths and weaknesses—or maybe he's playing you against one another."

"You think he'd do that?"

"I don't know," Peter said. "I've lived with him for as long as I can remember, and I don't have a good idea of what he would or wouldn't do. I don't *know* him. But I know you three." He gestured around the greenhouse. "And I know you're all badasses, and the *only* time I'd be scared of losing a fight is if I were fighting one of you. The four of us together? Moving in the same direction? We're *invincible*."

The group stood around. More silence elapsed.

"You didn't have to yell," Hal grumbled.

"We were just talking," Athena said.

"You two are the worst," Erin said. "But I think Hal is right. Regardless of the Temple's intentions, I want to help Morgan." She gave Athena a meaningful look. "I think maybe we're supposed to."

"What makes you think that?" Hal said. "Not that I'm complaining to have your support."

Athena sighed. "She's saying she thinks it's destiny because I finished my summer project, and it might be the key to helping your cosmic elemental girlfriend."

"She's not my girlfriend," Hal said.

"You finished your project?" Peter asked Athena.

"Yeah. I created a command that opens doorways between places far apart. I've only used it to do local stuff, like sneak me and Erin into the movies, but there's no reason to think it couldn't work over a longer distance, or help us find a prison whose entrance moves. But I think it's dangerous to assume the higher power at work here is benevolent. That's what Marsh is always warning us against. Pretending the Abrahamic God is guiding us. We can't absolve ourselves of our choices by saying it was written in the stars or God made us do it. We have this power and we're responsible for how we use it. If we try to rescue Morgan and it turns out to be a trap, or a mistake, that's our mistake, not destiny."

"If it's a mistake, it's the right kind of mistake," Hal said. "I'd be okay dying trying to help someone."

"Me too," Erin said.

"Same here," Peter said. Erin could've kissed him, then. She *would* kiss him later, when they'd sorted all of this out.

"I'm outvoted," Athena said. She sat back at the table. "If we're going to do this, we might as well make a plan."

Hal

In the weeks since she'd lost the job at KART, Lorna Isaac had yet to find new employment. Instead, she'd let Reggie move into the apartment, and now she slept during the day while Reggie worked, and spent the evenings smoking and drinking with him. Hal had never seen his mother smoke before, and was disgusted how easily she picked up the habit. It was like she had no personality of her own.

Then there was Reggie himself. Reggie didn't hit, or yell, but he always seemed like he might, if things didn't go his way. Also, there was something creepy and possessive in the way he touched Hal's mother. Lorna never seemed to touch Reggie back, but rather allowed herself to be touched and owned, seeming neither to like nor dislike it.

The night after the intervention at Marsh House looked like a rerun of the usual at the apartment. Reggie and Lorna sprawled across the living room couch, legs tangled, eyes glassy, their cigarettes winking at one another in the dark. Hal watched them for a time, feeling disgusted and wishing he was all grown up, free of his mother forever.

But the upshot of Lorna and Reggie's alcoholic, tobacco-fueled sexual drama was that they were distracted when Hal swiped Lorna's keys off the hook by the front door and snuck out of the apartment. With all the bravery his new license allowed, he drove away from the apartment complex, only turning on the headlights when he hit the street.

When he pulled into the driveway of Marsh House a little later, his friends stood on the porch waiting. Erin looked excited, Athena worried, and Peter—well, Peter looked chilled out.

"Everything go okay?" Peter said, as Hal got out of the car.

"No problem," Hal said. He climbed the steps to the front porch. "What about you three? Ready to play Justice League?"

No one answered.

"I'll take that as a unanimous 'meh,' " he said.

They went around the back of the house. Athena placed a hand on Hal's shoulder. "Since this isn't a place I've ever been, I can't promise my doorway command will work."

"You don't know how to fail," Hal said.

She let go long enough to punch him in the arm, hard. "Shut up," she said. But she smiled while she said it, and then opened her hand to put it back on Hal's shoulder. Was it his imagination, or was she gripping him tighter now?

"Close your eyes and picture Morgan's cave," she said. "Fill in as much detail as possible, but only real detail—not embellishment."

Hal shut his eyes and sketched Morgan's cave in his mind. The crystal ceiling, with its stone stars. The blue light in the pool. Morgan herself, floating in the middle, only her eyes visible above the water. He tried to ignore Athena's touch, the sound and smell of her Dissonant command taking shape, the feeling of energy gathering between them like an electric charge.

A wave of Dissonant energy swept past him like a wind, and an ozone stench singed the air.

Athena let go of his arm. "You can open your eyes."

She drew a rectangle, starting above her head and closing it in the grass at her feet. Her fingers left trails of sparking, hissing green light in the shape of a door. When she finished, she stood and thrust a palm through the center of the shape. A hole opened in the world, and a fishy smell wafted out, along with the sound of someone singing. Athena looked half-surprised and half-impressed with herself.

"Athena's Doorway," Hal said. "Told you you could do it." He walked through the portal and into the cave that had haunted him for weeks now. It was just as lovely and otherworldly as he remembered, the blue light from the water dancing on the crystalline ceiling, Morgan the undine floating in the center of the pool, her hair a black, undulating halo around her head. But it smelled worse, like fish sticks that had been left out in the sun all day.

Despite the stink, Morgan's song still sent a wave of gooseflesh across Hal's arms and legs, and a prickling sensation in his eyes.

"Hal," Erin whispered. "She's beautiful."

"Of course she is," Athena grumbled.

Hal kept his eyes on Morgan, and was grateful that the undine stopped singing, so he didn't have to cry in front of his friends.

"It's you," Morgan said.

"It's me," Hal said. "And I brought friends."

"I see." She kept her place in the center of the pool, far from the edge. She looked paler than when Hal had seen her last. Was she sick?

"Is something wrong?" he said.

"I don't like large groups of humans I don't know. It never goes well for me."

"I've been trying to get back here since we first met," Hal said. He gestured at his coven. "These three are the ones who helped make it happen."

"We're here to rescue you," Erin said.

Morgan lazily kicked her legs and waved her arms through the water to stay afloat. "I don't think you understand the implications of your offer. If I step out of this pool, this place will do its best to put me back. If we fail, there will be consequences for all of us."

"Those consequences haven't met my coven," Hal said. This seemed like a good moment for a dramatic gesture, so he extended his left arm from his side. A cascade of fire ran through his body and the Blade materialized in his hand. It was always a rush, and it always, *always* hurt, but this felt like the moment to do it.

"I have a magic sword," Hal said. "And I'm the least powerful member of this group. That should tell you something."

"I don't know how powerful you are," Morgan said. "But you are brave, and I am desperate. As long as you understand the risk—and are willing to give me your word about something."

"What's that?" Hal said.

"If it looks like we're going to fail, you have to kill me. I would rather die on my feet than spend another second in this prison."

"You bet," Athena said, before Hal could answer. "Now can we go? Keeping this doorway open isn't easy." She rubbed her temple with one hand, as she used the other to maintain the portal.

"Are you okay?" Hal said.

"Fine," she said, through gritted teeth. "Feels like someone is trying to shut the door behind us."

Hal stepped to the edge of the pool and kneeled to offer Morgan his free hand. She swam to meet him. Her touch was clammy and cold, and sent a buzz into his body, not unlike the jolt he'd gotten once when he'd been bored and licked the end of a nine-volt battery.

Morgan rose over the lip of the pool and landed on her knees. Hal hadn't seen the undine's legs before—human in shape, with webbed feet, not unlike the Creature from the Black Lagoon. As soon as Morgan touched the stone floor, the blue light beneath the pool turned red and the floor began to shake as part of the cave wall split along a previously invisible seam. Hal almost toppled into the water, and would have, if not for Peter's steadying hand.

The split in the wall widened to reveal a tiled corridor that would look at home in any hospital or office building. Beige walls and fluorescent lights on the ceiling clashed with what Hal had assumed until now was the natural formation of the cave, and the clash became stranger as the fluorescents went dark and a flickering orange light appeared at the end of the corridor.

"Is that fire?" Erin said.

Peter stood transfixed, mouth open like a small child.

"Peter," Hal said. Peter didn't respond. Hal shook his arm and Peter shook him off. He scrunched his face and swiped his hands through the air. The water in Morgan's pool rose as a single body, leaving an empty bowl on one side of the cavern. The mass of fluid hung in the air, a rippling sphere that seemed alive. Not a single drop fell on the floor.

Peter raised his arms above his head and made a throwing gesture toward the hallway. The ball of water rocketed through the seam in the wall like a bullet from a gun, flooding the hallway from top to bottom. The orange light sputtered out.

Hal shouted with triumph, but the shout was cut short as Peter's eyes rolled up into his head and he collapsed.

Athena

Athena Watts—who had invented and now held open a door through space, a door that possibly bridged multiple realities—knew a miracle when she saw one. She also knew miracles came with a cost. Take the doorway she was holding open. Opening it and keeping it open had given her the worst migraine of her life, and the pain was getting worse every second.

So she wasn't surprised when Peter's own miracle caused him to crumple to the ground like paper trash. Through her own near-blinding agony, she saw Hal panic and drop the sword, which disappeared into null space. Erin was observing these proceedings with the same absent, engrossed expression she wore whenever watching a movie, and Athena knew she needed to take charge.

"Erin," she said, through clenched teeth. "Shield the boys."

Erin came alert at Athena's command, and drew Haley's Dome over Morgan and the coven. She helped Hal pick up Peter, gathering the tall boy's legs while Hal lifted his shoulders. Together they carried him out the door. Morgan followed them. Athena crossed through last, but not before she looked down that oddly mundane hallway one more time. It might be her headache playing a trick, but she thought she'd seen that orange light flickering again. The fire reawakening.

She snapped the door shut as soon as she was through, and sat down hard in the grass behind Marsh House. Her head throbbed and the pain clogged her thoughts. The doorway had taken everything she had. Luckily, she didn't need to give anything else. The adventure was over. The good guys had won.

Then she noticed the quiet. Instead of the sounds of people moving, or Hal's and Erin's chatter, there was only the rustling of the trees in the breeze. She was alone in the yard. For a second, she thought she'd left her friends behind, alone with the fire—but no, that wasn't right, because she'd seen them exit through the doorway. Christ, her head hurt. It was hard to think.

She dropped her face into her hands and groaned. The trees rustled their susurration, but she'd been mistaken in thinking there was a breeze. The night air was hot and sticky. She looked up and wondered if she'd given herself an aneurysm, because the trees seemed closer than usual, and larger, their branches hanging lower, as if offering to help her up.

A twig scraped her cheek, and before she could scream, gangly wooden digits closed around her head and lifted her off her feet, the muscles in her neck howling in protest. She grabbed the branches clamped around her skull. She tried to pry them apart, but she might as well have tried to bend steel. The harder she pulled, the tighter the tree gripped. She finally did scream, and the sound was muffled by the wood. If this thing squeezed much harder, her head would burst like a grape. Let it be quick, let the pain end—

"Nope!"

The wood muffled this voice, too, but she recognized it as Hal's. He grunted as he grabbed her legs, trying to keep hold of her. The tree tightened its grip and Athena screamed. Hal let go of Athena, and a second later there followed another of Hal's grunts. The pressure on her head stopped, and she hit the ground, the breath knocked from her lungs.

She sat up, gasping for air. The branch which had been crushing her a moment ago lay severed in the grass. The tree swayed as though in pain, then leaned forward. There was something almost familiar in its bearing, which was ridiculous, because trees didn't have bearings. They were fucking trees. More of its branches touched the ground and skittered toward her, digging troughs in the earth. Athena crab-walked backward toward the house, some primitive impulse telling her to get inside, as if the feeble walls and doors there would—could—protect her from this nightmare.

Why did its movement look so familiar? It was almost like a—

Hal stepped between her and the trees, Blade held at long point guard, feet spread like his beloved Conan the Barbarian.

"I am in a violent mood," he said. "And I haven't gotten to kill *any-thing* yet tonight. I will chop down this entire forest if you don't back the fuck off and leave my friends alone."

One tree—Athena wasn't sure, but *thought* it might be the one that had grabbed her before—swiped a thick limb at Hal. Hal stepped forward beneath the blow, and the Blade slid through the tree's trunk as smoothly as if sailing through empty air. Hal followed the swing with a kick to the trunk, and the attacking tree crashed backward into its fellows. The other trees stood still, their branches wavering in the nonexistent breeze as they sized him up.

"Who's next?" he said.

The parliament of trees groaned and cracked as they retreated to their customary line at the edge of the yard, and blended with their fellows. Except for the felled tree, the gouges in the earth, and the severed branch that had snatched Athena a moment ago, there was no evidence of anything out of the ordinary.

Hal knelt beside Athena and cradled her head in his hands. He turned it back and forth, examining her.

"Hey," he said.

"Hey yourself," she said, and slapped his hands away. "That hurts."

"Sorry," he said. "I guess we know why Marsh told us to stay out of the woods."

"We already had good reasons not to go in there," Athena said.

"Fair. But I wonder why the trees never attacked before?"

"I have a theory," she said. "I'll tell you later when my head doesn't hurt so much." She rubbed her face. "How bad do I look?"

"A couple of scrapes," Hal said. "But I don't know how we explain this one to your dad."

"I'll tell him the truth: a gang of sentient trees attacked me."

Hal laughed and helped her to her feet. "Please let me be there when you do it."

She leaned against him, arm around his waist. "Where are we going?"

"My mom's car. We have to get Morgan to a body of water so she can activate her powers and go home. The creek is too low, and Peter's exhausted his nature tricks for the night, so we're taking a little road trip."

She groaned. "Leave me here. I did my part. I want to sleep." Every step jostled her head and made it worse.

"You were amazing," Hal said. "You deserve all the naps in the world. But the trees are probably still mad, so I think it's best if we give them some time to cool off. Also, if you're concussed, I don't want to come back in a couple of hours and find you in a coma."

She was too tired to press her case. Anyway, it was nice here, beside him. She surrendered control, trusting him to be in charge for a little while.

"Girl could get used to this," she said. "Chivalrously carried or half-carried every time we have an adventure."

They came around the front of the house to find Peter and Erin and Morgan waiting anxiously in the car.

"We thought you were right behind us!" Erin said.

"Gang of sentient trees," Hal said. "I'll explain later."

He helped Athena into the passenger seat. Morgan stank like an indoor seafood market, and Athena's stomach flip-flopped as Hal tried to buckle her in. She leaned out the open door and Hal jumped aside as she vomited in the driveway.

"Why don't we drive with the top down?" Hal said. "That sounds nice, right?"

Erin

Erin sat in the rear passenger seat of Lorna's convertible, behind Athena. Morgan was in the middle, with Peter behind Hal on the driver's side. Erin wished she'd given the seating arrangement more thought before they left. Morgan smelled awful, and Peter was semi-consciously trying to manage a killer nosebleed. She wanted to sit next to him, to help, and feel him close to her.

Aside from the rotten seafood smell and her separation from Peter, it was a good drive—one of those times that seemed both endless and far too brief, like something from a movie—a good one, where the editing and music swept you up in feelings bigger than you knew what to do with. A movie that reminded you why you were happy to be alive.

Up front, Hal poked Athena every few minutes, and peppered her with endless questions to keep her awake. He was being so nice, after Athena had accused him of being a cosmic accident. Did Athena understand how much Hal cared? Erin hoped so. After years of watching her parents dance around the truth and lie to one another, she wanted to know people could be honest. That some loves could strengthen, rather than weaken. That there was a point to trying.

They arrived at Lake Murvaul around midnight, a coven of would-be heroes and a creature out of myth in a stolen car stained with dried vomit and stinking of fish. Athena and Peter stayed in the car while Hal and Erin walked Morgan down to the water's edge. The undine's steps were awkward and unsure, and she gripped their arms for balance. Once in the water, she stood straighter, squared her shoulders, and continued under her own power. Hal and Erin stayed at the water's edge to watch.

When the water was up to her waist, Morgan tilted her head toward the night sky, her hair lustrous, her skin almost silver in the moonlight.

"It's been a long time since I last saw stars," she said. "I've missed them." She turned to face Hal and Erin. "You and your friends did a noble thing tonight."

"We couldn't have lived with ourselves if we hadn't tried to help," Erin said.

"You have my thanks. In return for your good deed, I offer you a boon."

"A boon?" Hal said. "What's a boon?"

"A blessing or a gift," Erin said.

"Cool," Hal said. "Like a suit of magic armor? A pet dragon?"

"I don't know," Morgan said. "The when, where, and what—those aren't my decisions to make."

"Rats," Hal said. "I wanted a dragon."

"Hal Isaac," Morgan said. "You carry the Blade of Woe. To carry the Blade is to stand in thrall to the Temple of Pain. That is no easy burden."

"It hasn't been too bad so far," Hal said.

"It will be," Morgan said. "I hope the boon, whatever it is, helps ease your burden."

"Thank you, Morgan," Erin said. And because the moment seemed to call for it, she leaned forward in a slight bow. Hal mimicked her but went farther, bowing at the waist.

"Farewell," Morgan said.

When Erin raised her head to look, the undine had disappeared beneath the surface.

They returned to the car to find Peter out cold, bloody Kleenex stuffed up each nostril, and Athena on the brink of unconsciousness. Hal honked the car horn and startled them awake.

"Oh, I hate you," Athena groaned. "You are such a fucking dick."

"I like you too much to let you slip into a coma," Hal said.

"Just let me be grumpy," Athena said. "Can't you do that?"

"Yes ma'am," he said.

They started the drive back to Clegg, Athena wide awake and complaining about her head. Somehow Peter slept through the racket, his brow wrinkled, lips moving as he spoke to a dream. Erin was wide awake, but not in the jittery, too-much-coffee way. Instead, she drifted in a rare stillness. For the first time all summer, she was calm.

When they returned to Marsh House, Hal and Erin carried Peter inside and put him in his bed. They pulled the Kleenex from his nose, ready to insert new ones, but the bleeding seemed to have stopped. Hal left to check out the backyard, but Erin lingered and tucked Peter under the blankets. Once she heard the door close behind Hal, she leaned over and kissed Peter's cheek.

He opened his eyes. "Where are we?"

"You're home," she said. "Marsh House."

"Did we win?"

"We did," she said. "I'll tell you about it tomorrow."

She stood and he grabbed her hand. "Wish you'd stay."

She leaned down to kiss him again, this time on the mouth. "Wish I could. Someday soon I'll stay until you get sick of me."

"Never happen," he said, already drifting off.

They took Athena home next. She was still woozy, but alert, so Erin and Hal helped her up the steps to the front porch, but she stopped them at the front door.

"I've got it from here," she said.

"You sure?" Hal asked.

"I'm fine. I'll call you tomorrow when I'm feeling better. And it had better be you who answers the phone this time."

"Yes ma'am," Hal said again. "But before you go—what about the trees?"

"Huh?" Athena said.

"You said you knew what the tree monsters were."

"Oh right," Erin said. "What happened out there?"

Hal quickly caught her up before returning his questioning look to Athena.

"Remember how you killed all those spider-things a couple of years ago?" Athena said. "On our first adventure?"

"Yeah," Hal said. "Wait. You think the ghosts of the spider-things are haunting the forest?"

"Not exactly," Athena said. "More like their blood infected the forest floor and the trees. I dunno, I don't have it all worked out yet. It's just a hypothesis. Ask me sometime when I don't have a giant headache." And with that, she went inside.

That left Hal and Erin. As they climbed back into the car, Hal was beaming.

"What are you so happy about?" Erin said.

"We did it," Hal said, starting the car. "We actually saved her. We're heroes." He grinned, and Erin couldn't help but smile in return.

They drove toward Erin's trailer first, but as they approached the neighborhood, Erin became aware of a smell—pleasant, almost, like a campfire—which quickly overwhelmed her entire olfactory sense. She glanced at the night sky, her subconscious directing her conscious mind toward what it already understood. The sky was two different shades of black. The second shade drifted and swirled and blotted out the stars even in the still air. Smoke.

"Look," she said, and pointed. "Where is that coming from?"

Hal didn't answer, but drove past the trailer park to his apartment complex. When they arrived the parking lot was already packed with emergency vehicles and flashing lights. Onlookers crowded the police barricades to watch one of the buildings burn. Hal parked illegally, in the middle of the lot, behind a cop car. Erin didn't say anything, because it was Hal's building on fire.

Hal leapt out of the car and sprinted toward the onlookers. Erin jogged after him, searching the crowd for Lorna's face.

Up ahead, an older woman caught Hal by the arm. He tried to pull away, but she held fast, and he stopped to listen to what she had to say. Erin saw the news enter his consciousness. The slump of his shoulders, the drop of his head. The retreat of nervous energy from his body. Something inside, some support beam, collapsing.

Later, she'd get the specifics. Find out the fire had started in Lorna and Hal's apartment. One of Reggie's or Lorna's cigarettes must've dropped on a stack of unopened mail during what was likely a blackout drunk. Two charred bodies on the couch. They probably suffocated before they burned. A mercy, as these things went.

But now, only suspecting the broad silhouette of the truth, Erin caught up to Hal and caught a glimpse of the unhappy man he would become. For the first time she understood why the Temple of Pain might have chosen him as its avatar.

She hugged him. "I'm so sorry, Hal."

He made a sick sound somewhere between a laugh and a sob. His voice sounded watery:

"Looks like I got my boon first."

2019
Memorial

Owen

All night Owen wanders from nightmare to nightmare, reliving Cole's murder, the sudden deaths of his best friend and classmates. He wanders endless dark caves, pursued by eyeless, wailing wraiths. And he is grateful when he is shaken awake and away from these phantoms, although when he first opens his eyes, he thinks he's wandered into another nightmare.

A rotting corpse that looks like Cole looms over him, its cold hand on his shoulder in a tight grip. He startles and tries to scramble away, but the corpse holds him fast.

"Relax," it says. "You aren't in danger. I just need you to wake up."

The world—his current situation—pours back into Owen like water into a basin. He remembers where he is—a musty room in a closed motel, with a magically restored A/C—and with whom he is traveling: the reanimated corpse of his murdered crush Cole White. A body possessed by something that at first seemed murderously insane and now seems calm and contemplative. The switch in demeanor hasn't eased Owen's fear.

Owen sits up and the thing lets go of his shoulder. He rubs his eyes and smacks his mouth. He can smell his own breath and it's awful. He should've stolen a toothbrush from that gas station the other day.

"Time to go," the Cole-thing says.

Despite a full night's sleep, Owen feels fuzzy and diffuse. He rubs his face, then puts on his shoes and ties them with numb fingers before walking out of the chilled motel room and back into the unforgiving August heat and humidity. The sight of the sky startles him—full of storm clouds, yes, but the clouds are a deep, bloody red.

"What the hell?"

"You can see it," the Cole-thing says. "The red?"

Owen nods.

"Interesting," the thing says.

They get into the car and Owen starts it, cranking up the A/C.

"You dreamed," the Cole-thing says. "You moaned in your sleep."

Owen doesn't deny it. "Nightmares." And because the Cole-thing seems to be in a calm mood: "During the ritual, before you came out of the ground and inhabited Cole's body, I stepped outside the circle of protection and seemed to go somewhere else. Like a cave? But there were all these weird ghost-things with their eyes and mouths sewn shut."

The Cole-thing stares straight ahead. "You saw the Unspeaking. Who saw evil and said nothing. Did nothing. They exist in blind panic for eternity, with no way to make their case or forgive themselves."

"Why did I see them? Do they have anything to do with you?"

"I don't know why you saw them. Perhaps it was a glitch in your ritual. Or they may have been attracted *by* the ritual. Perhaps they thought you could help them. You couldn't have, but they don't know that. Most of them don't know where they are or what's happening. It's part of the punishment."

"They killed some of my friends, before you arrived," Owen says. "But not me. Why not me?"

"Because I was already on my way," the Cole-thing says. "I needed you, singled you out for survival." It waves its hand, impatient. "Go, go. We have a little more driving to do today."

"And then?" Owen says, almost too afraid to ask. "Then what? You'll let me go?"

"No. But the driving part will be finished."

Owen puts the car in gear, pulls back onto the highway, and heads east.

Erin

Erin wakes relaxed and peaceful. Almost happy. She slept better than she has in months—possibly years. She feels safe here—because of her protection command, sure, but also because her coven is just upstairs. Nothing too awful can happen with Athena and Hal nearby.

She left the TV on when she was going to sleep. Last night, the movie channel had been playing *Remains of the Day*. This morning, it's showing the end of *Hackers*. Angelina Jolie and Jonny Lee Miller's characters on their first date, swimming together in their clothes in a rooftop pool. Jonny Lee says, *"Anyway, you're pretty good. You're elite."* And Angelina responds, *"Yeah? You know if you'd said so at the beginning you'd have saved yourself a whole lot of trouble."* The city skyline lights up with their hacker names "Crash and Burn," and then the gorgeous movie stars are kissing and the credits are rolling.

"Kismet," Erin murmurs.

"Hmm?" Philip rolls over, awake at the sound of her voice. Not unlike a pet. She dislikes that she has the thought, but it's there, right in the front of her mind. She wishes she weren't the kind of person to have thoughts like this. She wishes a lot of things about herself, but she is who she is: a woman with unkind thoughts, and one who is also very nervous about introducing her beau to her old friends today.

She runs a hand over his face. The swelling seems to have gone down a little. "Nothing. How are you?"

"I still hurt a little," he says. "But I think I'm okay."

"Good," she says. "Let's get dressed and meet up with my friends. Maybe we have time for breakfast before the memorial."

She texts Hal and Athena to see if they're amenable, and both say they are. She and Philip take hurried showers and dress—Erin in a muted black dress, Philip in an off-the-rack suit they bought on the drive here. It's an odd fit on him, too tight in the shoulders and loose around the middle. They'll need to get the jacket tailored when things calm down. They fumble with his necktie, just like in the movies— except she has no idea how to tie one, either, so they end up watching three YouTube videos before they fashion something that doesn't look like a giant clown knot.

During the third video, she receives a text from Hal: We're in the lobby.

On our way, Erin texts back.

She grabs her purse, triple-checks she has her room key, and ushers Philip out of the room in front of her. Hal and Athena stand at the base of the stairs on the far end of the hallway—Hal in a suit that looks a little too snug on him, Athena in black pants, flats, and a suitcoat. They're standing awfully close to one another, Hal with his hands in his pockets, Athena giving him her *You fucking idiot* smile. They haven't noticed her yet, and watching them, seeing her friends like they used to be, Erin feels almost whole. Then she remembers who she's with, and what she's about to have to explain, and the feeling disappears.

No use putting it off any longer. She walks down the tiled hallway, her heels clacking on the floor, catching her friends' attention. Hal's and Athena's smiles vanish at once. Hal gapes. Athena looks astonished, then offended.

"Hey guys," Erin says, the cheer in her voice faltering. "I want to introduce you to—"

"Peter?" Hal says.

Erin's heart drops into her stomach with an acid splash and she understands that this is going to be much more awkward and uncomfortable than she'd anticipated. Philip gives Hal a puzzled but friendly look, which is a perfect copy of Peter Marsh's old *I'm confused but want to be polite* expression.

Erin takes a deep breath. No going back now.

"Hal. Athena," she says. "This is my companion, Philip. Philip, these are my friends, Hal and Athena."

"It's nice to meet you," Philip says. He extends a hand, just like they practiced. Hal shakes it, still completely confused, his good manners running on autopilot. Athena, however, recoils from the offered touch.

"Erin," she says. "What the *fuck* did you do?"

Hal

Hal has always assumed the insanity of his adolescence prepared him for anything, but it turns out he was wrong. He was *not* prepared for Philip.

Philip hurts to look at, and not only because he looks so much like Peter Marsh, had Peter lived to see his late thirties. For Hal, looking at Philip is like trying to read with someone else's glasses. Instant headache. He grimaces, astonished, through a handshake with the man, whose touch also feels *wrong* somehow, but in a way he doesn't understand and can't articulate.

"Erin," Athena says, her voice icy as she ignores Philip's proffered hand. "What the *fuck* did you do?"

Philip steps back from the refused handshake and puts a protective hand on Erin's shoulder.

"Don't talk to Erin that way," he says.

Athena doesn't acknowledge him. She turns to Hal. "You see this, right?"

Hal glances at the reception desk. The receptionist is staring at the coven with open interest.

"Let's maybe take this outside," Hal says.

Athena storms out onto the front porch, and the rest of the group follows. The air is thick and humid, but at least there's no one else around.

"Okay," Hal says. "What I see is a man who looks a lot like Peter Marsh."

Athena, first of the coven to read Dissonant and the smartest person in most rooms, shakes her head. "This isn't a man."

Philip looks at Erin, confused, and Athena makes another intuitive leap, one which seems to compound her frustration.

"He doesn't know, does he?"

Philip gives Erin an inquisitive look. "What don't I know?"

"Yeah," Hal says. "SparkNotes for the non-geniuses, please."

Erin's fingers worry at the strap of her purse. "I was going to tell him. When he was ready."

Athena throws her hands up. "Now seems like the time."

"Philip," Erin says.

"Yes?" Philip says, expectant.

"Sweetheart," Erin says. She grimaces, sighs. Sits down in one of the chairs on the front porch and then immediately stands up again. "You know I love you, right?"

"Of course," Philip says. "I love you, too."

She gives him a pitying smile and Athena says, "Spit it out already."

Erin takes Philip's hand, and based on the look on her face, something about it weirds her out, too, because she lets it go.

"Oh for fuck's sake," Athena says. She throws an arm up and gestures at Philip. "It's a tulpa."

"What's a tulpa?" Hal asks. It sounds like some sort of flower. He's also perturbed at Athena's use of the word *it* rather than *he*.

"A concentrated thought-form," Athena says. "Slightly more real than an imaginary friend. Usually incorporeal, but Erin has given this one a body."

"That's not true, is it?" Philip says. "I'm not imaginary?"

Erin continues to play with her purse strap, pulling on a loose thread.

"What's your first memory?" Athena asks.

"Talking to Erin," Philip says. It doesn't appear odd to him that his first memory is his current lover, and Hal feels an even deeper sense of unreality.

"What were you talking about?" Athena says.

Philip considers. "We were introducing ourselves. Getting to know each other. Like you and I are doing right now."

"Where did you have this conversation?" Athena says.

He opens his mouth, then closes it, and frowns. "I . . . can't remember. It was dark."

"Because you weren't anywhere yet," Athena says.

"You were a voice in here," Erin says, finally joining the conversation and tapping her temple. "Something—someone—I created to keep me company."

Philip's frown disappears. "You like my company."

Erin smiles, but it's strained. "I do. I like it so much I wanted to bring you out of my head and into this world. So we could be together for real."

"How did you do it?" Hal asks.

"How do you think?" Athena says.

"Wait, wait, wait. You're saying Erin can still use the Dissonance?"

Erin shakes her head and fiddles with her purse. "Sort of. Not like when we were kids."

Athena's jaw works, and Hal's teeth ache in sympathy. "Grafts," she says.

"Grafts?" Hal says. "Like skin grafts?"

"Same basic principle," Athena says. "Back-alley Dissonant surgeons. A transplant of cells from a healthy Dissonant. Sort of like hair plugs, but way more dangerous. People die if it goes wrong. I mean honestly, Erin, how fucking stupid can you be?"

Erin throws her purse on one of the tables. It lands with a jangling thump. "You don't know how lonely I've been."

"No," Athena says. "No one on this porch has *any* idea what life has been like for you. None of us are coping with loss and loneliness every single day. Only Erin is suffering."

"It's different for me," Erin says. "You're only lonely because you're a coward."

Athena looks ready to unload—like she's been stockpiling choice adjectives for this conversation for twenty years—but Hal interrupts.

"Stop it, both of you," he says. "And someone explain to me why this guy"—he points at Philip—"is a problem? What's wrong with a tulpa? It's weird, but so what? It's also kind of cool."

"Thank you, Hal," Philip says. "I think you're cool, too."

Athena takes several deep breaths and closes her eyes before she responds. When she speaks, she seems barely in control. "There's nothing wrong with making a tulpa. Non-Dissonant people have been doing it for centuries. It's like meditation. You create a presence, a personality that lives in your mind. Someone to challenge your thinking, or keep you company. Eventually, if your mind and imagination are strong, the tulpa takes on a personality and inner life of its own. It develops a voice and appearance in your mind's eye. All of this is completely fine. What's bad is, Erin took the process a step further, and put her tulpa in a physical body. See, we live in a universe of rules. When we were kids, we used the Dissonance to bend some of those rules, but we never broke the big ones, like time travel, for example. One of those inviolable rules is that every living creature has a soul. The soul animates the body. In this case, Erin has created a living creature without a soul."

Hal finally understands. "Philip being embodied—that's why the red skies and the earthquakes?"

"My guess is it's the whole reason." She gestures at the scabs on Erin's arms. "And I'm guessing it explains the rain of pigeons at her apartment."

Erin no longer looks angry. She looks frightened. "I didn't think it was Philip. I thought someone was trying to kill me."

"The world is trying to kill Philip," Athena says. "You threw it out of true, and it's trying to put itself back in balance. It won't stop until Philip is dead."

"It won't?" Philip says.

Hal is impressed. The tulpa is following the conversation better than he would expect of an imaginary friend. Erin has created something remarkable. Childlike, but intelligent.

"What if I leave my body and go back into Erin's mind?" he says. "Will everyone be safe? Everything back to normal?"

"It depends on how Erin made you," Athena says. To Erin, she adds, "I assume you didn't conjure him from thin air. Not with grafts."

Erin winces, and now Athena sits down at the table. She puts her elbows on the tabletop and buries her face in her hands with a groan. "You used some of your own hair and blood, didn't you?"

Erin closes her eyes, mouth tightening.

"What does that mean?" Hal says, although he thinks he understands. "If Philip dies—"

"I die, too," Erin says. "We're linked."

Hal collapses into a chair beside Athena. "Fuck."

"Yes," Philip says. "Fuck." He sits down, too, although more hesitantly, self-conscious of himself and his movements.

Hal gives himself a moment of despair, then moves on. "Okay. So what do we do?"

"Do?" Athena says.

"Sure. What's the plan? How do we save the day?"

"There is no 'save-the-day' scenario this time," Athena says. "Either Erin and the tulpa commit suicide, or we wait for Mother Nature to finish the job herself."

Erin grabs her purse and runs for the stairs to the parking lot. She stumbles and nearly trips, but Philip gets to her in time to catch her. As she stands up straight, she shoots one last betrayed look at Athena, then lets Philip lead to her little hail-damaged Toyota.

Hal waits until the car has left the parking lot before he turns on Athena. "What the hell is wrong with you?"

"How is this my fault?" Athena says. "I didn't create this situation. I told the truth. We all have to take responsibility for our actions."

He steps back as if she's hit him. "I'm sorry we can't all be perfect like you."

He turns and follows Erin, leaving Athena alone on the porch.

Athena

Athena stands on the porch of the Saunders Inn, trying to decide what to do. She should get in her car and leave. She could be back in Oregon day after tomorrow. Let Erin figure it out for herself, and if Hal wants to waste his time hanging around to watch, that's his business.

Running again?

The words come from deep inside, but they don't sound like her. They sound like a voice she hasn't heard in twenty years, and they settle like stones in her chest.

She's already here. She'll put off any decisions until after the memorial. She can do that much: she can sit in the Baptist church and mourn her dead classmates and teachers, be the mascot for the town's pity and grief. She owes it to the dead. She owes it to Peter Marsh. Once she's paid her debt, she can decide whether to leave or stay.

She gets in her car and drives downtown, to the church. A sizable crowd (all white) has already gathered on the steps and is shuffling into the building. Athena feels their stares as she gets out of her car. She stands up straight and pretends she doesn't notice.

As she passes through the front doors and into the entryway, she sees women posted at each entrance to the sanctuary, handing out card stock printed with the order of worship. The older woman at the head of Athena's line looks familiar, and she appears to recognize Athena, too, because when Athena holds out a hand for a copy of the order, the woman pulls the stack to her chest.

"Athena Watts," the woman says. Not a question.

"Yes ma'am," Athena says.

"Oh, sweet girl," the woman says, and pulls Athena into an unsolicited hug. Athena is short, but this woman is shorter, and her head pushes into Athena's bosom. "It's so good of you to come."

Athena returns the woman's hug, and because she doesn't know what else to do, she rubs and pats the woman's back.

"I wouldn't have missed it," she says.

The woman hangs on to Athena until a voice comes from the line: "Mrs. Blackwood."

Jordan McCormick stands a few paces behind Athena. He's changed from his uniform to his Sunday best. He's broad and handsome, dark hair shiny with product, and glasses perched on his nose. He looks like Clark Kent on a job interview.

Blackwood. Athena knew a Judy Blackwood in school. If it's the person Athena is thinking of, she'd have been a senior in 2000. A year away from graduating and being safe. This must be that girl's mother.

Jordan approaches now and gently pries Mrs. Blackwood off of Athena.

"I'm sure Athena wants to get inside and find a seat," he says. "But I'll bet she'd love to talk with you after the service."

Athena fights off a smile. How did Jordan know she needed to be rescued? Was she so obvious? Or does he just remember her that well?

"It's so, so good of you to come, dear," Mrs. Blackwood says, wiping her eyes as she steps back to her place in the line.

"It's the least I could do," Athena says. *Literally the very least,* she doesn't add.

Athena's legs shake as she enters the sanctuary. She lowers herself into the last pew on the left side of the sanctuary, far from the center aisle. She's barely gotten settled when Jordan approaches.

"Okay if I sit with you?" he says. "It's all right to say no. I could understand if you need some space after . . . that." He gestures back in Mrs. Blackwood's direction.

"No," Athena says. "I mean no, I don't mind. Yes. Please sit, deputy. I could use a friendly face and protector nearby."

He settles in beside her. "Would you mind calling me Jordan?"

"Sure," she says, only half-listening. She scans the crowd for familiar faces, but all she can see from here are the backs of people's heads. Toward the front, she spots Erin and Philip. Hal sits by himself near the aisle in the middle of the sanctuary.

"Mrs. Blackwood has had a rough go of it," Jordan says.

"I knew her daughter," Athena says. "Poor woman."

"Doesn't give her the right to cling to you like a body pillow," Jordan says.

"If it made her feel better, it's fine," Athena says.

"Well, I'm glad you're here, too," he says. He sounds earnest, but when she looks at him, he seems way too interested in the order of service, and his ears have turned pink.

She can't help it. She laughs. She doesn't want to—feels awful about it, in fact—but the sound escapes her chest, loud above the murmurs in the church. People turn to glare at her as she tries to play it off as a coughing fit. Jordan's entire face flushes. She's embarrassed him.

"Sorry," she whispers, voice strained as she clamps down on a second fit of giggles. She grips his right wrist. "That was a sweet thing to say. I'm anxious, and when I get anxious, I react in inappropriate ways."

"No big deal," he says, with clear relief. Then he puts a hand over the one she's using to grab his wrist. She glances down at it, then back into his eyes. "What are you doing after this? We could get that cup of coffee."

She doesn't get a chance to answer, though, because at that moment, the sanctuary doors are thrown open and the thunderclaps begin, and then she's not there anymore, but rather, is reliving the worst day of her life.

Owen

The Cole-thing and Owen sit in the station wagon and watch the crowd of mourners file into Clegg Baptist Church. Well, Owen watches. He's not sure what his passenger is doing. It pinches its borrowed face and stares forward with what might be concentration or discomfort. Owen wonders if the thing knows these people. He doesn't understand what this has to do with saving the world.

He doesn't want to piss off his abductor, so he doesn't ask. He feels better after a night's sleep, but wishes he'd asked for a shower. His clothes are crusted with dried mud and sweat. He can smell himself, and it's not pleasant. At least he smells better than the Cole-thing, which now gives off the stench of sandwich meat weeks past its sell-by date.

When the ushers close the front doors of the church, the Cole-thing leans forward and turns to Owen.

"We're going inside," it says. "Stick close."

"Why?" says Owen.

"Never mind," the Cole-thing says, waving a dismissive hand. "Just remember: what happens in there is up to you. I'm prepared to frighten these people, not hurt them—so long as they do what I want."

It climbs out of the car and limps toward the church. Owen follows, watching as the Cole-thing jogs up the stairs with its weird, halting, jerky gait, and yanks open one of the front doors with so much force that it snaps from its hinges. The Cole-thing looks at the broken door in its hand, surprised, then tosses the debris aside and enters. Owen hurries to follow.

An old man in a suit sits in the entryway. He's probably there to usher in latecomers. He stands when Owen and the Cole-thing enter. His mouth moves without sound as he tries to find words for what he's seeing.

"Run now," the Cole-thing says, "and I won't kill you."

The man flees through the hole where there used to be a door. Owen and the Cole-thing move on into the sanctuary. The crowd is still settling in. The minister hasn't stepped up to the lectern yet. No one seems to have heard the ruckus from the entryway. The people chat like congregants at any given Sunday service.

The Cole-thing gestures at the ceiling, and sets off a resounding *bang*. It's as loud as a thunderclap, but indoors. People, confused about what they're hearing, start to look around. A few of them spot the Cole-thing standing at the back of the sanctuary.

"Oh Jesus," someone says, their voice sick with horror at the sight.

The Cole-thing gestures at the ceiling again, and then again, sounding off more thunderclaps.

"He's got a gun!" Owen yells.

Finally, the congregation begins to panic. There's shouting, and screaming, and the roar of too many bodies trying to move at once. People stampede the doors. Some make it out. Others fall and are trampled. Owen and the Cole-thing stand out of the way and let it happen. The Cole-thing keeps its eyes closed and traces green characters in the air. Owen's seen him do the trick before, but it's every bit as interesting now. More interesting, really, because a couple of the characters look familiar. Is he just getting used to seeing them? Or has he seen them somewhere before? The latter *feels* correct, because the sight fills Owen with a sense of déjà vu. Anyway, it makes a nice distraction from his own discomfort as people continue to struggle toward the exits.

Owen's so interested, so engrossed in the magic trick, he doesn't notice the one man who isn't running, despite the fact that he's sitting only a few feet away in the back pew, next to a Black woman who appears to have fallen asleep. This man stands and turns toward Owen. He's tall, broad, and handsome like a cartoon character, his square jaw clenched as he reaches for something in his suitcoat.

Here's the good guy with the gun. He has his pistol out of his coat pocket by the time Owen sees what's happening. The Cole-thing must see it, too, because it stops its closed-eyes magic trick and flicks a hand at the man with the gun. There's another *bang* as some invisible force hits the man and sends him sprawling backward over the pew behind him. He falls with a cry, and there's a sound of wood cracking with the force of his impact.

Owen looks at his abductor, then at the place where the man disappeared from view. The man doesn't get up. Whatever the Cole-thing did seems to have incapacitated him.

The sanctuary is mostly clear. A few rumpled figures litter the aisles, either unconscious, too injured to move, or dead. Only four people remain slumped in the pews—two men and two women. They look like they're asleep. The Cole-thing leans over the back pew and lifts the closest sleeper—the Black woman who'd been next to the dead good guy with the gun.

"Is that what we're here for?" Owen says. "Just her?"

"Not just her," the thing says. "Get the man at the front. The tall one next to the other sleeping woman." It points.

Owen moves forward on shaky legs to the pew indicated. He finds a skinny woman in a black dress. Her bare arms are sleeved with tattoos and her ears are gauged. She leans against a tall, handsome man with blond hair, a small bow of a mouth, and a patrician nose that should be homely but somehow isn't.

The Cole-thing, apparently having finished carrying off their first prisoner, returns to the church to help Owen pick up the beautiful man. As they carry him toward the church doors, toward Cole's station wagon, Owen glances at the remaining two sleepers.

"What about them?" he says.

"Leave them," the Cole-thing says. "Their part in this story is over."

1999
Field Trip

Athena

Around 1 a.m. on the night before the field trip—the one that would take Athena and her friends out of this world and into another—Athena woke from a light sleep, to the sound of a tap at her bedroom window.

With a few quick hand motions, she conjured a ball of eldritch green light and sent it to part the curtains and illuminate the window. Hal stood on the other side of the glass, waving. Athena got up and opened the window. The seal of the air-conditioning broke, and a rush of July heat smacked her the rest of the way awake.

"What are you doing here?" she said.

"I'm here to rescue you," Hal said.

"From what?"

"Um. The boredom of a good night's sleep?"

"Sleep isn't boring for me."

"Come on. Let's go for a ride."

He smiled at her, and she knew she couldn't say no to him. Not when he smiled at her like that. She told him to give her a minute and meet her out front. He gave her two thumbs-up and disappeared into the dark around the side of the house. She shut the window, put on some jeans, pulled her hair out of its bonnet and into a loose ponytail, and went out the front door as quietly as possible.

Lorna's convertible stood at the curb, top down, Hal stationed in the driver's seat. He'd inherited the car, his mother's sole surviving possession, after last summer's fire. The intervening year had not been kind to the vehicle. These days, in addition to the physical shortcomings like a lack of rearview mirrors, the instruments had gone wonky, too. Sometimes the fuel gauge picked a spot and stayed put, regardless of the tank's contents. The speedometer lay limp most of the time, only fluttering up from the baseline when Hal floored the accelerator.

If anyone else had asked her to get in this car, Athena would have refused, gone back inside, and gone to sleep. But for Hal, she climbed into the passenger seat and buckled her seatbelt.

"I guess Brofur was busy tonight?" she said.

Hal had been dating Cynthia Brofur most of the summer. Athena had barely seen him for the last several weeks, aside from Dissonant lessons at Marsh House.

"Couldn't tell you," Hal said. "We broke up."

"Sorry to hear it," Athena said.

He smiled a little as he started the car, and she looked out the window so he wouldn't see her smile in turn.

When they were a couple of blocks away from the house, he turned on the stereo. He had his Discman hooked up through an adapter in the tape deck, and turned the volume up to noise-violation levels. They drove through town, arms out the open windows, breeze and velocity tangling their hair. Athena settled in to the simple but effective sensations of loud music and forward momentum. The AFI CD in the player set her heart racing, the way music only worked when you were young and your emotional nerve endings remained intact. Twenty years from now, Athena would forget the name of the band, and the lyrics to the song, but she'd never forget feeling free and invincible at forty mph, with only good things ahead—or how that thrill died when the car turned onto Haven Street, coughed, sputtered, and died.

"Uh," Hal said.

"What's wrong?" Athena said.

They were losing speed. The street, lined with closed stores and restaurants, appeared deserted, the entire town asleep. They came to a red light and Hal stopped the car.

"Stupid fuel gauge tricked me," he said. "I thought I had more gas."

"Citgo's up the street," Athena said, and pointed. "Do you have any money?"

"My wealth isn't, shall we say, currently liquid."

Athena dug into the pockets of her jeans, and produced a crumpled bill.

"Is this enough to get us home?" she said.

"Yes?"

"You have no idea."

"I do not," he said.

"Do you have a gas can?"

"I don't even have a rearview mirror."

"Then we get out and push. Station's only another couple of lights down."

He put the car in neutral, and stood by the open driver's side door as Athena stationed herself behind the trunk. The light turned green and they leaned into the push. The car rolled. Sweat formed on her brow, in her pits, on the back of her neck. Her left leg cried out in protest and her back complained.

"What do we do if the next light is red?" Hal said.

"Try to hop in and hit the brake," Athena said. "Or run through and hope for the best."

"Like a motherfucking outlaw," Hal said. "I like it."

The car rolled past a strip mall, and a closed liquor store, and the town cemetery. As they passed the cemetery's darkened gravel driveway, blue lights flared and a siren chirped. A sheriff's deputy, waiting for late-night mischief-makers.

Hal got into the car and shifted into park. Athena walked up beside him as the cruiser pulled in behind.

"If he asks," Hal said, "we're on a date tonight, were on our way home, and ran out of gas."

Athena's face, warm from the effort of the car push, flushed warmer still.

"I thought this *was* a date," she said, mock indignant.

His mouth remained open as he tried to decide how to respond.

"I'm kidding," she said. "Are we in real trouble?" Despite the flush in her face, she couldn't stop an icy feeling in the pit of her stomach. She'd snuck out of her parents' house to go carousing, and now the cops were involved. Athena's parents had coached her on how to behave around police officers—always do exactly what you were told; never argue; be polite, even if you weren't doing anything wrong. They'd told her to always treat every interaction with the police as life-or-death.

Hal leaned over to the glove box and opened it. A bottle of Wild Turkey fell out onto the floorboard. The icy feeling in Athena's gut spread through her body as Hal swept the bottle under the seat and out of sight, then grabbed his insurance paperwork from the box.

"Of course not," Hal said. "Let me do the talking."

The deputy climbed out of his cruiser. Hal caught Athena's eye and winked.

"Good evening, deputy," he said, leaning past her.

Athena turned. She knew all the deputies in town, but this one she knew better than most: Deputy Jordan McCormick, her old neighbor, who'd graduated Clegg High in May and joined the department right after. She relaxed a little.

"Car trouble?" Jordan asked.

Hal launched into his spiel about their date, the myriad problems with his car (including a faulty fuel gauge, which he intended to fix at the earliest opportunity), and how they were on their way to remedy the gas problem now. McCormick listened to all of it with a half-smile, then turned to Athena.

"This true?" he said. "You on a date with this miscreant?"

"You've seen the pickings in my class," she said. "What am I supposed to do?"

Jordan's half-smile remained firm through Athena's weak joke before he returned his attention to Hal. "I could write you a ticket for all the things wrong with this car, you know. Or, I could be a decent human being and lend you my fuel can to get some gas and get you home."

"Do we get to vote?" Hal said. "Because I vote for the second choice."

Jordan got the can from the trunk of his cruiser, directed Hal to remain with the car, and then walked with Athena to the Citgo up the road.

"Athena Watts dating Hal Isaac," Jordan said, once they were out of earshot.

"He's a good person," Athena said.

"I didn't say he wasn't. You can do better, though."

"You're just being nice," Athena said.

"I'm not."

They arrived at the gas station and Athena gave her crumpled money to the deputy. He handed it back.

"This one is on the Sheriff's Department." He swiped a credit card through the reader and knelt to put the nozzle into the top of the gas can. "So. You'll be a senior in a few weeks?"

"You have a good memory," she said.

"Imagine you have big plans after graduation. College in some big city."

"Is that a problem?"

"Ask me again after you're old enough to vote or buy a gun."

Jordan finished filling the can, put the nozzle back on its hook, and tightened the lid of the can before he stood. They started back to the car and Athena tried to find her next words. She must've misunderstood. There was no way this older boy—man—was flirting with her.

"Maybe I will," she said. "Ask you, I mean."

He smiled again, but it was fleeting, and quickly replaced with a frown. "You understand you're the reason Hal isn't getting arrested tonight?"

She stopped walking. "No. I didn't know that."

"I don't want anything going on the record that could affect your future," he said. "But your friend reeks of booze. You must've noticed. You do the driving on the way back, okay?"

"Okay," she said, as she started walking again. She hadn't smelled anything in the car, but she wasn't a drinker, so she wouldn't know, would she? Did Hal always smell that way, and was she just used to it?

"Consider making some new friends," he said. "Guy like that will ruin your life if you let him. I've seen it happen to other girls we went to school with. Girls who got stuck."

"Thought you didn't want me to leave," she said.

"I sure as shit don't want you trapped here, either," he said.

They came back to the car. Deputy McCormick poured the donated gas into the tank and sent them on their way. Athena drove, as promised. Hal stayed oddly quiet, as if cowed, waiting for her to speak.

"I didn't know you'd been drinking tonight," she said at last.

"You couldn't tell?" He sounded genuinely surprised.

"Where'd you get it?" she asked. Hal had been living with Professor Marsh and Peter since his mother died, and as far as Athena knew, Marsh didn't even keep alcohol in the house.

"Don't worry about it," he said.

"You asked me to get in a car with you when you were drunk. That's not okay."

"I'm sorry," he said. "I should've told you."

"Don't apologize. Promise me you won't drink and drive again."

"I'll think it over, *Mom*," he said.

"Jordan could have arrested you," she said. "He didn't, because he didn't want *me* to get in trouble." She pulled the car over to the curb and killed the engine. "Take this seriously, okay?"

"I hear you," he said.

"And the next time you ask me on a midnight drive, I don't want it to be because you're drunk and sad you broke up with another girl."

She started the car again, and drove the rest of the way back to her parents' house. Hal remained cowed and quiet. When she got home, Athena parked and got out, then remembered something else the deputy had said.

"Promise me something," she said.

"Haven't I promised enough for one night?" Hal asked.

"Promise me we'll get out of this town, and that once we're gone, we'll stay gone."

"Try and keep me here one day—no, one *hour*—after graduation." He looked out the window and seemed to realize where they were. "Are you calling it a night?"

"We have an early day, remember?" Athena said. "The professor said he'd leave without us if we're late."

"Bullshit," Hal said. "He can't leave without you."

"You're welcome to test that assumption," she said. "*I'm* going to get some sleep."

"What about me?" Hal asked.

"I'm not sneaking you into the house."

"I'm not suggesting any funny business."

"Good," she said, meaning the opposite. "Sleep in the car. You'll be okay to drive by the time you wake up."

"I can't sleep on the living room couch?"

"Good night, Hal."

"Wait wait wait," he said. "Before you go."

She let go of the door handle and turned back to Hal with a sigh. "What?"

"Can you show me the sign for *air* again? I've been trying to remember and I'm drawing a total blank."

"Why?"

"Because I want to remember, and when you're with me, I sort of can."

She leaned over, so close she could smell the sweat on his body. It was somehow both repellent and irresistible at the same time. She gently took his hands into her own. She lifted them both, then positioned his fingers just so.

"Hold like this," she said, dizzy with the scent of him. "And then, just . . ." She slowly put his hands through the motions. At first, nothing happened, but by the time they finished, yellow-green light trailed their fingers through the air.

Hal smiled. "There it is," he said.

She let go of his hands, but more slowly than she had to, her fingers sliding along his until they were separated once more.

"My fingers always feel so tingly after you do that," he said, flexing his hands.

"Okay weirdo," she said. "Good night for real." She shut the driver's side door, jogged across the lawn, and slipped back into her parents' house. She waited until she'd undressed and gotten back into bed to let the night wash over her. Deputy McCormick wasn't wrong to be concerned about Hal. He'd always been a slacker and a goof, but since his mother had died, there'd been a new intensity to the goofing off. A hard edge.

But tonight, at least, Hal was safe. In fact, he was just outside in Lorna's car. She closed her eyes and conjured him lying with his seat reclined, the top and windows down, his arms crossed over his chest like a vampire in an oversized coffin.

What was love but the willingness to endure unpleasantness for another? Cynthia Brofur might've been Hal's latest make-out partner, but tonight Hal slept in a car because Athena had told him to.

She flexed her hands in the darkness. She hadn't admitted it in the car, but moving his hands through the motions of a Dissonant sign made her fingers all tingly, too.

Erin

The night before the field trip, Erin received special permission to sleep on the couch at Marsh House, provided that Professor Marsh vouched for 1) the presence of adult supervision, and 2) his grandson's conduct. Peter and his grandfather had offered solemn vows to protect Erin's virtue, but once Erin's father dropped her off, the professor had retreated into his study and left Erin and Peter alone to order pizza and watch rented movies. First up was *Warlock*, then *The Ninth Configuration*, which was based on William Peter Blatty's other, non-*Exorcist* novel. Both movies were pretty good, and best of all, Erin hadn't seen them before. That was her key criterion for renting a movie these days—finding something she hadn't already seen.

They ate their pizza in front of the TV in the den, and Erin felt terribly grown up. This could be regular life for her in another five years. Friday nights with junk food and movies and her sweetheart. The hard part, it seemed to Erin, would be to make sure she and Peter still liked one another in ten years. She couldn't imagine ever tiring of steady, quiet, handsome Peter, but she imagined most couples felt that way in the early days. Hell, even her own parents had been in love once upon a time.

As they neared the end of *The Ninth Configuration* now, she ran a hand along Peter's thigh. He took her hand in his without looking away from the screen. Another thing she liked about him: he wanted to watch the movie on a movie date. They'd get into the spicy stuff after.

Professor Marsh made one more appearance in the den, to say he was going to bed, and to extract another vow of celibacy from the teenagers. He reminded them of tomorrow's early start, then left them alone.

The movie ended not long after, and in the blue light of the VCR's standby screen, they skirted the edge of their vow, lips parted, tongues exploring, teeth nipping. It'd been a slow ramp up with Peter since last summer. Sweet Peter. Shy Peter. Quiet, smiling Peter. Peter, who seemed to desire and fear touch in equal measure. Peter, whom Erin had gradually coaxed into a comfortable place, one touch, one caress, one kiss at a time.

Tonight, Erin encouraged his hand up her shirt and over her bra, to show how she wanted to be touched. She wriggled the fingers of her other hand past the waistband of his shorts, and squeezed his erection. She tried to tease him with her fingers, but the tight confines of his boxers made grace a secondary concern, and she settled for pawing at him like an animal as he found and gently pinched her nipple.

It went on like this awhile longer, their breathing increasingly labored and hitched, but just when Erin thought Peter would give in and take the last plunge with her, he put his hands on her shoulders and pushed her away.

"What's wrong?" she said.

"Nothing. Sorry," he said. "It's just enough for now. If that's okay."

She tried not to let her frustration show. She wiped her fingertips on the denim of his shorts and kissed him on both his warm cheeks and forehead. "There's no rush," she said.

They set up their separate beds for the evening. Erin on the couch, Peter on the floor. They lay beneath the ceiling fan and cooled down, letting the hormonal wave pass as they talked. Another thing Erin loved about Peter—the talking was as good as the kissing. He thought and felt deeply, and in the last year, he'd let her into his secret world.

Tonight, all either of them wanted to talk about was tomorrow's field trip.

It felt like serendipity. Like destiny, no matter what Athena said. Last summer, right after their rescue of Morgan the undine, Professor Marsh had returned from his weekend trip with an old book about a place called "Deoth." No one—not even the book's authors—were sure about Deoth's location. Was it on Earth? A parallel Earth? Or somewhere in the Milky Way? Or maybe out in Andromeda? According to the book, it was home to an ancient, vast source of energy, and could hold the answers to many of the secrets of the Dissonance.

When the coven told Marsh about Morgan, and about Athena's Doorway, he'd gotten so excited he'd forgotten to be angry with them for going into the woods without permission. After watching Athena perform the command a few times, he'd determined that the doorway was essentially a wormhole through space—one which, theoretically, could bridge any distance, as long as you knew where you were going.

Athena and Marsh had spent the better part of the last year in his study, gathering every detail about Deoth they could. It wasn't much, even with the entire book at their disposal, but they hoped that, tomorrow, their assembly of ephemeral detail would be sufficient to conjure a doorway to another world.

The coven was already packed for the trip. Marsh had bought a bunch of new camping gear and photography equipment. Athena and Erin had pitched this trip to their parents as a camping expedition on some fictional land Marsh owned in Oklahoma—out in the woods, where they wouldn't have access to telephones for the better part of a week.

In reality, tomorrow morning they would walk into the Clegg woods together, and perform the doorway command there. Marsh had a theory about the woods: if the Many Worlds theory was true, then the woods might be a porous place, where things could pass through. It was the best explanation for the strange creatures wandering in them, as well as the entrance to the bizarre prison where Hal had found Morgan. Marsh hoped that performing the doorway command in a porous place would help their odds of success.

There were a lot of "ifs" surrounding this adventure, but that was what made it an adventure. They didn't know how it would turn out.

"What do you think it will be like?" Erin said now. "Deoth, I mean."

"Who knows?" Peter said. "The professor says there are a lot of references to sand, so at least part of it is either beaches or desert."

"What if the air is poison gas or something? We could be walking to our deaths."

"If anything goes wrong, the professor will call it off and bring us home."

Erin lay awake for a long time. She sensed Peter beside her, their Dissonance flames linked, their emotions disrupting the house's usual placid energy. When she slept, her dreams were sweet, for the last time in her life.

Athena

Despite her late-night misadventures, Athena woke early the next morning. When she went to the kitchen to start a pot of coffee, she peeked out the window over the sink to see if Hal was still parked at the curb. He was.

The cicadas were in fine voice when she stepped out of the house and crossed the lawn to where the car was parked at the curb. Hal was sprawled in the passenger seat, head at an awkward angle, skin shiny with dried sweat. Sunlight glinted off the bottle of Wild Turkey, abandoned, empty, on the driver's seat.

She rapped on the window and Hal startled awake.

"Can I help you?" he said, rolling down the window.

"Why did you sleep with the windows up?" she said.

"I didn't want bugs flying into my mouth," he said.

"If a bug is desperate to get into your mouth, I don't think your roof and windows will stop it."

"Maybe not, but it might give them pause. And pause might be enough to save me from having a tummy full of spiders and moths."

"Do you want some breakfast?" she said.

He pulled his seat into the upright position, rubbed his eyes, and ran a hand through his hair. "I could go for breakfast," he said.

She led him inside and sat him at the kitchen table with a sleeve of Pop-Tarts, then finished getting ready. When she returned to the kitchen half an hour later, showered and dressed, she found Hal chatting and laughing with her mother. You'd never know he'd been hungover half an hour ago.

Athena grabbed a sleeve of Pop-Tarts for herself. This summer, she'd finally given up starving herself. She'd immediately gained back ten pounds, which had been tough, but she was tired of trying to look like a white girl. This was her natural shape, and besides, being hungry all the time made it hard to think straight. Once she'd realized hunger was making her stupid, she'd given it up as a lifestyle—though guilty, shameful thoughts still sometimes intruded when she indulged herself, or even simply ate normally.

Pop-Tarts in hand, she kissed her mother goodbye, and made Hal drive them to Marsh House in Lorna's car. It reeked of booze and sweat inside, so they drove with the top down.

"Think Professor Marsh will be mad at you for staying out all night?" Athena said.

"I doubt he even noticed," Hal said. "As long as the police aren't bringing me home, he doesn't care what I do."

It was the verbal equivalent of a shrug. Lorna hadn't been the most attentive or present parent, so maybe it didn't bother Hal. At least in his new home, he had a friend sleeping down the hall, and Marsh had money to keep Hal in new clothes and school supplies for the rest of high school. He'd probably even pay to fix up Lorna's car, if Hal asked. But as far as Athena knew, Hal hadn't asked. He seemed to prefer his mother's car as it was.

As the beat-up convertible pulled into the driveway of Marsh House, Peter and Erin sat on the front porch steps, their hips so close they could've been sewn together.

"Where were you last night?" Peter asked.

"I was at Athena's," Hal said.

"Oh?" Erin said.

"He slept in his car outside my house," Athena said.

"That's what I said," Hal said.

"You have a bed here," Erin said. "You don't *have* to sleep in your car."

"Yeah, but I like it," Hal said.

They joined Professor Marsh in the backyard. He was dressed in "grandpa on safari" clothes, sitting in the driver's seat of a green ATV, the bed packed with food and camping gear. He held a leather book open on the steering wheel before him.

"About time," Marsh said, marking his place in the book. "I assume, late as you are, that you're all prepared?"

The coven voiced their assent. They weren't late, but it was better not to argue with the old man about anything.

"This is a colossal risk, for me and all of you," he said. "I have educated guesses about what we'll find on the other side, but that's all they are. Genuine uncertainty and possible danger lie ahead. Assuming we make it safely to Deoth, there are rules I need you to follow. First: don't go anywhere alone. Ever. If you have to answer nature's call, you bring someone else. I don't want to have to explain to your parents that I lost you on a fictional camping trip. Second, don't touch anything. And most important"—he looked at Hal—"we are explorers, not warriors. We want to learn, not fight. Do you understand?"

"Hal no hit things with sword unless smart man say so," Hal said.

"Good," Marsh said. "Now let's go discover the secrets of creation."

Marsh slowly drove the ATV out of the backyard and into the woods, and the coven followed. As they did, Athena looked back at the house and something fluttered in her gut. She hadn't been deep into the woods since their first adventure, back in 1996. Despite all the knowledge and power she had gained in the last three years, she wasn't thrilled to return here. She faced forward, refusing to jump at stray sounds, or give away her discomfort, and worked to keep up with the group.

They went deeper into the forest than Athena had ever been. The heat was oppressive, the air thick. Soon, Athena was slick with sweat, and Hal was taking long pulls from his water bottle. She almost warned him—there was no promise of water on Deoth—but he was a big boy. He could waste his water if he wanted.

"Does anyone else feel like we're going in circles?" Erin asked.

"We might be, geographically," Marsh said. "I can't prove it yet, but I think we share this forest with at least one other world—and the ratio of ownership changes, so you face a constantly shifting space. Part of what makes the woods dangerous."

"Then how do you know where we're going?" Athena asked.

Marsh opened his right hand. Something small and round glowed green in the center of his palm.

"What is it?" Hal asked.

"Some kind of Dissonant compass?" Athena guessed. "Instead of pointing north, it points toward the strongest source of Dissonant energy?"

"Very good," Professor Marsh said.

They stopped in the middle of a small clearing, where Marsh turned a circle and waved his little compass around, then seemed to decide on something.

"This is likely the best spot we'll find," he said. "Can you feel it?"

Until now, Athena had been distracted by the heat and her own physical discomfort. But as she began to pay attention, the power in this place set her brain tingling, and caused the tiny hairs on her arms to stand on end.

She didn't have to look at her friends to know they felt it, too. She sensed them around her as extensions of herself. She'd known the members of her coven shared a connection, but now, that truth manifested as a physical sensation. These weren't her friends. They were the rest of her soul. That was why she only ever felt complete with these three people. It wasn't sentimentality. Their connection was as real as gravity, or time.

"It's powerful," Erin said, in a cracked voice.

"Overwhelming," Peter agreed.

Hal said nothing, but rather wiped at his cheek with the back of one hand.

"Focus." Marsh's voice cut through the gauzy perfection of the moment. Athena's buzz retreated enough to put her back in a semi-recognizable reality. "Athena, this is your part."

Athena removed two books from her backpack. The first was *Athena's Cookbook;* the second a much older leather-bound volume with brittle yellow pages. This was the book Professor Marsh had brought back from his trip last summer, after they'd freed Morgan. It contained the accounts of Dissonants who claimed to walk between worlds. Who had been to a place called Deoth.

Athena placed the two books side by side on the forest floor and kneeled in front of them. She looked between the books as she worked her doorway command—a bigger, more complicated variation, because rather than opening a wormhole through earthly space, she was moving five people and their assorted belongings to a place none of them had ever been before. The air, which was already buzz-ing, seemed to take on physical dimensions and vibrate with haze.

The forest became a green and brown blur. The heat drained out of the morning, replaced with the harshest cold she'd ever experienced—colder than the chilliest snow day, or the worst walk-in freezer. And unlike those colds, which had both texture and flavor, this cold expressed itself as absence, lack, nothingness.

She resisted the urge to reach for her friends, to touch them and reassure herself they were there. She couldn't stop now. If she did, she might strand them in this awful freezing absence. She concentrated on her knot of light and meaning. The Dissonance moved through her, and she gave it shape. She finished the last flourish of her command, then released her hold on it.

The cold took on a smell and taste. The world had turned more purple than black, and the dirt beneath her shoes had been replaced with gray sand.

"We're here," Marsh said.

Hal

The world around Hal sharpened. The black void turned gray, then resolved into sand dunes, stretching away in all directions. They'd arrived in a desert at night, and the switch from a damp heat to a dry cold was a startling one.

"We're here," Marsh said, a note of quiet wonder in his voice.

Hal took a deep breath and didn't die. "Air seems okay."

Erin cast Haley's Dome over the group and some of the cold bled off.

Athena looked thunderstruck by what she'd accomplished.

"You okay?" Hal asked.

She stirred and licked her lips. "Water."

Hal opened his canteen and handed it to her. She drank and seemed to come back. He felt a pang, watching her take so much of his remaining water, but banished the feeling as disloyal. If she needed it, he'd happily die of thirst.

"That was intense," she said. "Not entirely pleasant."

"Look around, though," Hal said. "Look what you did."

She took in the landscape. Professor Marsh was walking the circumference of the dome, penlight in his teeth as he took notes, and Peter and Erin held hands as they gazed at the stars above.

"It could almost be Earth," Peter said.

"Or the planet in *Stargate*," Erin said.

Hal looked up at what he assumed were alien constellations and made an involuntary sound: "Huh."

"What?" Athena said.

He pointed up. "No moon."

Athena looked, too. "How about that?"

Hal's heart swelled with a feeling he didn't have a name for, and it caused him to do something that surprised even himself: he took Athena's hand, in an imitation of Peter and Erin. Athena started, then squeezed his hand in her own and then held on tight.

"Incredible," Marsh said. He'd finished his notes and turned his eyes up as well. "And only the first of the things I think we'll see here. But we have a long trek ahead of us, so we might as well start now. Move at night, sleep through the heat of the day."

They wrapped scarves around their faces, stuck goggles to their eyes, tucked their hair into hats, and marched alongside Professor Marsh in the ATV as he guided them with his compass stone. Like Tolkien heroes, they walked. And walked. And walked. They crested dune after dune after dune. There wasn't much to look at. No strange creatures poked their heads above the sand or moved across the horizon in herds. No alien architecture reached heavenward. The wind blew sand at them, but Erin's shield kept most of it out. The continuous onslaught made a gritty sound against the barrier.

Marsh didn't call a stop until the sky lightened and blotted out the stars. He called Erin to help him reinforce the protective barrier while the others set up tents facing the center of the camp. In that middle space, they gathered for a dinner of prepackaged foods—Pop-Tarts, bags of chips, MREs the professor had bought from a military surplus store. When they finished, they gathered the trash and turned their attention to Marsh, who drew in the sand with his fingertip as he spoke.

"I don't have any doubts we've made it to Deoth. I believe we came through about sixty miles west of this world's energy source. We walked twenty miles last night, and if we can maintain this pace, we should reach our destination in two more days. Assuming time works the same here as it does in our world."

"What do you think we'll find?" Hal said.

"I'm not sure, but I'd bet we'll know it when we see it. Now off to bed. I've had enough of you four for one day."

The girls went to their tent and the boys to theirs. The professor had a tent to himself, for which Hal was grateful. After a full year living with the Marshes, he still felt uncomfortable around the old man.

Maybe it was because he grew up without a dad, but Hal found himself ill at ease around most men. Peter was the exception, a gentle, friendly presence minus most of the hard edges and casual cruelty common among other guys Hal knew.

Tonight, even Hal was too tired to stay up chatting. He let the exhaustion sweep over him and carry him down. He was almost asleep when someone unzipped the tent flap and startled him awake. Peter sat up on his elbows as Athena popped her head in.

"Erin wants to see you," she said to Peter.

Peter didn't seem surprised. He sat up, pulled on his boots, and let himself out of the tent, leaving Athena and Hal alone together.

"You'll be here awhile," Hal said. "Might as well make yourself comfortable."

She crawled over to lie down on Peter's sleeping bag. "Oh my god," she said.

"What?"

"This is the most comfortable sleeping bag I've ever touched in my life. Like a feather mattress you can carry with you. Have you noticed?"

The only thing Hal had noticed about Peter's sleeping bag was that it looked newer than his own. Hal had been using the same one since grade school, and because he'd gotten into the habit of leaving it at Marsh House, it was one of his few possessions to survive the apartment fire. It was a rough old thing. The zipper had been broken since sixth grade, which made it more of a blanket with teeth at the edges.

"Feel this," Athena said. She took Hal's hand and pushed it down on the fabric of Peter's sleeping bag. What Hal noticed was the dry cool of Athena's hand, the proximity of his fingers to her round hips, her stomach, her face. She'd gained some weight this summer, but he thought it looked good on her.

"Peter gets the best stuff," he said, forcing himself to pay attention. "Must be nice to be rich."

"I'm sure the professor would buy you a new sleeping bag if you asked," Athena said. She left her hand atop his, and, after a hesitation, moved her thumb back and forth across his knuckles.

"What I have is fine," Hal said.

"My mom said between the insurance money from Peter's parents and what he'll inherit from the professor, he'll never have to work a day in his life. Can you imagine?"

"I can," Hal said. It was one of his favorite games, planning how he would live if he had Peter's money. "I know Marsh probably lives in Clegg because of the woods and the Dissonant connection, but honestly, if I had that kind of money? I wouldn't waste it all on this nonsense. I'd get a house at the beach and another at a ski lodge, and a big condo in New York. Also, I'd buy a badass car."

"You already have a convertible," Athena said.

"Har-dee-har," Hal said. "I mean a good car. Something that has all its mirrors. I'd take care of it, keep it clean." He looked at her thumb moving on his hand. "What about you? What would you buy?"

"If I had that house and everything in it, and enough money not to have to work, I'd try to grow the library and learn more, but that's it. Everything else I would leave the same. No thoughtless husband, no shitty kids. All to myself."

"You wouldn't let me keep my room?" Hal said.

"I thought you wanted out of this town."

"That was before you were rich and had a big house of your own."

"You *have* a friend with money and a big house already," Athena said.

"Yeah, but I get tired of him. I never get tired of you."

The conversation died as he realized the truth of what he'd said. He'd spoken to her, unguarded, free of the veil of sarcasm and banter.

"Do you get tired of me?" Hal said. "I'm always waiting for you to."

She considered. "I get mad at you. I get annoyed. But no, I never get tired of you." She looked surprised at herself, and he understood she had also spoken without guile, without having meant to. He held her gaze until she cleared her throat and pretended to rediscover Peter's sleeping bag.

"Anyway, enough mushy stuff. Check out this sleeping bag. You don't get the full effect by touching it with your hand."

Hal scooted onto Peter's sleeping bag beside her, their bodies pressed together, faces less than an inch apart. Hal lay on his back, hands behind his head. Athena settled onto his chest. It felt comfortable, correct.

"Hey," he said.

"What?" she said.

"Will you show me the sign for *water* again?"

She took his hand, manipulating his fingers into the correct positions, and then began to move, slowly guiding his hand through the air. As it had the night before, some small light trailed from their entwined fingers. Hal smiled at the afterglow as their hands dropped to his chest, still clinging to one another. His hand tingled, and the tingling spread up his arm and through his entire body. He squeezed her fingers. She didn't squeeze back, but also didn't let go.

"So you've come to an alien world," she said. "What do you think?"

He lifted his head to look at her and tried to think of a funny answer, but was distracted by her beauty: the soft curves of her body, her wide, generous mouth, the softness of her hair against his cheek. He experienced the same thing he did whenever he looked at Athena—fear. Not a fear he might love her. He knew he loved her. He was afraid because he also knew Athena loved him back. That if he were to kiss her, she'd be glad.

But sex and love had been fraught propositions for him so far, and even at seventeen he was self-aware enough to suspect they always would be. He was broken at the core. Why bring his favorite person into that mess?

He realized he owed her his thoughts and it was his turn to clear his throat.

"Honestly? This is my favorite part," he said.

Erin

In the girls' tent, Peter and Erin opened her sleeping bag and spread it across the floor, then collided at the mouth, kissing and caressing one another, their breathing loud and urgent. It felt different from last night in the living room. Last night had been sexy, but this was heavy. Important. There was no hesitation on Peter's part. Tops slid over heads, pants shimmied off hips. She reached for him, meaning to guide him inside of her, but her fingertips only brushed the sides and head of his erection as he kissed her cheeks, her forehead, the tip of her nose, her mouth and chin, then worked his way down her body, planting soft kisses on her neck, and clavicles, pausing to gently cup each breast and suck on each of her nipples. He seemed to know the perfect mix of tongue, lip, and teeth, and she moaned a little with happy frustration as he left her breasts and kissed his way down her belly, pausing to run his tongue over the hollows of her hips before at last pressing his lips to the cleft between her legs, then parting them to run his tongue from the bottom of her labia up to her clitoris. They moaned in unison as he tasted her for the first time.

"Is it okay?" she said. She hadn't been expecting him to go down on her, and she'd been walking through a desert all night, and hadn't showered.

"Perfect," he said, his voice muffled against her. The sound sent pleasurable little shocks outward through her body, and she gasped and pushed her hips forward. She cupped the back of his head in one hand and grabbed a fistful of his blond hair. It was gritty and greasy from exertion, but gave her a good grip to angle herself and keep him close.

He seemed to welcome her bid for control. He wrapped his arms around her thighs and pulled himself flush against her, working his tongue up and down again and again, in torturously slow rhythm, pausing to lavish attention on her clit at the top of each stroke.

He took direction well—slowing down when she asked, and speeding up when she wanted that instead. Varying his rhythm, using his fingers, moaning into her and pinching her nipple with his free hand as she bucked and shook and came. It wasn't the most intense orgasm of her life, but it was the first she'd ever had with someone else. In all her fooling around with Randy, she'd never been able to get off.

In that sweet aftermath, almost mad with desire and gratitude, she yanked Peter up and at last he let her guide him inside. The strange sky, the alien world, the existence of the Dissonance and the multiverse fell away outside this cocoon of pleasure and warmth and closeness.

The sex-sex part was awkward and short, but sincere in its brevity. She held Peter's face in her hands as he came, and something in his expression—a mix of pleasure, startlement, and grief—surprised her with its intensity. She pulled his head down into her neck so she didn't have to see it. She couldn't say why, but that look changed the experience. Her chest tightened, and she struggled to control her breath. She couldn't let him see her sudden panic. She wouldn't.

As they lay tangled in the afterglow, Peter propped himself up on one elbow. "I'm glad it was with you," he said. "My first time."

"Me too," she said, but she couldn't look at him. She closed her eyes as he pulled her close and kissed her. He seemed content to remain here in the tent with her, but she wanted him gone. Out.

"We'd better get some sleep," she said. "Big day tomorrow. Go to bed, goofball."

"Oh. Sure." He sat up, looking confused, but dressed in silence and then kissed her once on the cheek before he let himself out of the tent.

She waited in the quiet, taking deep breaths, trying to figure out what the hell was wrong. Why couldn't she breathe? She needed to get out of this tent. She had to move.

She yanked on underwear, shorts, boots, and a T-shirt, and stumbled, gasping, into the middle of the campsite. She landed on her hands and knees. She wanted to scream this too-big feeling out of her chest, and almost did when someone touched her shoulder.

"What's wrong?" Athena said.

Erin waved her hands in front of her face. She heard herself taking deep breaths, but had no idea where the air was going, because her chest felt like a vise.

"Should I get Peter?" Athena said. She started back to the boys' tent, but Erin grabbed her.

"No, don't."

"Did he do something?" Athena asked, her face hardening.

Erin shook her head and clenched her eyes shut. She felt Athena hunker beside her, and startled when the other girl enfolded her in her arms. Athena didn't ask any further questions. She didn't try to figure out what was wrong, or make it okay. Instead she held Erin and rocked her in the late-morning heat.

Erin cried as quietly as she could, unsure why it was happening, knowing only that something inside needed out, and Athena was helping. She'd almost regained control of herself when Athena lifted an arm and pointed at something far off.

"Look."

Erin wiped her cheeks and followed the direction of Athena's finger. In the distance moved a beast for which Erin had no name. It walked on four legs which seemed too spindly to support the barrel-shaped body atop them. It had no tail, and its head looked like an alien battle helmet, sharp as a blade and tapering to a proboscis in front like a bent, segmented straw. As this thing skimmed across the sand, the proboscis flexed like a many-jointed finger and curled up toward the creature's face.

Erin and Athena watched in mute fascination. They'd seen strange life-forms before, but never anything on this scale. Part of Erin wished the boys and the professor were awake so they could see it as well. The other, truer part of her was glad she and Athena were the sole witnesses to this dark wonder.

The girls watched the creature until it disappeared, obscured by the dunes. Then they went back to their tent and slept.

Athena

After the bizarre sighting outside the tent, Athena had trouble falling and then staying asleep. The daylight was intense, and Erin, usually a quiet sleeper, moaned and tossed. Athena didn't know what had happened while Peter and Erin were alone together, but she worried.

These things made good rest difficult, so when the professor summoned the coven at sundown, Athena remained exhausted and achy, her bad leg grumbling, her back sore from sleeping on the ground. Her friends and teacher said little over a breakfast of instant coffee and Pop-Tarts before they packed up the camp and started the second night's walk.

The silence persisted. Peter walked next to Erin, but Erin kept her head down and shoulders hunched, hands on her backpack straps, her posture communicating clear discomfort. Not even Hal ran his mouth. Was he exhausted, too? Or was he pondering their conversation in the boys' tent yesterday? She hoped it was the latter, because she couldn't stop replaying it in her own mind.

She had been so *sure,* for a moment, that he was going to kiss her. Why hadn't he? She'd never known Hal to be shy. She'd seen him with other girls at school.

The answer was clear: he didn't like her that way. It was the only logical explanation. Maybe he'd been trying the idea on for size, since he and Cynthia Brofur had broken up, but when the moment came he couldn't force himself to go through with it.

But if that was true, why had he said *Honestly? This is my favorite part?*

Her thoughts circled this way for hours as she put one foot in front of the other and forced her body to endure the long walk to the next campsite. As the stars faded and the second morning dawned on Deoth, the coven came down out of the dunes and onto a flat plain of hard-packed sand. Less than a mile ahead stood what looked like a village of clay buildings alongside a small pool of water and a sparse gathering of purple cacti.

All the buildings in the village were identical small clay structures with domed roofs, except for the one in the center of town. Where the other buildings were soft and curved, and colored a dun brown, this central building was comprised of sharp angles that almost hurt to look at, and had been carved from a black stone. The severe building stretched at least three stories into the sky before it reached a tapered spike, like a church without a cross.

"What is this place?" Hal said. "Is this what we came to see?"

Marsh pointed his compass toward it and frowned. "I don't think so. Maybe it was an outlying village. A place where travelers stopped."

"I don't see anyone now," Peter said.

"They could be hiding," Hal said.

"No," Marsh said. "This place is long-abandoned. If people lived here, there would be evidence. Beasts of burden. Gardens. Tools for daily toil."

"Should we look around?" Athena said. The appearance of the village had dulled her aches, pains, and sleepiness. Curiosity hit her like a simultaneous painkiller and shot of espresso.

"We'd better not," Marsh said. "I might be wrong, and I don't want to pay for it with your lives. We'll risk the big source when we find it, but not this." He studied the village a little longer. "I'd like to leave this place behind, but I can't go any farther today, and it would be foolish to go back. Besides, anything hiding in there has already seen us, and could follow if it wanted to. We'll take turns on watch today."

They made camp within sight of the oasis and ate another meal of prepackaged junk. The preportioned stuff reminded her of her previous dieting habits, and she experienced a moment of deep discomfort. She wished they could've brought real food. As they ate, she and Erin gave an account of the creature they'd seen the day before. After breakfast, Marsh assigned the coven to take the watch in pairs. Peter and Athena went first, Hal and Erin second, with Marsh himself third.

Athena wondered if the professor had noticed footprints between the boys' and girls' tents yesterday, and was pairing them this way to prevent further hormonal teenage mischief. But, she had to admit, this theory gave Marsh a lot of credit she wasn't sure he deserved. Did he actually notice anything about his students beyond their performance?

Hal, Erin, and the professor crashed in their respective tents, while Peter and Athena circled the camp, moving in order to stay awake. Peter, usually as calm as stone, looked grim today.

"You okay?" Athena asked.

"Yeah, I'm fine," he said. "Why? Did Erin say anything to you about yesterday?"

"No," she said. "Did Hal say anything to you?"

"No," he said. "We went to sleep as soon as I got back to the tent."

"Yeah," Athena lied. "Us too."

They circled the camp a few more times. Athena's eyes were drawn to the village from every point of the perimeter. The people who had lived here must've been poor. Lived simply. What had they eaten? Had they grown food, or imported it? Where would they have imported it from? And what the hell was that stone building in the middle? A church? Some sort of temple?

She ached to leave the protection of the perimeter, to take a closer look. Marsh might be right about it being unimportant *and* dangerous, but what if he was wrong on either count? What if this place—that temple in particular—held answers to at least some of their questions? It seemed irresponsible *not* to investigate.

But Athena also understood there were rules, and said rules existed for a reason. She was a rule follower. It was something her parents had indoctrinated her with early on. They'd explained that, because of the color of her skin, people would always look for any excuse to disqualify her or kick her out. She had to be better than perfect if she was going to survive, let alone thrive. So now she stayed inside the perimeter with Peter, both of them uneasy about the strange sight before them. She formulated theories and guesses, about the temple, about Hal, and about Erin and Peter, but none of them made sense. She was still confused when her shift ended and she went to wake Erin.

Erin

Erin had hoped to feel better after some sleep, especially since she was getting the tent to herself for a bit. She'd hoped the panic in her chest would abate and she'd be herself. But when Athena woke Erin for her watch, and Erin shuffled out into the blinding daylight to see Hal, bleary-eyed and grumpy, doing the same, she found she still felt tense and irritable. She wished she could call off this stupid field trip, go home to sleep in her own bed, and get sorted.

She and Hal waved to one another, slathered sunscreen on their exposed skin, mixed two cups of instant coffee, and paced the perimeter of the camp.

"Anything interesting happen while we were asleep?" she asked. She swallowed a mouthful of coffee and tried not to gag. It was awful.

"Peter didn't say anything," Hal said. "What about Athena?"

"She seemed grumpier than usual, if that means anything."

"Who the hell knows?" he said.

He seemed grumpier than usual, too. Erin didn't ask him what was wrong. She didn't want to know, or share. She had her own shit to deal with. She gulped down the rest of her coffee and rinsed her mouth with bottled water, spitting into the sand.

"I hate this weather," Hal said. "You'd think the professor could do something about the heat and the light."

"I think he *is,*" Erin said. "He added something to my barrier command. This is Deoth through tinted glass."

"Christ," Hal said.

Erin pointed to the village. "Think Christ knows about this place?"

"It could be a scene from his life story," Hal said. "Except for the creepy evil-looking castle in the middle of town, I mean. But if you subtract that, maybe find a barn, and a manger? You'd be set."

"Who knows, maybe both of those things are in one of the buildings."

"Shame we won't ever find out."

"I know, right? It's *right there*." She made a wide gesture with her arm.

Hal pulled a small bottle from his pocket and offered it to her. "Want a drink?"

She took the bottle, looked at the picture of the turkey on the label. "Where'd you get this?"

"Don't worry about it," he said. "The question is if you want any."

Normally she wouldn't. But today, confused and unhappy, she welcomed the chance to deaden a few nerve endings. She twisted off the cap and tipped the bottle back to drink in a mouthful of fire. It set her throat and stomach ablaze. She coughed into her fist as she handed the bottle back.

"Holy shit," she said.

Hal laughed. "You're supposed to sip it, not gulp it."

Erin leaned forward and put her hands on her knees. She waited for her stomach to decide if she was going to throw up.

"Shit's awful," she said.

"Yeah, but it's cheap and it gets the job done." He said it like an older man—but not a real man. More like a sketch of a man, a composite of burned-out soldiers and cops from movies. It was almost adorable. She studied his profile as he took a drink.

"You psyched for senior year?" he asked her.

"I don't know." She stopped walking as they came to the part of the perimeter closest to the strange village. She looked at the purple cacti only a few yards away. She felt an ugly twinge, her chest and stomach playing a sour song of discomfort. "Just another rung on the ladder they drop you on at birth. You ever get tired of climbing?"

He pointed toward the temple in the village. "What do you think it's made of? Obsidian?"

"Or some other shiny black rock native to this place. I'm sure they have—or had—their own name for it. I'm more interested in what's inside." She took the bottle and drank again. This gulp went down no smoother than the last. She almost dropped the bottle as she coughed.

"Easy there," Hal said. "This bottle has to last me the rest of the trip."

She pressed her hand to her mouth, afraid her stomach would trampoline the whiskey onto the sand. She remained absolutely still until the nausea passed, then cleared her throat and drank more water.

"That *also* has to last the rest of the trip," Hal said. "Go easy."

"What *do* you think is inside, though?" she said. "I guess church-type stuff. Pews. Altars. Some graven images of their gods."

"You think there's more than one god?" Hal said.

"What if there's a god in every single world and reality? Or if some gods exist in some worlds and not others? What if some gods are kind and benevolent, some are sinister, and some are stupid? And there's no real order to how any of it is arranged. It's pure chaos. I mean, look at you. You wield a sword in the name of the Temple of Pain. You don't think there's some deity in charge of that?"

"Fair point," he said.

"And speaking of gods and temples . . . any word from the Temple recently?"

Hal shook his head. "Nothing since the day it told me to go into the woods."

Erin wasn't sure whether to feel relieved or unsettled at this. "You'd think it might have something to say about us coming here."

"I'm taking it as a 'no news is good news' situation," Hal said. "Like I must be on the right path, and they'll speak up if it turns out I'm not?"

"I guess that makes sense," Erin said.

"But that said," Hal said, "I'm dying to get the lowdown on some other temples. Should we check out that one over there?"

"Are you joking?" Erin said.

"We've got like two hours before we have to wake the professor. We can come back before anyone knows we're gone."

"What about the barrier?"

"You made it," he said. "I bet you could get through it easy."

Maybe it was the alcohol, or her thoughts about ladders, or her recently scrambled feelings about Peter. Whatever the reason, she felt reckless.

"Fuck it," she said. "Let's go to church."

Hal

Erin cut a small door through the dome, allowing them out into the blazing day. She made it look easy, as he'd suspected she would.

He noticed the difference in temperature and illumination immediately. The sun, obnoxious before, became a physical presence. The light and heat pressed down on him like a weight and after only a few moments, his head ached with pressure.

Erin groaned and shaded her eyes. "How can I feel so hungover when I'm still drunk?"

They closed the few yards between their camp and the oasis. No hordes of creatures emerged from the buildings to greet or devour them. The village remained quiet and calm, its silence as powerful as the sunlight above. Hal glanced back at the camp. It already looked far away, and he felt a pang of foreboding—which, he, of course, ignored. Instead he pointed at the purple cactus closest to them.

"Want a closer look?" But when he turned to get Erin's reaction, he caught a glimpse of her disappearing into the nearest hut. She reemerged a second later, shaking her head.

"Nobody's home," she said.

Hal went into another hut. It didn't appear anyone had *ever* been home. It was a space without furniture, cookware, books, art, or tools. Just an empty building. It put him in mind of the generic town streets movie studios kept on their back lots. Looked real enough from your couch, on a nineteen-inch screen, but wouldn't stand up to in-person scrutiny.

"This is weird," Hal said, meeting Erin outside.

"Let's check the temple," Erin said.

Again Hal experienced that pang of foreboding, more powerfully this time. Part of it was the temple's appearance—sinister as hell—but also its presence didn't diminish with proximity, the way the huts had. As they got closer, it seemed somehow *more* real, *more* present. He could see imperfections in the black stones comprising the building—uneven masonry, chips in the rock.

"Seems like the sand should've worn it down by now, don't you think?" he said, as he ran a hand across a wall. "It shouldn't be so glossy, right?"

As his fingertips lingered on the stone, he had another thought: *We need to turn back.* The instinct was as bright as a neon sign. But Erin walked past him up the steps, her pace quick and almost aggressive. Hal followed her so she wouldn't have to enter alone.

The interior of the temple was cool and dry and dark. Hal took the flashlight from his belt and turned it on to help Erin find her own. Then they split up, exploring the interior.

It did look like a church. Long columns of pews stretched forward on either side of the entrance. They appeared to be made of the same stone as the rest of the building, and, when he got close, Hal realized the benches weren't standing on the floor. They appeared to have grown up out of it like a natural rock formation. The whole place reminded him of the Temple of Pain. It was smaller, and less empty, but gave off the exact same vibe.

When he told Erin about this, she summoned him to the front of the chamber, where she was pointing her light at the wall behind the pulpit. As Hal approached, he realized what she was looking at: a bas-relief carved into the stone.

Even with both their flashlights turned on, it was impossible to see the whole image at once: only pieces. From what Hal could tell, it depicted a ship on a tempestuous sea, surrounded by creatures hidden beneath the waves.

"A water scene in a desert temple," Hal said. "Does that make sense to you?"

"I don't know," she said. "If water was the rarest, most precious resource in your world, wouldn't you make it part of your version of heaven?"

Hal turned back to the bas-relief. There was something familiar about the creatures in the water around the boat. He tried to get a better sense of the image, but either his light was failing or something else had gone wrong, because it grew harder to make out.

"Oh," Erin said.

Hal turned back to her, thinking she'd come to some realization, then understood why the bas-relief was suddenly harder to see. The temple door was closing—not like a regular door, but from top and bottom, like a pair of jaws.

The world around Hal turned sideways and he lost his footing. Erin cried out as she dropped her flashlight, and he lost his grip on his own. It bounced away into the dark as he fell and slammed into a hard surface. Just like the Temple of Pain three years ago. Falling through darkness. Getting beat up by a building.

There might have been an interesting connection to make, but he wasn't capable of making it. His head spun from the impact and the liquor. He was definitely drunker now than when he had walked in. Nothing pinned him down, and none of his bones felt broken, but he couldn't make himself sit up. It was as if the gravity had increased in direct proportion to the darkness in the church. He struggled for a moment before he realized it was fruitless, and let his head drop to the floor. It landed with a wet, sticky sound, and when he tried to lift it again, he felt something tug at his hair. So, nothing on top of him, but definitely something underneath.

"Erin?" he called.

"'M'here," she said, voice thick.

"Is it sticky where you are?"

Sounds of damp suction came from somewhere to his left as Erin experimented.

"Yup," she said.

"I don't know how to tell you this," he said. "But I think we've been eaten by a building."

"Maybe it's an alien monster disguised as a village," she said. "To lure in curious seekers like ourselves." She giggled, and Hal couldn't help but laugh, too. Some quiet part of him wondered about the oxygen levels in here. Were they suffocating? Was this sticky stuff on the floor pumping some drug through his skin, to keep him calm during the digestion process?

Erin's giggle became a full laughing fit. "This is so fucking stupid. What an awful way to go."

"At least I'm an orphan," Hal said. "Nobody will miss me. But how will the professor explain this to your parents?"

They both laughed until Hal's insides ached and tears ran down his face.

"Stop saying funny things," Erin said. "You're gonna get us killed."

He bit down on another fit of giggles. This was *not* funny. It wasn't. This was serious shit. He focused on taking smaller breaths, while also attempting to calm down. It was difficult. Also, was it his imagination, or was the air heavier now?

Green sparks flashed in the dark, providing still image glances of Erin, trying to make a Dissonant command.

"How do we get out of this?" she mumbled.

"Set a fire?" Hal said. "Like in *Pinocchio*?"

"We have no idea what we're breathing," she said. "It's making us goofy, and it could be a flammable gas. We start a fire and we might blow ourselves up."

"Okay, that's a fair point."

Sparks of green flashed and faded, and Erin groaned.

"I can't," she said. "Can't think straight."

"It's okay," Hal said. He meant it. He felt oddly peaceful. Relieved. "It's funny. I go into these adventures half-hoping to die."

"That *is* funny," she said.

"I'm not suicidal or anything," he said. "I wouldn't swallow a bunch of pills or jump in front of a train. But I don't mind being eaten by an alien monster. Or hell, I should probably have died in that fire last summer, with my mom. At least when you're dead, you can relax, right?"

"We'd miss you if you'd died," Erin said. "Me and Athena and Peter."

"I know," he said. "I'd miss you too. But then I wouldn't feel this way all the time."

"What way?"

"Sick to my stomach. I mean, when I'm with you guys, I feel good. But when I'm by myself? I feel like I'm going to throw up all the time."

"So marry Athena," Erin said. "Then you could have one of us around all the time."

"Is that your plan?" Hal said. "Marry Peter after high school, happily ever after?"

"We're talking about you," she said.

"Now I want to talk about you. I talk too much anyway."

"Sure," she said, a bitter tinge in her voice. "If we survive this, I'll go marry Peter right away. It'll be great."

"You sound super pumped about it," he said.

"Don't ask me to talk about it. I'm all fucked up on monster tummy gas."

"Me too," he said, realizing that his head was spinning. "Forget I said anything."

"Please don't tell Peter I talked this way about him."

"I can keep a secret like a motherfuckin' riot," he said, which sent them into peals of uncontrollable laughter. It wracked Hal's body like a terrible coughing fit, and when it finally tapered, both he and Erin were groaning with pain.

"Want to know a secret?" Erin said. "Since you can keep them?"

"Sure," Hal said.

"I noticed you first. In kindergarten. Before Peter, I mean."

"Yeah?"

"You were the first one I wondered what it would be like to kiss."

"Do you still?" Hal said. "Wonder, I mean." This was a bad avenue of conversation. He needed to reverse right the fuck out of here, but he seemed to be riding passenger in his own mind. He couldn't stop picturing her, two summers ago, all dressed up for the mixer at the Dissonant convention. In her white dress, legs long and shapely, her smile an absolute killer.

"I'm wondering now," she said. "Since we're probably going to die in a minute."

"Should we give it a go?" he said. "Kissing. Not death. Although both are obviously on the menu."

"What the hell," she said. More sparks flashed, and a floating ball of yellow-green light coalesced above Erin's outstretched hands. Hal squinted in the sudden flare to see Erin lying a few feet away, goofy grin on her face. "Hey, it worked. Guess horniness is a powerful spark."

With great effort, Hal rolled onto his stomach. He dragged himself forward on his elbows like an army man under enemy razor wire. His head swam, and his stomach burbled, but he managed not to throw up on Erin as he came to a stop beside her, lay back down, and took deep, ineffectual breaths.

"All right?" she said.

He raised one hand in a silent thumbs-up. With a grunt, Erin pushed up on one elbow, but lost her balance and landed on Hal's chest with a thud.

This was the moment, right? Caution to the wind, carpe that fucking diem. He lifted his head and kissed her. She kissed him back with surprising intensity, and within seconds, she'd jammed her hand down the back of his pants to squeeze his ass. Taking this as permission, he ran a hand up under her shirt and cupped the flesh of her breast through her sports bra. He was dimly aware of the fact he wasn't hard at all—his cock was as soft as a silk pillow—which was embarrassing. Luckily—or perhaps, more accurately, unluckily—he didn't have a chance to explain or remedy the situation, because as he came to the realization, the ground heaved beneath them.

It felt like a trampoline double bounce. Hal and Erin soared up, shaken loose from the sticky temple floor, limbs entangled. Light burned through the dark and momentarily blinded Hal. He fell and this time he landed in sand, Erin atop him, both of them covered in viscous gunk, her hand down his pants, his hand up her shirt. Hal squinted up into the light. The temple had risen into the sky, revealing itself as a head on a long, curving black neck of scales. Its aspect had changed from faceless building to an angry countenance out of myth.

It swooped down as though it meant to bite Hal, but its arc was interrupted by a burst of green energy. Stone exploded off the creature's face, and it bellowed in pain. Hal turned toward the source of the energy. Athena, Peter, and Professor Marsh stood shoulder to shoulder a few feet away. Athena's hand was raised, wreathed in light, leaving no doubt who had wounded the creature.

Hal knew he should move, but his head continued to spin, and he was afraid he'd puke. The temple beast reared back, and for a second Hal thought it would attack again, and this time it would not back down until it had torn the entire coven to pieces, regardless of how much power Athena threw at it. But it seemed to think better of this course of action. Instead, it turned its back on them and retreated toward the horizon.

"What was that?" Peter said.

"A trap," Marsh said. "For idiots who can't follow instructions."

Hal realized Erin was still on top of him, and that they were still groping one another. He freed his hand and pushed her off of him. He rolled up onto his knees, woozy and sticky. Not only had the temple disappeared—the huts and cacti and oasis pool were gone as well, leaving only flat gray sand in their place.

"What the hell were you two thinking?" Marsh said. "You're lucky Athena couldn't sleep, or you'd be dead now. We'd never have known what happened to you."

"We're sorry," Erin said.

"Give me one reason not to send you home right now," Marsh said.

"Erin and I have discovered a valuable piece of information," Hal said, trying not to vomit. "Here on Deoth, creatures can disguise themselves as buildings, so they can eat you. Imagine if we made that discovery walking into what we thought was the power source we're looking for? All five of us? That would be it for our coven. All our lives over." He snapped his fingers to emphasize his point.

"Bullshit," Marsh said. "None of the rest of us would be as stupid as the two of you. But at least it's thoughtful bullshit." He waved a dismissive hand and walked away.

"Thank you for saving our lives," Erin said to Athena.

Peter looked at Erin like he wanted to say something, but instead he followed his grandfather back to camp.

"He's probably freaked out," Hal said to Erin. It sounded flimsy, and he regretted the words at once.

"Or," Athena said, "maybe he's wondering why you two snuck off together while the rest of us were asleep. Maybe he's wondering why you were pawing at each other when the temple threw you up."

She didn't wait for them to answer, but turned and followed Peter back to camp.

Athena

The next night's trek passed in uncomfortable silence. If Professor Marsh was right, this would be the last march before they reached their destination. A day ago, Athena had been excited. Now she felt sad and angry and basically ready for this whole damn trip to end.

As the stars faded and the night sky changed from black to purple to gray, she began to make out shapes on the horizon, so slight she wondered if she'd imagined them. When the horizon brightened, however, the shapes remained visible and took on definition—three tall, narrow shafts thrust up out of the sand, evenly spaced. About two thirds of the way up the height of each shaft hung what looked like a large bucket.

"Is that it?" Erin asked, and pointed.

Marsh opened his fist. His Dissonant compass stone jittered and hopped in his hand, straining toward the shapes in the sand.

"Looks like the masts on an old sailing vessel," Peter said. "Like the *Pequod* in *Moby-Dick* if all the ropes and sails were removed."

"I think you're right," Marsh said.

"Huh," Erin said.

"What?" Marsh said.

"We saw something in the temple last night," Erin said. "A sort of bas-relief carved into the wall. It was a picture of a ship. I thought the whole thing was an elaborate trap, but maybe we got some legitimate clues while we were in there?"

Marsh considered. "Why would there be legitimate clues in a creature posing as a temple?" he said.

"Maybe it started life as a real temple, like the Temple of Pain, and then went feral?" Hal said.

Marsh laughed. "I suppose it's possible."

As they got closer, it became apparent the masts were still attached to the hull of the ship—it was just that the ship was mostly buried in sand. Only its stern pointed diagonally out of the earth, as if it had come to a halt on the downside of cresting a wave.

"The hell is an old-timey sailboat doing in a desert?" Hal said.

"You've fought a giant spider and sentient trees and were almost eaten by a temple yesterday," Athena said. "Desert sailboats are where your credulity ends?"

That shut Hal up, which was gratifying, but it didn't make the discovery itself any sweeter. She'd hoped for a Gothic castle, or a massive cyclopean city at the end of the journey, not a boat she'd seen in boring old movies or picture books. This was pretty lame, as far as Dissonant discoveries went.

They made camp within sight of the not-that-strange boat, and Marsh asked if he could trust the coven to stay put within the barrier. An abashed Erin and Hal gave their word to behave.

"Watches today will be same-sex," Marsh said. "Girls, you're up first."

They pitched their tents, checked the barrier's integrity, ate a hurried meal of unperishable junk, and the boys went to sleep. Erin and Athena stared at the derelict before them.

"What do you think we'll find?" Erin asked.

"I don't know," Athena said. "Maybe some books or scrolls if we're lucky. Records of what the ship was. Where it was going. Why it's giving off so much Dissonant energy."

"So, answers," Erin said.

"Sure. Otherwise, what the hell are we doing here?"

"Sightseeing?" Erin said.

Athena glanced at her, and the other girl flinched.

"Be honest with me," Athena said. "How did you and Hal end up . . . doing whatever you were doing at the temple?"

Erin didn't answer right away, which told Athena everything she needed to know. All that remained were the words to give the betrayal shape and specificity.

"We thought we were going to die," Erin said. "It was hard to breathe. The creature did something to us. Something in its digestive gasses got us high, like when the spider-things poisoned you. We were out of our minds. We made out a little, but I didn't like it, and I don't think Hal did either. We'd probably have stopped in another moment, but that was when you rescued us."

"I guess that makes it okay, then," Athena said, voice dripping with sarcasm. She looked at the boat and tried to force an interest. She'd been excited for this all summer, after all. Instead, all she could think about was how much she hated her best friends right now. How it wasn't enough for Erin to have Peter. She'd just had to take a shot at Hal, too.

"I'm sorry, all right?" Erin said. "Peter and I had sex for the first time the other night. It was . . . I don't know. It was a lot. I got overwhelmed and did something stupid and I wish I could take it back."

Athena remembered Erin's tears, that first morning in the desert. Her high-pitched, shallow breaths. What Erin said made logical sense, but Athena couldn't untangle her own knotted stomach.

"I'm sorry Peter's steadfast love is so confusing for you," she said. "That must be tough."

They passed the rest of their shift in silence, and after, for once, Athena was able to sleep. Professor Marsh woke them in the early evening for another meal. They packed up camp and dropped the barrier, since Marsh worried it might interfere with their ability to investigate. Anyway, this was the risk they were here to take. They approached the ship, Marsh holding a camcorder, the coven armed with cameras. Nothing emerged to greet them or turn them away. Nothing stirred. The vessel appeared unoccupied. But so had the fake village yesterday.

"The wood seems to be in good shape," Athena said. "You'd expect a boat that looks this old to have rotted by now, right?"

"Desert aridity would preserve it for a time," Marsh said. "But you're right. By now, a ship this old ought to have decayed."

The sand had covered enough of the ship that they were able to climb over the bulwarks and onto the deck near the center mast. The area near the front mast was completely buried, so they walked up the diagonal incline toward the stern.

Near the apex of the incline, Marsh squatted and set his compass stone on the deck. It vibrated, shook, and rolled forward, upward, toward the companionway that led belowdecks.

Marsh and the coven followed the stone. The old stairs groaned beneath their feet, but held as they came down into a narrow room lined with wooden bunks. There were no blankets or pillows on the beds, no dramatically splayed skeletons wedged in for an eternal nap. Just the wood itself.

On one of the beds, Athena found a leather-bound book, its pages yellowed with age. "Look at this," she said, lifting it to show the others. She opened it to a random page in the middle, and shone her flashlight on it.

"What does it say?" Hal said.

Athena frowned at it as she tried to translate. "I'm not sure," she finally said. "It's definitely Dissonant, but maybe it's like another dialect or something? Like I almost recognize the characters, but not quite. And check this out."

She held up the book so the others could see an illustration spread across two of the pages. It seemed to be a picture of a ship—perhaps the very ship they were standing in? There was a man-shaped figure on the deck, surrounded by jagged lines. Almost as if he were on fire. There was a smaller man-shape before it, also surrounded by those jagged lines. Behind both figures was another group of jagged lines, bigger than either. Within this third set of lines there was a scene—a modern-looking building and a few trees.

"What are the lines?" Hal said.

"Some sort of energy or force field, maybe?" Erin said.

"And maybe this is a portal?" Hal said, pointing to the trees and building within the third set of lines.

"Huh," Athena said. "Maybe."

Hal smiled at her, the question of forgiveness plain on his face, and she was torn between the desire to smile back and to smash his face in with a rock.

"Bring the book," Marsh said. "Let's keep moving."

As they continued their exploration of the ship, Athena's body buzzed with Dissonant energy, even more than on the day they'd crossed over in the Clegg woods. She closed her eyes. She felt like she could dissolve here: spread her consciousness thin and join this energy, forget her name, her friends, her life. She could tune in with this cosmic music and become a note in the larger melody.

She let go of this fantasy with reluctance, as the coven followed the compass stone into another room with a hatch in the center of the floor. Marsh bent over to scoop the stone back into his hand, and directed Hal and Peter to open the hatch. It revealed a ladder down into the dark. Hal descended first, without needing to be asked.

They entered what Athena assumed to be the hold. Their flashlights, though powerful, only illuminated a few feet in front of them. They crept forward. The wood groaned around them, louder than the stairs down into the crew quarters. The creaks sounded almost human. Like a person in pain.

"I don't think there's anything in here," Peter said.

"Maybe the crew took everything they could and left," Hal said.

"Left to where, though?" Athena said. She tried to imagine sailors running across the sands with folded-up sails full of cargo. It was possible. Maybe all of it was buried out in the dunes somewhere. She'd probably never know.

Erin cried out in alarm and stepped back, bumping Athena's chest. Near the back of the hold was a dark silhouette, somehow darker than the space around it.

The uncertainty of the light around the shape gave the impression of movement, and for a moment, Athena believed that there was something alive down here with them, something which had been lying in wait. Making out only pieces, she saw what could be an arm near the ceiling, and two legs spread in a fighter's pose.

"Hold, all of you," Marsh said. He directed them to point their flashlights in different directions, so they shone in the figure's general direction, but weren't pointed straight at it. Now a more solid image emerged: a statue in the middle of a stone circle, anthropomorphic in shape, slight and androgynous, its head bulbous and dented at the crown, sagging forward as though too heavy for the delicate neck below. Its narrow arms were clamped to the sides of its head like a child covering its ears. It had no face.

Lights flashed as the coven photographed the figure.

"Any mention of a light-sucking statue in your book, Professor?" Hal asked.

Marsh studied the statue through the viewfinder of his camcorder. "No," he said. "But what's stranger is the statue doesn't show up on the camera, even with the night vision filter turned on." He offered the camcorder to Athena. She traded him her flashlight and peered into the viewfinder, where the ship's hold was lit a neon green almost the color of the Dissonance. She turned the camera back and forth. She could see the professor and other members of her coven, but no statue.

"That is strange," she said, as she handed it back.

"We've discovered something new. A brand-new Dissonant phenomenon."

"Or something so old no one remembers it," Peter said.

"It looks familiar," Erin said.

"Yeah," Hal said. "It's in the exact same pose as the illustration in the book."

Athena didn't know why—maybe she was exhausted and overwhelmed—but the statue hurt to look at. Its posture communicated pain, but also a desolation, a loneliness. She looked away, eager to put her gaze on something—anything—else. She wandered past it toward the back of the hold. She found nothing, and took pictures of the emptiness. She tried not to remember her first impression of the statue, that things were darting out of sight at the flash of the camera. It was a trick of the light. That was all.

"Professor?" Peter said. Athena paused her documentation and watched as Professor Marsh stepped into the stone circle surrounding the statue. He walked the circumference twice, and after the second orbit, stopped before the figure and set the camera down.

"What are you doing?" Hal said.

"I'm trying to concentrate," Marsh said. "Kindly shut up."

Green sparks flashed from his fingertips, and Athena knew immediately that her teacher had made a mistake. She sensed it in the surrounding air, the charged energy which changed from a humming, blissful constant to something surprised and angry. The light trailing from Marsh's fingertips shone brighter and purer than any Dissonant energy Athena had ever seen before. She opened her mouth to warn her teacher and her coven.

She was too late.

Hal

Hal saw a flash of light and felt a wave of heat and then, for the second time in as many days, he was thrown through the air and slammed into a hard surface—this time the wall of the hold. The light blinded him, the explosion deafened him, and the impact knocked the air from his lungs. He couldn't see, couldn't hear, couldn't breathe. He only knew he was alive because the wood behind him had snapped and he felt the sand pour onto his exposed neck and down his shirt, where it stuck onto his sweaty back.

He managed a long, ragged gasp. It sounded far away. He was dully aware that his entire body ached as the world returned to him: walls and support beams cracked but holding for now; shards of plastic and metal and film scattered where there were formerly flashlights and cameras; the limp figures of Professor Marsh and the others on the floor; and at the center, the light-sucking statue.

"Hey," he said. "Everybody okay?"

No one answered. Hal moved on shaky legs toward Peter, who lay closest, facedown on the floor. Hal rolled the other boy onto his back. Peter's eyes were closed, his forehead cut and bloody, but he was still breathing, so Hal moved on to Erin, whose right arm bent at an awkward angle. She screamed when he touched her.

"I know," he said in his most reassuring voice. "I know. Stay here while I check on the others. We'll get you fixed up."

Marsh was already stirring by the time Hal got to him. The old man grunted and waved away Hal's proffered hand. Hal suppressed the urge to give the old fuck a kick in the ribs. It was Marsh's fault they were here, and his fault that everyone (except Hal) was hurt. But sure, wave off Hal's offer of help. Very manly thing to do.

Hal moved on to Athena, who lay on her back, her face a bloody crisscross of lacerations.

Hal knelt beside her. "Athena?"

She made a small, weak sound.

"She needs help," Hal called.

"We all need help," Erin said.

"Not me," Hal said, looking himself over. It wasn't a brag, but a statement of surprise. The blast had mutilated his clothing, but he couldn't find a single cut or bruise. "I'm okay."

Professor Marsh had gone to Erin to examine her arm. "I can fix this, but we have to get away from this statue first. Hal, can you carry the others out? I'm not strong enough to lift any of them and I can't use a Dissonant command to do it."

Hal reckoned he could. He started with Athena, and somehow managed to carry her up the ladder and stairs out of the ship. He followed Marsh back to the campsite, set her in the sand, then went back. He meant to get Erin next, but upon his return, was surprised to meet her walking up onto the main deck, her broken arm dangling at her side. So instead he went down and grabbed Peter. Peter was taller and heavier than Hal, so it was a struggle, but somehow, with the help of desperation and adrenaline, pure stubbornness and an unusually high threshold for pain, Hal managed to bring the other boy back as well.

He joined Marsh and the others inside a newly drawn protective circle, where Marsh was fixing Erin's arm with a Dissonant command. She screamed as the bones reknitted, but then it was over and she could move again.

Next, the professor tended to Athena, who was still unconscious. He drew a few commands in the air, then used bottled water and a rag to wash away the blood. When he'd finished, Athena's face looked as though it had suffered no injuries whatsoever.

Finally, Marsh crouched beside Peter. He drew a command line in the air, but Peter remained unconscious. Marsh drew another, with similar results. He tried two others—visibly different to Hal, although he couldn't have explained how—and Peter responded to neither. Marsh's gestures grew sharper, his face tauter. Hal settled onto his knees beside Marsh, and took Peter's hand in his own. Marsh murmured several words in a tongue Hal didn't recognize, drew in the air, then clapped his hands, collapsing the green light between them.

Peter's eyes flew open and he rolled onto his side, coughing.

"Peter!" Erin cried.

Peter blinked at her, confused, as Erin held his face in her hands. Hal let go of Peter's hand and stepped back. He knew he was still in the doghouse for what had happened in the faux-temple. He didn't want Peter to think that he, Hal, thought all was forgotten and forgiven.

And anyway, the ruckus had woken Athena as well. She sat up on one elbow and scowled as she looked around. "When did we leave the boat?"

"You're lucky to be alive," Marsh said, as he hauled Peter to his feet. "Can you walk?"

Athena let Hal help her up, but stepped away as soon as she gained her feet. She swayed like a drunk person. Hal reached out to steady her, and she swatted his hand away.

"I've got this," she said.

"I want to go home," Peter said.

"Yes, I think that would be best," Marsh said. He touched the boy's shoulder, a rare gesture of affection. "Athena, are you strong enough to open a doorway for us?"

"Don't we have to return to our point of entry?" Hal said. "Like sixty miles back?"

"I designed the doorway to take you where you want to go," Athena said. "We didn't know exactly where we wanted to go when we came here, but we know exactly where we're going now. It should be easy."

"Then please," Peter said. "Take us home." For once he didn't look calm, or Zen. He looked like someone who's woken from one bad dream into an even worse one.

Erin

The coven emerged onto the back lawn of Marsh House and staggered inside, out of the stultifying afternoon humidity. They gathered in the kitchen and ate a lunch of sandwiches, chopped carrots, and canned sodas. They inhaled the food without conversation. After days of chips and Pop-Tarts, the carrots were the best thing Erin had ever tasted.

They demolished a loaf of white bread, two bags of deli meats and cheese, and made a sizable dent in the house's peanut butter and jelly stores. Then, stuffed, they lay around the living room with the A/C on blast, while the professor disappeared into his study. The sweat on Erin's body turned cold and she shivered happily before drifting into a doze.

She woke later in the day. The sun had almost set, and without the lights on, the living room was dim. The others were already awake, sitting far apart from one another on couches and chairs, alone with their own troubled thoughts. Erin wanted to say something. To break the tension, start to heal the gap. But she could think of nothing, and the silence persisted, and the sun set, and then they sat together in the dark.

Hal spoke first. "What do you think the statue was supposed to be?"

"I had a dream about it," Peter said. "While we were napping."

"Me too," Athena said.

Outside the living room, the hallway light snapped on, and a moment later, Professor Marsh appeared in the entryway, backlit, mostly silhouette. Erin experienced a flash of panic as she was reminded of the statue.

The professor had changed back into his usual sweater-vest over a button-down and pressed khakis. He held a book in one hand. Erin recognized it as the one Athena had found on the ship on Deoth. Marsh must've grabbed it before they left.

"How do you feel?" Marsh asked.

"Lousy," Hal said.

"We went all that way, and the trip was a total bust," Erin said.

"A bust?" Marsh said.

"Sure," Erin said. "All our cameras destroyed. No photos, no video. No evidence or answers about what that place is or what it means."

"True," Marsh said. "But we walked on the surface of another world. We know that, despite the orthodoxy's claims, the Many Worlds theory is fact, even if we can't prove it yet. We found this book." He brandished the book at them. "And yes, there was an explosion and people were hurt, and that *was* unpleasant, but it also provided us an invaluable bit of information." He leaned in the doorway, arms crossed. "We suffered some setbacks, but you've done well. Be proud of yourselves."

Erin didn't feel proud, and none of the others looked happy either. Marsh lingered in the doorway for a moment, then moved on to the kitchen.

Athena got up off the couch. "I should get home," she said.

"I'll give you a ride," Hal said.

"I'll walk," Athena said.

"But your leg," Hal said.

She waved to Peter. "See you guys around."

Peter walked Athena to the front door, where they spoke in voices too soft to make out.

Erin looked at Hal, who stared at his lap, frowning.

"It's been a rough trip," she said.

"Yeah," he said. He didn't meet her eye. "We could all use a break from each other." He stood and walked out, toward his own bedroom.

Erin was alone in the dark when Peter returned, and the sight appeared to surprise him. He rocked on his feet, as though caught between approach and flight.

"Hey," she said. "You don't have to run."

He remained at the edge of the room. She crossed to him and

wrapped him in her arms. Even after days in the desert he smelled good to her. He stank the right way. He did hug her back, eventually, but the hug was cold. Perfunctory.

"I'm sorry," she said. "For what happened at the temple."

"Me too," he said.

His embrace remained distant, but she pressed on. She had to make him understand. "After the other night, I freaked out. I lost control. I didn't know how to stop it, how to calm down, how to talk to you, and I did something stupid." *What my mom would've done,* she didn't add.

"Okay," he said. He let her go and stepped away, leaving her a clear path to the front door.

What did *okay* mean? Okay, she was forgiven? Okay, he'd heard her and would consider it? But she lacked the courage to ask.

"I guess I'll head home," she said.

"That's a good idea," he said.

She saw herself out. The sun had set, and despite the relatively straight road ahead, Athena was already out of view. Probably for the best. What the fuck would they talk about tonight?

Erin walked home alone, to the trailer where she lived with her father, where she had a room of her own, a door to shut, a place to hide until she was ready to face the world again. As she walked, she thought about the illustration from the book they'd found on the ship. It had almost looked like a "how-to" diagram. But what was it trying to show them how to do?

2019
The Last Adventure, Part One

Athena

Athena struggles back toward consciousness, but it's like swimming with weights tied to her ankles. Each time she nears the surface, she takes in a little more information: her bad leg aflame with pain; the comforting rumble of a car engine; the gritty sound of rocks and dirt spanging off the underside of the car; the angry patter of rain on windows and roof.

When she comes fully awake, she finds herself in the hatchback of a station wagon, her cheek pressed into the carpet. Philip lies beside her, unconscious, mouth open and snoring softly. He could be catching an afternoon nap.

The fabric under Athena's cheek smells faintly of marijuana but it's drowned by a more powerful stench, sickly sweet like a Christmas ham left out of the fridge too long.

She sits up and looks into the front seat. A white teenage boy sits in the driver's seat, his posture stiff, his dark hair greasy. Kid needs a shower. In profile, he doesn't look any older than seventeen or eighteen.

The source of the stench rides shotgun: a rotting corpse (which had probably also been a white person, at some point in the past) in a dirt-caked black T-shirt. Its head hangs forward, chin to chest, long hair in its face. Its hands move through the air and leave yellow-green tracers of light behind, casting a heavy-duty concealment command.

Athena sits all the way up and rubs her face. Her mind is fuzzy, her thoughts vague, misty shapes.

The boy at the wheel glances at her in the rearview, then away again. The gesture is enough to tell her he's nervous, doesn't want to be here.

"Who are you?" she says.

Again that nervous look, at and away. "Owen," he says.

"Who's your friend, Owen?"

"He's not my friend," Owen says. He blinks a few times, as though trying to clear something from his eyes. "He killed my friends and took me hostage."

"Where are we going?" she says.

"Some house," the boy says. "Outside of town."

She looks out the closest window. Even through the heavy rain she recognizes the tree-lined road to Marsh House. When they come to the chained gate that stopped Athena's car yesterday, the corpse in the passenger seat flicks its wrist. The chain breaks and the gate swings open. Owen drives over the fallen chain, the metal barely making a sound beneath the tires.

The road ends at the circular driveway of the rambling single-story home that seems, from the front, to extend on into the dark woods behind it forever. The place where Athena discovered the Dissonance. The gateway to all her happiest, best memories, and most of her worst. What could her abductor want with the place?

"The house is empty," she says. "I looked yesterday."

The passenger stops moving its hands and turns to look at her. Its eyes are hidden behind dark sunglasses and the muscles in its neck groan and creak, and the bones click. How can this thing be alive? It stinks, looks, and sounds like something dead, a meat puppet being used by some animating force.

"Are you sure you saw what you think you saw?" it says.

It unbuckles its seatbelt and gets out of the car. "Owen, open the door for our passengers."

Owen comes around to open the hatchback door.

When Athena stays put, the corpse says, "Get out of the car."

"No," Athena says. Not because she likes it in the car, but because she wants to see what will happen if she refuses.

"I won't ask again," it says.

"You didn't ask the first time," she says. "But do me a favor and leave me the keys while you're inside. I want to listen to the radio."

The corpse's mouth stretches open in a toothsome grin. It lunges forward and grips her bad leg. She grabs the headrest behind her and kicks with her good leg. She lands a blow on the corpse's chest and hears something crack inside as it stumbles back, trips, and lands on its ass with a grunt and another audible crack. Its grin is gone, its face blank. Did she kill it?

No such luck. The thing blinks and looks to Owen. "Help me up."

Until now, Owen has been holding the tailgate open like a wet, filthy chauffeur. He lets go of the door and offers the corpse a hand up. It reapproaches the car, freshly soaked and dirtied.

"I am in this body, but this body is not me," it says. "I don't feel its pain, and it doesn't matter how many of its ribs you just broke. What *does* matter is that you defied me."

It draws a command in the air, and Athena tenses, braces for pain. None comes. Instead, Owen sprints away from the car and runs full speed, face-first, into the closest tree. He bounces off the trunk and falls onto his back, blood arcing through the air behind him. His hands fly to his face as he screams.

"What the fuck?" Athena says.

"You aren't afraid for yourself," the corpse says. "And I need your help, Athena. I don't need Owen anymore, strictly speaking. I will do worse to him if you test me again." Something about the coldness and the practical nature of the cruelty in the corpse's speech. It rings a bell of recognition deep in Athena, but she doesn't look too closely at it. She doesn't want to.

Athena scoots out of the car until she stands in the driveway. She turns back and shakes Philip's leg. His snore turns into a startled snort as he wakes, blinking.

"Time to get out of the car," Athena says. "Come on."

As Philip climbs from the car, he spots Owen bleeding on the ground. He doesn't ask permission, but goes to the boy and helps him up. The tulpa says something Athena can't hear, and strokes the boy's back.

"Fix the kid's face and I'll do what you want," she says to the corpse.

The corpse whips one hand in Owen's direction. The air cracks as though with thunder, and Owen falls back in the grass with a sound of pure agony that gives way to a gasp of relief. He sits up, face, hands, and chest still a bloody mess, but his expression implies more bewilderment than pain.

"Are you okay?" Athena asks him.

Owen touches his nose. "I think so?"

Philip helps Owen to his feet and touches the boy's face. Owen startles, but doesn't recoil.

"I'm disappointed," the corpse says. "All these years later and you still haven't absorbed my first lesson: there are some people you can help—"

She can no longer refuse to acknowledge the truth. It's looking her in the eye, and demanding she finish its sentence.

"And some people who will drag you down with them," Athena finishes. She feels sick to her stomach, and there's a burning sensation behind her eyes. Why would she cry at a time like this? It makes no sense.

"Professor Marsh," she says. It's not a question.

That terrible smile widens. "You always were my favorite, Athena."

Erin

Erin wakes from an awful dream to the feeling of rain on her face. When she opens her eyes and comes all the way awake, she finds herself strapped to a stretcher being carried down the church steps by EMTs. The people of Clegg, Texas, stand in clumped groups, eyeing her curiously.

"What happened?" she asks. Her voice is scratchy, her throat dry. The last thing she remembers, she was sitting in the church, and there were loud noises, and then she entered a dream that felt so very real. A dream about the worst day of her life. Now she's here, outside in the rain, surrounded by onlookers and the flashing lights of Sheriff's Department cars and ambulances.

"You're okay, ma'am," one of the EMTs says. "We just need to get you to the hospital."

"No," she says. Unless something has changed, the nearest hospital is a twenty-mile drive from Clegg. They'll keep her for hours. She knows somehow that she can't afford to lose that time. Something awful has happened. She can't feel Philip or Athena anymore. Hal's presence is faint and small.

"Stop," she says. "Let me off."

"Ma'am," the EMT says, with practiced calm.

"I'm not hurt," she says. Aside from a headache and a dry throat, she feels fine. "And I don't want a $1,200 ambulance ride or ER visit. I. Want. Off."

The EMT looks over Erin at his partner, a woman with curly dark hair. The woman shrugs. They stop the stretcher at the bottom of the stairs and lower the side rails. Erin hops onto the pavement. Her head swims, but only a little.

She looks around. The townspeople eye her curiously, as though silently begging her to make this make sense. A second ambulance finishes loading its own passenger and speeds down the street, siren blaring.

She walks back into the church, which has mostly cleared out. She finds her purse on the floor where she left it and fishes out her keys. She's halfway back to her car when her phone rings. It's Hal. She accepts the call as she climbs into her car.

"Erin?" he says.

"I'm here," she says. "At the church. Where are you?"

"I went on some sort of *Doctor Strange* trip," he says. "But I'm back now. Athena's not answering her phone. Can you see her where you are?"

Erin scans the crowd. She can't see Athena or Philip, and tells Hal so.

"That can't be good," Hal says.

"Agreed," Erin says.

"Will you come get me? I'm at Kinney's and I could use some help."

She could make the drive blindfolded. She leaves at once, and when she pulls into the parking lot, she finds Hal outside next to the ice freezers, brown paper bag in hand. He hurries over to get in the car, and tucks the bottle between his legs, hand covering the cap so she can't tell if he's broken the seal or not.

"I could go for a drink," she says.

He reaches into his pocket and pulls out a small blue chip. She's watched enough movies and TV shows to recognize AA paraphernalia when she sees it. She wonders why he didn't say anything about his sobriety at dinner the other night.

"Do you want to give me the bottle?" she says. "I can get rid of it."

"No," he says. "Not yet, anyway."

She nods. "What should we do?"

"Find the others," Hal says. "But I have no idea where to start."

"Okay," Erin says. Her thoughts are racing, but not going anywhere useful. She forces herself to take a deep breath. "Why don't you leave the bottle in the car and come inside with me? I need some fucking cigarettes and junk food to think this problem through."

They go into Kinney's and load a handbasket with sodas and chips and beef jerky and candy. At the counter, Erin adds two packs of yellow American Spirits to her total. When they reemerge into the parking lot, the rain has stopped. Does that mean anything about Philip? He can't be dead, because she'd be dead, too, right? So where is he? Why can't she sense him through the Dissonance, the way she senses Hal now?

She drives them back to the Saunders Inn, where they set up camp on the front porch with their snacks and sodas and proceed to smoke and binge. The cigarettes are heaven, but the soda and food leave Erin's throat sticky, her stomach upset. From the sour expression on Hal's face, she guesses he feels the same way.

"Remember when we could eat this stuff and not get sick?" she says.

He takes a swallow of Mountain Dew, smacks his mouth open and closed a few times, and makes a face. "We could put away a twelve-pack in an afternoon."

"I'd go into a diabetic coma if I tried it now," Erin says.

The joke lands with a thud, the momentary lightness gone. They each smoke another cigarette, and listen to the wind crinkle the plastic wrapper graveyard between them. Erin glances at the bottle in the brown bag, which is also on the table. Hal hasn't touched it. The cap remains sealed.

He catches her looking, and she tries to play it off, staring into the parking lot and taking a drag on her cigarette.

"Remember how I kept a bottle of Wild Turkey in my backpack during the trip to Deoth?" he says.

"Sure," she says. "You were mourning your mom, and I was fucked up after Peter and I had sex. You and I got drunk and into trouble, and broke the coven."

"That wasn't a mourning phase for me," he says. "It's been my whole life since Lorna died."

She grunts a humorless laugh. "I can identify. I've been mourning Peter for twenty years now."

"Yeah, but you didn't wish Peter dead and get that wish magically granted. You aren't the cause of your own pain."

"Aren't I?" Erin says. "If I hadn't left camp with you, if we hadn't fooled around, maybe things would have gone differently. We could have functioned as a team and won, instead of splintering and losing almost everyone we knew. It's my fault Peter is dead."

"If it's your fault, then it's mine, too," Hal says. "Lorna was my fault. Peter was our fault. And there's a third person on my conscience, too."

Erin smokes and waits for him to go on.

"Something happened about a year ago," he says. "Got hammered at my favorite bar. When I was leaving, I met some guy getting aggressive with his girlfriend in the parking lot. I stepped in, he fought back, we got into it. I don't remember what happened next, but when I woke up, the guy was dead and I didn't have a mark on me."

"Hal. I'm sorry."

"I met with my attorney earlier this week. He told me they're offering a plea deal of five to ten years. He thinks it's the best we'll get on an intoxication manslaughter charge. The guy's girlfriend saw the whole thing. They have me dead to rights. No wiggle room."

"Are you going to take the deal?"

He spreads his hands in an *I don't know* gesture. "Haven't decided yet. I got the invite to the memorial right after I walked out of my lawyer's office. This sounds silly, but it felt like a sign. Like maybe some higher power was pointing me in the right direction. Stupid, right?" He looks at the bottle and away.

"Not stupid," Erin says. "My life hasn't been great either. I'm thirty-six years old and working in a coffee shop. I've never had a relationship that's lasted over a year, or a job that's lasted more than two, and I missed my high school boyfriend so much I created a living fuckdoll replica of him, and thereby put all of reality in danger. You hurt one person, but if we don't solve this, *everybody* in our reality could end up dead, and that will be on me."

Hal stubs out his cigarette. "And we're the two walking around free, while the innocents, Athena and Philip, have vanished."

"Philip is an innocent," Erin says. "Athena's something else. She's carrying something, too. She just hasn't admitted to us what it is yet." She uses the end of one cigarette to light the next. She offers Hal the pack, but he declines. "You're right, though. It should've been us that disappeared, not Athena and Philip. We're the real fuckups, and we're out here smoking and stuffing our faces while they're god-knows-where. But what can we do?"

Hal frowns into the middle distance. Erin, offended, slaps his arm.

"Are you even listening to me?" she says.

"I am," he says. "But I think I might have an idea." He turns and smiles at her. "What do you think about the fuckups saving the day for once?"

Owen

The Cole-thing (which Athena calls Professor Marsh—she *knows* this thing?) leads its captives into the house. From the outside, it didn't look like anyone had lived here in years, but inside, it smells like Owen's grandma's house—old and musty, but lived-in.

Marsh turns on lights in the entryway, and then in a wide, sunken living room full of comfy-looking couches and chairs. An old tube TV sits on the floor, and vinyl records line the shelves.

"Owen, tulpa," Marsh says. "Shower is up the hall. There are clothes in my grandson's bedroom next door." He points. "Athena and I have things to discuss."

"His name is Philip," Athena says.

Philip, Owen thinks. It's a nice name.

"Is there anything to eat?" Owen asks.

"I couldn't tell you," Marsh says. "But anything you find, you're welcome to eat. It should be safe."

Athena follows Marsh down the hall into what looks like an office or study, and shuts the door behind them.

Owen goes into the bedroom Marsh indicated. It looks like its occupant might return any moment. The bed is unmade, and there's an open paperback book facedown atop the snarled blankets. The closet has two folding doors, one of which stands open. Its promised cargo of shirts and pants and coats hangs exposed on the rack.

Except for the rumpled bed, it seems a strange room for a teenage boy. There are no posters or decorations. Only a bed, a desk, a chair, a dresser, a nightstand, and stacks upon stacks of books. It's almost monastic.

"Hello."

Owen turns and finds Philip in the doorway. The man's beauty strikes him anew—the dimpled chin, wide blue eyes, and mop of fair hair. The broad spread of his shoulders. And most of all, the openness on his face. Owen's never seen anything like it. Everyone he knows wears a guarded expression. They're all on the lookout for how others might hurt them. But here is a man whose face contains no calculation, or shrewdness; just open, plain emotion. And right now, the emotion on display seems to be anxiety.

"It's okay," Owen says. "You can come in."

Philip takes two more steps into the room and wrings his hands. Owen isn't sure if *man* is the right term for Philip. When he first saw him at the church, he'd have sworn Philip was nearing middle age, but now he realizes he's probably in his mid-twenties.

"Are you hurt?" Owen asks.

"I've been separated from my—" Philip stops and puzzles over the next word. "My person," he finishes, although he doesn't sound satisfied with this answer. "And I am afraid."

Owen guesses Philip is referring to the woman who was asleep beside him in the church. The blond lady with the tattoos. A girlfriend? A wife? A sister?

"I bet she's worried about you, too," Owen says.

This idea appears to be a new one for Philip, and seems to increase his discomfort rather than lessen it. Owen's sorry he said anything. He thought it sounded right, but clearly it was wrong. Maybe he should keep his mouth shut. He's finally feeling the weight of the last few days, the toll on his body and mind. Exhaustion urges him toward collapse.

"Do you want the first shower?" Owen asks.

"You're covered in blood," Philip says. "You go first."

Owen grabs some clothes from the closet and goes to the bathroom to shower. It's glorious, the water hot and firm, unknotting his muscles and sending cascading waves of pleasure down his naked body. He stands beneath the showerhead and lets the flow massage his scalp for what seems an unconscionable length of time. When he's had his fill, he climbs out, dries off, and dresses in the borrowed clothes. They're a little big on him, but at least they're clean.

When he returns to the bedroom, he finds Philip at the desk, studying something in his hands. He turns to look back at Owen, and again Owen wonders how he could've thought this person was over the age of twenty-five. He's in his early twenties at the latest.

"Hello again," Philip says.

"Shower is all yours," Owen says.

"Thank you," Philip says.

When Philip leaves the room, Owen approaches the desk to see what Philip was looking at. It's a framed 3x5 photograph from an old film camera, and depicts a boy who looks like a younger version of Philip—well, almost. The boy in the photo has a slightly more hooked nose, and his eyes are a little too close together. He looks more like a first draft of Philip, with his arm around a pretty blond girl in sunglasses and cut-off jeans. She could be the woman he saw in the church today—the one he and Marsh didn't kidnap. Same mouth, same chin. Philip's person from the church, maybe, but fifteen or twenty years earlier.

Owen puts the photo on the dresser, tightens his belt around the ill-fitting jeans. He stands in the room, waiting for someone to come tell him what to do. Marsh has given him nonstop directions since their first meeting in the cemetery, and now he feels at loose ends, terrified of doing the wrong thing.

But eventually boredom wins out, and he wanders the house. Supposedly abandoned, but the electricity is on, the A/C is working, and Owen can't find a hint of dust. Has someone been taking care of the place? Do other people live here, individuals Owen hasn't met yet? No one comes out to greet Owen, so he guesses not.

He goes to the front door and opens it. No one stops him. He could do it. He could walk out the door right now. The car keys are still on the kitchen table. He could get away from here.

Sure he could. He could sneak off, leave all of this behind. And go where? He just assaulted a church.

So yes, he *could* flee. But there aren't too many places he could go right now. He doesn't know what to do.

Voices draw his attention toward the rear of the house. Owen follows the sound down the hallway, which ends at a set of heavy-looking double doors. Light streams from the small gap between. Owen is careful not to obstruct it as he creeps forward to eavesdrop.

"Has it ever been done before?" Athena is asking.

"No," Marsh says. Is it Owen's imagination or is his control of Cole's voice weakening? "Or not in any book I've read."

From behind him he hears the sound of breaking glass, followed by a sickening thud. Owen runs toward it, his footsteps muffled on the thick shag carpet. He throws open the bathroom door. Philip lies on the floor in a mosaic of broken glass, his body a crosshatch of cuts. Jagged shards of glass hang where the shower door used to stand. Water continues to spit from the showerhead, washing blood down the drain.

Athena

Athena can't quite believe she's finally back at Marsh House. It doesn't seem real, but rather like a dense dream. The smell of the house—a potpourri of old person and wood paneling—brings back a flood of memories, a sense of deep comfort commingling with the deep unease she's carried the last few days. Her eyes sting with sudden tears, and she wipes them away as Marsh directs Owen and Philip to shower and make themselves at home. She follows Marsh into the study, where the magic and terror took shape for her so many years ago.

Marsh shuts and bolts the door behind them and limps to the massive wooden desk. He runs a pale, translucent hand along one edge of the surface. The wood shines as if someone polished it this morning.

She remains near the doors. There's no point in trying to escape, but she can't convince her body to come closer to the thing.

"How is this possible?" she asks.

Marsh walks around the desk to his old high-backed chair. "Me, or the house?"

"Either. Both."

Marsh sits in the chair. His posture—the stiff shoulders, the elbows on the desk—identifies him, unmistakably, as her old teacher.

"You tell me," he says. "If you were trying to solve the mystery, what would be your hypothesis?"

Her mind grabs on to the puzzle, hungry, grateful for something to work on, and she feels calmer at once. This is her sweet spot.

"Starting with the house?" she says. "It could be a simple illusion command, right? Make it look abandoned from the outside. But." She stops there and frowns.

"Yes?" Marsh says. He sounds pleased, and God help her, she's pleased he's pleased.

"But," she says. "That can't be all. It doesn't explain the inside of the house. Why the power is on. Why there's no dust." She licks her lips, realizes she's thirsty and has been for a while. "Have you somehow slowed time on the interior of the house?"

"Basically," Marsh says.

"But how?" she says. "I thought time travel was one of the big, inviolable rules of the Dissonance?"

"Time travel supposedly is, yes," Marsh says. "But like so many Dissonant commands, slowing time is merely *bending* the rules, not breaking them. It's something Peter was working on before he died. I borrowed it from his notes. Quite brilliant, once I worked the kinks out."

"But again, how?" she says. "You severed your own connection to the Dissonance after you severed us." She stares at him. "You didn't, though. Did you?"

"No," Marsh says. "I continued my studies for another ten years. I couldn't give up when I was so close. Same old story, isn't it? Moses wanders in the desert all his life, only to die within sight of the promised land. I was close to answers of my own when I discovered I had cancer. So I put my affairs in order, cloaked the house, and waited to die."

"You could've called me," she said. "When you got sick. Before the end."

He looks mildly surprised. "Would you have come?"

"Yes," she says. "I would have. I bet Erin and Hal would have, too. You were our last tie to the best part of our lives. I spent years after Peter's death waiting and hoping you would change your mind, call us back together, and make us whole. We'd have come because we wanted to be forgiven."

"Then I made another mistake," Marsh says. "Another in an endless parade."

"What was it like to die?"

He sighs. "It was like sliding into the most wonderful nap. For a little while. Then I woke up. What came after wasn't fun."

"You didn't go to heaven, I take it?"

He shakes his head. "You don't learn the things I've learned, or grow as powerful as I became, without hurting and crossing people. It's the price you pay for greatness. I don't know if there's more than one hell, but the one I went to was staffed by bored, incompetent bureaucrats."

"That does sound like hell for you," Athena says.

Marsh grunts with what might be a laugh. "They put me to work doing data entry. Recording the sins of the living. Adultery. Lies. Fraud. Theft. I once spent eight hours tallying the number of sticky notes a man stole from the bookstore where he worked. And I watched the tapes—I'm pretty sure he never did it on purpose.

"When we weren't working, they put us in cells, but they were inattentive, and it only took me a few days to escape. I don't think they bothered to search for me, and why would they? They were receiving fresh souls every day."

Athena finally overcomes the worst of her revulsion to Marsh in this rotting body. She takes her old seat in the armchair before the desk, curled up like she's sixteen again, and listens.

"I made friends with refugees in the mountains beyond the city," Marsh says. "Most of them were scum—rapists, murderers, child molesters—but there were a few people of vision like me, made to pay the price for doing what was necessary. They welcomed me into their enclave, and there I dwelt, looking for a chance to return. The laws of the multiverse make a return from the dead almost impossible, but there are occasional openings. The surprise—although perhaps it ought not have been—was that one of my former students made it possible. When Erin created her tulpa, she threw off the balance of universal rules. All I needed was a back door, and a body. Through luck or fate, a group of teenagers in Alabama—Owen, and the boy who used to live in this body"—he gestures to himself—"decided to perform a necromancy ritual in a cemetery. It was internet nonsense, but because reality was in flux, and because Owen is more powerful than he knows, I manipulated the ritual, made it temporarily true. The return . . . took a toll on my mind. I didn't know who or what I was, only that I was frightened and wanted to live. I killed Owen's friends, took this body for my own, and made Owen drive me here. I hurt others along the way. I regret that. I wasn't in complete control." He grunts. "But I don't think it was chance that Erin opened the door that brought me back. I think she was meant to, the same way I was meant to return and find you."

"You're saying this is the will of God?" Athena says. "After all you taught us, you're a believer?"

"Call it whatever you want. The will of God. The natural unfolding of reality. Something is moving us around on a gameboard. I think this thing, this power, wants us to return to Deoth."

"Why?" Athena asks, meaning both *Why would you think that?* and *Why would the multiverse want us there?* But there's a bigger question she speaks aloud: "Why approach it like this? Why not call and ask for help? Why not bring Hal and Erin, too? Why knock me out, make me dream the worst day of my life, and abduct me?"

"What did you dream?" Marsh asks. He seems interested, which is a surprise. He caused the dream, so shouldn't he know?

"I dreamt about the day Peter died."

"I suppose that's to be expected," Marsh says. "Regardless, reality is a china plate less than an inch from shattering on the kitchen floor. I didn't have time to be polite. Hal and Erin would only slow us down. You're the one I need. If we succeed, we'll help everyone, Erin and Hal included."

Maybe he's telling the truth. Maybe he can save Erin's life without destroying reality.

"What do you need me to do?" she says.

"You still read and speak Dissonant," he says. "I have a vision, but I don't know how to execute it. I need you to write the code."

"You don't have my old grimoire with the doorway command?" she says.

"Oh no, I kept everything you did," Marsh says. He opens the desk's top drawer and there it is: *Athena's Cookbook*. Athena's heart catches in her chest. She didn't expect the book's reappearance to cause such a surge of emotion.

"A record of an extraordinary mind at work," Marsh says. "I was sorry Peter fell in love with Erin. I always thought you were the better match. But that's in the past." He looks up from the book. "I don't need your help with the things you've already done. I need you to write something new. Your ninth symphony. Your masterpiece. A ritual you will perform before the statue, in the derelict ship on Deoth."

"We nearly died the last time we used the Dissonance there," she says.

"That's why you're going to figure out a way to direct that energy and focus it." He pulls a stack of loose-leaf paper from the same drawer where he kept the *Cookbook*. He extracts several pages and arranges them on the surface of the desk. Athena crosses the room, curious.

The pages, placed together, comprise a crude diagram, a scaffold of wires and metal piping above two gurneys, all of it built around the bizarre statue that's haunted her dreams for the last twenty years. She opens her mouth to tell her old teacher this is ridiculous—a comic book daydream—but interrupts herself with a thought. The first vague shape of an idea.

"What do you need so much power for?" she asks. She thinks she already knows, but she wants him to say it without all the grand language about purpose and destiny and saving the world.

"The tulpa in my bathroom has no soul," Marsh says, pointing into the house behind her. "I have a soul, but no viable body. I want you to solve both our problems by moving my soul into Philip and healing reality."

"Has it ever been done before?"

"No," Marsh says. "Or not in any book I've read. If my guesses are correct, we'll need nuclear levels of Dissonant energy to make it work. The ship on Deoth is the only place I've ever encountered that much power."

"I thought that power was focused around the statue in the hold," Athena said. "After what happened at the high school in 1999, why would you think the statue would still be there?"

"I've seen it," Marsh said. "From hell, I was able to see other worlds. I don't know how it got back there after the destruction of the high school, but it's there again."

She wants to ask for more information—particularly, she wants to know why he had this design sitting in his desk before he died—but before she can voice this question, a muffled crash sounds behind her. There follows the sound of footsteps, retreating down the hall from the study, and then Owen is shouting for help.

Athena runs out of the room and up the hall to the bathroom. What she sees through the open door looks like an accident or crime scene photo. The shower door has shattered from the inside, and Philip lies curled in the fetal position on the floor, naked and bloody, his head in Owen's lap.

"He won't wake up," Owen says.

Hal

After changing out of their formal wear and into more comfortable clothes, Hal and Erin walk through Clegg City Park for Hal's Hail Mary play. The walk is longer and more tiring than Hal remembers. Middle age continues to creep, making a simple nighttime stroll slower and more painful.

He pauses now to put his hands on his hips and crack his back. "Almost there," he says.

"You sound winded," Erin says.

"I need to get in shape," he concedes. "I hear prisons have superb exercise facilities."

"Something to look forward to."

He laughs, and his laughter turns into a coughing fit—his punishment for the cigarettes they smoked earlier. "Fuck you for making me laugh right now."

They resume their trek through the park and come to the creek in its middle. Normally it would be completely dry by now, but the storms of the previous days have left the water high.

Hal pulls his keys and cell phone from his jacket pocket and sets them on the ground. He strips down to his boxers and looks into the water below. This would be a lot more fun and less embarrassing if he could have a drink. His throat feels dry and he thinks of the bottle of Maker's Mark back at the hotel. Oh well. He's come too far now.

He tries to lower himself down the embankment, but loses his balance and tumbles into the water with a cry and a splash. It's humiliating, and not at all how he meant to get here, but it will serve. He remains beneath the surface, hands and feet pushing into the soft dirt of the creek bed. He lets the water flow around him until the shock wears off, then opens his mouth and expels a single word like a comic book thought bubble: *Morgan.*

He rises from the water and wipes his hair out of his face.

"Everything okay down there?" Erin says. He can't see it but he hears the smile in her voice. She sits on the embankment with her arms around her knees.

"I feel like an idiot," he says.

"That's funny—you look like an idiot."

"I'm glad one of us is having a good time."

"For real, though. What now?"

"I called to her, with no guarantee that this is how she receives calls, or if she even can. Now we wait and hope she comes."

He looks up the length of the creek into the woods. This is so stupid. A grown-ass man in this filthy-ass water, praying he can summon supernatural aid? And iffy supernatural aid at that. The last time Hal got a boon from an undine, his mother ended up dead.

Because the water is moving, its surface is turbulent. He doesn't see the figure approaching until it breaks the surface and rises before him. It is unmistakably an undine, slender and silvery in the moonlight, a fairy tale from another life, brought into the hell he's living now. But it's not the undine he knows.

"You're not her," he says. "You're not Morgan."

"Morgan was my mother," the undine says. "I am her daughter. Sybil."

"Was?" Erin says from her spot on the embankment. "She died?"

The undine appears to notice Erin for the first time. Her shoulders tense and her mouth scrunches down.

"It's all right," Hal says. "This isn't an ambush. We're friends. My name is Hal Isaac, and that's Erin Porter."

"Hal," Sybil says. "Erin. I know these names. My mother told me about you."

"What did she say about us?" Hal asks.

"She told me you saved her life. And that a friend of yours saved mine."

"I remember saving Morgan," Erin says. "But when did we save you?"

"Neither of you were part of that event," the undine says. "It was the other boy. Peter. I was barely more than a baby. I am sorry he died before I could truly meet him. My mother said we owed Peter a second boon for his service. Since he has died, that boon passes to you."

Fix it, Hal wants to say. *Make it so my accident never happened. Bring back the man I killed. Save my life.* The thought is followed immediately by a wave of shame. This is no time for selfishness.

"Do we get to pick the boon this time?" Erin says. "The last time your mother offered a boon, Hal's mother was killed."

Sybil frowns. "I don't think that's right. When my mother died, your boon had not yet been bestowed."

Hal, who has been contemplating a literal "get out of jail free" card for the last several seconds, finds his train of thought derailed. It crashes and bursts into flames against the mountain wall of this revelation.

"Are you telling me," he says, "it was a coincidence that my mother burned to death the night we saved Morgan's life?"

"I can only tell you it wasn't the boon," the undine says. "How or why it happened had nothing to do with my mother."

Hal sloshes over to the embankment, climbs out of the water, and plops down with a squelch. He needs a minute to process this.

"Your boons are imminent," Sybil says. "You will receive them soon, as will the others of your coven. Athena, and the one she travels with—the one who has emptiness where his light should be."

"Philip?" Erin says. "He's not part of our coven."

"A new coven forms," Sybil says. "With new members, and new agreements. But we're running out of time. We have a journey ahead of us. The first part of your boon."

"Are you going to help us save our friends?" Hal says.

"I can give you a chance," the undine says. "Not a guarantee. And this boon will render my debt paid. You won't be able to call on me for help again."

Hal stands and forces himself to focus. He looks at Erin, his question unspoken. She takes his hand and stands up beside him.

"Last march of the fuckups," she says.

"We understand and accept," Hal says.

"Then Hal Isaac, I suggest you reclothe yourself," Sybil says. "You'll most likely require pants for the journey ahead."

Owen

Athena helps Owen move Philip into the kitchen, because it's the only other room in the house with a tile floor. Marsh hobbles in a moment later with a book under one arm. He kneels, tendons groaning, and studies the unconscious tulpa.

"The damage is mostly cosmetic," Marsh says. "I can fix that. What I don't understand is why he flew through a glass door or why he won't wake up. Breath and pulse seem normal. I thought that, here in this house, he'd be safe from nature's attempts at correction, but perhaps I was mistaken."

He picks up the book he brought with him, flips through the pages until he finds what he's looking for, then hands the open book to Owen.

"Hold this for me," he says.

Owen squats next to Marsh as Marsh reads to himself, lips moving. He raises his hands in the air like an orchestra conductor, murmurs and draws shapes, each finger stroke leaving a tracer of green light in its wake.

The light grows brighter and more defined as Marsh draws. A sound rises to join it—something between the popping of a campfire and the crackle of electricity. There's a smell, too, familiar but hard to place. Earth and stone and something else.

The crosshatch of cuts across Philip's body thin as the skin knits itself back together. At first there are light scars, but they quickly flatten and fade into unblemished flesh.

Owen notices the miracle, but distractedly. He's more interested in the symbols Marsh draws in the air. His mind falls quiet for the first time in days, and in this stillness, he recognizes part of the symbol Marsh has drawn. One part means *body*. Another means *whole* or maybe *entire*. There's plenty in the sigil Owen can't make sense of, though. He focuses on these unclear parts, and scries for meaning, but the lights flash and vanish before understanding arrives.

All of this—the comprehension, the reading—happens in the space of a breath. When it ends, Owen finds Athena watching him, rather than the miracle on the floor.

Marsh, on the other hand, doesn't seem to have noticed anything. He pulls his borrowed mouth into a smirk.

"Quite a thing, isn't it?" he says.

Philip's head lolls to one side, eyes closed.

"He's not awake, though," Owen says.

"I've healed his body, but I can't reach his mind. He'll have to find his way back on his own. I have other important work to do tonight."

Marsh goes back to the study, leaving Owen and Athena to tend to Philip. Owen cleans the blood off the unconscious man, and only feels a little guilty for enjoying the task, the chance to brush the toned arms, the broad chest, the long, muscular legs, and the face somehow innocent and adult at once, almost angelic.

Athena and Owen carry Philip back to the teenager's bedroom. Together they work boxers and a T-shirt onto him. Owen does his best not to look. Then, the sleeping beauty having been dressed, they put him in the bed.

"Watch over him," Athena says. "Let me know if anything changes."

She starts to leave, then pauses in the doorway. She looks like she has more to say, but stops herself from saying it. Then she does leave, and allows Owen to focus on Philip. He looks peaceful in the bed, his chest rising and falling in a slow, steady rhythm. Owen thinks of Snow White in her coffin in the forest, waiting for true love's kiss.

He turns away. It's rude to stare at unconscious people's junk, and you shouldn't kiss them, either. These are all chapter one lessons in the "Don't Be Creepy" handbook. He busies himself exploring the bedroom. Who knows, maybe if he makes enough noise, Philip will wake up.

He starts with the closet, where he finds a bunch of old No Fear and Mossimo T-shirts, and a box of *Real Ghostbusters* toys on the top shelf. He moves on to the bookshelf, which is stocked with fantasy novels by Ursula K. Le Guin, R. A. Salvatore, and Michael Moorcock. There are a few graphic novels—*Watchmen, Kraven's Last Hunt*—and a few gardening books as well.

Next Owen examines the desk. The top is free of clutter, and the first drawer contains a neatly arranged collection of pens, paper, highlighters. The middle drawer is full of drawings, crude sketches of what look like desert landscapes, an old sailing ship stranded on the dunes, and a statue with a humanlike figure in its center. There's something unsettling about this last one. Its posture is off, and the proportions seem wrong, the limbs too thin, the head too large. The figure communicates immense pain.

He puts the sketches back where he found them. In the bottom drawer, he finds a VHS tape, still shrink-wrapped from the store. A movie called *Hackers*. The box art features two beautiful, familiar-looking people. If Owen weren't so tired, or if he had his phone, he'd recognize or at least look up the faces. (God, he misses his phone.) He flips the VHS over to read the synopsis on the back. He finds a scrap of paper taped over it, and on the paper, a brief note:

> *Erin*
> *You are elite.*
> *Love always,*
> *Peter.*

Owen replaces the VHS, grabs the desk chair, and drags it in front of the bed. He sits in it with a sigh, props his feet on one corner of the mattress, and crosses his arms. He watches Philip sleep, flat on his back, arms at his sides like a corpse.

He isn't aware he's fallen asleep until a hand on his shoulder shakes him awake. It's Philip, leaning out of the bed, concerned.

"You're awake," Owen says.

"Why are you sleeping sitting up?" Philip says.

"I didn't mean to sleep," Owen says. "I was watching you. To make sure you're okay."

Philip lets go of Owen and rubs his eyes with the heels of his hands. "Do you want to trade places? I can sit up and watch while you sleep."

Owen laughs. "You don't have to watch me sleep. I was only

watching you because of what happened in the bathroom. Do you remember?"

Philip drops his hands in his lap. "I was in the shower, and then I was in a terrible dream. Then I woke up here and found you asleep in the chair. You looked like you were going to fall over, so I woke you up."

Owen stands and stretches. "I should let Athena and Marsh know you're okay."

Philip grabs him by the wrist. "Don't go." He scoots back on the mattress until his back is against the wall and half of the mattress is empty.

"It's big enough for both of us," he says.

It's not, but Owen is so damn tired, and the bed looks so damn cozy, and the person inviting him into it is so damn handsome. He plops down on the bed and rolls onto his right side, but startles when Philip drapes an arm across his chest.

Philip withdraws. "Was that wrong of me to do?"

"Not at all," Owen says. "Just wasn't expecting it." He tries to relax as the arm drapes over his side again, and the warm body scoots up behind his. Owen puts his own arm on Philip's. He marvels at its smoothness.

"You smell good," Philip says.

"Thank you," Owen says. "So do you." He tries to force his breath to come normally, without hyperventilating. He fails. He's wide awake now, completely aware of his own body and Philip's: the warmth, softness, and comfort of being close to someone who wants to help you feel better, rather than worse. It's too much. Finally, days after watching his best friend and classmates murdered in a church graveyard, Owen's entire body shakes and he cries.

"Are you okay?" Philip says. "Is it me?"

"No, Philip. It's not you." He pulls Philip's arm tighter around himself. "And no, I am not okay."

1999
The Day Of
(and What Came After)

Hal

Hal didn't technically move out of Marsh House after the coven's return from Deoth. He still had a room and a house key, but he stopped making use of either. There were no words exchanged with Professor Marsh or Peter. Instead, Hal packed his clothes in a duffel bag, got into his car, and looked for other places to sleep.

The first two nights, he slept in his car, and it sucked. The backseat of Lorna's convertible was too narrow to spread out, and the front seat didn't push back far enough to lie down comfortably. Also, it was the time of year when it remained unbearably hot until three or four in the morning, and he couldn't afford to leave the car running all night. Without A/C, he never sank deeper than a mild doze. It was terrible, and he hated it, but after cheating on two of his best friends with his other best friend, he felt he deserved it. So he sweated, and he stank, and he drank whiskey. This last didn't help with the perspiration, but it helped him care less about everything, which was almost the same thing.

When he woke on the third morning, his bottle empty and his stomach rumbling, he counted the meager contents of his wallet: seven dollars. He drove to Kinney's convenience store to buy soda and chips. He'd rather have had more alcohol, and he knew the clerk would sell it to him (Hal guessed the clerk felt sorry after Lorna's death, and was helping Hal in his own small way), but he needed to eat something.

The bell over the door jingled as he entered, and the clerk and the customer at the register stopped their conversation to look at him. The customer was Erin. She looked like she'd had a rough go the last few days as well. Her face was puffy, her eyes clouded and vague with exhaustion.

Hal stopped in the entryway, unsure whether to flee or enter. The door bumped into his back.

"In or out," the clerk said. "We're not trying to air-condition the whole damn town."

Hal headed down one of the store's three aisles. He already knew what he wanted, but he browsed air fresheners and cans of WD-40 so Erin had time to leave before he picked out his 20-ounce bottle of Dr Pepper and two bags of Doritos.

When he left the store with his makeshift breakfast, he found Erin on the sidewalk outside waiting for him.

"You look like hell," she said. "And you smell like a whiskey barrel that just ran a marathon."

"Yeah, but I feel great," he said, and tried to smile.

"Did Peter kick you out?" she asked.

Hal stopped at his driver's side door and let his head drop. "Not technically, no."

"Then why do you look and smell like that?"

He turned to face her. "I've been roughing it."

"Sleeping in your car, you mean," she said.

"If you want to get technical."

After a moment of quiet, she spoke again. "I've tried to call Marsh House. To tell Peter it was my fault. But no one ever answers."

"It was both our faults," Hal said. "But it doesn't matter. What matters is that it happened, and we got caught."

From the shocked look on Erin's face, he guessed he'd said the wrong thing, so he threw up his arms in a *who knows* gesture. "But what the fuck do I know? I've never been in a relationship that's lasted."

"I haven't spoken to Athena since we got back," Erin said, seeming to read his mind. "Her I haven't called."

"Me neither," Hal said.

"You should at least try," Erin said.

"Yeah, maybe," Hal said. He planned on doing nothing of the sort.

He opened the car door and got in, but instead of leaving him alone, Erin came to stand next to his rolled-down window.

"Don't sleep in your car," she said. "You can stay with me and my dad. We have a pull-out couch in the living room."

"It's nice of you to offer," he said. "But that wouldn't look good."

"It doesn't matter how it looks," Erin said. "What matters is you need help." He didn't answer right away, so she continued to make her case. "Please. I need to do something good right now. I need to believe I'm capable of being a good person." Her free hand wavered over her chest as she spoke, in the same spot where Hal had carried his own pain for the last few days.

He told Erin to get into the car. They drove back to her father's trailer. He moved his duffel bag of belongings inside, and slept on the living room couch for the rest of summer break. He and Erin spent their days getting ready for the new school year, and their evenings watching movies on TV. No lingering touches or suggestive looks passed between them. Whatever had sparked between them on Deoth had burnt out, thank the gods. What remained was friendship, camaraderie, and a mutual sadness they never talked about.

Every night at about midnight, Erin would help Hal fold out the couch before she went to bed. Hal would listen to her get ready—the telltale sound of brushing teeth, mouthwash, the flush of the toilet. He was patient. He waited until the trailer fell silent (save for Mr. Porter's snores in the front bedroom), then opened Mr. Porter's liquor cabinet. He paced himself, with small sips from varied bottles, so nothing disappeared too quickly. He only drank until he grew comfortably numb, at which point he rebrushed his teeth and went to sleep.

This time with Erin was a gift. An intimacy without romance or sex, since both he and Erin were lonely for other people. At least they could be lonely together. And this had to be a good sign, right? That they could spend so much time alone together and not be all over one another? Hal began to hope. It wasn't like he and Erin had had sex on Deoth. They'd just made out a little. Not a big deal in the grand scheme, not compared with lifelong friendships.

Never in all this time did Hal try to call Athena.

To be safe and send the right message, on the first day of school, Hal and Erin arrived separately—Hal driving, Erin walking. When Hal got out of his car in the Clegg High parking lot, he didn't see Peter or Erin out front, but he spotted Athena climbing from Mrs. Watts's Hyundai.

This was it. Time to try. He cupped his hands around his mouth and shouted Athena's name.

She looked at him. He smiled, waved.

She turned her back and speed-walked up the stairs into the building.

Athena

Athena spent the final week of summer vacation in bed, her phone unplugged, her curtains drawn as she reread her favorite books: *Otherwise Known as Sheila the Great, The Tombs of Atuan,* and the entire Madeleine L'Engle oeuvre. She relived the stories she had escaped into as a kid, when magic was a fantasy rather than another flawed reality in this hopelessly broken world.

The novels' magic remained mostly intact, and Athena slipped into these borrowed dreams like a warm bath, let them massage the knots in her heart and mind. She was still young enough to disappear entirely into a book—a skill she'd lose in adulthood, as smartphones and the internet became more pervasive, and her thought patterns turned into a series of constant skips and interruptions. But here, now, she could read and forget herself for a few days.

No one came to visit during her week of books. Athena told herself this was a good thing, though in truth, she was stung no one had *tried* to make amends. Had they all ditched her? Were the rest of her coven hanging out without her now? Not even Professor Marsh had reached out yet, and she had thought herself his favorite student.

She slept poorly on the last night of summer vacation, worried about how life would look from now on. Her first day as a senior dawned gray and muggy, the kind of weather that, in Texas, came with a false promise of rain. Athena's mother gave her a ride to school, and even with the A/C on blast, Athena was a sweaty mess by the time they arrived in the parking lot.

Worse, she got no time to compose herself, no time to prepare. Two seconds after she shut the car door, she heard Hal calling. She saw him jogging across the parking lot, waving. She did the only thing she could think to: turned and hurried up the stairs into the school as fast as she could without actually running.

He seemed to take the hint, and didn't chase after her. She made it to her first class unmolested, and there, in physics, she found her center. She took notes on the syllabus, contemplated the challenges of the year ahead, and was able to focus through both this class and the one that followed (precalculus). It was almost a good morning. Almost.

Things took a turn during third period, in the middle of Mrs. Goolsby's AP English class, when Peter Marsh darted into the room, sweaty, his hair disheveled. He looked worse than Athena had felt getting out of the car this morning. Much worse. He wasn't wearing a backpack or carrying any books.

Mrs. Goolsby squinted at him from behind her thick glasses with a mix of annoyance and curiosity.

"Good morning, Peter," she said. "So happy you could join us."

Peter nodded and licked his lips, but seemed unsure how to respond.

"Are you all right?" Mrs. Goolsby asked.

He took a long time before he nodded again. "Yes ma'am. Sorry, ma'am."

Mrs. Goolsby pointed toward the rows of desks facing her. "Go have a seat then."

He shuffled between rows of already seated students and took a desk one row over and one seat behind Athena. She could smell him from where she sat. He positively *reeked* of fish, and was breathing like he'd run a marathon. His anxiety shone brightly through the Dissonance, as did his desire for Athena's attention.

She faced forward, and tried to focus on Mrs. Goolsby. Whatever was going on, she didn't want to know about it.

Then something poked her in the back of her arm. It was Peter, passing a folded-up note. Athena clamped down on a heavy sigh and unfolded the page.

I'm not staying, it read. *I'm only here for you and the others. We have work to do today.*

Athena wrote back, *I'm not ditching school.* And then, after a second's consideration, she added, *Especially not with Erin and Hal.*

She handed back her reply while Mrs. Goolsby's back was turned. Peter made a face, wrote another line beneath it, and passed it to her.

Give me two minutes after class. Please.

She folded up the paper and gave him a grudging nod. If it would shut him up so she could pay attention, she would agree to say no to his face. She was allowed to listen to the rest of Mrs. Goolsby's explanation of the importance of studying *The Canterbury Tales,* and the MLA formatting required for senior themes. Her attention remained fractured. She couldn't stop glancing at the clock.

Twenty minutes before the end of the period, the floor trembled. It was so slight you could have mistaken it for the building settling, or the air conditioner struggling. Then the tremble became a shudder, and a full, un-ignorable shake: awkward, but steady. Like the footsteps of something massive.

The other kids noticed, too. Glances were exchanged. Mrs. Goolsby stopped her monologue and looked out the window, puzzled.

Athena turned to Peter. "Is this us?"

"I think so," Peter said.

They stood and headed for the door.

"Excuse me, Ms. Watts, Mr. Marsh," Mrs. Goolsby said. "Where do you think you're going?"

Peter paused. "Act like it's a tornado drill," he instructed. "Hunker down in the library until the noises stop." The school library was housed in the center of the building and had no windows. It was the safest place to be right now.

"I haven't given you permission to go," Mrs. Goolsby said.

"Then give us all detention when we get back," Peter said. "But please, for now—go to the library."

Athena followed Peter out of the room. A few feet from the door, he broke into a run, and she chased him down the hall, her bad leg crying out with each footfall. Teachers and students poked their heads out of other classrooms as Peter and Athena ran past. Athena repeated the advice about the library over and over as the ground shook with increasing frequency and intensity.

Peter paused at the top of the stairs to the first floor and looked back. No one had taken their advice. All the classroom doors were shut.

"It's not enough to shout at them," he said.

"Maybe they think it's a prank?" Athena said.

"We need to get on the intercom. Can you be extra convincing?"

Athena had a command for that, and said so. They started down the stairs, holding the railing to stay upright with each new mini earthquake.

"What is it, Peter?" she asked as they came to the office door. "What's making that sound?"

"I'm not sure," he said. "But it's bad."

Erin

Erin was having a pretty lazy third period. She'd taken tech theater for this exact reason: unless there was a play to put on, the teacher, Mrs. Flores, basically let the class do whatever they wanted. She was doodling in a spiral notebook when the shaking started, and in the ensuing ruckus, as the unsupervised students crowded toward windows to see what was happening, she had no trouble exiting through one of the auditorium's side doors and into the main hallway.

As she stepped out, she almost ran directly into Hal, and was so startled by his sudden appearance that she gave a shout.

"Easy," he said. "It's just me."

A fresh tremor rocked the building. They ran side by side toward the sound, which led them to the front doors of the school. They found Peter there, looking through the glass at the front lawn. The sky had turned from hazy white to a mass of full-bodied red clouds. Pink light flashed between the formations, and the ground shook.

Peter gave the new arrivals a wan smile. "Took you long enough."

Hal wrinkled his nose. "Dude. You stink. Did you fuck an entire fish tank this morning?"

Although Erin was happy to see her (ex?) boyfriend, she had to agree. Peter smelled awful.

"You finally caught me, Hal. I stand exposed in my perversity," Peter said.

"Where's Athena?" Erin asked.

"In the office," Peter said.

As if on cue, the school intercom screeched to life. The three members of the coven clapped their hands over their ears at the feedback.

Athena's voice came through speakers all over the school. "Attention, students, faculty, and staff. I suggest, strongly, that you all calmly but quickly make your way to the library. This is not a drill. This is a matter of life and death."

Every classroom and office door in the main hallway opened at the same time. Students and teachers poured out, walking toward the library. None of them seemed to notice Erin, Hal, and Peter at the doors.

Erin felt a sudden urge to head to the library alongside her classmates and teachers. She pushed past the desire, but it took an effort to clear and refocus her thoughts, and the initial impulse scratched at the back of her mind like a small alarm. Athena was damned good at that command. Erin would be in real trouble if the other girl ever decided to use it against her.

Peter stepped through the doors, toward the approaching storm. Hal and Erin followed in time to see that bizarre pink lightning flash again. The earth shook so hard Erin had to grab the railing to keep upright on the front steps.

She was still bent over, clutching the bar, when the clouds parted, and something fell out of the sky. It landed near the edge of the school property, maybe two hundred feet away. It was a twelve-foot-tall object, roughly human in shape. From its posture, Erin recognized it at once.

"Holy shit," Hal said. "Is that the statue from the ship?"

"I think so," Peter said, as the air around the statue began to darken. "It's here for me. I don't understand why, but it is."

"That's sort of presumptuous," Hal said. "It could be a transfer student."

Erin appreciated Hal was trying to lighten the mood, but she wished he would shut up so she could think straight and ask some questions. Why would anyone be after Peter? Did it have something to do with how he smelled?

The statue took its hands away from its head, and looked down at them. It tilted its head, as if confused by what was happening. Then it looked across the lawn, saw Peter, Hal, and Erin. It raised its arms and began to draw Dissonant characters in the air.

"Oh shit," Peter said. "You guys should go inside."

"And leave you to fight this thing by yourself?" Hal said. "Absolutely not. I'm the one with the magic sword, remember?"

"That's why I need you to go with Erin to the library," Peter said.

"What?" Erin said.

"Are you fucking kidding me?" Hal said at the same time.

"Erin, I need you to put up the biggest dome you can," Peter said. "Around the entire school. Hal, you're the best fighter—"

"Which is why I should be out here with you," Hal said.

"—Which is why I need you inside," Peter said. "I've got an idea for how to get rid of it without hurting anyone, but if things go bad out here, you need to be ready to finish the fight." He looked as unhappy saying it as Erin felt hearing it. She didn't want to leave Peter alone.

"How can you stop that thing?" she said. "I don't think a ball of water is going to do the trick this time."

Peter's shoulders sagged. He looked exhausted, and more than a little irritated. He never looked irritated, and certainly not with her. That stung, and pushed her away from him just a little farther as he wiped the sweat from his brow.

"I have some tricks you haven't seen yet. Now please, go."

Erin wanted to argue, but she also wanted Peter's forgiveness. And anyway, his idea for a shield was good. She decided to trust him. She grabbed Hal by the arm and pulled him toward the doors.

"We're on it," she said. "But Peter?"

He looked away from the approaching creature. "Yeah, Erin?"

She wanted to tell him she loved him, that she was sorry; that her feelings for him were so large she'd sabotaged herself. But she couldn't make the words come.

"What about Athena?" she said instead.

"If you see her, send her my way," Peter said. "Now go."

Hal let Erin pull him up the steps to the front doors. As they went inside, Erin spared one last glance back at Peter. He looked so small, standing by himself before the statue.

It was the last time she ever saw him.

Hal

Hal and Erin hurried to the library. Most of the students and faculty inside were hunkered along the walls. Some appeared frozen, nearly catatonic. Others were on the verge of hysteria. As Erin and Hal passed, classmates and teachers asked if they knew what was happening. Was it a storm? Was it a shooter like those boys in Colorado this last spring?

"Stay where you are," Erin said to their interlocuters, as they ducked behind the checkout desk. "Cover me," she added, to Hal.

It only took Erin a moment to throw up a barrier. Hal never tired of watching his friends use this primordial language to change the world. It was the great jealousy of his life. What good was a magic sword when your friends could alter the fabric of reality? A few quick strokes in the air, a crackle, that familiar smell, and the school was safe. He hoped.

Erin kept her arms up and her eyes closed. Sweat beaded her forehead. Her hands shook with effort. She'd never done anything this large before. Hal was wondering if he ought to summon the Blade, just in case, when something hit the building and knocked him off balance. Erin gritted her teeth. The lights went out. People screamed.

"Are you okay?" Hal asked Erin.

She shook her head and shushed him. The building rocked. Freestanding shelves in the middle of the large room dominoed into one another, the paper and wood colliding with soft, heavy sounds. Hal watched teachers and students scatter out of the way. Most of them made it, but a few tripped and fell beneath the last of the tipping shelves. They shouted with pain, and caused more chaos and disruption in the room. Hal wanted to go help, but had promised to cover Erin. He couldn't leave her side, no matter what. They would deal with injuries later.

Erin gasped, then groaned. Her whole body shook. She opened her eyes, a look of panic on her face.

"What's wrong?" Hal said.

She grabbed his hands and yanked him down to the floor in front of her. She wrapped her arms around him, but he felt her hands continue to move, drawing, trying to shield and protect.

"Close your eyes," she said, and he did.

There was a roaring sound, a wave of warmth, and then a sharp pain in the back of his head, and darkness took hold. Hal was gone for a time, unaware of anything. Perhaps it was a mercy he didn't see what happened next.

Athena

Athena had every intention of joining the fight once she finished her announcement on the school intercom. Her coven—she couldn't quite think of them as friends, not anymore—needed her help. Everyone in this building needed her help.

She exited the office and marched toward the front doors. Through the glass, she saw Peter at the top of the steps, facing off against the object that had haunted her nightmares for weeks. The statue from Deoth, somehow transported to the lawn of Clegg High School.

Erin wasn't there. Hal wasn't there. Peter wasn't even fighting, per se. The statue stood frozen in the act of swinging a fist toward Peter's head. Peter's arms were raised. Something strange was happening in the air in front of him. A force rippled from his hands, almost like water, and spots of golden light winked in the waves. She recognized the Dissonant energy, but couldn't tell what it was actually doing.

She pushed through the doors and stepped outside.

"Peter?" she said.

Then she realized the statue wasn't frozen. Its arm continued to descend toward Peter's head, inch by inch. This impressive display had slowed the thing, not stopped it. And where were Erin and Hal? Had they already fled?

Peter turned his head to look at her. She saw real terror in his eyes.

"I don't know how much longer I can hold it," he said.

Athena tried a hard wind command. It bounced off the statue and lifted her off her feet and tossed her back into the front doors of the school, hard enough to knock the breath from her.

Then the statue spoke. It said a single word, slowed down like a record played at half-speed: *"Athena."*

She looked from Peter to the statue and back again. She saw the terror and plaintiveness in her friend's eyes, and understood. He was going to die. Whatever was happening here, she wasn't strong enough to stop it.

You can't help Peter. He will drag you down with him, if you let him. The voice came from deep inside, and she recognized the truth of its words. Hal and Erin had apparently already abandoned him. All Athena could do here was die beside her friend. She'd die a hero, sure, but she'd still be dead.

She scrambled to her feet, gasping, and did the smart thing. She ran away from Peter and the statue, back through the school halls, past the library, and out the back doors onto the athletic fields. She ran until she came to the chain link fence surrounding the field, and jogged along it until she found the gate, fumbled with the latch, and then was off school grounds, arms and legs pumping, heart pounding, sweat stinging her eyes, her bad leg *screaming*. She had no destination in mind, only away.

For a short, unathletic person with a chronic health condition, she made good time. She was almost two blocks away when the school exploded.

Erin

The cemetery was an oddly lively place the morning of Peter's funeral. Due to the unprecedented number of deaths at the high school (every single student, teacher, and staff member, aside from Hal, Erin, and Athena), the town cemetery had to knock down one of its barriers and expand farther north into its field. In addition to the construction crews, there were several funerals taking place at the same time as Peter's. Clumps of people sweated at randomly placed intervals around the cemetery, arranged like pieces on a bizarre gameboard.

There was no burial for Peter, because there was no body. Professor Marsh elected to plant a headstone in the family plot anyway, alongside those of Peter's parents. Because the town clergy were overwhelmed, they'd called in outside help to meet the demand for officiants. The man in charge of Peter's farewell was a minister from two towns over. He didn't know Peter, but did his best with the usual platitudes. Then, service concluded, the man sensed he was no longer wanted, shook the professor's hand, and left.

Erin and her coven formed a circle with the headstone that marked a life but not a grave. They stared around like small children who expected to wake up from a bad dream. Only Professor Marsh wore the grim expression of a person who accepted and understood this present reality.

"This is my fault," he said. "I thought the Dissonance had chosen the four of you. That it wanted me to train you. Instead I turned you into targets."

"We made our choices," Athena said.

"You are children," Marsh said. "You aren't capable of making an informed choice. I was the adult. I made the mistake, and it's cost me everything. I won't let this happen to you, too."

"You won't teach us anymore?" Erin said.

"I won't," Marsh said. "But that won't be enough to keep you safe. This mistake calls for a more drastic solution. I have to sever your connection to the Dissonance."

Athena stepped back and bumped into the iron fence around the plot.

"No," she said. When no one else chimed in, she turned to the group. Erin looked away. "Erin. Hal. Back me up here."

"Maybe it's best this way," Erin said.

"How can you say that?" Athena said.

"If we hadn't messed around in stuff we shouldn't have, none of this would have happened," Hal said. He swept his arm to encompass the sea of new headstones.

"You know it's the right thing," Erin said.

"I don't," Athena said. Erin could understand why she'd argue this way. After all, Athena was the one who'd found the little green book back in 1997, and showed it to the rest of the group. She'd pushed them forward, relentless in her pursuit of knowledge and power. This, to some degree, was her fault, and she needed to be absolved.

"You do," Erin said now, and reached out to touch Athena's arm. Athena backed away, unmollified.

"What about you?" Athena said to Marsh. "After you sever us, what happens to you?"

"I'll sever myself as well," Marsh said. "I can't trust myself not to be weak. I have to shut that door forever."

Athena seemed to understand then—this was going to happen whether she consented or not. She was strong, but not strong enough to take the old man in a confrontation. A weight pressed on Erin's heart, but it came alongside a massive sense of relief. She could let go of this now. Try a normal life.

"Join hands," Marsh said.

Athena stepped away from the fence, and after a moment's hesitation, took one of Erin's hands, and one of Hal's. "Will it hurt?"

"I don't know," Marsh said.

Erin lowered her head as if in prayer while Marsh drew out his command line.

The severing didn't hurt, not in a physical sense. It was more like when you fiddled with the settings on a TV and desaturated the image. Vibrancy drained and the world became a little duller. The accompanying sensation was worse than pain. This morning, she had felt Hal, Athena, and Marsh around her in their misery. She had felt the grass wilting under her shoes. She was so used to this constant connection, she didn't notice it most of the time. Now she was cut off, isolated within herself. Everything outside her body was other—and would be for the rest of her life.

Finally, almost a week after Peter's death, Erin looked into a future without him, without the Dissonance, and cried—partly in mourning, but also in mistaken relief, thinking that the most confusing time in her life was finally behind her.

2019
The Last Adventure, Part Two

Athena

Athena looks up from the desk to check the clock on the study wall, but she can't see past the stack of books beside her. She's been working since sundown, writing and rewriting Dissonant by hand. The process soothes her, takes the low-grade fear she's carried since that first Dissonant earthquake, and replaces it with that all-systems-go flow she falls into when she engages with an interesting problem. It's been years since she experienced this perfect marriage of intellect and instinct, the place where she does her best work. And despite the circumstances, she knows she's doing the greatest work of her life tonight.

She flexes her hand and shakes her head, attempting to refocus. The building blocks of Marsh's demands are all here in this haphazard manuscript, but it's up to Athena to string them together in a way that works: create an orderly procession of miracles starting with Giuseppe's Reservoir and Li's Funnel, and then Huntley and David's Soul Locator—and that's only on the first page.

Her hand aches, the muscles cramped from trying to keep pace with her mind. Not for the first time, she laments that no one has created a Dissonant font for Word or Google Docs. Or a Dissonant keyboard. She understands it would be a tricky device to make. Dissonant isn't like the Roman alphabet. It more closely resembles Hanzi in its construction and variability. There are keyboards capable of Hanzi. Would a similar solution work for Dissonant? Would the underlying power of the universe cooperate with a computer?

Her bad leg aches, which means it's time to get up and move around. She stands, puts her hands on her hips, and cracks her back. She's written and rewritten her symphony several times now. The wastebin

beside the desk overflows with discarded drafts. She wishes for cigarettes. She kicked the habit a few years ago, but now regrets doing so.
The ritual of stepping outside with a fresh (or refreshed) cup of coffee,
lighting up, and taking that first drag. The gorgeous burn at the back
of the throat. Best fucking feeling in the world. Better than sex.

Oh well. She comes around the desk, where Marsh sits on the floor,
surrounded by his own stacks of books. He sifts through them, hunting for anything useful. His hands shake as he pages through the volume in his lap. He's losing control of his stolen body. He looks up as
she pops her hip and groans with satisfaction. He grins at the sound,
and she's not sure what to make of the expression. Maybe it's lack of
control, but the look seems almost lascivious.

"I need a break," she says. "Figure I'll check on the boys."

He looks back at the book before him. "Don't be long. We leave
at dawn." She's almost out the door when he speaks again. "You are
doing the right thing. I know the tulpa seems like a real person. You
have to remember: it is not. It is a problem you are helping to solve."

Athena pulls the study door shut behind her and pads up the hall to
Peter's old bedroom. She finds Owen and Philip spooned together on
the bed, fast asleep. Philip has one arm over Owen, and her heart aches
at the sweetness of it.

Looks like a person to me, she thinks.

She tells herself he's not. Philip is a convincing facsimile. A *very*
convincing facsimile. Although—is it just her own perceptions,
warped from being awake too long, or does he look younger? Almost
like Peter at sixteen. The same age he was when he died.

The impression rattles her, and she retreats to the study. She returns
to find Marsh at his desk, thumbing through her manuscript.

"That's not ready," she says.

"It's good," he says, without looking up.

She tamps down on the rush of pleasure the compliment brings her.
"The boys are okay. Both asleep."

Marsh continues to read, and doesn't answer.

"Do you have any idea what happened to Philip?" she says. "In the
bathroom? The way the glass broke, it looked like more than a slip
and fall."

"I have several theories," Marsh says. "He's a copy of Peter's body, occupying Peter's former home, using Peter's shower. It's possible those things alone could cause some minor Dissonant disruption. I'd be happy to investigate once we've finished the business at hand. I might need to, unless I want to get pitched out of the shower myself when we get back from Deoth."

For the first time, Athena tries to picture Marsh in Philip's body. Something about the image, so soon after seeing Philip and Owen asleep in one another's arms, bothers her deeply.

Marsh steps away from the desk so she can return to work. She buries herself anew and doesn't look up until the sky turns gray with pre-dawn light. A sizable stack of loose-leaf paper sits to her right, covered in her tight, controlled hand. She leans back, flexing her fingers and massaging her wrist. Marsh has been lying on the sofa for the past few hours, to preserve whatever meager strength remains in his body. She has to touch his shoulder to wake him, and a hard shudder runs through her as her hand wraps around his cold flesh. Her chest heaves and her throat tightens, and only relaxes once she lets go and takes a full step back.

"I'm finished," she says, as he opens his eyes.

He shuffles to the desk and sits to read through the manuscript. His motions are jerky now, like a marionette operated by a clumsy puppeteer.

"It's a masterpiece," he says. "So elegant that it makes the formerly impossible seem simple. Future generations will study this and wonder why no one thought of it sooner. You're lucky, Athena. You secured your legacy in your original lifespan."

"If it works," Athena says. "Remember, it's still all theoretical."

"If it doesn't work, you and I won't be around to be disappointed." He stands and something in his host body cracks. He's running out of time. "Come with me. I have some things to show you."

She follows him down the hall, past the bedroom door where the boys sleep, and out the back door of the house. He limps across the grass to the toolshed. Athena's never seen the door open, and is surprised by how easily Marsh unlocks the ancient padlock holding it shut now.

The door swings open and reveals what seems at first to be a normal shed, full of power tools and landscaping equipment. As Marsh walks inside, however, his body begins to disappear from the feet up. Looking at both things at once—the everyday shed, and the vanishing corpse—twists something in her mind out of true.

"Follow me, but maybe keep your eyes shut," Marsh calls back.

Athena takes his suggestion. She makes small steps forward, lets her body tell her what's real. Her feet find stairs, and her right hand discovers a rail. She hobbles forward and down, counting twenty, thirty, forty steps before she emerges on a landing.

"Open your eyes," Marsh says.

She's in a large room with a concrete floor and a low ceiling. Gurneys stand at regular intervals, each bearing a lump beneath a white sheet. The white is almost blinding beneath the intense overhead lamps. Metal drains line the floor. The room looks like a morgue.

"What is this place?" she asks.

"This is part of my laboratory," Marsh says. "Where I performed autopsies of Dissonant creatures." He points to a shelf mounted in a corner, lined with notebooks. "I was working on a sort of bestiary, but it probably contains less than a hundredth of a percent of what exists across the multiverse."

"Did you kill these creatures?" Athena asks, indicating the sheeted lumps.

"When I needed to, yes," Marsh says. "I apologize that the grimmest chamber of the lab is also the entrance, but that's the way we built it. Necessity first. Come. I have kinder sights to show you."

They go through the door on the far side of the room. The next chamber is dim and atmospheric, with ceiling-mounted track lights illuminating the exhibits. Instead of paintings or sculptures, however, the exhibits are otherworldly creatures in terrariums. Neon cats stalk the other side of the glass and watch Athena with suspicious, hungry eyes. Snakes with spiked skulls hang from artificial tree limbs. A creature that appears to be nothing but mouths and tentacles spins slowly in midair like a disco ball. A humanoid figure of muck slumps in a muddy cell, reading a water-warped copy of *Swann's Way*. The muck figure turns from the book and regards her with intelligent brown eyes. It raises an oozing hand in greeting.

Next door to the muck lives a creature that stands upright like a person, but bears the face of an orange-eyed wolf. It wears a blue robe of rough-hewn fabric. This wolf on two legs bares its teeth and growls. An overwhelming sadness hits Athena, a sense of utter futility and hopelessness like a punch in the heart. She lowers her gaze.

"You don't have to be afraid," Marsh says. "If it could hurt you, it already would have."

"What is this place?" Athena says. "A private zoo?"

"I prefer to think of it as a multiversal ark," Marsh says. "A place to gather and preserve life and knowledge. To bring us closer to solving the core mysteries of existence."

"You built all this yourself?" Athena says. "How did no one in town notice? How did *we* never notice?"

"I didn't do it all myself," Marsh says. "And this place isn't precisely *below* my toolshed. The shed is how we arrive here from our world. We're in a pocket dimension outside of time."

That explains why these creatures are alive and haven't starved to death in the last decade. They wouldn't *need* to eat or drink as long as they arrived healthy.

"A workshop that requires no upkeep," she says, impressed. "Where the rules of life don't apply." And this revelation leads to another: "You used to have an undine here. Named Morgan."

"I did," he says. "Until *someone* set her free while I was away on business in 1998."

"Were you mad?"

"Oh yes."

"Is that why you killed Peter and blew up the high school?"

He leans away from her, surprised.

"Don't lie to me," she says. "Not about this."

"I was angry to lose Morgan," he says. "But I thought the doorway command a fair trade, so I let it go. I always figured I could catch more undine, but you had created or rediscovered something entirely unique."

That wasn't a denial. "The day he died, Peter showed up to school late, in a panic," Athena says. "He seemed sure something bad was headed there."

"I had nothing to do with what happened that day," Marsh said. "Think better of me, Athena. Would I risk exposing myself and kill my own grandson in public? My hope was to win him over to my way of thinking when he got back that afternoon. To win all of you over. But then things went sideways, somehow. I'm still not sure what really happened, and that's the truth. If I'm to believe the story I got from you, Hal, and Erin, it sounds like the statue from Deoth arrived at the school. I have no idea what to make of it. Perhaps Peter was trying to send it back and somehow destroyed the school in the process? I don't know. But while we are exchanging honesties, here's a chance for you to earn my trust: why weren't you at the school when it exploded? Hal and Erin were in the library, you were in the front office, and then you weren't? It makes no sense, unless you fled."

She drops her gaze, her face aflame with humiliation and embarrassment. The great shame of her life, laid out in plain words.

He touches her arm, and she's too upset to recoil. "You did the right thing," he says softly. "Running. It's what I would've done."

She's so desperate to hear these words. To be absolved. But something inside her won't accept it, and now she does step back. "Don't say that to me. I'm not like you."

"You couldn't have won that fight," Marsh said, voice still soft. "If you'd stayed, you'd have died, too. Instead, you lived. You continue the search for knowledge. For truth. You have to be ruthless if you want to unravel the mysteries of existence. Let lesser people keep their consciences clean while they follow paths people like *us* hew. You knew it then, and you know it now. And that's why I've chosen you for this."

She frowns as something occurs to her. "But then why did you die? You could've stayed here in your fortress outside of time and avoided death altogether, couldn't you?"

"I considered the possibility," Marsh says. "But even with my reclusive tendencies, it wouldn't have been much of a life. It would have been a compromise, and I spent my life trying to resolve the problem of compromise. It's why my associates and I built this place. Why I braved the wrath of a lower-case 'h' hell instead of cowering here. I needed to see beyond, and trust myself to find a way back. It's all part of the quest to untangle the rat's nest of the multiverse and find its fundamental truths."

Athena laughs. "Oh, is that all?"

Marsh doesn't share her mirth. "Do you know what I discovered during my first lifetime, through all my explorations, experiments, and autopsies?" He walks her back to the morgue and pulls a notebook from a shelf along one wall. He flips it open to a page near the back and runs a stiff finger along the text and diagrams until he comes to a Dissonant character drawn in black ink—a character Athena doesn't recognize.

"What is that?"

Marsh points to a sketch on the opposite page, which depicts a creature that could be a missing link between zebras and monkeys. "I found it in the DNA of this thing." He flips the page to a drawing of a lizard with six eyes. "And in this one." He flips through the book. Each two-page spread contains a sketch or diagram of an animal, and on the page opposite, a drawing of that same new Dissonant character.

"Every creature you've examined carries this Dissonant character in its genetic makeup," Athena says.

"That's not even the most interesting part," Marsh says. "If you take blood from multiple species and look at them side by side, the characters are infinitesimally different."

"To account for differences of physiognomy or personality," Athena says. "How quaint. We really are all special snowflakes."

"Do you know your Bible?"

"Okay, of all the things I've heard in the last few minutes, that *has* to be the most incredible. Professor Elijah Marsh, quoting the scriptures."

"There are a pair of verses I've been turning over in my mind for years now. Here's the first: 'In the beginning God created the heavens and the earth.'"

"Yeah, I've heard that one," Athena says.

"Here's another: 'In the beginning was the Word, and the Word was with God, and the Word was God.' John, chapter one."

"Sure," Athena said. "They made a big deal of that one back in 1997, at the Dissonant Conference."

"Well, maybe they were onto something," Marsh says.

"Your trip to hell made you a Christian?" Athena says.

"I never denied the *possibility*," Marsh said. "What I had a problem with was the absolute certainty of those religious idiots. I always wondered if early mystics and primitive believers understood something. In that first verse from Genesis, language brings light to a darkened world. In subsequent verses, God speaks every living thing into being.

And in the second quote, from the Gospel of John, God *is* language. Language is the prime tool of creation. There must be a speaker, or speakers, who gave shape to all of this." He points back toward the menagerie in the other room. "God. Lower gods. Nephilim. Call them what you like. If I and my partners hadn't been willing to do the work, to get our hands dirty, we'd still be ignorant. Progress in any field requires pragmatic ruthlessness. Knowledge is your only ally. Everything and everyone else are tools or obstacles in your path." He sets the book down to focus on her. "You were the only one of my students who had the potential to see this. It's why you were my favorite, and why I'm partnering with you now. You see, in all my experiments, although I could change the shape of life, I could never *create* life. I could never make that particular symbol come alive. And I would bet you American dollars that if we took a sample of Philip's blood, we wouldn't find that symbol in his DNA, because he's not really alive, any more than I am. What I'm hoping is that, by transferring my soul into his body, that character will form and the world will realign. Everyone wins. And I need your help to complete the task."

"I wrote your ritual," Athena says. "My part is done."

"No it's not. Follow me."

He leads her out of the room, back through the maze of the menagerie, and into a much larger chamber beyond. Fluorescent lights hung from exposed rafters above a floor of dull concrete and lined with floor-to-ceiling racks of boxes and crates. It reminds Athena of the warehouse from the end of *Raiders of the Lost Ark,* but with better lighting.

"What the hell is this place?" she says.

"It's my storehouse," Marsh says.

"Why in the world do you need a storehouse this large?"

"If the creatures I keep in captivity represent the past, then this warehouse represents the future. The next step in my grand design. I have everything I need to outfit a small army here."

"An army for what?"

"We can discuss the specifics later," Marsh says. "In the meantime, we should focus on the task at hand. Come look at this."

She follows her old teacher into one of the wide aisles. He stops a third of the way down and points to a small black case on a shelf right above eye level. It looks like it might contain a drill or tool set.

"Open that for me," he says. "It's taking all my strength to hold this corpse together."

She takes the case down, sets it atop a crate, and unclasps the lid. Inside, she finds three vials of a green fluid, an injector gun, and a small package of needles, all nested in a foam rubber bed.

"What is this?" Athena asks.

"Something I was working on before I died." He gingerly frees one of the tubes from the rubber and holds it up to the light. The liquid inside looks like Mountain Dew infused with tiny fireworks. "Another discovery from my autopsies. Every living creature contains a portion of Dissonant energy. That energy dissipates when the creature dies and rejoins the Dissonance. In a few cases, I captured that energy and distilled it. These three vials contain all the Dissonant energy I've been able to capture."

Athena looks at the needles and the injector in the case. "So I give myself a shot and get the Dissonance back?"

"Maybe. Even if it works, it won't be permanent. But for a time, you'll be supercharged with Dissonant energy. You'll have all your old strength back and then some."

"So for maybe a couple of hours, or minutes. Maybe seconds," she says.

"Or days, or weeks. Or years," Marsh says. "We won't know until we try it."

She wonders if this is Marsh's big solution to her severance. Three more hits of her favorite drug, which might collectively last the length of a sneeze?

Her dismay must show, because Marsh says, "This is only a down payment. A stopgap for the task at hand, because the journey back to Deoth is going to demand more strength than I have left to spare in this body. The boy, Owen, seems to have the talent, but I don't have time to train him. I need someone I can trust to lead the journey and ensure our safe arrival. If we make it back to the ship and your symphony works, I'll have an entire new lifetime to find or create a reconnection ritual."

She takes the vial from him and feels a dry ache. The thing she's missed more than anything else, these past twenty years, dangling in front of her. Despite her mixed feelings—her conflicting desires to save reality and her friends and her deep misgivings about putting Marsh in Philip's body (to say nothing of what he plans to do once he's *in* the body)—Marsh has her by the short hairs. He knows how much she's missed the Dissonance, and is offering her a chance, however brief, to connect with it again. He knows that if she can taste this power three more times, she'll take it, no matter the cost.

"Okay," she says, staring into the vials. "I'm in."

Erin

Hal and Sybil climb out of the creek. Hal makes a face as he pulls his dry jeans over wet legs.

"Ready for this?" he asks.

Erin stands as Sybil loosens a cord from around her waist and feeds out several lengths to hand to Hal.

"Tie this around your waist," the undine says. "The dive will be taxing and this will keep you safe with me."

Hal fastens it around himself and extends the rest to Erin. It has the texture of a damp bedsheet pulled straight from the washer. She squeezes it and looks skeptical.

"Are you sure this will hold?" she asks.

"It will hold," Sybil says. "And will prevent you from suffocating in the vacuum."

"Are we going to outer space?"

Sybil considers. "One culture referred to it as tehom. In modern parlance, you might call it 'the deep.'"

"Let's stick with tehom," Hal says. "Sounds more mythic."

Erin finishes knotting the cord around her waist. Sybil double-checks the knots, then steps back.

"Once we dive there's no stopping."

Erin grabs Hal's hand and holds tight.

Sybil turns her back on the creek, spreads her arms, closes her eyes, and tips backward. The world around Erin stretches in all directions until it becomes lines and colors, and then she's falling through space in darkness. She screams, but the sound is ripped from her mouth and lost amid a roar that seems to combine running rapids, TV static, and the hiss of a dial-up modem.

She squints into the dark, and is rewarded with the most incredible thing she's seen across a lifetime highlighted with incredible images: tehom. The waters of the multiverse flow around her, a mix of sights familiar and strange, merging into a medley of colors and light. Erin is in the presence of the infinite, and for the first time in twenty years, she is genuinely happy and alive. She's been holding tight to the cord and to Hal. Now she lets go of both and raises her arms like a kid on a roller coaster. Something unbuckles in her chest and she cries out in exhilaration, in happiness, in relief.

Sybil takes them ever deeper. The descent slows. The roar quiets and the flood of light and color grows dimmer, the worlds presented murkier, harder to see. The images around her ripple, like something is swimming beneath the surface, just out of sight. Things trying to break through to this between place, where Hal, Sybil, and Erin are.

The between grows quieter and darker until they slow and alight on a floor of wet sand. There's light from the universes above, enough for Erin to see her companions, but not much else.

"We're here," Sybil gasps. The undine sits down hard next to Hal and nearly yanks him down, too. Her nose is bleeding.

"Where is here?" Erin says. "The ocean floor? It looks like nowhere at all."

"My mother called it the Source. She said I would bring you here one day because there was something you would need to see, and do."

"I don't suppose she said what that was?" Erin asks.

"No," Sybil says. She wipes the black blood from her upper lip with the back of one hand. "This part is a mystery to me as well."

"How are we supposed to get back to our world?" Erin asks.

"I don't know if you are," Sybil says.

Something shifts in the air and the ground trembles. Erin grabs Hal to keep her balance and remain upright. Yellow-green light shines up through a new-made opening in the sand. The hole is as long and wide as an average doorway, and leads belowground.

Sybil produces a dagger from somewhere on her person and severs the cord attaching her to Hal and Erin, then severs them from one another.

"Good luck," she says.

"Thank you for your help," Hal says. "I'm sorry about your mother. I didn't know her long, but she meant a lot to me."

Sybil's face wrinkles into a hard-to-read expression which resolves into a tight smile. "You were special to her, too. I'm glad I got to meet you, Hal Isaac. I hope our paths will cross again." She bends her knees and rockets up into the darkness, kicking up a puff of sand in her wake. Hal stares after her with his own hard-to-read expression.

"I guess she wasn't glad to meet me, too?" Erin says.

Hal gives the joke a slight smile but doesn't stop staring. Erin squeezes Hal's arm. He takes her hand in his and squeezes back. Together, they start down the stone steps, out of the dark and into the light of the Source.

Owen

Athena wakes Owen before sunrise. The first thing he notices is she's changed from her church clothes into drab olive slacks, black boots, and a forest green tank top. She's gathered and tied her hair behind her head. The second thing he notices is a change in her countenance. When Owen met her, she looked afraid. Now she looks scary.

"Time to move," she says, and there's a hardness in her voice that wasn't present before. She'd been tough, but not this tough.

Philip stirs behind him, and Owen becomes aware of something warm poking against the back of his thigh. He tries to keep the surprise from his face and focus on Athena.

"We going somewhere?" Owen says.

"One more leg on this trip," Athena says. "The most dangerous part. Get Philip up and meet me at the shed behind the house."

After she leaves, Owen scoots out of bed and takes a moment to compose himself before he wakes Philip. Philip gives Owen a bleary smile as he comes to, and an invisible fist squeezes Owen's heart.

"Is it morning?" Philip says.

"Yeah," Owen says. "Time to go."

Philip doesn't move. "Go where?"

"I don't know," Owen says.

Philip sighs and rubs his eyes. "Fine. This place gives me bad dreams anyway." He sits up, but appears to notice his erection and rolls back onto his side. Owen heads to the bathroom to give him some privacy. He brushes his teeth with a toothbrush and toothpaste that look old enough to be his father's (but which nevertheless feels and tastes fresh). He splashes water on his face, then waits in the living room while Philip does the same. Together they trudge out the back door, and across the lawn to meet Athena at the shed.

"Follow me," she says. "Owen, keep your hand on my shoulder. Philip, you hold on to Owen. And you both might want to close your eyes."

Owen hesitates. He's already suffered one injury since coming to this house, so he's not keen on making himself extra vulnerable. On the other hand, it was Marsh who hurt Owen. Athena was the one who'd insisted that Marsh heal the injury. And it's Athena asking him for vulnerability now, even if she does seem changed somehow. Owen decides to trust her. He closes his eyes and puts one hand on Athena's bare shoulder. Philip takes hold of Owen's, his hand warm through the fabric of Owen's shirt. Together they walk into the shed and down a flight of stairs, following Athena's directions to keep from stumbling. When they reach the bottom, she instructs them to keep their eyes closed a little longer, and leads them across a flat surface for some time.

When she tells them to open their eyes, Owen is surprised. He expects to see a witch's hut, or the dungeon where Mickey Mouse worked as a sorcerer's gofer. Instead, he stands in a vast, well-lit space that reminds him of an airplane hangar or an industrial warehouse. Aisle after aisle, lined with racks full of boxes.

"What is this place?" Owen says.

"Professor Marsh's storehouse," she says.

"What was he storing up for?" Owen says. "World War III?"

Athena leads them to one of the middle aisles, and points out boxes of army surplus boots and clothing. She tells them to grab three sets each, pack them into a duffel bag, switch their shoes out for boots, and come find her when they're finished.

Owen has to help Philip, who apparently doesn't understand the concept of clothing sizes. Who is this strange man—or rather, this strange boy? Last night, he looked like someone in his twenties. Today, he looks like he might be a year or two older than Owen, at the most. Owen wonders if he's going to keep aging backward until he disappears, like Brad Pitt in that movie. The thought makes him shiver. He supposes they'll all find out.

Once they've found enough stuff in the correct sizes, they change, switching their tennis shoes for heavy boots. Then they pack the rest and go find Athena at the far end of the storehouse. She's crouched beside what looks like a sarcophagus built from the carapace of a giant black insect. It glistens and pulses with red light, like a heartbeat. Athena seems to measure that pulse, checking it against the watch on her wrist.

"What is this?" Owen says.

She finishes the count before she turns to answer. "Marsh needs to save his strength. This keeps him and the host body intact until we reach our destination."

"Why are you helping him?" Owen says. "Why not let him die in there?"

"His is the only plan that doesn't end with our reality tearing itself apart."

"And he offered you something," Philip says, with a frown. "Something you want."

Athena appears both impressed and chagrined. "Yes, that's true."

"So where are we going and what are we doing?" Owen asks again, his tone sour. Apparently she's allied herself with his tormentor.

She tells them they're going to travel to another world, named Deoth, where they'll perform a ritual to save Marsh and the rest of reality. It sounds insane, and she's vague on the details of this ritual, but after everything Owen has seen the last few days, he's ready to believe anything.

"If we pull this off, Marsh will be in your debt," Athena says to Owen. "And he's aware of that. You'll be in a position to ask for favors in return."

"He's already in my debt," Owen says. "My friends and I raised him from the dead. He's living in my crush's dead body, and I've driven him all over creation."

"I'm sure you'll think of a worthwhile compensation for your loss and effort," Athena says.

Until now, Owen has considered Athena to be someone like him, a good person trapped in a bad situation. Now he sees the ice and steel in her. She can play nice, but houses a deep ruthlessness.

The trio load their duffel bags and Marsh's sarcophagus into a small trailer, which has been hooked up to an olive green ATV. When the packing is finished, Athena pulls a black case from the passenger seat and opens it. Owen expects the case to hold a gun, but what Athena removes instead looks like a sort of injector. Athena takes a vial from the case, full of a light green fluid, and loads it into the injector. Then she presses it into her left arm and squeezes the trigger. The injector clicks as the needle pierces her skin and she squeezes her eyes shut.

"Are you okay?" Owen can't help but ask.

When Athena opens her eyes, they glow a bright yellow-green. Her lips pull back to reveal her teeth in what could either be a smile or a grimace.

Athena

The injection rushes through Athena as a wave of heat. Her skin prickles, and her mind, which has felt small and fuzzy for years, cracks free from its shell of suffocating numbness. The Dissonance sparks about her, tickling her nerve endings. She is fully awake and online for the first time in twenty years.

"Are you okay?" Owen asks, dragging Athena back to the immediate, corporeal world.

She opens her eyes and grins at the boy. She feels feral, like a wolf. Hot tears burn down her cheeks.

"Fine and dandy," Athena says. Even her own voice sounds closer, more real.

She stands, ejects the empty vial from the injector, and replaces it in its case. She tucks the case into the bed of the ATV and begins work on the doorway—her first original command. She has her old *Cookbook* with her, but she doesn't need to review the contents. Her fingers remember. She draws patterns of light, layering them atop one another. The air shimmers like a ripple in a pond, spreads outward from her fingers into a dome that spreads over her, Philip, and Owen. She closes her eyes, pulls the memory of Deoth into focus. She doesn't picture the ship, because she worries what might happen if they arrive too close. Could there be another explosion? Instead, she recalls the endless sea of dunes where she and her coven arrived in 1999.

Athena's feet lift from the floor—another thing that's never happened before—and something yanks in her stomach, the way it does when a roller coaster plummets from a peak. But unlike the roller coaster, there's no sensation of falling.

The warehouse disintegrates around them, as does the feel of warmth, replaced by an empty, flavorless cold, and a vast darkness. There's a terrifying second of abyss, which stretches far enough to worry Athena that she's failed, and stranded herself and her companions in some awful empty void, and then the expanse of sand fades in like a scene in an old-fashioned movie. The dunes take shape beneath a starry, moonless sky. Sand fills in below her, and she lands on it softly. Owen loses his balance and falls over.

Philip has remained upright, and helps Owen to his feet. The ATV and trailer appear to be intact.

"Is this it?" Owen asks. "Did we make it?"

"We made it," Athena says. She takes a long pull from her canteen, then sets about her second task—the creation of a protective dome over the ATV and the travelers. When she's finished, she sits, exhausted, eats a protein bar, and waits for her body to recover. The Dissonance didn't used to take this big a toll. Could it be the side effect of using it like a drug instead of being naturally connected to the source? Or is she just getting old?

When she regains her equilibrium, she produces the professor's old compass stone from the ATV's glove box, and moves the object through the air until it hums, pointing her toward the strongest source of Dissonant energy in the area. Then she starts the vehicle, and they begin the trek toward the ship.

It's slow going. The boys have to walk because the ATV is already pulling more than it should, with Marsh's sarcophagus and the equipment for the soul transfer ritual. The world is as boring as Athena remembers, an endless landscape of shifting sands. The barrier keeps out the worst of the winds and the nighttime cold, but the shield is not enough to keep them comfortable. They take small, rare breaks, and only stop for the day when the sun rises, making camp and settling into their tents.

Athena sleeps poorly and wakes too early, in the late afternoon. Unable to fall back asleep, she makes a cup of terrible instant coffee, sits in the ATV driver's seat, and reads through the manuscript of her symphony. She looks for flaws, holes in the logic. But like any first draft, they're hard to see without proper distance.

Sounds of rustling and groaning come from the boys' tent. She freezes up, thinking she's overhearing something intimate and private, then considering: does Philip have a sexual preference? Is he pansexual? Or is he designed to provide physical comfort to whoever is close by? The last is the explanation she finds most comforting, because it lines up most cleanly with the professor's point of view. The tulpa isn't human.

She relaxes when she hears Owen grunt in pain. She's not hearing sex, but rather the discomfort of waking up with sore muscles.

"I hear you in there," she says. "Might as well get up if you're awake."

Owen crawls out of the tent, scowling at the sunlight.

"Sleep okay?" she says.

"Sleep was fine," the boy says. "The waking up is sort of a killer."

Athena offers him the rest of her coffee. "It's instant, and lukewarm, and doesn't have any sugar or milk, but it *is* caffeinated."

"No thank you," he says. He looks away and shoves his hands into his pockets.

"Are you sure? Might help you wake up."

"I said no thanks."

She realizes now what's wrong: he doesn't trust her. And who can blame him?

"Look, kid," she says. "Don't be stupid. You look like hell. Maybe you can get some use from it."

Owen takes the cup and sits down in the ATV passenger seat. He takes a sip, makes a face, then chugs the rest. It seems to wake him up a bit. He points at the symphony manuscript in her lap.

"What are you reading?" he asks.

She looks at the pages, and decides. She only has two doses of Dissonance left. He has some talent. She might need him before the end.

"Last night when Marsh was healing Philip," she says. "I saw you watching."

"He was doing magic," Owen says. "Who wouldn't have watched?"

Athena gives him a *Give me a break* look. "You saw something familiar. Something you thought you recognized, only you couldn't remember where from. A happy spark, like when you run into a friend. Or an unhappy pang, like you see your secret crush kiss somebody else."

Owen stares into the cup, but he doesn't disagree.

"It's the pull of the Dissonance," she says. "The disharmony of the multiverse—the gap between how it ought to be, and how it actually is. Most people have some vague existential dread, an ennui they can't name. But people like you and me? We see the worlds as they are, and call things by their true names. Well, you can, anyway. I can't anymore, because my connection was severed."

"How did that happen?" Owen says.

"Marsh did it," she says.

Owen makes a disgusted sound and shakes his head. "So he mutilated you."

"That's certainly one way of putting it."

"And now you're working for him."

"Look, he did what he thought was right at the time, and now he's trying to undo it. That's the thing about the Dissonance. A life spent facing reality is difficult. You make choices, and you're not always sure they're the right ones. There are lots of ways for a Dissonant to go wrong, to lose her way. Many do. We did."

"So you forgive him for what he did?" Owen says. "Because he thought it was right?"

"Ask me again when the adventure is over," she says.

She stands and stretches. The sky is almost dark. She puts the manuscript in her backpack and pulls out the *Cookbook*.

"We should wake Philip and get a move on," she says. "But the next time we take a break, look through this." She hands her old notebook to Owen.

"What is it?" Owen asks.

"Call it my grimoire, or book of shadows," Athena says. "Useful commands I found in Marsh's library, plus some homebrew stuff. A lot of it is theoretical, but the book will give you an idea of the basics, what's possible. I wrote all of it when I was about your age."

Owen flips through the book. "This ritual you and Marsh are going to do at the boat. The one that will save reality and leave Marsh in my debt." He frowns. "Is it something to do with Philip?"

She doesn't see any reason to deny it. If she's going to teach this kid, she'd better start with honesty. "Yes."

"Why?" Owen says. "You could let Marsh die in that pod. We could go home, and you could leave Philip alone."

She grips the side of the ATV bed and squeezes hard. "Consider this your first lesson in facing the worlds as they are. Philip is a tulpa. A concentrated thought-form given a physical body. He has no soul, so his very existence has thrown reality out of balance. To restore the balance, we have two options: either we can kill Philip, which would mean also killing one of my best friends, or we can try Marsh's plan."

"Which is?" Owen asks.

"To transfer Marsh's soul into Philip's body. If we're right, putting a soul into Philip's body will restore the balance and save the world without hurting my friend. It's the closest to a right thing that there is."

"I don't think the right thing involves hurting an innocent person," Owen says. "Ever."

"If you have a better plan, I'm open."

"How would I know?" Owen says. He waves her grimoire at her. "I'm not the one who wrote a damn cookbook. Seems like the woman smart enough to fill this thing could imagine a better way."

"The *girl* who wrote that cookbook had a lot more power and options than I do," Athena says. She stalks away and dismantles her tent. She feels Owen stare at her back for a while before he finally goes to wake the tulpa.

The second night's march is much the same as the first. More cold, more sand, more long stretches of eerie quiet. Athena had hoped to spot some of this world's denizens, as she had back in 1999, but this time she and her companions seem to be the only living things here.

Every time they take a break, Owen reads the *Cookbook* by flashlight. He looks interested despite his better judgment. Athena waits until they've been moving a few more hours before she asks him what he thinks.

"It looked like a bunch of gobbledygook," he says. "At first, anyway. The more I look at it, though, the more it seems like it might make sense."

She's impressed. He's quick, same as she was at that age.

"Show me," she says.

"Do you want me to read to you?"

"I had a more practical demonstration in mind. Can you work any of the commands you've read? Something simple maybe?"

Owen flips through the early pages and finds one he likes. He holds the notebook open with his left hand, and with his right he draws in the air. No sparks accompany his movements, no light. Just a bunch of finger work.

Athena tries not to show her disappointment. "That's all right. Pretty common for a first attempt."

Owen doesn't answer or look up from the book. He puts his right hand flat in the air, like pressing a reset button. His frown deepens into something like a grimace. This time when his hand moves, light flows out of it upon the first stroke. The eldritch light grows brighter from there, turning from a dull green to a near-white. The light rises and coalesces into a ball, a tiny sun that floats above his head.

"Let there be light," he says, with a little flourish.

He's joking, but Athena hears an echo of Marsh's theory—the insistence on a first speaker or speakers—and it sends a pang of discomfort through her arms and chest. If there is a first speaker, what must they think of what she and Marsh are attempting?

"Impressive," she says. "Keep at it."

As the night passes, she spots distant lights and movement on the horizon. The world's inhabitants? Other travelers like themselves? Or illusions, traps like the temple that tried to eat Hal and Erin?

She turns her attention away, focuses instead on her new pupil. She lectures Owen on the basics of Dissonant theory. Things she remembers from high school and can repeat extemporaneously. On breaks, she teaches him, makes him proficient with commands to summon and banish light, and to muffle sound. To enhance his senses, see farther, smell more. How to throw up a personal shield like the barrier protecting them now. How to summon a burst of wind to stagger or knock down an assailant. He only needs one or two tries to get anything right.

The training passes the time, makes the long slow trek across the dunes more bearable. He's a good student, eager to learn and impress. He reminds her of herself at that age. Most kids she can't stand. They're loud and filthy and obnoxious and far too impressed with both themselves and the world. But this boy—this quiet, thoughtful boy—she likes. She's old enough to be his mother, if barely, and she wonders what her own children would be like, if she chose that life.

Aside from any sentimentality and connection, she's also glad that the training seems to be distracting Owen. She doesn't want him thinking about Philip. She doesn't want him getting more attached. The boy needs to let go when the time comes, and she'd prefer he do so willingly.

Is that what you hope? she wonders. *Or are you trying to give Owen the tools to stop Marsh and save your soul?*

She has no answer for herself.

The night is almost two-thirds gone when Philip cries out. He's been silent for hours, his face a blank mannequin stare as he trudges forward through the sand. His shout comes during a lull in Athena and Owen's conversation, so there's nothing to muffle the sharp, terrified sound. Athena brakes, throws the ATV into park, and gets out to see what's wrong.

Philip lies flat on the desert floor, like he's tripped. There's something wrapped around his ankle, almost invisible—a tendril of living shadow that tightens its grip as Philip whimpers.

Athena stands still and motions for Owen to do the same. Sudden movements could make this so much worse. She tries to think of what to do, what the tendril might be, why the Dissonant barrier didn't keep it out.

Before she can come up with a plan, the sand behind Philip shifts and ripples and Philip is yanked backward in the direction they've come.

Owen bolts after the tulpa, shouting his name. His speed is impressive, especially after two nights of walking up and down the dunes. He closes the distance between himself and Philip, then dives forward to catch him by the hands.

Unfortunately, this does nothing to stop the thing in the sand or disrupt its grip on Philip. The smoky tendril zigzags, trying to shake Owen loose. It doesn't seem to want them both, only Philip. Of course. It can probably sense whatever is special or off about the tulpa, and wants that for itself.

In another moment, they'll be too far for her to see, out of sight and her ability to do anything. Athena pulls the black case from the bed of the ATV. Only two doses of Dissonance left. She knows there's no other choice, but she hesitates a moment anyway before she loads the second vial into the injector and shoots it into her arm.

She experiences a lance of pain, and then that amazing feeling, like stepping into sunlight after two hours in a cold, dark movie theater. Warmth flows through her arms, chest, ears, and cheeks, and she is fully herself once more.

She dashes after the boys and their abductor, drawing commands in the air beside her for strength, speed, enhanced eyesight. The world slows and she has time to observe Owen and Philip like a living painting, clinging to one another, mouths open to scream. The black tendrils of smoke have burned through the leg of Philip's pants. The skin visible around it is blistered and pink.

Athena circles the screaming boys and moves toward the writhing mass beneath the sand, the tendril's source. She stomps down with her good leg as hard as she can.

Her booted foot sinks into and through the mass as softly as if she were kicking over a sandcastle. Sand flies up and obscures her vision. She steps back as a shape rises into view, a long serpentine ribbon almost invisible against the night sky. It rears back to glare at her with two yellow pinprick eyes.

She hits the thing with a gust of hard wind, throwing it off balance, then draws her hunting knife from its sheath on her waist and jumps. As she reaches the apex of her leap, she swings the knife as hard as she can.

The creature might be made of shadow or smoke, but it can be cut like solid flesh. Athena's blade shears through the monster's neck and separates head from body. As she falls, she has time to see the head tumble through space with her. She smells something burning and looks at her knife hand. The skin is puckered and warped with blisters. It's her. She's what's burning. The knife guard has melted onto her hand, and the blade smokes.

She lets go of the enhanced speed and vision, but keeps her strength. As soon as her body and mind resume their normal human speed, she realizes she's made an error. Owen has stopped shouting, but Philip has not. His cries sound worse than before, and the smell of cooking meat hangs in the air. The shadow serpent hasn't released Philip's leg, but rather tightened its grip. The tulpa's howls are almost unbearable.

"Help him!" Owen says. He's wriggled up to his knees and holds Philip's hands.

Philip's cries become choked sobs. Athena kneels in the sand beside him. The leg looks like something from the butcher shop and smells like a steakhouse kitchen. She grabs his foot with her free hand and brings her smoking knife down at the place where the tendril holds on to the leg. The shadow splits, but the blade falls off and sinks into the sand. Athena looks up, meaning to ask Owen for his knife, and is surprised to see the boy's look of horror.

Before she can ask what's wrong, he points behind her.

"Move," he says.

Athena looks over her shoulder in time to see a face of shadow lunge at her. It could be the twin of the one she just severed. Is there more than one out here? Did its head grow back, like a worm, a hydra? It's moving too fast to dodge. She doesn't have time to consider, as the thing darts forward, mouth agape.

Light flashes, and Athena loses her grip on Philip and falls onto her back. She looks herself over, doesn't see any new injuries. Owen stands beside her, arms raised. He's used hard wind to interrupt the creature's lunge.

She has to end the fight fast. She can't count on Owen to save her a second time, and her own strength could fail any second. She scrambles to her feet and runs toward the shadow serpent. Its head darts forward. She braces herself, injured right hand balled in a fist. She focuses all her remaining power into this clenched mass of muscle and bone. She imagines it as a brick of dense stone.

The serpent head collides with her punch. Its teeth break beneath her knuckles and her fist is halfway down its throat before it understands what's happening. Athena's right arm burns with agony as she wraps her fingers around the serpent's tongue. She yanks as hard as she can and brings its face down level with hers. Both she and the serpent scream in tandem. Her entire arm is on fire. The meat is going to melt off her bones if she doesn't let go.

She waves to Owen with her free hand.

"Your knife," she manages.

Owen fumbles at his belt and produces a twin to the knife Athena lost a moment ago. He hands it to Athena and she stabs it into the serpent's neck. She can already feel the Dissonance leaving her body. She won't have the strength to finish this. She's losing her grip on the tongue. It's slipping between her fingers.

The blade sinks into the serpent's neck and lodges there as the last of the Dissonance drains and leaves her human. Her grip on the tongue fails, and it slides through her fist like a shot of flame. The world turns white, and reduces her to a howling clump of nerves. Is she dying? Right now she'd do it gladly if it meant ending this agony, too.

She doesn't die. She doesn't even pass out. She's too damned tough. The white of pain fades to the deep purple of the Deoth night sky. She becomes aware of the desert wind, and her own sharp, rasping breath, along with Philip's whimpers and Owen's soft, soothing voice, cooing reassurances to the tulpa.

"Athena," he calls. "Please help. I think Philip is dying."

Owen

Athena's battle with the shadow-monster happens so fast Owen can barely follow it. He watches his would-be teacher behead the thing *twice*, then collapse, screaming, the flesh of her right hand sizzling and smoking like a fajita plate. The creature dissipates like a cloud, its grip on Philip loosening at last. Philip continues to scream, and when Owen gets closer, he sees why. The other boy's leg has been severed below the knee. Blood spills from the wound and darkens the sand.

How did this happen? Athena put up a shield around them. Was it weak, since she doesn't have her full powers anymore? Did it only extend aboveground and leave the party vulnerable to attacks from below? He'll have to ask Athena later, if there is a later.

"It's okay," Owen murmurs, as much to himself as to Philip. "It's okay. We'll fix this." But he has no idea how.

He looks over at Athena, who lies in the sand, eyes open but unfocused. "Athena. Please help. I think Philip is dying."

Athena doesn't move. Her eyes are closed. She's either passed out, or, worse, she's dying, too.

Owen unfastens his belt, yanks it off, and ties it around Philip's severed leg. He hopes it's tight enough to serve as a tourniquet. He's only ever read about stuff like this. Never seen it in real life.

He runs to the trailer behind the ATV, opens it, and pulls a couple of extra shirts from his duffel bag. He wraps one around the stump of Philip's leg, and the other he wraps around Athena's right arm, which has now shriveled and blackened from fingertip to elbow.

He needs to do more. He needs to clean the wounds with disinfectant. But he can't sit still. He has to keep moving, get away from the spot where all of this happened. He drags Philip and Athena back to the ATV, and lifts Athena into the passenger seat. He tries to lift Philip, to put him in the little bed at the back of the vehicle, but Philip is heavy, and Owen has never been physically strong. He lowers Philip back to the ground and leans over next to him, breathing hard and thinking. As he catches his breath, he pulls *Athena's Cookbook* from his backpack and rifles through it until he finds a page marked "A Simple Strength Command." The ritual is near the front, so he assumes it must be one of the simpler, easier ones.

He draws the symbols in the air with his right hand, but his fingers shake, and he can do little more than make faint green lights. He forces himself to stop. To breathe. To focus on nothing else but his breath until a calm spreads through his body.

He makes a second attempt. This time his hands remain steady, the light from his fingertips strong and bright. The symbols burn in the air when he finishes, then blow into him like a breeze. He looks down at his body. It doesn't look any different, but he feels the change. His muscles have hardened. The world feels farther away, less consequential. Less a thing to be afraid of.

He kneels beside Philip. Philip's eyes dart beneath closed lids and he mumbles incoherently, as though gripped by an awful nightmare. Owen picks him up and sets him in the ATV bed. This time, it's easy.

Then he consults the way-finder stone Athena has hung from the rearview mirror, figures out the direction of the strongest Dissonant energy in the area, and starts the engine. He knows he'll need to look in Athena's grimoire for healing commands, but right now he needs to be far away from where the bad thing happened. He got the strength command right, but healing will probably be more complicated, and he needs to be calmer before he tries it. A mistake could kill his companions.

He sighs: here he is again, chauffeuring fucked-up crazy magical people around on errands he doesn't quite understand. He drives through the night and into the dawn. He doesn't stop to make camp. He's afraid of what else might lurk beneath the sand. His progress is slow, the ATV struggling up and down the hills until they finally give way to flat, hard-packed earth.

The fuel tank runs dry not long after, so he parks the ATV and checks on his passengers. Both are wan and clammy to the touch, but breathing. His hands shake as he examines them. He realizes he hasn't eaten all day. He digs through the trailer until he finds some beef jerky, then collapses back into the ATV and eats until the bag is empty and he's downed an entire bottle of water.

Afterward, it's a little easier to think. He takes the binoculars from his backpack and scans the landscape. They've been following this path for a few days. Their destination, whatever it is, ought to be visible by now, right? When he raises the binoculars to his eyes, he spots a parade of figures marching in a straight line along the lightening horizon. Some are tall and spindly, others squat and loping close to the ground. Some walk on two legs, others on more. One figure appears to float above the sand like a ghost. The parade jerks back and forth, prancing, leaping. Dancing. The sound of music comes to him now, barely audible above the desert wind, faint and far away—a calliope, like carnival music in a minor key.

Owen watches the parade in mute wonder. What is this place? Whatever it is, he'd happily leave it and its weird mysteries behind for a return ticket home, the day before the ritual. He could say "no" when Cole and Lucy asked Monica if they wanted to come along.

He continues to scan the horizon in other directions, and at last sees something promising—three wooden poles that stick up out of the earth. They could be the masts of a ship, right? Maybe?

"I feel like hot garbage."

He turns to find Athena blinking in the morning sunlight, looking weak.

"I think we're here, wherever here is," he says. "Unless there are other big boats stranded in this desert."

He hands her the binoculars and she looks in the direction he points. "Not bad, kid. I thought we were dead back there." She lowers the binoculars and looks back to find Philip in the ATV bed.

"Fuck me," she says. "Where's the rest of his leg?"

"Gone," Owen says. "That was a whole day ago. How's your arm?"

Athena unwraps her makeshift T-shirt bandage. That cooked meat smell wafts toward Owen. His stomach full of beef jerky does backflips. Her skin looks like a fried turkey, scorched black and wrinkled.

"Can you move it?" he asks.

She holds the hand up in front of her face. "I'm sitting here, talking to you, telling my fingers to flex, and this is what's happening." The arm remains motionless in the air.

"Does it hurt?"

She frowns. "No. Which is bad, but I'm not sure how bad. Bring me my *Cookbook*. Maybe there's something we can do for me and Philip."

Owen produces the book from his bag. He holds it in front of Athena and flips pages as directed until they locate a simple healing command. Athena shows Owen how to use it on Philip's leg, cauterizing the wound with new pink skin and stopping the blood loss.

They try the same command on Athena's hand, but it has no apparent effect. "I'm sure Marsh will have some ideas," she says. "We can ask when we wake him up."

Owen's heart sinks as he remembers why they're here. In the excitement, he momentarily forgot Marsh's plans for Philip.

"You've done well to get us this far," Athena says. "I think we should camp and sleep and wake Marsh at sundown. Can I count on you?"

In other words, will Owen behave himself during whatever they plan for Philip? Part of Owen, the part which has kept him in the closet and relatively safe in his father's house for the last eighteen years, wants to agree to cover his own ass. But another part of him—the part only now waking up—hesitates.

"Marsh killed my best friend, and a bunch of other innocent people," he says. "I watched him do it. Now he wants to take another life, but in an even worse way. Not just killing, but living life in another person's place. It's wrong. If I help you help him, that makes me a henchman. I don't want to be a henchman."

"I appreciate your candor, Owen," Athena says. "I'll reward yours with some of my own. With my arm injured, I can't assemble Marsh's machine by myself. I need your help. If you behave and follow directions, I will do whatever I can to help you once this is over. But if you don't help? If you sabotage this? Marsh will kill us both. I know he seems weak now, but we're talking about a man who literally escaped hell. He's more powerful than you think. I also know you've taken to Philip, but you have to remember *he is not real*. He's a shell, made to look and sound like someone who's been dead for twenty years. An empty shell that will destroy our world if we don't do something about it." She can tell she's not convincing him and makes a frustrated sound. "There's not a choice here. You're young. You think in terms of good and evil. Life—adulthood especially—is more complicated. It's a lesson you have to absorb if you're going to study the Dissonance. You have to accept that there are some people you can help, and some people who will drag you down with them."

It *sounds* right but *feels* wrong. Owen stews, trying to reconcile the two things. He thinks again of the creature he saw during the ritual that brought Marsh back to life—the gowned figures screaming a high-pitched whine, eyes and nose stitched shut. The unspeaking. Who saw evil and did nothing.

"Sleep on it today," she says. "See how you feel tonight. In the meantime, do you want to see the ship, since we have the light?"

"What about Philip? Is it safe to leave him? What if something else comes after him?"

"We'll keep the ATV close," Athena says. "So if we hear anything we can be back in a flash."

Owen can't deny he's curious about it. They refuel the ATV, lower their Dissonant barrier, and slowly drive to the edge of the break in the earth, out of which extends the body of a remarkably well-preserved wooden sailing vessel—the kind of boat that would've been at home in one of those *Pirates of the Caribbean* movies. It juts up out of the earth at an angle, as though cresting a wave, its nose pointed down, its posterior up in the air.

They shuffle down the incline, holding hands to keep their balance and step onto the deck where it meets the earth.

"How do you think it got here?" Owen asks.

"I have no idea," Athena says. "Well, I take that back. I have some vague ideas of how, but not why."

He follows her to a doorway near the front of the ship, and down the stairs.

"Use a regular flashlight here, not the Dissonance," she says. "This place is—"

"Powerful," Owen says. He can feel it. A pleasurable hum in the air that seeps through his body, connecting him to the wood and sand around him.

Athena closes her eyes at his interruption. Like she remembers what he's feeling but can't feel it herself. He tries to imagine losing this newly discovered experience, this expansion of self. What it would be like to have it taken away.

"I shouldn't have talked over you," he says.

"No worries," she says. She switches on her flashlight and leads him into what looks like it might have been crew quarters. There are no signs of life whatsoever, and yet he can't shake the impression of being watched. Whenever he glances into dark corners, he finds them empty, but this does nothing to reassure him. The back of his neck prickles.

"Not much to look at, I know," Athena says. "The real goods are down in the hold." She kneels to open a hatch in the floor and climbs down a ladder into what Owen at first mistakes for an endless empty space. From the bottom of the ladder he can only see about six feet ahead. He checks to make sure his flashlight hasn't turned off or dimmed, and follows Athena forward. The farther they go, the less light there seems to be.

"There," Athena says, and points. "Still here, just like Marsh said it would be. Can you see it?"

He can, but barely. A figure mostly human in shape, androgynous, genderless. It's bent forward, hands clamped on either side of its head. It seems to be absorbing the light and putting out darkness in its place.

"Is that a statue?" he says.

"I still have dreams about that thing," Athena says. Her tone implies the dreams aren't good ones.

"This is what's giving off all that power?"

"We think so."

Owen wishes he had his phone so he could take pictures. Assuming he survives this ordeal, he wants to preserve every detail. He wonders what this statue would look like in open daylight.

"And you're telling me *this* is our best hope for saving the world?" he says.

"Unfortunately."

"We should check on Philip," he says. The silence down here is as unnerving as screams would be up above. He's eager to be away, to lay eyes on the other boy and make sure he's okay.

They leave the boat, and make their way back to the ATV. Philip is stirring, but is still asleep, so Owen uses the time to set up the tents. When he's finished, he approaches Philip and shakes him awake.

"What's happening?" Philip asks.

"We're here," Owen says, and points at the boat.

Philip scowls at the sight. "Oh."

The word sends a sharp pang through Owen. "How's your leg?" he asks.

Philip touches the bandaged stump. "Hurts. I can feel the part that's gone."

"I'm sorry," Owen says. "Maybe Marsh can heal it?"

"I know what he's planning to do to me," Philip said. "I overheard you talking to Athena. I don't want him to heal me. I hope I've ruined his prize."

It's the first time Philip has acknowledged it aloud. Owen doesn't have a suitable response, a way to make it better. Instead, he helps Philip into their tent, tells him to rest some more, and then he and Athena take the ATV and trailer as close to the ship as they safely can. First they drag out Marsh's sarcophagus and set it on the ground. Next come the crates, which have to be carried onto the boat one at a time. Owen has to do most of the work since he's the one with two working arms and legs. He unpacks the crates in the crew quarters, and carries the contents—mostly metal pipes and wiring—down to the hold, where he arranges them according to Athena's instructions. He assembles the pipe and erects a metal structure interlaced with wires. Some wires he ties together using exposed copper ends. Others have inlets and outlets which snap together like Lego bricks. Small, clear glass spheres attach to the wiring at intervals, like a string of Christmas lights.

As the structure takes shape, Owen realizes it was designed with the statue in mind. The piping surrounds it like a jungle gym built around a Gothic masterpiece. The final two bits are elevated metal slabs, one placed on each side of the statue, at the base of the piping. Owen supposes Marsh will lie on one and Philip will lie on the other, and somehow the DIY edifice will harness the Dissonant power of this place and facilitate a soul transfer. If it works.

Owen is a sweaty mess by the time he's finished, and Athena tells him to return to Philip and get some rest.

"This next part I have to do on my own," she says. "If this goes to shit, I don't want you two exploding."

"What about Marsh?" Owen says.

"If I explode, Marsh gets to explode, too," she says. "Go on. I'll come get you when—when it's time."

When Owen gets back to the camp he finds Philip outside the tent, looking through a box of food and water. He settles in next to him and they pick out some bottled waters and a couple of MREs. Neither speaks until their meal is done and Owen is gathering the waste in a plastic grocery bag.

"I don't want to die," Philip says.

Owen finishes tying up the bag and sets it on the ground beside him.

Philip stares down at his lap. "Until now I thought I would be okay with things. You know, as long as I knew it wouldn't hurt Erin. But something's changed. I don't want her to be hurt, but that's not the main thing I care about anymore. I care about me. And what I want." He looks up at Owen, and Owen feels like the other boy can sense the frustration and desperation in his own heart.

"It's okay," Philip says. "There's nothing you can do. They'll kill you if you try, and I'd rather that not happen."

"How can you be so calm?" Owen says.

"It's the last day of my life," Philip says. "I can be however I like."

Owen couldn't explain why if asked, but this is the moment he finds the courage to kiss Philip. The other boy's lips are dry and cracked like his own, and they both have awful breath, but Owen goes with it, pushes his dry mouth to Philip's. He's shocked by his own force-fulness, his need, as if his body has been impatiently waiting for this moment.

Philip cups Owen's stubbled cheeks, runs hands through Owen's hair. Said hair is dirty and stiff after three days in the desert, and Philip's fingers catch in the tangles, sending little spikes of pleasure across Owen's scalp.

They stop to breathe, and lean their foreheads together. "Do you want to help me into our tent?" Philip says.

Owen does. He drapes one of Philip's arms around his shoulders and together they run the three-legged race to their tent, laughing as they sway between balance and urgency. They make it without falling over, but it's a near thing.

Owen has wondered for years what it would be like, to be with another boy. He's skittish about touch—when you grow up with a father like Owen's, it's hard not to be. He has worried he would be too nervous to enjoy the moment, to sink into it. That his anxiety would keep him from getting a hard-on. That he might throw up on his partner.

But after the last few days, he's too tired, too full of need and pain to worry about anything but the beautiful body here with him in this tent.

"Is this okay?" he asks, as he tugs at Philip's shirt.

Philip nods. "I want you too. I want you for *me*."

Owen yanks Philip's shirt up over his head and pushes him onto his back and proceeds to kiss his neck, his collarbone, the hollow of his throat. These exploratory pecks become something rougher and hungrier as he works his way down Philip's muscled torso, reveling in the texture of his flesh, the salty taste of dried sweat. When he comes to the waistline of Philip's pants, Philip tries to sit up and help with the belt.

Owen pushes him back down. "You relax. I've got this."

He can't take Philip's pants all the way off without dislodging the makeshift bandage at the end of Philip's severed leg, so he makes do by wriggling them and the underwear just beneath Philip's hips. Philip appears to be as excited as Owen, his tumescence arcing up and toward his belly. A single fat drop of pre-come crystallizes and leaks onto Philip's stomach.

Owen doesn't give himself too much time to think. He takes Philip into his mouth.

"Oh," Philip says, in a half-gasp.

Owen stops and looks up at him. "Does it hurt?"

"No," Philip says. "It's . . . amazing."

Owen returns to the task, trying to be gentle, to use the tips he's read online but never practiced. He covers his teeth with his lips, and moves his hands in gentle sync with the motion of his mouth. Every few strokes he pauses to wriggle his tongue around the head of Philip's cock and the sensitive spot on the bottom where it connects to the shaft.

He sinks into a rhythm, lost in the pleasure of giving pleasure, enjoying the gentle stroke of Philip's fingers across his cheek, through his hair. The other boy's eyes are closed and his head is thrown back. His Adam's apple bobs in his throat as he swallows between sharp breaths. Again, although Owen has never ceased to recognize him, he feels that Philip's appearance has changed. He seems more *here*. More himself than ever before. In full stereoscopic, glasses-free 3-D.

Owen picks up the pace, uses his free hand to explore, to squeeze Philip's thighs, the soft curve of his ass, his flat stomach. When he massages the soft area behind Philip's balls, Philip's intact leg begins to shake, and the shake spreads to become a full-body tremor. His hips clench and his balls tighten. He cries out, lets go of Owen's hair, and bunches the fabric of his sleeping bag between his fingers as he spills into Owen's mouth. Owen gently guides Philip through climax and down, down, down, until he seems to be completely still, and at peace.

Owen goes outside, spits in the sand, and rinses his mouth with bottled water, then returns to the tent and pushes his sleeping bag up next to Philip's. They lie together, sweaty and exhausted, Philip curled into Owen's chest as the sun sets.

"That time was different," Philip says, absently stroking Owen's side. "From all the other times, I mean."

A spear of insecurity jabs Owen's heart. "Because it was with a boy?" Or does he give such terrible blowjobs that even the not-real boy has notes?

"That, yes," Philip says. He sits up a little so he can look Owen in the eye. "But also, all those times with Erin. They were nice, but never like that. Something different happened at the end this time. Like an explosion."

The lance in Owen's heart melts. "That's what normally happens for people with penises at the end of sex. If the penis-haver is having a good time and all. It's called an orgasm."

"Oh," Philip says, looking thoughtful. "Then I'm glad I got to have normal sex before the end, and I'm glad it was with you. I like you, Owen. More than anyone else I've met in my life."

"More than Erin?" Owen says. "Your person?"

"I care about Erin," Philip says. "Very much. But what we have is . . . different. She's far away, even when we're together. You feel like you're here."

Owen strokes Philip's cheek. "I like you too."

What he means is *I'm in love with you.*

Athena

Athena savors her third and final injection of Marsh's Dissonant elixir. Her senses expand and brush the surrounding ruins as she prepares for the soul transfer ritual. She moves slowly at first, drawing symbols, on guard for any sign that the air around her will combust, but Marsh's contraption seems to work as promised. The glass bulbs positioned along the metal pipes fill with green light as they siphon energy out of the air and store it. She finishes preparation with power to spare.

She leaves the ship, heads back to the camp, and slaps the side of the boys' tent.

"Time to begin," she says.

"Be right there," Owen calls.

He and Philip emerge a moment later, both flushed, their hair tangled and standing on end. They look somehow joyful and terrified at once, and Philip looks different overall, although Athena can't quite put her finger on *how*.

Nor does she waste time worrying about it—although something about their giddiness nags at her. She and the boys head back to the ship. No one says anything during the trip. Athena worries one of the boys might cause a scene—might beg for Philip's life, or even turn violent. She would be in real trouble if she had to endure another battle before the ritual. But her charges are docile. She should feel grateful they're making this easy. Instead, she worries.

"Are you planning something?" she asks.

"Like what?" Owen says.

"You're being awfully quiet, considering. I just want to make sure you aren't about to make the worst mistake of your life and do something stupid."

"You don't have to worry," Philip says. "Isn't that right, Owen?"

Owen doesn't answer, but his expression sours into something a bit more appropriate for what's about to happen. Athena hates to feel relief at his resignation, but she does.

When they get to the base of the ship, Owen helps Philip down to the hold below, while Athena opens Marsh's sarcophagus. She nearly gags on the stench that wafts out. She has time to wonder if the old man miscalculated, or if his hibernation was interrupted. Did one of the boys sabotage it? Is that why they're so calm?

Then the corpse's eyes open and Marsh looks up at her.

"We're here," Athena says.

She helps him climb out of the sarcophagus. He turns a slow circle, takes in the night sky, the sea of sand, and the ship. His mouth stretches in what might be a smile.

"I've dreamed of this for so long," he says. "In the final years of my first life, and through my years in hell. And now here I am." He turns to Athena. "Better, I'm here with you. Together, you and I will find the cure for your condition. We'll both have the second chances we deserve." His weird fake smile fades as he sees her blackened, withered hand.

"We had adventures while you napped," Athena says. "I'm not the only one who was damaged."

Athena tells him the story of the shadow serpent. He's clearly unhappy. "That is unfortunate. I don't suppose you saved the severed leg?"

"Afraid not," Athena says.

"No matter," Marsh says. "Either we can find a command to regrow it, or we can't. The important thing is that we made it here alive."

"Alive? Seriously?"

"You know what I mean," he says. "The point is that the ritual can proceed. Let's not waste any more time."

Athena leads Marsh down into the ship's hold. Owen has already strapped Philip onto one of the metal slabs, and the boys are now holding hands. Owen brings the tulpa's fingertips to his lips and kisses them. Athena suppresses a sigh. She told the kid not to get attached.

She lowers Marsh onto his slab and straps him in. He grabs hold of her good arm.

"I'm proud of you," he says.

Athena looks at Owen and Philip, and her gut wrestles with her mind. The plan—this ritual, the reason they've come all this way—*sounds* right, but it *feels* wrong.

"You were my favorite part of all of this," Philip says to Owen.

Athena looks away. It's obscene to watch such an obviously personal goodbye. And the words remind her of something. Something she can't quite place, although she feels like it was here, on Deoth.

She feels rather than sees Owen leave Philip to come stand beside her.

"You can leave if you want," she says. "This next part is going to be dangerous. And you might find it hard to watch."

"I'll stay," Owen says.

"Will it hurt?" Philip asks.

"I don't know," Athena says. "I'll try to make it quick." She hands the sheaf of paper containing her symphony to Owen. "Hold this and turn the pages when I tell you."

Owen holds the paper before her as she conducts her masterpiece, left-handed. She goes slow, because she needs to get this right, because this might be the last time she gets to do her favorite thing in the world.

There's that word again. *Favorite.*

She needs to focus. She closes her eyes and reaches out through the Dissonance to touch Marsh's machine. Her mind runs along the wires and piping and locates a warmth in the chest of Marsh's meat puppet. She wraps invisible fingers around this warmth and pulls. It resists, clings to the dead body with little red tendrils. She is gentle yet unyielding. Somewhere far away, she hears a gasp as Marsh's soul leaves the corpse.

A bright light appears in the darkness of her mind. The soul in her grasp wriggles and stretches its tendrils toward this light. Athena tightens her grip, aware she's not concentrating as well as she ought to be. She's distracted with thoughts about that stupid word and its stupid déjà vu. *Favorite.* Favorite what?

Her head aches. She grinds her teeth. Sweat forms on her brow, her neck, her pits, and her back. She pulls the soul along the intricate network of piping and wires, resisting both its struggle and the overwhelming gravity of the doorway of light. She threads her cargo through the machine and pushes it toward the slab at the other end where Philip is strapped. As it nears Philip, the soul turns its struggles toward the tulpa instead of the doorway. Its tendrils strain for the boy's chest, and she can hardly believe it, this is going to work, she's pulled off a dark miracle. No matter what else happens, she's cemented herself as one of the great Dissonants of all time.

Then, that word pinballing around her head finds a slot where it fits, and she remembers why *favorite part* struck a chord. Nineteen ninety-nine, the coven's trip to Deoth. Erin and Peter off in their tent, losing their virginity, while she and Hal lay together atop Peter's sleeping bag, joking and talking about everything except what mattered. Her head on his chest, his arm around her shoulders, not because she was injured or needed the support, but because he wanted to hold her.

So you've come to an alien world, Athena had said. *What do you think?*

Hal had lifted his head, and for a moment she was sure he meant to make a joke. Then his face shifted and he looked at her with something like pain. This handsome, sad, lost boy, showing her his truest face.

Honestly? This is my favorite part, he'd said.

The wriggling soul in her grasp touches Philip's body. A blinding flash of pain rips through her mind.

Owen

Athena's symphony begins as a dazzling light show, something out of a big-budget movie. Owen wants to keep his eyes on Philip the entire time, to be with him through the end, but as soon as that red light comes out of Marsh's chest and starts its journey through the machine, Owen can't help himself. He has to watch the thing progress through the pipes.

When Marsh's soul emerges from the machine over Philip, it washes his body in red light. Philip lies still, eyes closed, as the soul sinks toward him, spreading tendrils like an ethereal jellyfish. *Now* Owen wants to look away. He doesn't want to see Philip go and Marsh take over. He doesn't want to watch the murderer gain more life.

Yet his gaze remains fastened, and so he sees it when the red jellyfish stops in midair between the tube and Philip's chest. The tendrils reach for Philip, straining. Something is holding it back.

Philip's face, peaceful until now, breaks into lines of pain. His lips roll back and his forehead wrinkles.

The red jellyfish flies back up into the machine as though thrown. It jets through the piping and wires the way it came, but halfway through the return journey, a fissure appears on one of the pipes. Light streams from the fracture and shines on Athena's face. She grunts and lowers her head.

"What's wrong?" Owen says.

On the slab, Philip opens his eyes, bewildered. Owen's no expert in soul transference, but Philip still *looks* like himself. The red jellyfish lingers in the machine, halfway between corpse and Philip, apparently trapped.

"Athena," Owen says. "Let go. Let the machine break. He'll die and we'll be free."

"If I let go," Athena says through gritted teeth, "we lose control of the power in the hold. It'll be like setting off a bomb." She opens her eyes and squints at him, and even in the reflected red and green light, he sees her iciness, her cruel steel is gone, replaced with the fear Owen saw when he first met her. That and a deep, profound sadness. The look of someone giving up. "Take Philip and the ATV and go. You can get clear in time. The doorway ritual is in my *Cookbook*. Go home."

Owen goes to the slab and loosens the strap across Philip's chest. He's almost got it unbuckled when the machine produces another groan. Something above and behind Owen snaps, and a voice— inhuman, cold and rough as stone—cries out.

Owen pulls Philip onto his remaining foot. Together they start hobbling up the ladder. They're only a rung away from freedom when a blast of energy hits Owen in the back. He loses his grip on Philip as his feet leave the ground. Philip falls over with a cry and Owen is thrown sideways. He slams into Athena, bowling her over.

They both hit the wooden floor of the hold with a painful *thump*. Owen rolls off her and watches the machine as it continues to break. Pipes snap out of alignment. They bend and twist in jerks and bursts, like a stop-motion or time-lapse video. And as all of this chaos unfolds, as the machine tears itself apart, the bulbs of green light burst, and the energy inside them seems to enter the jellyfish. The red light floats toward the statue at the center of this storm. The stone figure with its hands on its head, communicating incredible confusion and agony. The jellyfish flies like a falling drop of water, reaching for the statue's chest.

With a sound like an avalanche, the statue stands up, and lowers its arms from its head. It examines its hands, turning them over. They look almost comical, like giant stone mittens.

Two red eyes appear on the statue's face, where previously it had no features. With a rumble, its blank countenance becomes a face, and its mitten hands split into fingers.

"Traitors!" the statue shouts, its voice a deep rumble.

Athena sits up, dazed, and rubs her temples. "I don't understand. It should have worked."

The statue picks her up and throws her against a wall.

"Don't lie to me," it says. "You ensouled the tulpa."

Athena turns her disbelief on Owen. From his place on the floor, Owen raises both hands. "I don't know what he's talking about," he says.

"I'm not stupid," she says. "You and Philip were alone together for hours. What did you do?"

Owen gets to his feet, hands still raised. "What did we do? While we were alone?" He glances at Philip, shy despite the terrifying nature of the moment. Philip smiles at him from the floor, and Owen begins to laugh.

"Not a great time to get the giggles, kid," Athena says.

"I know," he says. "I'm sorry. But. Oh god. When Philip and I were alone, all we did was fool around. Nobody told me blowjobs were magic." Owen bursts into a fresh gale of laughter.

"They're not," Athena says.

"Maybe you've been doing it wrong?" Owen says, tears streaming from his face. "Every boy I blow grows a soul!"

Marsh doesn't share in the mirth. "Years of planning, of suffering, wasted." The statue takes a step forward on thick legs of rock.

Athena's too weak to do anything, and Owen is too frightened to try. He looks at Philip. He wants Philip to be the last thing he sees before he dies. He smiles at the other boy, tries to tell himself he's ready, that at least they got one stolen afternoon together before everything is over forever.

The world behind Marsh tears, and bright daylight comes flooding into the dark of the hold. Owen shields his eyes with his hands and squints as a blast of hot, humid air hits him in the face.

A hole in the world has opened behind Marsh. Marsh turns to look at it.

"What the hell?" he rumbles. He barely has time to say it before he's yanked up into and through the air. He passes into the portal, and it shuts behind him with a *whoomph*.

Before Owen can react to any of this, something makes a thunderclap sound above him.

The ceiling of the hold crashes inward and an object rolls along the ground and up onto its feet in one smooth motion. At first Owen thinks it's a woman, but there's something otherworldly about her. Her skin is silvery, her eyes are black orbs. She's more than human. She offers Athena a hand and helps her up.

"Morgan?" Athena says. She sounds dazed.

"Athena Watts," the not-a-woman says. "Your boon is at hand."

The world bends around them, and both figures disappear, leaving Owen and Philip alone together in the hold.

Athena

Athena falls for a long time. First through darkness, and then through blinding white light. Eventually, the plummeting sensation stops, but there's no abrupt end, no crash. There's no landing at all. When the white light fades, she finds herself back in Marsh House, in Peter's old bedroom. Early-morning light streams through the curtains and turns the white walls a creamy yellow. The bed is a mess, recently slept in.

"Athena?"

It's Erin. She and Hal stand in the room as well, looking every bit as confused as she feels. Even more shocking, however, is the presence of Peter Marsh beside them. It's definitely Peter, not Philip. Slightly less handsome, slightly more real-looking. Peter at sixteen, his presence as distinct, welcome, and familiar as a favorite jacket.

"Peter?" Athena says.

"Hi guys," Peter says. He gives them a bittersweet smile. "You grew up."

"What is this?" Athena says. "Are we in heaven?"

"No, you're in my bedroom. The morning of the day I died."

"Why?" Hal says.

"There are things you need to see, since I'm not alive to tell you myself. So pay close attention." He disappears as the bedroom door opens and another Peter Marsh walks in, towel around his waist, brushing his teeth. He goes about his business, doesn't seem to notice the coven.

The room vanishes, replaced with the hallway leading to Professor Marsh's study. Peter stands in the study doorway with his back to the group. He's dressed for school, his backpack slung over one shoulder. He looks in at Marsh, bent over a book at his desk.

"I'm off to school," Peter says.

Marsh looks up. He takes off his glasses and pinches the bridge of his nose. When he puts them back on, he seems a bit more present, if weary.

"It's not too late to transfer," Marsh says. "We've got the money. You've got the grades. You don't *have* to go back to them."

Peter kicks the carpet with the toe of one sneaker. "I should probably at least go today."

Marsh looks back at his book, dismissing the boy. "It's your life."

The coven follows him out of the house and down the driveway. They're halfway to Peter's little red CRX when Peter stops and looks into the woods. A few seconds later, Athena's older ears pick out what Peter has already noticed: a voice, singing a plaintive tune in a language she doesn't understand.

Peter drops his backpack beside his car and follows the sound. He runs past the tree line and into the woods like something is chasing him. Athena understands why. The song has reached into her chest and squeezed her heart. She'd do anything to stop that pain.

What she *doesn't* understand is how she and the others are able to keep up with a sixteen-year-old boy at full speed. Her old injury doesn't pain her the way it should as she jogs behind him. Is it the Dissonance? Is she not actually in her own body right now?

Peter finds the singer in the creek bed. It's been a hot summer, and the creek is dry. Waters will rise in the fall, but for now it's a grassy ditch. She sits in the dried mud at the bottom, her mouth wide in song, her dark hair snarled with dried leaves. Morgan the undine looks ill, her skin rough and blotchy, lips cracked.

She stops her song as Peter approaches. "I hoped your friends would be with you."

Peter flinches at the word *friends*. He climbs down into the ditch and kneels so they're at eye level. "You look like you need help."

"My daughter," Morgan says. "They took her from me."

"You have a daughter?" Peter says.

"I didn't have her the last time we met. She's a hatchling."

"Who took her? Where?"

"Poachers," Morgan says. "I don't know where they took her. I came here because this is close to where I was held. Where your friend Hal found me."

Peter frowns as he thinks. "Hal found you by accident. We only located you with Athena's Doorway and Hal's memory of you."

"I have plenty of memories of Sybil," Morgan says. "You open the door and I'll do the remembering."

Peter nods. "Okay. Can you walk?"

She can, but needs help. She drapes an arm around Peter's shoulder and he holds her by the waist as they trek back to his grandfather's house. Athena can smell the undine from several feet away. She stinks like fish left out in the sun.

As Marsh House comes into view at the edge of the woods, Morgan halts.

"We're not going in there," she says. "It feels *wrong*."

"It's probably one of the safest places in the multiverse," Peter says. "Nothing bad will happen to you in there."

Morgan scrutinizes his face, her gaze intense. Peter holds eye contact, calm. She allows herself to be led forward into the house.

Peter calls for his grandfather as they enter, then takes Morgan into his bathroom. He shows her how to plug the drain, and how to work the hot- and cold-water knobs. He leaves her to draw a bath and, since Professor Marsh hasn't yet appeared, he goes to the study. The door is shut, so he knocks and calls out. He receives no answer.

He visibly braces himself—he knows better than to enter his grandfather's sanctum uninvited—and pulls the door open.

An unfinished mug of coffee and a plate of toast crumbs sit on the desk. A journal stands open, pen abandoned at the crease between the pages. The desk itself is unoccupied.

He goes back up the hall, stops, and ducks into his bedroom. He pulls a Mead spiral notebook from the top drawer and flips through it. Athena's never seen Peter's grimoire before. It contains sketches of plants, tables charting rainfall and weather patterns. Dirt smudges cover the pages. Toward the back, he comes to a section of copied out rituals and commands. He stops on the page marked "Athena's Doorway." He marks its place with a finger, and takes it with him to the bathroom.

He finds Morgan in a tub so full the water almost reaches the lip. Her skin looks less blotchy, her expression less wan.

"Better?" he says.

She points to the notebook in his hand. "Is that what we need?"

"I think so." He kneels beside the tub and flips to the page with the copied commands. "Hold on to my shoulder and picture Sybil. I'll do the rest."

Morgan grabs him with one damp hand and closes her eyes. He takes a deep breath, and with his free hand he draws. He focuses on the text, rather than the light show, like a proficient Dissonant should. The air fills with a crackling hum and a dark rectangle rimmed in green light takes shape behind him.

"Time to go," Peter says.

He and Morgan stand and pass through the doorway together. Athena and the others follow into a cool, dark room, the air humid and thick with strange smells.

Athena already recognizes it. They've come to Marsh's menagerie.

"This is where they brought me when I was first captured," Morgan says.

"Do you want to go back to the creek?" Peter says. "Maybe I can find Sybil and bring her to you."

"No," she says. "Mine should be the first face she sees."

They pass terrarium after terrarium. One contains a potbellied centaur with dark circles beneath his eyes. In another sits a mannequin shaped like a woman with two heads, her arms bent in the wrong direction. In a third stalks an enormous cat with mouths in place of eyes.

Eventually Peter and his fellow traveler move into what appears to be the aquarium in this menagerie. Tanks full of blue, green, and, in one case, red water. Fish that dart in and out of sight. There's a tank containing an otter with a near-human face. And toward the back of the room, a cylindrical tank that stands apart. It's less than five feet tall and contains a mock-up of a stone shelf. Through the glass Athena sees a creature who could be Morgan in miniature, chubby little fingers pressed to the glass before her, huge eyes plaintive and miserable. Then the baby sees her mother and shouts her surprise in a flurry of bubbles.

Morgan jumps into the tank with her daughter. Water splashes up over the side and onto the floor as they spin beneath the surface, a flurry of black hair and silvery limbs. Something of their song passes out of the tank, loud enough for Athena to hear—a melody of surprise and delight that vibrates through the air and sends a joyous shiver through Athena's body.

In the tank, Morgan and Sybil stop their song as Morgan locates the manacle around the girl's ankle. She's chained to the floor of the tank. Morgan gathers the chain in her hands, plants her feet on the glass wall, and pulls. The glass cracks beneath the balls of her feet as the chain tears free. Peter, Athena, Hal, and Erin dance out of the way as the tank shatters and everything inside rushes out to soak the floor.

Athena is so intent on watching Peter help the undines to their feet that she doesn't notice the man enter the room until he speaks.

"Peter?" Professor Marsh says. He wears an apron tied around his front. The fabric is dark with blood. A few drops have stained the professor's cheek as well. He looks harried, a man interrupted in the middle of something important. He's just come from the morgue.

Peter stares at his grandfather, and Athena sees something break in her old friend—a long-suspected, long-denied truth finally escaping confinement and cementing itself as reality.

Morgan looks at Peter. "You know this man?"

"You did this?" Peter says. He points to Morgan, and to Sybil. "You took them?"

"Calm down, Peter," Marsh says.

"Run," Peter says. He and Morgan dash back toward the still open doorway.

"Peter!" Marsh shouts. "Come back here right now!"

The scene around Athena changes in another flash of light. Now she's riding in the backseat of Peter's car. Morgan sits up front and the rest of the coven is jammed three across in the back. Sybil sits in Morgan's lap. The girl, barely more than an infant, looks terrified. The car reeks of seafood, and Athena's stomach clenches as she remembers throwing up outside Lorna's convertible the first time they rescued Morgan.

She tries not to think about it. Instead, she focuses on the girl's face. There's something familiar about it, something that goes beyond her resemblance to Morgan.

Peter pulls into the parking lot at Lake Murvaul, gets out, and opens the passenger side doors. An hour's drive in the August heat appears to have sapped much of the undines' strength. He wraps his right arm around Morgan's waist and uses his left to hold Sybil clasped to his chest. She clings to him, chubby little arms around his neck. Together the odd trio walks out into the water. Morgan submerges first, dipping her head beneath the surface. She reemerges a few seconds later, her arms out for her daughter. Peter walks in up to his knees to hand Sybil over. Morgan dunks the girl, and the baby comes up looking considerably more cheerful.

Morgan cradles Sybil on her chest and inclines her head toward Peter. "Once again I find myself in your debt."

"The man we saw when we fled. He's the one who imprisoned you?" Peter says.

"He is," Morgan says.

"That man is my . . . my teacher. So freeing you and your daughter was my obligation. You owe me nothing."

The water gently undulates around Morgan, as she studies Peter.

"He's more than a teacher, isn't he?" she says. "He's family."

"Yes," Peter says, head low. "The only parent I've ever known."

"You're not him," she says. "And with your friends' help, you can stop him from hurting anyone else."

Peter grimaces. "I'm not sure they are my friends anymore."

"The four of you are bound. They are your forever people. Forgive them and allow them to help you."

Peter lifts his head. "Speaking of family. I know Sybil's father, don't I?"

Morgan touches his cheek. "I hope I'll see you again, Peter. Under happier circumstances." She backs into the water until it covers her head, and then she's gone.

The world flashes white around Athena and when the light fades, the coven is hurrying up the steps to Clegg High School behind Peter. He stops in front of the doors and turns to look at them again.

"You all know how the rest went," he says. "I came inside to get you, and then—the statue arrived."

On cue, the statue drops from the sky. It appears to take in its surroundings, and then, after a moment's consideration, it starts moving its hands through the air, its fingertips leaving yellow-green light in its wake.

"I thought it was casting an offensive command," Peter says. "Something meant to hurt us. So I cast one of my own."

His hands move quickly through the air, and a blast of green light shoots across the lawn, slamming into the statue. It staggers back a step, shakes its head as though dazed, and then comes storming toward Peter.

"I panicked," Peter said. "So I cast a slow command on it, to buy some time until you came back, Athena. You know the rest."

His words hang there, waiting for her to say something. She thinks for a moment that she won't be able to respond, that even now she won't be able to voice her great shame. She drops her head, no longer meeting his gaze. Still Peter waits for her, and she understands that nothing else is going to happen unless she speaks.

"I know you needed my help," Athena says finally. "I came out and tried to fight. I really did. But then I realized what we were up against, and—" She braces herself, and her voice breaks as she continues. "I was afraid. I ran. I'm so sorry, Peter."

She raises her head to risk a glance at Peter. His expression seems to express sympathy, understanding, if not quite forgiveness.

"If I had it to do over," Peter says, glancing at Hal and Erin, "I would've listened to Morgan. I wouldn't have split us up. What about you? Would you do it differently if you had the chance?"

"Yes," Hal says.

"Yes," Athena says. Her voice still sounds watery and weak, so she nods emphatically to drive her point home. "Yes," she says again.

"Let's see," Peter says. He turns to them. "The me outside the school won't remember this conversation. You'll have to make him understand who you are, and why you're here. Good luck."

He and the school disappear in a flash of light. When it fades, Athena finds herself alone, about a block from the school, running. She's running now like she ran then. Trying to save her own skin.

She stops and looks back at the school. It's still standing. She looks down at herself, realizes she's still in her thirty-seven-year-old body, with all its attendant aches and pains. The undine had told her, *Your boon is at hand.* Here it is. She understands intuitively that the guided part of the tour is over. She seems to have traveled back in time to 1999, and she's now being given a choice: to continue running, to save her skin like she did the first time, or to go back, and stand with Peter on the school steps as he fights the statue from Deoth—the one, she now knows, which contains Elijah Marsh's soul.

The stern schoolteacher who lives in her mind clears its throat. *You can't defeat Marsh. You're not even Dissonant any longer. You'll die if you go.*

"Fucking good," she tells the teacher. "I'd rather be dead than do the last twenty years all over. Seems like a fair trade."

Athena Watts sprints back toward her old high school, to do battle, and, if necessary, die.

Erin

After the last flash of light, Erin finds herself back in Clegg High School, in the hallway right outside the library. Through the glass in the doors, she can see students and teachers huddled inside. Although she can't see herself, she knows, the way you know things in dreams, that the seventeen-year-old version of herself is behind the checkout desk, arms in the air, trying to maintain a shield around the school while the battle out front shakes the building.

This again. If there's a hell, this is what it would be for her. This place, this day, over and over and over again.

Hal Isaac stands beside her—not sixteen-year-old Hal, but the Hal who she met in the diner the other night. The Hal who held her hand as they walked into the Source together. A bit of gray in his dark hair, crow's feet and laugh lines on his stubbled face. This Hal doesn't look panicked. He looks pretty fucking serene, considering.

"I can't believe we're back here," Erin says.

"Let's try something different this time," Hal says.

Instead of entering the library, they walk through the silent hallways of the school. Their footsteps are loud, the rubber soles of their shoes squeaking. As they near the front doors, Erin slows.

"I don't know if I can go out there," she says.

"Sure you can," Hal says.

"I can't. Not on the day he sent me away."

He takes her hands and turns her to face him. "We asked for help. This is what we were given. It's our turn, remember? Last march of the fuckups and all that."

She swallows, closes her eyes, and takes a deep breath. "Let me go first? Wait here for a minute, okay?"

She lets go of his hands and walks ahead to the school doors. Peter stands outside, alone, hands in the air like a teenage Gandalf as he faces off against the statue from Deoth. There's a strange quality in the air. It crackles with energy and as light passes through this energy, it distorts somehow, goes wavy like the surface of water on a windy day. The crackles happen slowly, like thunder played at one-quarter speed, endless rumbles and scratches reverberating in the air.

Peter's face is a grimace of agony as the stone statue swings a giant arm down toward him. It's not frozen, but moving very, very slowly.

"What were you doing?" she says. She says it mostly to herself, and is surprised when Peter blinks at normal speed and turns to look at her.

"Who are you?"

His confusion stings, and she takes a step back despite herself. Has she grown so old?

Then his face wrinkles anew with concentration. "Erin? Is that you?"

"Hi Peter," she says. "It's me."

"I don't understand. What's happening?"

"It's a long story," she says. "From my perspective, twenty years ago today you . . ." The next words are hard to say.

"I what?" Peter asks.

"This day—today—is the day everything went wrong for all of us," she says. "You did your best with the statue, but it wasn't enough."

"What do you mean?"

"I mean . . ." Jesus Christ, why is this so hard? "We lost the school, and everyone in it, except for me, Hal, and Athena."

"What about me?" Peter says. "What happens to me?"

Erin shakes her head, can't say the words. Peter seems to understand anyway.

"I die today?" he says.

She nods.

"But you and the others lived?"

She nods again.

"That's something, anyway," Peter says. He seems to gather himself. "So why are you here now?"

"Twenty years from now, something else has gone wrong. Or maybe it's all the same thing. I don't know. But we asked Morgan's daughter for help, and here we are. I think this is her boon. We've been sent back to help you."

"We?" Peter says.

Erin beckons toward the school and Hal emerges. He looks uncharacteristically sheepish.

"Hey Peter," he says.

"Hey Hal," Peter says. The devastated look on his face—the knowledge of his own impending mortality—lightens a little, and he smiles. "It's good to see you both."

Erin nods toward the statue. "What are you doing to it?"

"It's a Dissonant trick I was experimenting with—slowing time within a confined space. I'm basically playing for time, because there's so much Dissonant energy in the air it's like a bomb is about to go off."

That tracks with what Erin understands of the statue. It's basically a nuclear-level Dissonant energy source. Last time they tried to use Dissonant around it, they all nearly died.

Before Erin or Hal can respond to what Peter's said, the statue seems to free itself from the time-slow. Its fist passes through the ripples of Peter's trick, intact, and plummets straight toward the coven.

Erin's hands are in the air before she realizes it. Her old instincts are strong, and her fingers move faster than her thoughts, making the old signs, invoking the old protections. Her mind races to catch up, to tell her she's made a stupid mistake, that even with her grafts she's no match for this thing and she needs to get out of the way *now*—

And then, in the moment she expects to die, she instead hears an almost laughable sound: a hollow *bonk*, like two rubber balls colliding in midair. The statue staggers back and the force of its blow shakes the world around them. Glass in the school doors shatters and falls to the ground.

"I didn't know you could still do that," Hal said.

"I can't," Erin says. "At least, nothing that strong. Yesterday, a piece of hail ripped my dome to shreds."

She looks at her hands, and as she does, she feels herself expand beyond the limits of her own body. She feels the bricks of the school, the grit of the concrete, the sharp blades of freshly mown grass. She feels her friends beside her—truly feels them for the first time in twenty years. Not as separate presences or bodies in space but extensions of herself. "Something's changed. It's . . . it's back." She's reconnected to the Dissonance, back online.

The statue stands back and cocks its head, peering down at the three Dissonants in the bubble. "Erin? Hal?" it says. The voice is strange, sounds like two rocks being scraped together, but its cadence is familiar. Erin has no problem placing it at once.

"Professor Marsh?" she says, incredulous.

"You're a statue now?" Hal says. "Or in 1999? How is that possible?"

"It's a long story," Marsh says. "But thank god you're here. I need your help."

Passionately, he recounts how he ended up here, how Athena betrayed him and sent him into a statue—and how, for whatever reason, the statue time-traveled here.

"Time travel is one of the fundamental no-no's of the Dissonance," Marsh says. "It's thrown the world out of true again. Me being here is like a bomb going off. No matter what, the destruction is already going to be immense. But if we act swiftly, I think we can keep from destroying the entire town, and save your lives in the process."

There's silence for a moment. Erin looks to Hal, to get his opinion, only to see her friend shaking his head.

"What do you mean, Athena betrayed you?" Hal demands.

"I mean she betrayed me. She said she would help, but when the time came, she banished me to this." Marsh gestures at the statue body. "Hal, you know her as well as anyone. You know how ruthless and cold she can be."

"I don't believe it," Hal says. "If she put you in that thing, I'm sure she had a damned good reason."

"Hal, don't be a fool," Marsh says. "We're going to kill so many people if you don't help me get out of here."

"Give us a minute," Hal says.

For a wonder, the statue steps back, giving them space to talk.

Hal leans in close to Erin. "What's the play?" he murmurs.

She shrugs. "I can't hold this for much longer," she whispers back. "Not if he attacks again. I'm strong, but Marsh—even as a statue—

is stronger. And he's probably right about what'll happen if he stays here."

"Okay," Hal says, keeping his voice low. "I'll distract him while you two come up with a plan to get rid of him."

"Are you insane?" Erin says.

"If you're reconnected to the Dissonance, maybe I can summon the Blade of Woe," Hal says. "Maybe finally bring that whole 'destiny' business I was promised full circle, you know? But I know I can't do it in this bubble. The Blade has to have a clear line to me, no interference."

Hal looks to Peter, who's been watching the conversation silently.

"Last time we did this," Peter said, "I sent you away because I wanted you to have a chance to meet your daughter."

"Daughter?" Hal says, nonplussed. Then it seems to dawn on him what Peter is saying. "Daughter," he repeats, awestruck. "Sybil?"

Peter nods. "Let's do it differently this time. Let's work together. Hal, you go distract it. Erin, you keep the shield up. I'm going to use Athena's doorway command to send it away."

"Hal, that thing could kill you," Erin says.

"It'll have to catch me first," Hal says.

Hal

Hal braces himself. Tells himself he's ready to die. That if this is his reward and/or punishment for his life, he accepts it.

Daughter! his mind cries. *You have a daughter!*

He's still in shock over the revelation. He's also confused, since he never slept with Morgan. But most of all he's delighted. He never knew he wanted to be a father, but now that he is, he wonders if it's what's been missing all these years. A child. In a perfect world, Morgan would have told him. He could've been a part of the girl's life. But at least he knows. And like Peter says, at least he got to meet her.

He steps out from behind Erin's shield. The statue is still standing a few feet away. Hal steps into one of the divots its heavy feet have made in the lawn and raises his left arm skyward. This is how it used to work. The call from his heart. The response from a power that chose him for reasons he still doesn't fathom.

"What are you doing, Hal?" Marsh says. The question sounds strange, coming from the statue—annoyance filtered through stone, but still unmistakably Hal's old teacher.

"What's it look like, genius?" Hal says.

"And why would you need the Blade right now?" Marsh says.

"To kill you, duh."

"Look at you," Marsh says, his rock face breaking into what might be a crude version of a sneer. He steps toward Hal, and Hal takes two steps to the side, up out of the divot but farther away from Erin's shield. "Slouching into middle age, as unremarkable a man as ever walked the earth."

"Could be worse," Hal says. "I could've been reincarnated as an ugly-ass statue." He starts to feel the strain of holding his arm aloft. Is he experiencing the telltale tingle, maybe? Or are those the nerves in his arm complaining? Hard to tell at thirty-seven.

Marsh swings at Hal. Hal dodges, but barely. Marsh stomps and drives a fresh crater in the grass. Dirt sprays up and Hal throws himself backward. He lands on his ass, and scrambles to his feet.

"I see you're still your coven's remedial student," Marsh says. "Your friends were always the special ones. You're the accident."

"No idea what you're talking about," Hal says. He flexes his fingers. *I'm here. I need you, dammit. Come to me.* "I have a destiny, remember? Maybe it's to kill you."

Marsh takes another swipe. Hal barely ducks to one side. He's running out of lawn. He glances up the steps to the school, straining to see through the ripples in the air, but it appears Erin and Peter are both casting.

Hal loops in a different direction, starts toward the far end of the lawn, toward town. Marsh follows. He doesn't seem to be in any great hurry. He's toying with Hal.

Behind Marsh's back, he sees a figure come around the side of the school. Even through the ripples in the air he recognizes Athena's silhouette. She's running, but stops when she sees Hal.

Despite Hal's desperate, silent cries, the Blade doesn't seem to be coming. Maybe the Temple has chosen another champion. It *has* been twenty years. Maybe Hal's boon was Sybil. Maybe it was the opportunity to be here and die with friends. To give the talented members of his coven enough time to save the day.

He stops backing up. Athena slants toward him, a look of concern on her face. He wants to wave her off, but he can't let Marsh know she's arrived. So instead he does what he does best. He runs his mouth:

"It must chap your ass," he says, and lets his arm fall to his side. "You studied and worked all your life. You dedicated your life to this shit. You put it above everything. And for all you gave, what did you accomplish? You managed to make a bunch of kids think that this"— he gestures at the bizarre tableau around them—"was their fault. And then you went and died alone, and unfulfilled. And yeah, my adulthood might be pretty terrible, and my best days might be in the rear-view, but me? This kid from the shitty apartment complex? For a little while, I was chosen by cosmic forces beyond your comprehension."

He smiles at Athena.

Marsh raises both arms above his head and swings them down at Hal. Hal tries to dodge again, but time has finally caught him—he is too slow. He hears Athena's scream, and then he sees and hears no more.

Athena

Athena watches Marsh kill Hal. It looks like something from a cartoon: the giant statue literally *pounds* her old friend into the ground, creating a dent in the earth. Hal is dead. She knows it. There's no question—and she realizes that she knows because she can't feel Hal in the Dissonance anymore. Which is how she realizes that she is connected to the Dissonance—not in a fleeting sort of way, but truly connected. Retethered to the perpetual motion machine at the broken heart of all things.

Something tears its way up out of her. Not a shout, nor a scream. A roar as primal as the Dissonance itself. She launches herself across the field toward the stone man, heedless of the miracle that has befallen her, the pain in her bad leg, or thoughts of her useless right arm. She casts with the left, gifting herself strength and speed.

Marsh turns, and despite his inability to make a face, his posture communicates alarm as Athena hurls herself into the air and hits him with a blast of hard wind. He stumbles back and she slams into him. He grabs her by the arm so that she falls alongside him and they hit the ground together. He yanks her off the ground and holds her close to his face.

"Look at what you did to me!" he shouts. "Forced into this—this monstrosity!"

"I am so glad this is how it ends for you," Athena says.

"Don't be foolish, girl!" Marsh says. "There's still time to make this right—to save your friends and yourself."

"And you," Athena says.

"Yes, goddammit, and me," Marsh says. "Why not me? You agreed to help me! You were supposed to be my right hand!"

"Right hand for what?" Athena says. "Why do you have that storehouse? What are you planning?"

"Oh, now you have questions," Marsh says. He lets her go and she drops to the ground. "Whereas before you were happy to do whatever I said, as long as it got you back to your precious Dissonance."

She snorts and rolls back to her feet. "And now I'm happy to die here with my friends, as long as it means you die, too."

He's gained his knees, but she tackles him again. One of his wild haymaker blows connects with the side of her head and the world wobbles around her. Then something yanks her into the air and she's flying. She expects to hit something—either a wall or the ground—hard enough to lose consciousness. Instead, she comes to a gentle stop and drifts to lie in the dirt.

"Athena." The voice could be coming from another room, directed at another, different person. "Athena, are you still with us?"

She blinks. Erin's and Peter's faces hang upside-down in the air over her.

"He killed Hal," she mumbles through a mouthful of blood.

"I know," Erin says gently. "But if we don't do something soon, he's going to kill us, too, and who knows if the explosion that's coming will actually kill him."

"Can you keep him busy for another minute?" Peter says. "Erin and I are going to open a doorway. All you have to do is push him through it."

They help Athena sit up. Marsh lumbers across the lawn toward them in his unblemished stone body. Athena thinks there's probably a good joke about arguing with a brick wall in there somewhere, but she can't find it.

"Yeah, I can handle it," she says. She blinks a few times, stands, and casts from memory. Marsh loses his footing, stumbles, and falls skyward. It's the same antigravity command she worked on Hal in 1996, but now she chains it to a second command, one she didn't know back then: a gravity command. She makes it double strength, so he slams into the earth face-first with a shout. She does it again. Then again. Each time, the ground shakes hard enough to stagger her.

"How do you like it?" she says, hammering him into his own impression in the earth. She glances back at Erin, who has her eyes closed and arms up, and Peter, who is still casting. They still need more time.

"You know what I think?" Athena says to Marsh. "I think you didn't want Peter to have friends. You wanted him all to yourself, so you could twist him into something like you. You were jealous of the coven. And when Peter died and we didn't? Your jealousy turned to fear. You wore the mask of grief to strip us of our gifts. But you made a mistake. You could've kept us around, kept us under your thumb. Instead, you *broke* us. And you should know better than anyone what gives a Dissonant power. In your arrogance, you've made us *insanely* powerful."

"Is that right?" Marsh wriggles out of her grasp and rights himself once more, but he doesn't approach the rest of the coven. He crosses to the spot where Hal's body lies facedown in the dirt. He bends and digs the corpse out of the ground with one hand. Hal hangs limp. "If the four of you are so powerful, then how do you explain this?"

Hal

Hal comes to in the dark, with the sensation of cold stone against his cheek. He sits up and looks around, trying to reorient himself. Then he spots a small light some distance away, and realizes where he is. Twenty-one years after his last visit, he's finally returned to the Temple of Pain.

He knows the drill here, so instead of wasting time, he stands up, crosses the wide stone floor, and thrusts his left arm into the light. The light clamps down on his hand like a pair of jaws, and his entire arm is engulfed in an almost overwhelming agony.

"Thought I already passed this test," he says, trying to keep his voice even.

Beg. The voice comes through his mind, clear as a loudspeaker. *Beg to be reunited with the Blade. Beg to become our champion again.*

"We've played this game before," Hal said. "You tell me to beg, I tell you I won't, you learn to respect me, and then I'm your champion. Right?"

You abandoned your duty to us. Let Marsh sever your connection. Why should we choose you again, after your dereliction?

"Why did you bring me here?" Hal asks. "If you don't want me anymore? I mean, I died, right? So that's it. Dunzo."

Your friends are dying. They need your help. Beg for our forgiveness. Pledge yourself anew to our teachings, and perhaps we will take pity on you. You will be allowed to complete your destiny.

"And what destiny is that, exactly?" Hal says. "You were never too clear on that."

To help Marsh. You will return to the field of battle and call a truce. You will convince your friends to help him return to Deoth. You will find a way for his grand design to move forward.

"What grand design?"

Marsh knows that pain is the great catalyst—that true, lasting change only comes with violence. He's planning a war on the Dissonant world. You are to stand at his side, as his general. His enforcer. Your anger—your deep rage—will make you a powerful aide. This is your destiny, Hal Isaac. This is why you were chosen. To help spread the gospel of pain through the entire world.

Hal's gut twists. All this time—he's been *serving* Marsh? Helping him start a war?

Despite his disgust, his need to help his friends almost wins out. He opens his mouth to do as he was told—to beg—but then, for some reason, he thinks of Sybil, and her mother, and finds he cannot.

Time is running out. If you have a plea, now is the time.

"I know," he says. "I know. But here's the thing. I don't think I want this gift."

The voice is silent for a long moment before it responds: *Excuse us?*

"Yeah," Hal said. "Your whole ethos—this 'ability to withstand great pain.' I get it, it's totally metal and badass, and as a teenager, I thought it was the coolest thing that could possibly happen to me. Like, by earning your mark of approval, I was showing how tough I am. But I'm not fourteen anymore. I'm almost forty. And spending my life bragging to myself about how much pain I can take? It doesn't suit me anymore. I found out today that I have a daughter, but I've missed out on most of her life so far. And I know her mother must've had her reasons for hiding her from me, but I can't help but think—if I spent a little less time trying to absorb pain, and a little more time just dealing with it—maybe I would've been worthy to meet my kid when she was, you know, still a kid? Maybe I could've told Athena how I really feel, instead of trying to protect her from me and my messed up, broken personality. Maybe I could have been happy all these years, or at least trying."

So you will not plead?

"I'm afraid for my friends," Hal says. "And I'm afraid for myself.

But I will not plead. I will not help that awful old man wage a war on innocent people. I reject the Blade of Woe. I'd rather die earnestly than saddle myself with the destiny of being your champion."

Very well, Hal Isaac. We send you now to your reward.

And before Hal can think or say more, the light spreads and engulfs his entire being. As he falls through the light, a single image comes to him: Peter's resurrected potato—the potato *Hal* resurrected back in 1998. Its glow pulses at him, consumes and becomes one with him, and as Hal vanishes into the light he thinks he finally understands what it means.

Athena

As Marsh approaches with Hal's body, Hal's limbs dangle and sway. His fingers almost seem to be wiggling, but it must be an optical illusion. Wait—no. They're definitely moving. Is it reflex? Some weird thing dead bodies do?

Hal's left hand opens and closes. Opens and closes. Opens. And then, as it closes, there's a new glow in the air, in addition to Peter's casting. A flood of yellow-green light bursts from Hal—pouring from his mouth, his eyes, his fingertips and toes. Athena hears several awful-sounding cracks. Bones resetting themselves? His body rises into the air, out of Marsh's grasp, and the flood of Dissonant energy severs Marsh's arm. Hal and the arm both fall—but while the arm hits the ground, Hal is gently turned and deposited on his feet.

Marsh freezes, looking at the space where his arm used to be. Athena doesn't waste the opportunity. She casts a set of ethereal armor for herself, runs at Marsh and slams into his middle, flipping him backward.

Hal, still glowing yellow-green, looks at Marsh, at Athena, and then at his hands.

"I thought you were dead," Athena says.

"I thought so, too," he says. "I'm not sure why I'm not."

"You're the champion of the Temple of Pain," she says. "I suppose you can take a beating."

"Actually I'm not," Hal said. "Not anymore. I just refused to reenlist."

"Then why are you covered in Dissonant energy?"

"If I had to guess?" Hal said. "I think the Blade of Woe was blocking my connection to the Dissonance all those years." He laughed, a loud, braying, unselfconscious sound. "I can *feel* you, Athena. Can you feel me?"

She reaches out and realizes she can—his presence brighter and more *there* than even Erin's and Peter's flames.

A hole in the world opens, obscuring Athena's view of Peter and Erin. Marsh, struggling to right himself, doesn't appear to have noticed. Hal and Athena approach, hands raised. Working in tandem in a way they never could have done as kids, they drive Marsh back, Hal with blasts of hard wind, Athena with hooks behind the legs, trying to trip him up. He staggers and skips, trying to stay ahead of their attacks, but can't find his equilibrium.

"It doesn't have to end this way," Marsh says, his voice high and panicked. "There's still so much I can teach you. So much you don't know. What do you want? Just tell me and it's yours!"

"You have nothing I want," Athena says.

As Marsh approaches the hole, she uses a hastily improvised rework of her symphony to reach inside the statue and grab hold of Marsh's soul. She manages to get a grip on the red jellyfish, but barely. The little fucker is strong, and she's about spent after the last few hours. Her head feels like it's made of pain as the statue falls forward, empty again, and the red jellyfish emerges, squirming.

"What am I looking at?" she says, gazing into the portal.

"Tehom," Hal says. "The deeps between worlds."

Athena struggles to keep hold of Marsh's soul, but the jellyfish is struggling back toward the statue, looking for a home.

"My grip," she says. "I can't keep hold of this thing much longer."

"Let me, let me," Hal says, stepping up beside her. He smiles at the jellyfish. "Hey, Professor. Want to see a magic trick?"

He closes his eyes, moves his hands through the air, and, a second later, a burst of pure green flame erupts from his fingertips, blowing the jellyfish out of this world and into the portal, into the deeps between worlds.

Erin

Erin might be imagining it, but she *thinks* she hears the jellyfish scream as it passes through the portal, and she allows herself a measure of satisfaction as Peter closes the doorway behind it, leaving only the sounds of Athena's harsh breath and the crackling of Dissonant energy in the air around them.

Hal kneels on the ground and braces himself with his hands. "Oh hell. That took a lot out of me."

Athena smacks him in the back of the head.

"Ow!" he shouts. "What was that for?"

"What were you thinking?" she says. "You don't get to die. You understand me? Not until I say so."

Hal stands up, rubbing the back of his head. Then he takes Athena by the waist, draws her to him, and kisses her. It's the bravest thing Erin's ever seen him do.

"I love you too," he says.

Peter sighs and tips forward. Erin catches him halfway through his fall and keeps him from hitting his head on the concrete. She sits down with him on the broken stairs, and he leans into her embrace, and hugs her back.

Finally. Exactly what she's missed all these years.

She startles as another pair of arms encircle both her and Peter. Hal has let go of Athena and joined the hug. Athena approaches from the other side, without a silly remark or snide comment, and squeezes as hard as everyone else.

This is home. Peter, yes, but Hal and Athena, too. Her forever people.

"I'm sorry I sent you away," Peter says, into her neck.

"We're sorry we let you," Hal says.

"Good news," Athena says, with a watery laugh. "We can all be sorry. We're all fuckups here."

They stay wrapped in one another, whole for the first time in half a lifetime. Exactly where they're supposed to be, vibrating in harmony with the disharmonious world.

Their happiness is interrupted by a deep rumbling noise. They look up in time to see the statue beginning to fade.

"What's happening?" Hal says.

"If I had to guess?" Erin said. "It's returning to Deoth. To the hold of that ship."

"How did it end up here to begin with?" Hal says.

"I'm not sure," Athena said. "When I put Marsh's soul into it, it disappeared into some portal. Like somehow the soul transference triggered a time travel event."

"Doesn't explain why it was drawn here," Athena says.

"Maybe because it already was here?" Erin says. "Like, because it was here in '99, it had to come here?"

"I already have a headache," Hal grumbles. "Don't make it worse."

"I guess now it's empty again it's returning home?" Erin says, as it continues to fade.

"Whatever happened and however it happened, it caused a major Dissonant disruption," Peter said. "I've slowed it down, but it's only a matter of time before the equivalent of a bomb goes off and time folds back in on itself. Hopefully it will send you home when it does."

Erin can't help herself asking the next question: "I don't suppose you'll come home with us?"

"I don't think he can," Athena says. "It would cause another time disruption. We could set off another explosion in the present."

"Oh," Erin says in a small voice. "So he has to stay here and . . ."

"Die," Peter finishes.

Erin's heart twists in her chest. She takes Peter's hand as Hal and Athena step back.

"So this is goodbye," Erin says. "Like, for real goodbye."

"We'll give you two a moment," Hal says.

Peter smiles up at Hal and Athena. "I hate fighting, but I'm glad I got to do it with you one last time."

"Us too," Athena says.

"We love you, Peter," says Hal.

"Love you too," Peter says, voice a little hoarse.

Hal and Athena walk into the school, leaving Peter and Erin alone at last.

"I never meant our last conversation to be so abrupt," he says. "I didn't think it would be our last."

He cups her face in one hand and she suddenly feels bashful. "You're just as beautiful as I remember," she says. "But I went and got old."

He doesn't let go. "Same eyes. Same smile. Still my favorite face in all the worlds. I wish, more than anything, we'd gotten a better chance. I think it would've been fun."

She leans into his palm—rough and callused from his garden. "I know you can't come back. But what if I went with you? Wherever you go next."

"I don't think it works that way, either," Peter says. "I think here in a moment everything that's supposed to happen will. I'll go on, and you'll go back to your time. Besides, Hal's a brand-new Dissonant. He'll need your help."

He glances at the sky. Erin notices it, too. The air is getting hotter. Time is almost up.

"I always told myself I'd give anything to see you again," she says. "But it's almost worse this way. Because I have to walk away and leave you, knowing for sure it's the last time."

He lets go of her cheek and brushes a lock of hair behind her ear. "We'll see each other again, Erin Porter. We'll have time when it's time."

"You promise?"

He kisses her cheek. She tries to savor it, to take in every detail of his hands in hers, his soft lips, his face scratchy with stubble. She freezes this perfect moment in her mind, this last kiss, and lets it carry her away, back home.

Epilogue:
The Next Adventure
(2019)

Hal

Hal and Athena leave Peter and Erin to walk through the doors of Clegg High School, but as Hal enters the building, he finds himself outside again—and in midair, no less. He falls a short distance and splashes into the creek bed where he met Sybil only a few hours ago. He shouts as he's soaked all over again, and scrambles up onto the bank, swearing. He pulls his phone from his pocket and checks it to make sure it hasn't been fried. According to the clock on the lock screen, it's about 6 a.m., and the air around him seems to confirm that. The sky is faint with predawn light.

His train of thought is interrupted as Erin appears in the air above the water and makes an identical pratfall back into this world with a shriek and a splash of her own. Hal laughs as she surfaces and glares at him.

"Not funny," she says.

"A *little* funny," he says, as she climbs onto the bank.

His phone buzzes with a text from Athena: *We're at Marsh House if you want to meet here.*

Hal and Erin decide to make the trip on foot, like the old days, to give their clothes time to air out. Their shoes squelch on the grass as they walk across the park and eventually come to the dirt road they've walked so many times before.

Erin says little, and seems pensive, so Hal gives her space, and takes in the morning. Clegg looks prettier to him than it did two days ago. Funny how your perspective can change so quickly. For the first time since the fight outside that bar, he doesn't mind being here—either in Clegg, or in this world, in himself—so much. It helps, knowing about

Sybil. Regardless of how any future conversations go, he knows he's done at least one good thing in his life: he saved Morgan, and somehow fathered Sybil. And now that he's fully Dissonant, he can *feel* the world around him in a way he never could before—can feel the grass beneath his feet, the trees, the molecules of oxygen in the air. He can feel Erin beside him, torn between grief and relief, and it's all beautiful.

When they arrive at Marsh House, Peter's doppelgänger, Philip, is sitting on the wide front porch beside a battered-looking boy of about seventeen or eighteen. Hal is taken aback when he realizes that Philip is missing part of his right leg, but even more startling, the guy now looks about seventeen or eighteen, like the beat-up kid. And that's not the only change. He also looks somehow *less* like Peter. The resemblance is still there, but, having just stood next to the real Peter Marsh a few minutes ago, Hal can see a difference between Peter's and Philip's faces. Philip looks less like a xerox of Peter now, and more like, well, Philip. Quiet and kind-eyed, but handsomer, and more haunted somehow. Like the kid has seen some real shit since Hal last met him.

Marsh House also looks a bit different. It's still grand, but with its peeling paint and sinking porch, it's gained a haunting, melancholy quality. *Time steals everything,* he thinks.

Philip rises with the battered boy's help, and, red-faced and stammering, introduces the boy as Owen.

Erin's face twists into a mask of concern. "What happened to your leg?"

"Can we talk?" Philip asks. "Just you and me?"

Erin looks at Hal. Hal looks at Owen.

"C'mon," he says. "Let's give them a moment." He doesn't need Dissonant powers to guess why Philip stammered during the introductions, or what it means for Philip and Erin's relationship. He doesn't think Erin will mind.

He and Owen walk around to the back of the house, to the yard where all the adventures began, twenty-three years before. The two of them stand in the grass, awkwardly not talking for a moment.

"Philip got his soul," Owen says.

"Did he?" Hal says, grateful for a chance to talk about something. "That's good news."

"So the world isn't going to end or whatever. At least not yet."

"That is also good news," Hal says.

Eventually, Philip and Erin walk around the side of the house, Philip leaning on Erin for support, then transferring his weight to Owen. The four of them go into the house, and join Athena at the kitchen table for coffee. There isn't anything to eat in the house except a box of saltines that somehow hasn't gone bad despite being in the house for ten years. They trade stories, and catch one another up on all the adventures they've had in the last few days.

Afterward, all five of them split off into different parts of the house and sleep—the boys in Peter's old bedroom, Athena in the study, Erin in the master, and Hal on the living room couch. When he wakes, it's dark outside, and the hallway light is on. The house is quiet but he can hear voices from the back. He heads instead for the front porch, away from the noise. He lets himself out the front door, and is surprised (but not unhappy) to find Athena already on the bench by the front door. She has the light off, and is smoking a cigarette.

"Don't judge me," she says. "It's been a long week."

"Judge you? I was going to bum one."

She offers him the pack and he takes a cigarette, but waves off her offer of a lighter. She gives him a puzzled look, which turns into delight as he performs his first magic trick, lighting the cigarette against the flint of his heart.

"When did you learn to do that?" she says.

"I'm not sure," he admits. "I think I was in my twenties when it happened for the first time. Long after Marsh supposedly severed us."

"He didn't sever you because he didn't know," Athena said. "Your abilities were cut off or muffled because of your deal with the Temple?"

"That's my current working theory," Hal says.

"Another question to add to the pile," she says with a heavy sigh. "Maybe now that we have Marsh's library, we can find some answers."

They smoke in companionable silence for a while, the cherries of their cigarettes winking at one another in the dark.

"How's your hand?" he asks.

"It doesn't hurt," she says. She holds it up and even in the dim light Hal can see that it remains shriveled and warped. The skin looks charred, like beef jerky left too long to cook. "I can use it for some basic things, but the nerve endings are shot. Like when your hand goes to sleep and it feels like you're operating a glove. But without the pins and needles to go with it."

"Can it be fixed?"

"If it can be, I'll fix it. If not? I guess one hand is a fair trade for what I got back in return. Being reconnected to you and Erin. Seeing the world in full color again, so to speak." She puts the hand down. "But you didn't really come out here to ask about my hand."

"I actually came out here for some fresh air, but now that I'm here . . ."

"Hal," she says. "Before you say anything else—thank you for the kiss. And for saying you loved me. I wish I could send my high school self a letter and tell her about it."

"What about present you?" he asks, shoving his hands in his pockets. "The one I actually kissed."

"What did you think would happen?" she says. "That you'd kiss me and everything would change?"

"This isn't about Morgan and Sybil, is it? Because Morgan and I never—"

"I know more about undines than you, Hal. They can reproduce sexually or asexually. In old myths it's a great honor to be chosen as the second parent to an undine's child. So no, it's not about that. It's about the years you spent coming to me for comfort while you dated and fucked other girls."

"It wasn't like that," he says.

"I'm not stupid," she says.

"I think you are. At least when it comes to me. Same way I'm stupid when it comes to you. When I was young, it didn't feel safe to care that much. So I distracted myself. Got into situations that wouldn't last." He pulls the cigarette out of his mouth and holds it away from his face, so he has a clear view of her. He swallows hard, surprised to find the next thing difficult to admit, even now. He forces the words in a cracked, dry voice: "But the truth is, I've loved you my whole life."

She takes a long drag on her cigarette. "I love you too," she says. "But not like that. Not anymore."

Erin

The next few weeks are like a monthlong version of the slumber parties Erin's coven had as kids. In the afternoons and evenings, she and Hal and the boys lounge in the living room and watch old movies on VHS. They sit at the kitchen table playing board games, and laugh late into the night every night.

During the days, she tutors Hal, Owen, and Philip in Dissonant, teaching them simple commands. Erin basks in her restored connection to the Dissonance, the wholeness it brings to her sense of herself. And it makes her happy rather than sad when she sees Philip and Owen hold hands, or sneak a kiss when they think no one can see. It's not what Erin created Philip for, but she's not especially proud of what she created Philip for. This is better. He has a soul now. He'll have a life beyond her.

There are a couple of dark spots in all this peace. The first is the news coverage of the incident at the church. Nobody died, but people were hurt. There are a couple of blurry photos of Owen and Marsh making the rounds on national television, which means Owen has to lie low for a while. If anyone were to find out that he's hiding at Marsh House, that could mean trouble.

To be safe, he stays out of town. Meanwhile, Erin keeps waiting for someone to show up on the doorstep and demand to know what they're doing in a house that doesn't belong to them, but as long as they leave Clegg alone, it seems content to do the same.

The other dark spot is Hal and Athena. Hal participates in all the lessons during the day, and leads the combat drills with the boys, and publicly he smiles and laughs a lot. But when left alone, he wears a look of sorrowful contemplation.

Athena sometimes joins in lessons or movie night, or plays games, but mostly she locks herself in Marsh's study, and sleeps on the leather couch where they took lessons as kids. Erin can tell Hal is concerned, but advises the others to leave Athena be. She'll emerge when she's ready.

On their last afternoon together in Clegg, Hal takes everyone to the creek bed and summons Sybil. Erin and Athena say their hellos to the undine, but mostly hang back in a patch of shade, close enough to watch without eavesdropping. Owen and Philip sit with Hal in the creek bed with Sybil. She seems otherworldly, almost unknowable like her mother, but when she smiles, she looks just like Hal.

Erin can't get over the idea of Hal as a father—and father to this strange, beautiful creature—but the new role seems to have settled something in him, the way her goodbye to Peter seems to have settled something in her. His old restless energy has been replaced with calm. Not happiness, exactly; more of a stillness.

That afternoon at the creek, Athena spends a long time watching Hal, the boys, and Sybil, a hard-to-read look on her face. She only turns to Erin with obvious effort.

"So what's next for you?" Athena asks.

"Hal's starting his sentence in mid-October, so I'm going to help him tidy up loose ends in Vandergriff," Erin says. "After that? I'm not sure. I don't think I should try to go back to my apartment in Iowa. They've probably already thrown out all my stuff, fixed the damage, and rented the unit to somebody else."

"You're welcome here," Athena says. "The boys and I are staying for a while."

"Is that legal?" Erin asks.

"I'm still searching for documentation. Anything to explain where the house's ownership lies. Someone may show up sooner or later to kick us out, but I guess until then we're okay."

"What about your store?"

"I can trust the staff to run it for now. The important work is here. I need to catalog Marsh's library, as well as that crazy fortress bunker-slash-zoo under the toolshed. I also need to see if there's a safe way to return the imprisoned creatures to their homes. And someone has to look after the boys. Philip has nowhere to go, and Owen's not interested in going back to Alabama. I don't blame him."

"Can't hide from your problems forever," Erin says.

"No, but it's okay to take a break," Athena says. "Owen's earned one."

"How do you think Marsh did it? Captured all those creatures? Built that huge warehouse-slash-menagerie? Did he do it all himself?"

"He mentioned 'associates' and 'partners' more than once. He even hinted at a 'small army' before the end. But he never gave me names. They could be lackeys, or former students like us. Or maybe Dissonants as powerful as he was—people like the Thorpes. They could be a threat to us all if they find out we're here, and reconnected. That's the other reason I need to stay. I need to guard this place from people like Marsh."

Both women fall back to observing their companions chat with the visitor. Something the undine says makes Owen laugh, and Hal turns and smiles at Erin and Athena. He waves.

Erin waves back. Athena keeps her arms crossed, bad hand hidden from view.

Athena

Athena remains buried in her work. When Erin and Hal leave to get Hal's affairs in order, she takes over Owen and Philip's education, giving them lessons in the morning, and enlisting their help for cataloging both the library and the menagerie in the afternoons. In the evenings she looks for answers to the big questions. What sort of command keeps the house and the bunker in stasis? Is it dangerous for humans to live here long-term? Who was Marsh working with? What were his plans for the coven, for Peter, before everything went to hell?

But she also makes sure to take breaks. She keeps up a steady text and meme exchange with Deputy Jordan McCormick, and it's a bright spot in her days. She stays up late and he gets up early, so they end up sending each other messages while the other is asleep, and Athena grows to love waking up to a bouquet of silly pictures and cat videos. She can count on it. There's never a question. Jordan seems as focused on her as she is on him.

They go for the coffee date. He asks about her hand only once, and when she tells him it was an accident and she doesn't want to talk about it, he acquiesces and doesn't bring it up again. It's his discretion as much as his charm which wins him a second, dinner date. She goes to movie night at his house, where they watch a dumb, fun superhero flick. In Jordan's darkened living room, lit only by the pale light of his big-screen TV, they share their first kiss, and it doesn't set off klaxon alarms of passion or desire, but it's pleasant. Gentle. And maybe, in the back half of her thirties, nice is enough. Especially if it's a nice you can count on.

In early October, two days before Hal is due to start his sentence, Erin calls to invite Athena to Vandergriff.

"He's surrendering at the Fort Worth jail before they transfer him to prison," Erin says. "Hal would love to see you before he goes in," Erin says. "Will you make the drive? Go with us?"

"I'm neck-deep here," Athena says.

"Athena," Erin says. "You can take a couple of days off. I'm sure Philip and Owen won't mind some time to themselves."

Athena promises to think about it and get back to Erin tomorrow. That evening, she goes out with Jordan. So far they've gone out of town for public dates, but tonight they go to the diner. Jordan thinks it's a good idea for people to get used to seeing her around town, to understand she's back, at least for a while. So she endures the looks of people she used to know, and eats a burger and drinks a milkshake, and talks with her almost-maybe-boyfriend about Erin and Hal.

"Why wouldn't you go?" Jordan says. "He's your friend. You guys were tight."

"You don't think it's weird?" she says. "Since," she says, using her straw to gesture at him, and then herself. "Us?"

"I mean am I jealous? Sure. But I'm also smart enough to know I can't keep you from anything you mean to do." He smiles and looks bashful. "It's one of the reasons I like you. You think for yourself."

"Shut up," she says, and it's her turn to look at the table. "I will dead-ass leave you here if you don't knock it off with the compliments."

He raises his hands and leans back. "Sorry," he says, not looking it.

After dinner, they linger in the parking lot, enjoying the almost-pleasant air. Athena leans against the side of her car and Jordan leans against the side of his, and their feet meet on the white parking space line between.

"Thank you," she says. "For being nice."

He leaves his hands in his jacket pocket as he spreads them, and he briefly looks like a flying creature. Something that could come out of the Clegg woods.

"How else am I going to be?" he says. "Besides." And here he drops his hands, and takes on a more serious look. "I want you to feel like you can tell me stuff."

It almost sounds like a scold, and she stands up a little. "I do tell you stuff."

He tilts his head and gives her an *oh-come-on* face. "Oh sure. Miss 'it was an accident and I don't want to talk about it.' Miss 'you can't come over to where I'm staying, I'm a private person.'"

"What?" she says. "I *am* a private person."

"And I'm a cop," he says. "And not a bad one. Definitely not a stupid one. So do me a favor and be honest with me now. Here, I'll start. Why do you think no one's come to kick you out of that house yet? Why do you think you haven't been grilled by the police about your disappearance after I got knocked out? I've been covering for you. Keeping the law from coming sniffing around," he says. When she doesn't respond, he prompts her: "Now you ask why I would do that."

"Why would you do that?" Athena says, although she thinks she might know why. Her heart is already sinking.

He stops leaning against his car and stands up straight, leaving Athena's feet alone on the white parking space line. His posture—no, his entire demeanor—seems to change. All of the "aw shucks" persona tossed aside, leaving behind an imposing man with a cold stare. "I *own* Marsh House," he says. "Marsh left it to me when he died. Technically you're squatting on my property, which I'm allowing."

So here it is: the first of Marsh's mysterious "associates" revealed. She would kick herself if she could. No wonder Jordan had been so attentive. No wonder he'd found her out at the property gate when she first returned to town. He'd probably been coming to check on the place and caught her trespassing.

"I used to work for him," Jordan says. "On the side, for a little extra money. I kept people from nosing into his business, and in exchange he taught me some things."

"You're Dissonant?" Athena says. She's hesitant to use the word, but also wants to see how it registers with him.

"No," he says. Clearly warming to his topic, he takes a step closer to her. He's now definitely in her personal space. He lowers his voice as he continues. "And that's part of the problem. See, I took care of him in the last years of his life. I assisted him. I did things for him. And when he died, he left me the house and everything in it. Only it turned out to be a shitty inheritance, because I couldn't get inside. He'd sealed it up with a command. One only a Dissonant could undo. I spent years trying to find a Dissonant. They're hard to come by if you're not already part of the community. Almost no internet presence at all. So when the twentieth anniversary of the school's destruction came around, and the town announced a memorial? I saw an opportunity." He smiles a little. "I hoped you'd come, and that, once you were here, I could convince you to open the place up for me, and now you have."

"Christ," Athena says. She wishes she could step back but she's already up against the car.

"Oh, don't give me that look," he says, with a dismissive wave. "I do like you. I've always liked you. Just because I used you doesn't stop that from being true. You studied under Marsh. You do what it takes to win. What's not to love?"

"Love?" she scoffs.

"By nature of where you live and what I legally own, we have a relationship," Jordan says. "But it doesn't have to be a bad one. We both have things the other wants."

"What kind of things did you do for Marsh?" Athena asks. "Did you ever hurt or kill anyone? Did you help capture and enslave all those creatures in his menagerie?"

He hesitates, and that's all the answer she needs.

"I don't want to hear from you again," Athena says. "Don't call. Don't text. And don't you *dare* come to Marsh House. If you do, I will kill you myself."

He lets out a short, frustrated huff of air, and looks genuinely hurt. "I don't understand. I thought you would be cool about this." A slight whine enters his voice. "This isn't how it's supposed to go. You and I—we're supposed to be together. To continue the grand design."

"Sorry I didn't follow your little script for you," Athena says. "But you know what? Marsh tried to come back. He tried to recruit me. And my coven and I sent him back to the grave."

He lets out another little huff, and balls his fists. "I know you're upset so I'll wait to call you until after your fake boyfriend is in jail," Jordan says. "Maybe by then you'll be thinking straight."

He's a good foot taller than Athena, so she has to punch up, but she lands a pretty solid upper cut to his chin. His head snaps back and he falls against his car. She gets into her own vehicle, and peels out so fast she burns rubber.

She goes back to Marsh House, and sleeps fitfully in the old study.

Part of her wants to run back to Oregon and leave all this behind, but the other, better part of her is tired of running from problems. And this house (and everything to do with it) represents a massive, tangled problem. One it's her job to solve.

One piece of Jordan's advice she does take: she calls Erin and promises to go along to the jail tomorrow.

"I'll be there first thing in the morning," she says. It will be a useful distraction from the Jordan issue. Besides, Hal *is* her friend. She can do this for him.

The next morning, she gets up before dawn and casts a fresh protection command on the house, one she hopes will keep Jordan from being able to enter. She leaves a note telling Owen and Philip to stay indoors, then makes the three-hour drive to Vandergriff. The sun is just rising as she arrives at Hal's apartment complex. Hal and Erin are already waiting for her on the front porch of Hal's unit.

Athena has a sudden suspicion—*They've been fucking*—and is surprised to feel stung by the idea. She tells her inner CW drama queen to shut up. She turned Hal away. His love life isn't her business. And anyway, there's nothing in her friends' postures or body language that suggests that level of intimacy. They sit together like old friends.

Hal bounds off the porch and into the parking lot, smiling and waving. He hops into the passenger seat, eager as a dog for a car ride.

"What are you so chipper about?" Athena asks.

"Happy to see you is all," he says, as he buckles himself in.

"He's a morning person," Erin grumbles as she climbs into the backseat. "In case you forgot." She fumbles in her jeans and pulls out a crumpled, folded-up piece of paper. "Check this out. Came in the mail yesterday. Hal's mail."

Athena takes the folded-up paper, which turns out to be an envelope. Inside is a short letter, typed on neat stationery watermarked with "THE COUNCIL OF THE WORD":

Dear Ms. Porter,

It has recently come to our attention that you have created a physical being without a soul. Per Council Law, this is both heretical and highly illegal, as it is a potentially world-ending offense. We are charging you with 1st degree world-tampering, which carries a

sentence of imprisonment and possible severance if you are convicted.
There will be a preliminary hearing on December 1, at which
you may enter your plea. If you do not attend, enforcers will be
dispatched to bring you in. Please surrender of your own volition.

"Oh shit," Athena says, when she finishes reading the letter.

"That's what I said," Hal says.

"Guess it's time to start boning up on the Council's laws," Erin says—lightly, despite looking wan and pale.

"I'll help," Athena says.

"Do you think you can?" Erin says.

"There has to be something in Marsh's library," Athena says. "I'll find it."

"Athena's got to be a better lawyer than I had," Hal says. He scowls out the window. "Fucking Robert K. Tuttle." But he doesn't actually sound too upset about it.

"After all we've been through, I'm not going to let the Council resever you," Athena promises. "Never gonna happen."

Erin takes the letter back. "Thank you. I guess we can worry about it later."

"Yeah, worry about it later," Hal said. "Today is my special day."

Athena can't help it; she laughs at his joke.

She lets Hal pick the music for the drive into Fort Worth. He picks Taylor Swift's *1989* and blasts it so loud Athena worries for her speakers. She refrains from adjusting the volume. It'll be some time before Hal can listen to whatever he wants—as loud as he wants—again. He can have this. Her eardrums will (probably) recover.

They arrive at the Fort Worth jail half an hour early. Athena's never been here before. It's a tall brick building, monolithic and imposing and generally unpleasant. It looks exactly like a place where you'd lock someone up, a drab version of the castle tower in a fairy tale. Worse, the jail faces an open street without a parking lot, and all the spots at the curb are full.

This—an iffy parking situation—is enough to snuff out whatever courage she's mustered for the event. Her heart starts to race and she licks dry lips. She can't go into the jail with them, can't watch Hal be taken away. She just can't.

"You two hop out," Athena says. "I'll circle the building until you're ready to come back out, Erin."

"You're not coming in?" Erin says.

"I don't know the area," Athena says. "I'm not sure where to park." It's a lame excuse, but she sticks to it and pretends not to see Erin's raised eyebrows.

"She's right, Erin," Hal says. "It's a nightmare trying to park around here." He squeezes Athena's right arm. "Thanks for coming. It was good to see you."

He gets out of the car and starts up the steps to the front door. Athena experiences a brief but intense sensation of déjà vu, remembers Peter Marsh on the steps of Clegg High School on his last day. The day she fled.

"You're going to be sorry about this," Erin says. "Eventually." She slams the car door and jogs to catch up with Hal. Athena wants to watch them go, but someone behind her honks. The light at the intersection is green. She pulls forward, takes one right, and then another, and then another. By the time she's rounded the block, her friends are out of sight.

That glimpse of Hal on the steps will be the last she has for a long time. Hal, squaring his shoulders to prepare for a test somehow more terrible than monsters and the undead. Acting like a grown-up.

She leaves the car parked illegally on the side street, and sprints around the block, jogs up the stairs of the jail, through the automatic sliding glass doors, and finds herself at the back of a line of people waiting to pass through a metal detector. She tries to prepare, pulls off her watch, belt, and shoes, and dumps them into a plastic tub with her cell phone and purse. As she shuffles forward through the line, she cranes her neck, trying to spot Hal and Erin, ignoring strangers staring at her injured hand.

When she at last passes through the detector, and into the large, depressing lobby with its rows and rows of molded plastic chairs, she hops forward, stepping back into her shoes, her belongings bundled in her left arm, panic growing in her chest as she tries to find her friends amid the strangers. Why are there so many people at a jail this early in the morning?

Then she sees Erin, in one of the lobby's plastic chairs. She sits with her elbows on her knees, head down. Athena calls her name, and she looks up, her face crumpled into a sympathetic grimace.

"I'm too late," Athena says.

"They're taking him back now," Erin says, and points.

At the front of the lobby, past a roped-off area, an armed bailiff escorts a handcuffed Hal toward a forbidding pair of double doors. Athena lunges forward, meaning to run after them, but Erin restrains her.

"You don't want to run at men with guns," she says.

Athena fights with herself, tries to reconcile the contrary impulses—her need to obey the rules, now in combat with the higher orders of the heart—until she comes to a compromise.

She cups her hands around her mouth and shouts. "Hal!"

Hal stops walking and looks back. So do his stony-faced escorts.

Okay, she has his attention. Now what? She can't go to him. They won't let her touch him now that he's property of the state of Texas.

She does the only thing she can think of: she blows him a kiss, with a sweep of her left, good arm.

He raises his cuffed hands to mime a low catch. Then the bailiff, fed up with the nonsense, turns Hal forward away from her, and pushes through the doors. Before she's ready for it, Hal's gone.

It's not how she wanted the moment to go. It's not how it should have happened, but it's what reality afforded her today, and if there's one thing Athena's good at, it's dealing with how things really are. But for once, as Athena looks at how things really are, she realizes that they're not so bad. Hal is gone for now, yes, and he'll be gone for a while, but he's not dead. There will be life for him, both in and after prison. There will be life for them both. And now that she knows what she wants—*who* she wants—she understands that it could actually be a pretty good life, for both herself and for Hal. One worth fighting for and through, despite the pain.

She blows another kiss at the closed doors, hoping that Hal can feel it. Then she turns to face the day, whatever it might bring.

Acknowledgments

Thanks as always, to my editor, Anna Kaufman, and my agent, Kent D. Wolf at Neon Literary, for helping to turn my mess of pages into something coherent and (hopefully) entertaining. Thanks also to production editor Kathleen Fridella, copy editor Fred Chase, proofreaders Chris Jerome and Chuck Thompson, interior designer Michael Collica, jacket designer Henry Sene Yee, publicist Demetri Papadimitropoulos, marketer Julianne Clancy, and editorial assistant Brian Etling, for making sure my shoes were tied and my shirt was tucked in.

Special shout-outs: to Austin Stephens, who was a great help in plotting Owen's character arc; to Sheena Barnett, who supplied me with the idea for a glow-in-the-dark potato; and to Holly Williams, who coined the phrase "potato power." This book would be poorer without your contributions.

This is a novel about friendship. I started writing it during the COVID-19 lockdown, when I was missing all of my friends, and I'd be remiss if I didn't thank them here, for keeping my spirits up through the insanity of the last several years. So to my friends—both the people I see in person *and* those of you I only talk to online—thank you. I couldn't do any of this without you.

A NOTE ABOUT THE AUTHOR

Shaun Hamill received his BA in English from the University of Texas at Arlington, and his MFA from the Iowa Writers' Workshop. His debut novel, *A Cosmology of Monsters,* was published in 2019. His fiction has appeared in *Carve* and *Come Join Us by the Fire 2.* His nonfiction has appeared in *CrimeReads* and *Tor Nightfire.* He lives and works in North Texas.

A NOTE ON THE TYPE

This book was set in Fournier, a typeface named for Pierre Simon Fournier *le jeune* (1712–1768), a celebrated French type designer. His type is considered transitional in that it drew its inspiration from the old style, yet was ingeniously innovational, providing for an elegant, legible appearance. In 1925 his type was revived by the Monotype Corporation of London.

Composed by North Market Street Graphics,
Lancaster, Pennsylvania

Printed and bound by Berryville Graphics,
Berryville, Virginia

Designed by Michael Collica